PELQUIN'S COMET

Also by Ian Whates

PELQUIN'S COMET

Book One
of
The Dark Angels

Ian Whates

NewCon Press
England

First published in the UK April 2015 by NewCon Press

41 Wheatsheaf Road, Alconbury Weston, Cambs, PE28 4LF

NCP 079 (limited edition hardback)
NCP 080 (softback)

10 9 8 7 6 5 4 3 2 1

ISBN:

978-1-907069-77-2 (hardback)
978-1-900679-78-9 (softback)

Cover illustration by Jim Burns
Cover layout by Storm Constantine

Book layout by Storm Constantine

For Helen

ONE

Maurice Hoffman the Third relaxed for the first time in several weeks. He knew himself to be a fortunate man living a privileged life – one which suited his sensitive nature – but of late financial concerns had overshadowed his affairs, bringing with them unaccustomed levels of stress. A temporary situation no doubt, one which would be alleviated in the fullness of time if only the banks – those cursed pecuniary vultures – could be held at bay for just a little while longer, allowing recent speculations to bear fruit.

It was a huge relief to forget about these matters for a while. All such worldly concerns were shed as soon as a patron set foot inside the grandeur of the Lexington Grove Pleasure Palace, abandoned at the door like tainted footwear set aside before stepping onto the tatami flooring of a traditional Japanese teahouse.

Wearing a deep blue silk yukata draped around his otherwise naked body, which was freshly bathed in waters scented with lotus blossom, he stood for a moment, curling his toes and luxuriating in the soft, deep pile of the carpet, before strolling into the bedroom. The whole suite was suffused with mellow light which had no obvious source, promoting a sense of tranquillity and relaxation, while harp music rippled quietly in the background, adding a subtle aural texture to the ambience. He pushed apart the silk veils that artfully hid the four poster bed and smiled on seeing who waited for him there. Annette and Aidan, his favourites.

Both were completely naked. They rested on their sides facing each other, Aidan nearest to him. Neither spoke, the young man – a muscular Adonis – not even deigning to look up, though the glaze in his eyes suggested that he might not actually be focusing on anything at all. Annette, though, smiled; a coy shadow of an expression which immediately brought a reaction as Hoffman felt his manhood stir. She knew exactly what she was doing, the little minx, as she languidly lifted a leg to drape it over Aidan's immobile thigh – her tanned skin several shades darker than his paleness – and brought her hand up to run well-manicured fingers slowly through the lad's golden hair.

Hoffman felt himself stiffen fully as the girl's gaze met his.

She rose from the bed sheets, a sensuous movement that saw her upper body flow into a sitting position. Her hand moved, slowly reaching towards him. A shrug of his shoulders sent his kimono sliding to the floor. He took a step forward, his breath catching in anticipation. His gaze never left her eyes.

The moment was shattered by the rasping sound of someone clearing their throat from behind him.

"What the hell?" Hoffman whipped around to find a tall, elegantly dressed man of thirty or so standing there – though rejuve made such assessments uncertain. The intruder was holding the drapes aside and peering in. His face was striking. Dark hair worn slightly longer than current fashion dictated, though still impeccably neat, framed darker eyes. Well-defined cheekbones and a smallish mouth, which appeared to be no more than a twitch away from either a pout or a sneer.

None of which made Hoffman any less indignant. "Who the fuck are you and how did you get in here?"

This space, this time, was supposedly inviolate. Lexington Grove guaranteed its patrons' privacy and interruptions were theoretically impossible.

Hoffman scrambled off the bed, half-bouncing to his feet as the mattress pushed him upward, his fury rising as swiftly as his manhood deflated. The intruder stepped away, allowing the drapes to fall back into place, and was waiting for him in the centre of the room as Hoffman pulled the veils aside and strode out, not deigning to retrieve the kimono. "Well? Start talking," he demanded.

The smug bastard just stood there, one hand nonchalantly resting on the silver handle of a polished rosewood cane, his finely tailored grey pinstripe suit making Hoffman abruptly conscious of his own nakedness. The man looked completely at ease in a situation where he had no right to be present. Hoffman suddenly remembered himself, realising where he was and what he could do about this. He reached up to his own forehead, grasped the pads he knew to be there, and wrenched them free of his skin.

The scene vanished. The bed, the deep piled carpet, even his nakedness – all were gone. He tugged off the state of the art visor and was already struggling to sit up – his physical body being a deal more corpulent than the virtual one he occupied in the Pleasure Palace's fantasy scenarios. In place of the idealised bedroom with its two young and pliant occupants, he found himself in the familiar plain walled room. He levered his body upright on the black leather couch, fumbling to rearrange his clothing and blinking at the sudden return of light. Only the gentle strains of harp music and the subtle fragrance of lotus blossom remained: sensory triggers designed to reinforce the mind's acceptance of the fantasy immersion.

Sven, his muscle-bound steroid-guzzling bodyguard, lay supine on the floor, either unconscious or dead, his head propped up against the wall as if pillowed. The intruder, this dapper stranger who had so outrageously interrupted his pleasure, stood at the foot of the couch, cane in hand, staring down at him with a supercilious air.

"To answer your question, Mr Hoffman, my name is Corbin Thadeus Drake, registered agent of the First Solar Bank."

"The bank?" Hoffman spluttered. "The *fucking* bank? And you dare to accost me *here*?"

"Need I remind you that you do owe my employers a considerable sum of money, Mr Hoffman?"

"I don't care how much frigging money I owe them! You can't just barge in here and interrupt a man's legally paid for pleasures. This is Lexington Grove for God's sake. It's sacrosanct, it's world renowned, it's a byword for discretion, it's…"

"…largest single shareholder is First Solar Bank, Mr Hoffman," Drake interrupted. "To all intents and purposes, we own this establishment."

"You own…?" No wonder this arrogant son-of-a-banker had been able to invade his private fantasy world.

"Now, I have no interest in your sordid little diversions," the man continued.

"Fantasies!" Hoffman snapped. "They're harmless *private* fantasies."

"Quite. As I say, not my concern. However, your recurring inability to meet your financial commitments is. With that in mind I am instructed to accompany you immediately to the bank's head office, just a few minutes from here, where you can have a cosy chat with a certain Terry Reese, one of our senior officers. There you can explain which assets you intend to liquidate in order to reimburse First Solar as swiftly as possible."

"I can do *what?*" Hoffman felt his cheeks burn with rage. "I categorically refuse, you posturing jackass. The only person your precious bank will be hearing from is my solicitor!"

Drake's answering smile was as cold as ice-snake venom. "Perhaps I haven't made myself clear, Mr Hoffman. I wasn't offering you a choice."

Unfailingly polite, but then the truly dangerous ones often were. The man's calmness was unnerving. Recovering a little from his initial shock, the businessman hesitated, deciding on a new strategy. All Hoffman had to do was keep this Drake talking for a little while longer. He'd spotted something which the banker evidently hadn't. Sven was waking up.

"Now look," he temporised, "there's no need for this to get unpleasant. I'm a reasonable man who prides himself on always honouring his commitments. There's no question of my *not* paying First Solar, it's just that now has proved a somewhat difficult time and..."

"I'm sure all of this will be taken into account, Mr Hoffman, along with the fact that you've already reneged on two agreed repayment schedules."

"Unfortunate oversights," Hoffman said quickly, willing the man not to look around and determined that his own gaze should not flicker down to where Sven was now gathering himself into a crouch. Just a few seconds more... "Quickly corrected," he added.

Mercifully, that was all it took. Uttering a roar that a wild bear would have been proud of, the burly bodyguard sprang at Drake's back, barrelling into the startled banker.

Drake was far slighter than the bodyguard and clearly outmatched, but Hoffman had no intention of waiting around to see the outcome of the tussle. He was already sidling past as Sven's massive arms engulfed the banker's frame. A few hastily shuffled paces and Hoffman was able to wrench the door open and dash out into the corridor beyond. If he now went to his left he'd be heading towards the front, the main body of the Pleasure Palace: reception area, bar, restaurant – places designed for patrons to gather and relax in the afterglow of their climactic fantasies. Instead he turned right, not knowing whether Drake had come alone and not wanting to run into any other agents of First Solar who might be loitering near the entrance. Ahead stood a large cream-coloured door, which flickered with the ghost of virtual flames as he drew nearer. Presumably this was for the benefit of anyone who couldn't read the words emblazoned upon it at around head height: 'Fire Door'. Perfect. Hoffman hurried up and thumped it with both open palms. Nothing happened. He tried again, harder, and this time the door responded, swinging ponderously outward as it was designed to when any anxious or panicked souls beat against it from within.

The full glare of daylight caused him to squint as he stumbled outside, looking right and left, trying to get his bearings. He was in an alleyway, at the back of the Pleasure Palace by the look of things. Tall walls faced him, while from the left the sounds of traffic drifted to his ears. The mouth of the alley was some distance away but beyond it he could see the blur of vehicles racing past. That had to be the main street. He headed in that direction, anxious to be gone as soon as possible, just in case, despite appearances, the banker somehow prevailed against his bodyguard.

He had taken no more than three or four steps when something gripped his arm, yanking him back. A loop of mottled green cable: thick, insulated, rubbery; it almost looked to be alive. These impressions barely had a chance to register before he felt a similar hold around his waist, this time gripping so tightly it was physically painful. His free hand automatically reached for the constriction, finding a muscular... tentacle? Before he could process the implications of that, he was pulled backwards and up, causing him to tip helplessly forward. He felt certain that his head was about to be dashed against the ground; but it wasn't.

Hoffman was hoisted into the air, dangling upside down, legs kicking impotently, blood rushing to his head, body wanting to right itself – gravity pulling at his well-padded posterior as if determined to tear him apart at the waist. He screamed. Not to attract attention, not for help, just in pure terror. The tentacle continued to draw him upwards.

Something large loomed above him. He looked up to see a huge maw opening, mucus stretching between curved, pointed teeth the size of his arm, while a thick grey-black tongue flowed out as if to engulf him.

Hoffman suddenly realised that he hadn't in fact been screaming before; that had just been him warming up. *This* was what real screaming sounded like. Terror blanked his mind, blotting out any hope of constructive thought. He became aware of warmth saturating the front of his trousers as his bladder vented, urine spreading to dampen the stomach and shirt that hung beneath.

A small part of his mind registered that he ought to be struggling, but his muscles had frozen and his limbs seemed leaden and unresponsive. This couldn't be happening. The monstrosity that held him, this mass of tentacles and teeth, was like something out of a bad children's space fantasy. It *couldn't* be real.

Fantasy: that was it! The thought freed his paralysed mental processes. None of this was real, he realised. The First Solar Bank agent had invaded his private fantasy and so had obviously infiltrated the Pleasure Palace's systems. This was still part of the game. Hoffman had only *seemed* to wake up. In truth he was still in thrall to Lexington Grove's virtual dreams, newly woven to become nightmare.

That might be true, of course, said a voice in his head, a voice he'd never heard before. *But it isn't.*

Hoffman found that he'd been lifted above that intimidating mouth and was now level with two huge, equally intimidating eyes. Great brown orbs with disks of darkest ebony at their centre. Somehow he knew beyond doubt that the voice in his head and these eyes were linked, that the same intelligence dwelt behind both.

You're nothing, Maurice Hoffman, the voice told him; *a speck of grit which has lodged in the wrong place and is interrupting the smooth flow of events. You've become an irritation. One that can no longer be tolerated.I need Corbin Drake to be available for other things, important things, not wasting his time on petty irrelevances such as you. So this ends* now, *understood?*

"Yes, *yes!"* Hoffman blabbered, his head pounding with the rush of blood, all thought that this might be anything other than wholly real banished.

Good, because precisely how this encounter ends is entirely up to you. Either I let go... Hoffman cried out as the tentacle around his waist loosened and his body was left unsupported, abandoned to the unforgiving tug of gravity. He started to fall, only for the grip to tighten again in an instant, his plummet arrested before it had properly begun. *...in which case you will be dashed to the ground and perish: case closed. Or, you go straight from here and liquidate as many assets as necessary to repay the sum owed before the end of the working day: case closed. Your choice. I have no preference either way. But this matter will be resolved today. Oh, and if you leave here and have a change of*

12

heart, please don't assume that distance will keep you safe from me, it won't.

"I'll pay!" he yelled. "Just put me down. *Please.*"

Good choice.

Slowly, mercifully, he felt himself lowered towards the ground. He risked one more glance at his impossible captor, seeing beyond the obvious features of mouth and eyes for the first time. In truth, there was little else *to* see. From Hoffman's admittedly skewed perspective, the monster looked to be nothing more than a great puff of brown-green fur, like filaments of some gigantic moss, fronted by those oversized facial features and supported by a mass of writhing tentacles. Again he was fleetingly reminded of some child's representation of what a monster ought to look like, yet surely no child's vision could ever have evoked such abject terror.

Remember, I'm inside your head, the voice said again as first Hoffman's shoulders then his back and finally his bum and heels came to rest gently on the ground, *so don't entertain the idea of a double cross.* The tentacle slithered off him, bringing blessed relief and the ability to breathe freely again. He was abruptly conscious of his face being covered in snot and spittle, which he hastily wiped away even as he scrabbled to stand up, while the urine-soaked areas of his trousers and shirt were cooling rapidly towards cold and uncomfortable dampness. Right then, he didn't care; the presence of firm ground beneath his feet more than made up for his tarnished dignity. A quick glance at the roof informed him that the monstrosity had disappeared from view, which was something at least, though nowhere near enough to make him feel safe. He wasn't sure he'd ever feel safe again.

A door slammed open and Drake charged out from the back of the Pleasure Palace. "Hoffman!" The man's suit might still appear to be barely ruffled but his temper clearly had been.

"Thank the Gods!" Hoffman would never have believed he could be so pleased to see the banker, but he was. "Look, forget about taking me to your bank's head office, that'll just waste time. I'll get the money, all of it, transferred across by close of business today."

As Drake strode across to him, Hoffman noticed the man's gaze shift just for an instant towards something behind him and to the left. He instinctively looked in the same direction and nearly jumped out of his skin. There, sitting atop an upturned wooden crate, was a ball of moss-green fur, small enough that he could have held it in his hands.

No gaping mouth and no tentacles, but two beady eyes that watched him with chilling intensity. This could only be the monster's smaller cousin, or perhaps even its offspring.

"Look, I'll get you your money!" he repeated, and he was stumbling past the banker, almost running in his haste to get away from this cursed alley. Already he was calculating which assets could be liquidated, what would be most likely to bring the highest return in the shortest time. No matter the cost in terms of his long term wealth, there was no way that Maurice Hoffman the Third was going to miss this particular deadline.

Drake frowned as he watched the overweight businessman scamper away. He would have stopped the man but for Mudball's reassurance. *Don't worry, Drake,* said the familiar voice in his head, *you can trust him on this.*

What exactly did you do to him? he thought back, in a form of communication that had become all too familiar in recent years, ever since he first encountered Mudball in a wrecked facility guarding a chamber of ghosts.

Hoffman was clearly terrified, and the additional horror that crossed the man's face on seeing Mudball hadn't escaped Drake either. Little did.

Me? Nothing. I did exactly what you told me to do. I waited to see if he appeared and, when he did, made sure he didn't get away, delaying him until you arrived.

Drake kept a firm lid on his thoughts as he went across and collected the small bundle of fur, scooping him up. He was conscious of the warmth of that compact body in the palm of his hand as the creature hopped off and then into the special pocket that all Drake's clothes now sported, just behind the left shoulder. *Sure you did. So why is he so terrified?*

Beats me. Guess you must have had him rattled. You can be pretty formidable in the right mood, you know, certainly a lot more terrifying than a puffed-up little tat of fur like me.

Drake knew there was no point in pursuing this right now so he didn't, content with filing the incident away for further reference. Some day he'd get an explanation for this and all the other little anomalies that seemed to occur around Mudball. Not today though; he would bide his time.

One thing he was increasingly certain of: there was a great deal more to his diminutive companion than met even *his* eye.

Two

Buildings cut the skyline like a fistful of razors. Even the clouds scudding above the metropolis held a rosy pink glow – as if some artist had added the hint of colour as embellishment, a suggestion of blood summoned forth by steel, glass, and concrete edges where the buildings scraped the heavens. It was one of two things Pelquin loved most about New Sparta, that skyline; the other being the inordinate amount of wealth sloshing around the place.

New Sparta was the banking capital of human space. In Pelquin's experience, bankers usually demanded blood before they would even consider parting with a fraction of the wealth they shepherded, so the sky's ruddy hue struck him as wholly appropriate.

He'd even seen an Xter here once; the very first of that strangely unsettling alien race he'd ever set eyes upon. To date, Xters were the only other intelligent species mankind had encountered, but the two races rarely mingled, warily eying each other across the mutually agreed boundaries that arbitrarily defined their respective 'space' in an uneasy peace founded on tolerance rather than welcome. Pelquin had gained no more than a fleeting glimpse, straining to see over the heads of a crowd as security ushered the gangly figure through a hastily cleared lobby. But it was a moment he would never forget. The Xter looked insectlike, abhorrent both in form and in its darting, stuttering motion, but fascinating at the same time; alien in every sense.

Doubtless the Xter had come to New Sparta for the same reason everyone else did: money.

Pelquin continued to head for the river, as he had been for much of the morning, though circumspectly due to the nagging sense that he was being watched. Part of him almost wished he'd been pounced on by now – shaken down by pseudo-muggers, found to have nothing of interest on him and left to get on with things. No such luck, just the incessant prickling at the back of his neck, the conviction that *someone* was following him. If they'd tagged him with a bug, he couldn't find it. If they were using a revolving tail there must have been a lot of them and they had to be very good. The only time he thought he might have spotted someone – a woman, middle-aged and nondescript – she'd slipped away in apparent innocence seconds before his suspicions could crystallise into certainty and well before he could discount his own paranoia as culprit.

Of course, under the circumstances, paranoia was to be expected, welcomed even as a goad to caution. After all, when someone bigger and tougher than you and with a far longer reach openly declares their intent to thwart your ambitions and pummel you, it pays to be careful.

For all his determination to remain vigilant, Pelquin's musings were almost his undoing. A streak of pink fur and fast-moving legs suddenly shot across his path, low to the ground, almost tripping him up.

"Binky!" a woman shrieked as Pelquin's footfalls stuttered and he was forced to swerve and skip on one foot to avoid colliding with the creature or stepping on it. A genpet, genetically engineered to its owner's dictates. The wretched things were all the rage on New Sparta at present. Pelquin hated them. He wasn't religious in the slightest; he had no qualms about mankind's tinkering with the genes of domestic animals on that score. He knew full well it was something that had been going on since the dark ages, long before the advent of spaceflight, but genpets struck him as a step too far. They were an affectation of the rich and foolish, a pointless abomination to titillate jaded palates and blatant testament to the fact that some folk had more money than taste. This one, with its narrow muzzle, flopped-over ears and long sausage-like body, had clearly been developed from canine stock, despite the pink fur and its three pairs of legs – front, middle and rear. Probably a bit of snake in there as well to judge by the sinuous way it moved.

The creature's owner, a slender, leggy woman in pencil skirt whose platinum hair was tied back to display a wrinkle-free face flush with the tell-tale glow of a recent rejuve, tapped frantically at her wrist perminal, reeling in the invisible leash that was supposed to keep her pet in thrall.

Pelquin had been momentarily distracted by the incident. He nearly missed the flash of steel as the kid in scruffy blue top came towards him, hood up, head down; and if he'd reacted a fraction slower the blade would have found its mark and lodged somewhere in his belly. As it was, he came to his senses in the nick of time and was able to sway and jump, allowing the steel splinter to thrust forward and slice through the air where he'd been standing a split second before. He didn't think, just reacted, grabbing hold of the assailant's arm with both hands. He dug his thumb into the wrist tendons so that the kid had no choice but to drop the knife. Movement in the corner of his eye warned him that the attacker wasn't alone. Still holding the arm, he swivelled, yanking the inept knifeman across and driving the kid's torso into the advancing form of a thicker-set youth dressed in grey, hood again pulled up as token gesture to anonymity.

Somebody screamed – a woman – more a yelp of surprise than of fear. Something else barked excitedly – quite possibly the same genpet that had distracted him. The sounds reminded Pelquin that there were others here, that he'd been walking down a crowded thoroughfare when the attack came. He stepped back, dropping into a fighter's crouch as the kids untangled themselves. A small knot of onlookers had stopped to watch. The attention evidently unnerved the two would-be muggers. The pair exchanged quick glances, as if seeking reassurance which neither was in a position to provide, before they turned and fled, the smaller one barrelling into an elderly man in a brown jacket who was too slow to react, nearly knocking him off his feet.

The cluster of people began to dissolve at once, clearly preferring not to get involved. All except for one man who stepped forward as if to help. "Are you all right?"

"Yes, I'm fine," Pelquin replied. He trusted this man about as much as he did the two muggers.

"If you hang around for a minute, security should be here and you can report those two hoodlums."

Of course they would. This was New Sparta, where cameras lurked at every vantage point and petty criminals could never be allowed to prosper. It was only the fat-cat corporate ones who had a right to do that. Bankers, for instance. The very sort he was eventually due to meet that day.

"No need," Pelquin assured the stranger. "I'm late for an appointment, and there's no harm done." He was already moving away.

Perhaps the two kids had simply been opportunists who somehow sensed he was new here, but perhaps not. Likewise the Good Samaritan with his sincere expression and neighbourly concern.

Pelquin walked swiftly for the next half hour, every nerve on edge, every sense straining to catch something out of place. He would stop suddenly to look in a shop window here, staring at whatever was displayed without seeing while checking reflections, cross the road for no real reason there, and retrace his steps at random intervals. He didn't glance upward much, didn't want to present his face any more than necessary to cameras that might be taking an interest in him after the fracas, but he did look around, surreptitiously checking for the two kids, the concerned man, for *anyone* who might be following him.

Eventually, despite the likelihood that the attack had been staged and the lingering concern that those tailing him might simply be better at this than he was, he arrived at the river. It was either that or miss the first rendezvous entirely, which wasn't an option.

Beneath the embankment a narrow track ran right along the river's edge, submerged during Spring tides but usable otherwise: the subbankment, which perhaps had been a towpath in the past – Pelquin couldn't have cared less about its origins.

He resisted the temptation to glance around again as he took the grey stone steps that descended beside The Crescent Bridge, fully aware that looking furtive was the best way to attract the sort of attention he was anxious to avoid. Instead he simply walked up to them and trotted down, as if this were the most natural thing in the world. The wall of the embankment hurried past until he stood on the narrow path below, which was all but forgotten by everyone except the tramps and the bargemen and the whores in search of a quiet place to take their johns, and the occasional hormone-laden teenagers looking for a quick shag somewhere their parents wouldn't find them.

It seemed cooler down here, as if the water sucked the heat from the air. Pelquin failed to supress a shiver that travelled up his spine. Smelt colder too; the river bringing with it a hint of the uplands that had birthed it. A buzzing insect landed on the back of his left hand. He squashed it with a deft slap of the right before the thing could bite, and then brushed away the small corpse, leaving a black smear.

Under the bridge itself, pushed up against the mouldering brickwork, a pile of rags and cardboard had been heaped in apparently haphazard fashion. Only as he walked towards it could Pelquin make out the shape of a man sitting in the middle of the small mound, head bowed, tatters and off-cuts of packaging material and clothing gathered around him like a flowing cape fashioned out of refuse.

He frowned, torn between conflicting urges to say something and to walk on. This didn't look anything like the person he was expecting to meet here. Then the figure glanced up and the eyes gave him away.

"Nate?" He barely recognised his recently returned second in command, the man who was the closest thing to a friend he'd known in a decade or more. Nate Almont looked filthy, his hair unkempt and his customary stubble sprouting towards ragged tufts of bristly beard – ginger peppered with grey.

"Shh..." the figure urged, staring down again. He was fiddling with something cradled on his lap, pressing keys with deft assurance. A console of some kind, Pelquin realised – an oversized perminal. Seconds later the man sat up straight, to stare past the new arrival, towards the river. Pelquin followed his gaze but couldn't see anything.

This parody of the man he knew grunted and said, "That's better." Only then did his attention return to Pelquin. "Spyflies," he explained. "Two of them. I hijacked their command frequency and ditched them in the river."

"Thanks." *Spyflies?* No wonder he hadn't spotted them, but since when had Jossyren grown so sophisticated?

"I thought you were going to be careful!" Almont snapped.

"I was… Or at least I thought I had been."

Pelquin let the other's tone go, this time. After all, the man had been living rough for the past few days, blending in, losing himself among the dregs of New Sparta's homeless, doing all he could to remain beneath the authorities' notice and enduring who knew what indignities for their mutual cause. Nate had jumped ship the moment they docked, smuggled off within the small cargo they'd delivered here. An endeavour whose success had taken a lot of planning, considerable discomfort on Nate's part, a pinch or two of good luck, and a well-placed bribe. However, all that would have been worthwhile if in the process they'd succeeded in getting one particular item off the ship unnoticed.

"You've got the gonk?"

"Of course I have. You don't really think I'd be sitting here dressed like this if I didn't, do you?"

"Don't push it, Nate," Pelquin advised.

Almont rummaged around among the rags that swaddled him and produced what looked to be a fist-sized ball of screwed-up greasy paper. He thrust the unsavoury object towards Pelquin, who took it gingerly. The weight immediately told him that there was something a lot more solid than mere paper at the ball's centre. He carefully pulled the bundle apart, to reveal a dull matt-grey object. Half an ovoid, like an egg sliced in two lengthways, the 'gonk', as Bren had christened the thing for no good reason anyone could think of, looked unremarkable in the extreme. Then again, the first indicator of so many fake artefacts was their artfully bizarre appearance. The genuine ones were often like this: mundane on the surface. It was only once you saw what they could do or tried to analyse what they were made of that their truly alien nature revealed itself.

Pelquin grinned and pulled the papers across to cover the thing once more before stuffing it into a pocket. "Good job," he said. "You'd better get back to the *Comet*."

"No kidding. Don't worry, I'll be out of here as soon as you're on your way. Don't look for me for the next couple of days, though. I'll be too busy soaking in a hot bath and catching up on some snooze time."

Pelquin grunted, pulled his collar up against the chill emanating from the river, and continued along the subbankment footpath. He emerged on the far side of the bridge and hurried up another flight of stone steps, taking them two at a time, to emerge once more in the sunlit world of the quadrant's financial capital.

He didn't dawdle, having left the rendezvous with Almont until the last possible minute. In fact, he'd have to hurry to avoid being late, which suited him just fine. Pelquin knew he wouldn't relax until the alien *thing* had served its purpose and, hopefully, left his possession. This was largely because of Jossyren. If, as seemed likely, the faceless corporates really did have men out in the streets, they'd presumably be making a beeline for this area now that the spyflies were down.

Ever conscious of the gonk's solid presence at his hip, he stepped out into the stream of people. Transport modules shot down the avenue at high speed, unerringly controlled by the network's AIs, while dampener fields protected pedestrians from both the wind and noise of their passage. Carefully choreographed light displays played along the sides of the endless stream of fast moving vehicles, gauged to match the 'average' walking pace of a person on foot in either direction so that the portrayed adverts could run their course. The one currently haunting Pelquin's every footstep featured a series of glossy images of mankind's noble endeavours, all fronted by women with faces as perfect as their physiques and men with biceps as broad as their foreheads. It was an ad for First Solar Bank, which struck him as ironic, given that this was precisely where he was going.

Moments later he stepped into the plush lobby of the imposing black-glass building that served as First Solar's head office and strode up to the reception desk. Human receptionists, two of them; as ostentatious a declaration of wealth as any investor could wish for.

"Name's Pelquin," he said to the pretty young thing whose smile might as well have been tattooed in place. "I've an appointment to see Terry Reese."

Pelquin wasn't remotely nervous. He'd dealt with bankers before – perhaps not with this particular one, but all such were interchangeable in his experience and he knew exactly what to expect. Reese was a capitalist by definition, and a successful one to have risen to his current position. He would be slightly corpulent, marginally the wrong side of middle age, his hair bearing an artful touch of grey – just enough to look distinguished in his own eyes – and his features would be a little waxy from rejuve treatments. He'd be dressed in an expensively tailored suit, with or without a waistcoat, and ensconced behind a completely redundant desk, there merely to impress upon those few privileged enough to be ushered into his august presence that this was *his* domain and they were there only at his tolerance. The man's worldview would be narrow but his mind razor-sharp in one particular area: finance. Pelquin knew how to play such men and had his strategy all worked out. He'd tantalise Reese, using greed to draw the banker in, holding back his trump card until precisely the right moment, revealing it only once he could see the currency signs dance in the whites of the man's eyes.

The pesky alien artefact that Bren had so quaintly christened a gonk had turned out to be more trouble than Pelquin had counted on. He couldn't wait to offload it, even if he was about to do so only in order to secure the funds to go and find a whole shipful *more* of the blasted things.

The final door slid open, admitting Pelquin into exactly the sort of office he'd envisaged. The huge desk might be absent but the room was plush yet modern, efficient and sparsely furnished, with a few understated personal touches – 3D image cube with a sequentially changing series of family photos, and a pot plant whose small verdant leaves spilled out to tumble down the pot and dangle over the shelf supporting it like an eruption of green yeast. It was enough to suggest that the interviewer might be human after all, to lightly smooth the edges of what could otherwise have come across as a wholly unsympathetic environment. Enough, perhaps, to throw the unwary off-balance, to tempt them to relax just a fraction; but Pelquin wasn't about to fall for that. The room's only occupant, however, was a different matter. At least he'd been spot on regarding the age. As for everything else...

"Captain Pelquin, I presume," said the tall, rod-slender woman who stepped forward to clasp his hand in a vice-like handshake. The eyes that assessed him from behind the perfunctory smile were as keen and bright as a console alarm. "I'm Terry Reese, Senior Loan Assessor for First Solar Bank. Do take a seat."

Three

Prior to Pelquin's arrival, Terry Reese had taken the trouble to skim through the file containing all the information First Solar had on the man, which proved to be a surprising amount. She gazed with jaundiced eye at the fields of text that scrolled across the air before her, while reflecting on a thoroughly unproductive morning. This was to be her third and final appointment of the day. The previous two had been a waste of time and she didn't suppose number three was going to prove much better.

This was an age of expansion, of hot heads and burning ambition, of genuinely heroic deeds sprinkled among the far more numerous foolish and ill-conceived ones. Mankind was stretching out to claim the stars, his reach greatly boosted by caches of ancient technology left behind by the Elders – an advanced civilisation which seemed to have abandoned this sector of the galaxy centuries ago. Not for her to speculate as to *why* they'd abandoned so much intriguing and useful tech, she left such matters to wiser heads with different priorities. Not that every cache held significant finds, of course; some proved to contain no more than baubles and trinkets, but even these were highly valued. The lack of an apparent pattern was frustrating to say the least – her job would have been so much easier if each haul was identical – but *any* cache was worth retrieving.

Then, of course, there were the guardian entities: programmed intelligences left behind by the Elders to protect the caches; or, at least, to protect *some* of them. Again, no one had yet figured out a way to predict whether a guardian was likely to be in situ or not; and that was a decidedly telling variable, since the guardians had proved to be tenacious, ingenious, and often deadly.

There was no doubting, though, that this was a good time to be a banker. Cache hunting had ignited the imagination of a generation, inspiring men and women to gamble on finding that elusive pot of gold at the end of a xenological rainbow. The pursuit of their dreams, successful or otherwise, required many things: dedication, faith, self-belief, courage, knowledge, resourcefulness, a dollop or two of good fortune and, above all… money. Which, of course, was where she came in.

Terry Reese saw her position as one of great privilege and responsibility. She and those like her were retained by the banks to separate the diamonds from the rubble, to decide which proposals merited support and which were black holes waiting to suck in funds without any prospect of a return. The substantial salary she received was merely a reflection of her success in making the right choices and the privileged lifestyle she enjoyed no more than just reward.

Of course, some cases were easier to assess than others.

The first person who had come to see her that morning with begging bowl in hand, for example, had required a judgement that was simplicity itself. A naïve rich kid with stars in his eyes and little more behind them. His family had grown wealthy on manufacturing a small but essential component of stardrive engines and he had more than enough credit to finance his own expedition should he wish to.

She still wasn't entirely sure why he had presented himself before her at all. Was it simply because he'd heard that the first thing you did when venturing forth in search of Elder artefacts was visit the bank manager, or because he had so little faith in this proposal that he didn't want to risk his own family's money on the venture? She suspected the former, doubting he was canny enough for the latter, not when fired up with the sort of zeal he'd demonstrated here today.

As it was, Terry had to resist the temptation to slap him down and tell him to go away and grow up. That would hardly have been the most diplomatic approach, bearing in mind the influence his family wielded. So instead she had smiled and let him down gently, explaining that unfortunately there wasn't enough substance to his proposal for her to commit the bank's support at this stage, suggesting that he should go away and conduct more research in order to bolster his arguments and present a stronger case. Once he'd done that, she assured him she would be happy to reconsider the situation, in, say, six months' time? By then, hopefully, his enthusiasm would have waned and his attention wandered on to some new project; preferably one that wouldn't bring him into her presence again.

Her second appointment had been a different matter entirely: a mother, desperate to mount an expedition to find her missing son. The lad had been crew on a ship that disappeared while on a cache hunt. To be specific, he'd disappeared while in search of Lenbya. Terry groaned inwardly when she heard this. If she had a credit for every time she'd heard *that* name, she could have retired a rich woman by now. The name was said to derive from the corruption of a word in the Elder language itself, which was patently ridiculous; no other Elder word had survived to Terry's knowledge, so why this one? Lenbya was nothing more than a deep space fable, the so called 'Ultimate Cache of the Elders', said to put every other cache to shame. Discovered by an ancient spacer who had never been able to find the place again, Lenbya's legend had become part of the whole Elder mythos, taking hold of the public imagination. Like El Dorado, Paititi, the Seven Cities of Gold and even Atlantis before it – Terry had made a study of such ancient Earth-borne myths in her youth, when she had still harboured secret hopes of discovering the ultimate cache herself – Lenbya had become a romantic goal and irresistible lure for the foolish and the gullible. As such, it was the bane of the older, wiser, and more cynical Terry's professional life.

Even so, she managed to smile compassionately with this obviously distraught woman, and even felt a degree of sympathy for the applicant, which surprised her. The woman at least possessed enough sense to do her homework and brought a well-constructed proposal to the meeting, built not around the missing son but rather around the hoard of Elder artefacts the son's ship had been searching for, which might or might not have been the ever-elusive Lenbya itself.

Unfortunately, inevitably, there was simply too little to go on. Calculations, carried out as the woman spoke and taking into account everything she presented, suggested no better than a 17% chance of actually finding the cache, *any* cache, which made the proposed trip financially unviable. Much as Terry might have liked to help, she couldn't, not with that sort of success profile.

The woman was gracious in her disappointment, which made it worse; almost as if she'd been resigned to hearing just such a response from the outset but had felt compelled to go through the motions and at least *try*, for her son's sake. Terry ushered her out with genuine regret, doubting that the day's third applicant would be anywhere near as brave or deserving. Not that such factors could be allowed to influence her judgement.

Even in the 3D file images displayed before her, this Pelquin character possessed a certain rakish charm. Stockily built, with a roundish face – the sort that carried the passing years deceptively lightly – dark hair cropped short, as most spacers favoured. He was far from handsome in any classical sense, yet there was something undeniably appealing about him. He had the air of a naughty schoolboy who had never quite grown out of the rebellious stage but instead developed into a loveable rogue. Perhaps it was the way his eyes stared straight at you in each of the three images, as if challenging the viewer to criticise. There was no ambiguity in those clear dark depths, which seemed to say: 'this is me. Live with it'.

She sighed, wondering if the man himself would live up to the image her fancy was building of him. Certainly Pelquin's record was colourful enough to fulfil the 'loveable rogue' tag. Little was known about his early years – there was nothing on file about his parents and family, or even his planet of origin – but he'd served on various trading ships before acquiring his current vessel, *The Sun Princess*, a few years previously. He immediately renamed her *Pelquin's Comet*, which said something about the man's ego. He paid for the ship with his share of the bounty from a respectable but hardly record-breaking Elder hoard discovery, registered to the crew of *The Silver Fish*, the last ship he'd served on. A few brushes with the law, mostly relating to alcohol and brawling, and the suspicion of black-market artefact trading without anything ever being proved... In short, exactly what she might have expected and there was certainly nothing in the files to concern the bank. The aspect that puzzled her most was why he was coming to see her at all. The morning's first applicant had his own resources, but this one had his own *ship* for crying out loud. So where did the bank fit in? Yet Pelquin's record argued that he wasn't an idiot and wasn't likely to waste either his own time or hers. Enough prevaricating; the only way she was going to find out was by interviewing the man and assessing this proposal.

The sweep of a hand wiped away the information suspended before her.

"Jay," she spoke into the air, knowing that vocalising the name would ensure the words were heard by her secretary in the anteroom. "Send Captain Pelquin in, please." At least this one appeared experienced enough not to try offering her Lenbya.

27

She enjoyed watching people's reactions when they met her for the first time, fully aware that most would suppose Terry Reese, banking executive, to be a man. Stepping forward to greet visitors as they entered rather than sitting back and having them come to her was another habit calculated to fly in the face of expectation.

Pelquin proved to be shorter than she'd anticipated, less imposing. It was difficult to judge such things from file images, of course, which were rarely life-size. He was stocky though; powerfully built, with broad shoulders and a barrel chest, while his handshake was firm and strong and his eyes held the same intensity the pictures had conveyed.

"Would you like a drink, coffee perhaps?"

"Ehh... no. Thank you."

She led the way to where two chairs waited. Hers was a little grander than the visitor's, higher-backed and more sumptuously padded, but the chairs faced each other at a jauntily skewed angle to avoid any sense of direct confrontation and no desk drew a demarcation line between them. Instead, a small table stood beside the larger chair, just enough to rest drinks or other small items on. The idea was to suggest to the subconscious that this was more in the nature of a cosy chat rather than the discussion of anything important.

Terry sat and smiled at Pelquin. She had a feeling that this one wasn't fooled for a moment.

Terry Reese was proving a difficult so-and-so to read. Pelquin endeavoured to be at his most charming as he made the pitch, explaining how Nate Almont had approached him a year or so after leaving the crew of the *Comet*, conveniently avoiding mention of how acrimonious that parting had been. Nate brought with him a bona-fide Elder artefact accompanied by a harrowing tale of struggle and narrow escape.

Pelquin could still see his friend now, exhausted and nervous, ready to jump at shadows. The two of them had been huddled in a booth at a crowded bar on some fringe world or other, their animosity forgotten. Nate had evidently been crew on a mining vessel, the *Southern Cross*, which had stumbled on a significant cache – the sort of thing that every trader and miner operating at the edge of human space dreamt of stumbling upon. Pelquin had no intention of acquainting Reese with the precise circumstances of its discovery; he didn't doubt the bank would dissect this interview and pore over his every utterance in the hope of gleaning enough information to locate the site themselves. All was fair in war and cache hunting. Better to say too little than too much.

The cache had proved to be warded by a fully alert guardian entity with a small arsenal of sophisticated defences at its disposal. Some of these the eager invaders bludgeoned their way through using mining equipment from their ship, others required a little more thought and subtlety, while the slightest miscalculation soon proved to be deadly. There had been nine aboard the *Southern Cross*. Only Nate and two others survived to reach the inner chamber, their shipmates having fallen one by one, picked off by the installation's defences.

Nate described the process as a sobering one. After the first death there had been heated debate about whether they should abandon the site and make do with selling knowledge of its location for a smaller return. Eventually avarice, thinly disguised within the excuse of ensuring their colleague's death wouldn't be an empty one, had won out. It became easier each time, until the excuses were worn away. There was nowhere for conscience to hide and by the time the surviving trio broke through they'd abandoned all pretence. Greed had brought them here, pure and simple.

Of course, these were far from the terms Pelquin employed when describing events to Reese.

That final chamber proved to be a vast storeroom. Nate had shown him some scratchy footage – relayed back to the ship from the suit cameras, the quality of the images compromised by the layers of Elder architecture and technology that lay between receptor and recorder.

The brief clip showed a tantalising glimpse of a room piled high with all manner of Elder devices and trinkets; a perfect teaser, almost as if it had been designed that way, though Nate insisted otherwise.

"These are the only images we came back with," he'd explained. "Only wish there was more, but soon after we breached the chamber we were hit with some sort of EMP blast that wrecked a load of the power tools, fried our comms and cameras, and wiped the suitcams. This was all we could salvage."

Pelquin played the footage for Terry Reese. Surely, as a banker, she couldn't help but be impressed by *that*? She watched impassively, and made a note in the air close to her face – sensitised space doubtless containing text visible to her but hidden from his perspective.

Nor was he entirely open about what had happened subsequently. He told her frankly of the final manifestation of the guardian Nate and his colleagues encountered within that inner chamber, about how it had scared the living daylights out of them because this one seemed responsive, adapting to their actions rather than just passively performing pre-programmed tasks. They were rare, guardians that could do that. They were the truly dangerous ones. According to what Pelquin proceeded to tell Reese, this final defence had accounted for both the other spacers and Nate had barely escaped with his life, snatching up a single artefact as he fled – his only tangible proof that any of this was real.

In fact, the way Nate had described events to *him*, two of them had escaped that chamber. Pelquin, however, reasoned that the bank wouldn't want to hear about this, reckoning that his case would hardly be helped by the knowledge that he had a competitor. At least *his* key to the cache was still breathing.

Both the survivors were determined to return to the installation – who wouldn't with such a huge cache to exploit? Both knew they couldn't do so alone, that they needed help, but they couldn't agree who from. Nate had wanted to turn to the devil he knew: Pelquin, but the other argued that it would be better to approach a mining concern, people who would already have the necessary equipment and manpower on hand. In the end Nate relented, and they approached Jossyren, one of the larger fringe mining companies.

This proved to be a costly mistake. They were double-crossed, Nate's colleague was killed, and he only escaped by the skin of his teeth – for a second time. With nowhere else to go and the hired guns of a powerful corporation after his blood, Nate had taken the only option left to him, swallowing his pride and approaching his old buddy Pelquin for help.

No, the bank definitely wouldn't want to hear about any of this. Jossyren might be small in galactic terms but they were highly influential on the fringe worlds; a powerful enemy.

So Pelquin presented a slightly abridged version of events to Terry Reese, one in which only Nate Almont had escaped the Elder installation. He did so smoothly and confidently. He was hardly a novice when it came to lying.

"This has to be the biggest cache of Elder tech to be discovered in decades, perhaps the biggest *ever*, and I have on my crew the only man who knows where it is," he concluded – exaggeration being an accepted part of the game. He then sat back, inviting Reese to comment.

She nodded thoughtfully, and then said, "It's a shame Mr Almont isn't here with you."

"Nate's not at his most comfortable in formal situations." *And trust me, right now you wouldn't want to meet him*, he thought but didn't say.

"Pity. Perhaps I could have a chat with him though, on another occasion."

"Perhaps."*Like hell.*

Had he overestimated his own powers of persuasion? Was he about to lose this because of Nate's absence? Surely the woman could see the opportunity he was offering her?

"So, to recap," Reese said, "you're not asking the bank to pay for the hire of a ship, since you already have one, but you are asking us to fund your purchase of a considerable amount of equipment, which you'll utilise to reach this inner chamber where a significant number of Elder artefacts are stored."

"Precisely. Nate got out of there with the guardian entity still fully functional. It'll have rebuilt the defences by now, maybe varied them and probably ensured they're nastier than ever. We need to be prepared for any eventuality and I wouldn't mind hiring one more crewmember – some of this equipment's heavy."

"Not to mention expensive," she observed, "judging by the amount you're after."

He shrugged. "A lot of this is specialist stuff and will have to be made to order."

"Hmm… and how exactly did you arrive at this figure?"

"All carefully calculated, I promise you."

"I'll want to see a full breakdown."

"Naturally." Pelquin struggled to suppress the thrill that coursed through him. If she was asking for figures, she'd bought into the concept already. The rest was just a matter of negotiation and bickering over the details.

"And what are you proposing to offer First Solar in return for this investment?"

Better and better – getting down to the nitty gritty already. "A legal charge over my ship, the *Comet...*"

"...which is next to worthless if you renege on the loan and choose to remain at the fringe, where finding the ship, let alone seizing it, would be too costly a venture to prosecute."

"True, but who wants to eke out a living from the piddling scraps of trade you can pick up around the fringe? You've got my history on record. That's not what I'm about. In addition, I'm offering a ten percent share in the profits made on all Elder artefacts we recover."

"Fifty percent."

"*What?* That's outrageous. Twenty percent, and I'm being more than fair. Don't forget I've got an entire crew to share the balance with."

Her fingers tapped the air in a manner which, from Pelquin's viewpoint, suggested she was conjuring a spell, but which presumably involved something less arcane – calculations, most likely. Seconds later she frowned and wiped her hand across the space, before starting to weave her fingers in a new pattern. At length she sat back and fixed Pelquin with an appraising look. "All right, given the size of the apparent find, I'm willing to come down to forty percent, but that's as low as I can stretch to."

Now it was time to play his ace. "Twenty five percent and I'll throw in this as tangible security." He produced the gonk with a flourish.

She stared at the innocuous seeming object. "Are you trying to tell me that *this* is an Elder artefact?"

He grinned. "You bet your sweet asset base it is."

Still she didn't extend a hand to take it from him. "Does it... *do* anything?"

"Sure does. Do you have anything with a flat surface that's solid but disposable?"

Reese stared at him, as if trying to decide whether or not he was being serious.

"Preferably metal," Pelquin added, "though it doesn't have to be; must be solid, though."

After a fractional hesitation, Reese spoke into the air, "Jay, would you bring in the silver tea tray please?" There was a further pause before she added, "No, the crockery won't be necessary. Just the tray."

Seconds later the door slid open and the secretary breezed in, his every step a study in precision, every footfall a pronouncement of dedication and efficiency. He presented the tray to his boss, who indicated with a nod that he should place it on the small table beside her.

As the secretary departed, Pelquin stared in fascination at what the man had delivered. The tray had a raised rim, with embossed flourishes around the inside edges, and it struck him as far more outlandish than any Elder artefact.

Reese gestured, inviting Pelquin to do his worst. He got up and stepped across, placing the gonk, flat surface down, on the tray. Glancing across at Reese, he saw she was watching him intently. He smiled and raised his eyebrows, milking the moment. The only thing missing was a drum roll. Then, before his dramatic pause could become too irritating, he reached forward... and stroked the gonk with the fingertips of his right hand. Once, twice, moving laterally along its tapering form.

In response, a golden glow emanated from the artefact's underside and the thing seemed to move slightly, to settle in much the same manner a cat might while being fussed. Seconds only the glow lasted before fading, and the suspicion of movement ceased.

Pelquin stepped back and grinned at Reese, who stared at him in amazement.

"Is that it?"

"Ah, don't be fooled. Pick the tray up."

With a sigh that suggested she was humouring him and didn't really know why, Reese did as instructed. The tray lifted clean over the half-egg lump, to display a gonk-shaped ovoid hole at its centre. The gonk was still on the table. Reese held the tray up and stared at it, her gaze meeting Pelquin's through the hole.

"Feel it," he suggested, "run your fingers along the edge. You'll find it's smooth and cool to the touch."

She did so and then picked up the gonk, examining its base. Beneath was nothing except the table: no molten metal, no residue, not even a mark on the table's surface, while the artefact itself remained smooth and unblemished.

"What happened to the missing silver?" Reese asked.

"Beats the hell out of me. It only ever goes through one layer, however thick, and it'll go through absolutely anything; well, everything we've tried it on at least."

"And the process is triggered by a simple stroke?"

"Two, front to back. We only found out by accident. Scared the life out of one of my crew, Monkey, first time it happened. He'd placed the artefact on a desk and sat down to study it, but noticed a mark and gave the thing a quick rub. The next thing he knew it was sitting on his crotch. I've never seen him move so fast nor yell so loud."

Reese gave no indication that she'd even heard the anecdote. Pelquin hadn't really expected the 'chummy' approach to work, but it came naturally to him.

"Does it have a purpose, do you think?" she asked

The question might almost have been rhetorical, but he answered anyway. "Again, no idea. It could be anything from a specialist tool to a child's game."

Her gaze shifted back from the gonk to him. "And you're offering this as security?"

"Yeah, that's right. It has to be worth at least ten percent."

"Please, Captain, don't insult my intelligence. This is a trinket. It has novelty value, certainly, and an inherent worth because it's an Elder artefact, but let's not kid ourselves that this is the key to Lenbya or anything."

Pelquin smiled. He found such directness refreshing, especially in a banker. "Of course it isn't, but it *is* tangible evidence of an Elder cache."

"Perhaps." She studied him thoughtfully. "And you consider this Nate Almont to be fully credible?"

"Yes. I'd trust Nate with my life – I've known him for most of it."

"Ah, but that's not the issue here, is it? You have to convince *me* to trust both his word and your judgement, with my employer's money."

Which, her words seemed to suggest, was far more valuable than a mere life. His turn to smile. "Quite. After all, that is what banks are here for, isn't it?"

She didn't respond directly, instead saying, "I'm still a little unclear why Mr Almont left your service after so many happy years together."

Pelquin made certain his smile didn't slip one iota. "We had a falling out." There was no need for her to know anything about Julia, who had caused the argument.

"And a year later he pops up again with an alien artefact in one hand and the opportunity for you both to get rich in the other."

"More or less."

"How convenient. And the matter you fell out about so dramatically, that's all been forgotten?"

Pelquin shrugged. "Time's a great healer. We've both had the opportunity to cool down and, when all's said and done, there's a lot of history between me and Nate, far more than a stupid argument could ever wipe away. Looking back now, the argument was nothing. So yes, it's forgotten."

Reese nodded, hopefully in acceptance. "It still seems a little odd that he should turn to you given the bad blood that clearly existed."

"Not really," Pelquin replied, wishing she'd stop nitpicking over what he saw as a minor detail and would concentrate instead on the bigger picture. "After all, he's known me and the crew for years, knows we're good at what we do and that we can all work together. Where else was he going to go?"

"Fair enough."

Thank God! There might have been an unspoken 'for now' at the end of her sentence, but Pelquin didn't care, so long as they could move on. Time to get back to business and close the deal. "Now, about your cut…"

They settled on the bank taking thirty five percent, which was higher than he'd hoped but lower than he'd feared. There remained a few 'procedural matters' to be dealt with – and Pelquin didn't doubt these would entail some furious background checking behind the scenes – but he didn't care. Jossyren were hardly advertising their interest.

Reese assured him the money would be available within a couple of days if everything checked out, and he believed her.

As he headed towards the door it was all he could do not to skip and kick his heels.

"Oh, one more thing," Reese said from behind, even as the door swished open. "I will of course be appending one of the bank's officers to your crew for the duration of the trip. Merely as an observer you understand, there to safeguard our investment."

"Of course," Pelquin replied, though a passenger was the very last thing he needed aboard his ship; especially one who might suffer from an overblown opinion of their own authority. One man alone made the decisions aboard the *Comet*, and it wasn't any banker. Still, this seemed a small price to pay for the credit line Reese had just agreed to extend to him. With that in place, Pelquin was confident that nothing could stop him from becoming a very rich man indeed.

Terry Reese sat back in her chair, deep in thought as she reviewed the interview with Pelquin in her mind. He hadn't overstated the case; well, not by much. This might not be Lenbya but it promised to be one of the most significant cache discoveries in recent years and the potential for profit was enormous. It was the sort of thing that could make or break a career.

The amount she'd agreed to lend was significant but well within her remit and, in any case, much of the risk would be offset to other institutions, as was the norm where large sums were committed. Gut instinct told her that this was a good investment... So why was she still hesitant? Because she was taking a gamble, no question about it. She'd learned to trust her instincts, but this was far from being a clear-cut case. Oh, the figures added up; the risk assessment gave a high enough success rating that she could comfortably justify the loan should her judgement ever be called into question, but that failed to take into account the man himself. Pelquin had not been fully open with her, she was sure of that; the risk lay in precisely how much he'd kept back and whether it was personal to him or pertinent to the expedition.

Reese had to wait for a few tense heartbeats before the call she'd been expecting came through.

"Nothing," a woman's voice told her. "Sorry, but the images are of too poor a quality to yield anything useful. Either that or they've been expertly scrubbed to present as if they are. I can't even pick up a hint of ambient quasar energy to help us get a fix."

"Thank you, Paula." Terry made a point of memorising everybody's name. She prided herself on such attention to detail and names were important; they were the key to dedication and loyalty. She could address even the lowliest of juniors by their first name after the briefest of encounters, and had been rewarded on more than one occasion with a smile of surprise and delight as a result.

Damn! No more than a long shot, perhaps, but she'd had high hopes that the brief footage Pelquin showed – retained by her office systems as a matter of course – might give him away. It was surprising how many would-be prospectors were tripped up in that fashion, by failing to take even minimal precautions. Images generally held a wealth of encrypted information, but not on this occasion it would seem. Thirty five percent of the cache glimpsed so tantalisingly in the scratchy footage would more than justify the bank's exposure, but a hundred percent would have been so much better.

So, it was Captain Pelquin or nothing. The man was an enigma, one which merited careful handling and a watchful eye. A major mistake was something Terry Reese could ill afford at this stage of her professional life; the potential plaudits on the other hand... She needed her best agent for this one, someone capable of thinking on their feet, of reacting to the unexpected and turning potential disadvantage into an asset.

"Drake," she spoke to the air, "I'm sending you across the recording of a recent interview. Please study it carefully. This is to be your next assignment."

FOUR

Drake was unusually distracted as he left the head office of First Solar Bank. He wasn't angry; he was determined *not* to be angry about being sent off world. *Again.* Another ship; another crew; another group of spacers forced to accommodate his intrusion and interact with him. He knew from experience that people tended to respond in one of several ways. Some resented his presence and weren't afraid of showing the fact, others viewed him as a necessary evil and made the best of things, while still others preferred to ignore him as much as possible and simply stay out of his way. A few, a very few, would accept him for who he was and extend a degree of friendship.

In truth, the latter could often be the biggest pains of the lot. Given the choice, he would prefer to be ignored, since this gave him the most scope for analytical observation and assessment unhampered by distraction, but he knew that was the least likely response. After all, he was destined to be locked away with these people inside a metal tube with limited space, walking the same corridors, breathing the same air, eating in the same galley. Under conditions like that ignorance required a considerable amount of effort, while resentment could fester in no time at all.

Drake hadn't anticipated a new assignment quite so quickly and could really have done without this one. It felt as if he'd only been back from the last trip a matter of days. Oh, he knew that in reality it was longer than that, but readjusting to life dirtside after a protracted period in space took time. He'd barely begun to pick up the threads of his life on New Sparta and here he was heading out to God only knew where again.

He was almost tempted to seek a quiet word with Terry Reese, to ask if she might consider someone else for this particular venture. Of course, he wouldn't actually do so. He was too conscientious, and too aware that such reluctance might cause Reese to hesitate when considering him for future jobs. Representatives were paid a decent enough basic salary but they were also in line for commission based on a percentage of anything brought back from an expedition, and that was where the real money could be earned. Assuming assignments were successful, of course, as his invariably were – a situation he didn't intend to see change. Also, despite his misgivings and a deep-seated weariness, he relished a challenge.

Drake did his best to ignore his unlooked for reputation but he wasn't ignorant of it. He was aware of the statistics, knew that he had a significantly greater hit rate than any other bank representative, but he refused to believe the hype. It was all down to blind luck. Surely anyone with a modicum of good sense could see that. How could it be anything other than pure coincidence? He didn't get to pick his own assignments but simply went wherever First Solar sent him, as all his colleagues did. It was true, though, that success had a knack of breeding success. Because he'd gained a rep for being lucky, he tended to be top of the list for the juiciest, most promising assignments; particularly if Terry Reese was involved. She seemed to view Drake as something of a personal prodigy, which he supposed he was, in a sense. After all, he owed his position with First Solar to her. If Reese hadn't spotted something in him and been willing to take a chance when he first approached her for a job… But she had, and he hadn't let her down.

As Drake crossed the mottled marble floor of First Solar's deliberately imposing foyer, his reveries were interrupted by a greeting.

"Drake?"

He looked up to see Archer, a fellow representative, coming towards him. Tall, blond, athletically built, and reputed to be equally sharp in both mind and dress sense, Archer was one of the rising stars of the department.

He also possessed a glaringly broad ambitious streak, which Drake simultaneously admired and was wary of. On the rare occasions they'd met, Drake had the impression that Archer's ready smile was disingenuous and that the younger man's true self lurked some distance back from the ever pleasant façade, observing and calculating; even as Drake tended to do. Perhaps that was why Archer unsettled him: the man reminded him too much of himself.

"Hear you've been assigned to a potential big one," the other man said cheerfully.

Word *did* travel fast. "I'm not so sure about that. It's another trip on another rust bucket chasing wild geese. I'll only find out what's waiting at the far end when I get there. You know what it's like; every pitch ever made to an assessor is for a 'big one'."

Archer laughed, as if they were the most intimate of friends and he was fully relaxed in Drake's company. "That's true. Can't say I've ever heard of an applicant seeking funds for an expedition to uncover a paltry cache of insignificant baubles."

"Quite."

"Well, best of luck in any case. I mustn't keep Those Upstairs waiting." With a final smile, Archer continued on into the building.

Drake stepped from the comparative tranquillity and subdued lighting of the head office's interior into the full-on glare and bustle of New Sparta's day, reviewing the conversation. The bank's field representatives spent so much time off world that casual meetings like this were rare. He didn't know Archer well, but then he didn't need to. Any fool could see that the man's good wishes had been hollow. Archer clearly begrudged Drake this new assignment, but why? Drake suspected this apparently chance encounter had a significance that escaped him at present and wouldn't become clear until he could define its context more effectively. Refusing to waste time on pointless speculation, he dismissed the incident from his thoughts.

After wending his way across a busy landing field Drake finally reached the designated berth, where a ship waited as promised: a squat silver beetle of a craft built around a bloated fuselage designed to provide maximum cargo space. The front of the ship tapered to a narrower prow where the living quarters and guidance systems were housed. That tapering and the stubby fins projecting to either side and ventrally at the rear of the craft were the only structural concessions to aerodynamics; as if to testify that here was a vessel that plied its trade far from any world's atmosphere and dipped down to grace the planet-bound only when strictly necessary.

Much of the ship's broad backside below the thrusters and exhaust vents was taken up by the cargo hatch, which currently gaped wide: the main door doubling as a loading ramp. A couple of the ship's crew were on hand – a man and a woman – though neither had noticed his arrival.

"Compact Tectonic Detector," the woman declared.

"Complete and Total Destruction," the man countered instantly, as if this were a competition being run against the clock.

"Controlled Thermonuclear Device," the woman said almost as quickly.

The two figures were hunched over a large silver metal case which stood at the foot of the loading ramp. Drake could see very little of the woman, who had her back to him, though her hair was a tumble of black-brown curls pulled back haphazardly and kept in place by a band. The angle might have hidden her figure but not her frame, which was broad and well-muscled, dwarfing that of the man beside her. A gangly individual with sallow complexion and a mop of ginger brown hair, the man wore dark blue work overalls belted at the waist, while his face was dominated by a prominent roman nose.

No question, this was the right ship, though the realisation filled Drake with little joy. He was back at the spaceport, amidst the clamour and the shouting, the whir of machines and the groan of metal and the dust and the colour and the chaos, as incoming cargoes were unloaded and outgoing ones delivered and brought aboard. No departures were scheduled for this section of the field until late that afternoon, so activity on the landing pads was hectic and constant. People and machines moved around each other in a stage-managed melee, to the accompaniment of shouted instruction and the warning beeps of large vehicles on the move. Drake knew that proceedings were far better coordinated than they appeared to the naked eye, but from his perspective the whole thing looked chaotic.

To reach the appropriate berth he had been forced to sidestep a long cargo train laden with assorted goods, detour around a particularly large crate that stretched across the width of the thoroughfare, and quickstep from behind a reversing lifter whose driver was clearly oblivious to his presence.

For a moment his attention strayed beyond the two crewmembers to the craft itself: an old comet class trading ship. It brought back a whole welter of memories that, given a choice, he would have preferred not to revisit.

Still, this was what they paid him for.

"Constant Tongue Dicking," said the man.

The woman punched him on the arm with something more than playful force. "Arsebrain!"

"Ow! What was that for?"

"Is there anything anywhere that you *can't* turn into something smutty?"

Drake could see the woman a little more clearly now, if only in profile; broad features on a face that he'd describe as pleasant rather than beautiful, dominated by dark brown eyes and full lips.

"I hope not," the man said, "I've got my reputation to think about."

"Central Transport Data," the woman said.

"Is that the best you can come up with? I give you tongue dicking and you give me transport?"

"In your dreams. There's no way that you giving me any sort of dicking and me still breathing are ever gonna happen in the same universe."

"Is that so? Sounds to me as if the lady protests too much…"

"Don't push it, Monkey."

This seemed an appropriate time to interrupt. Drake cleared his throat and announced in a clear voice, "Corbin Thadeus Drake."

The man jumped as if startled, looking up as if noticing the banker for the first time; his pale blue eyes wide. "Who the fuck are you?"

"He just told you, Arsebrain," the woman supplied.

"Stop calling me that!"

"I represent First Solar Bank," Drake continued. "I believe you're expecting me."

The woman also straightened, stepping away from the silver trunk to reveal the letters CTD clearly embossed on its metal lid.

She examined him, a stare that fell short of hostile but was equally distant from welcoming. "I think, my friend, that you've come to the wrong ship," she said. "We don't do passengers here on the *Comet*."

He recognised these two from their infofiles, but dry facts and snippets of tri-D recordings were poor substitute for meeting the real thing. The woman was Brenda Jayne Bearman, youngest of three siblings; father dead, mother remarried and no longer in contact; brother and sister both gainfully employed. Brenda, the black sheep of the family, had been in and out of trouble throughout her teens before she was eventually conscripted into the army. A reluctant recruit, she had subsequently thrived in the military environment, serving with distinction during the Macinairy Campaign, which had provided a coda to the Auganics War; a flexing of military muscle that finally quashed the lingering discontent left over from that bitter conflict which had threatened to tear the coalition of worlds apart.

Since her discharge, Brenda had lived at the fringes of society, spending a couple of years drifting from place to place and picking up odd jobs in security or as temporary crew before settling – for reasons the files failed to explain – as a crewmember aboard a freelance trade ship currently registered as *Pelquin's Comet*.

The profile of the man beside her, Malcolm 'Monkey' Palmer, was a little more straight forward. Palmer had enjoyed limited formal education but had gained a wealth of experience souping-up engines for illicit street races and getaways, a pastime which saw him graduate from bikes to cars to ships. A dozen Malcolm Palmers could be found hanging around the bars of almost any spaceport, but Brenda Bearmans were a little harder to come by. Bearman was dressed casually in military-style fatigues with cut-away arms, worn tight enough to both display her biceps and accentuate a well-toned figure. He caught a whiff of perfume and she wore makeup, subtly applied. Here was a woman who had taken considerable care with her appearance but didn't want to be obvious about it, which led him to conclude that there was somebody on board she was keen to impress. Not Monkey Palmer, that much was obvious.

"Today we're making an exception," a new voice declared. The instantly recognisable form of Thomas Pelquin stood at the top of the ramp. Drake noted the fleeting look in Bearman's eyes as she first saw the ship's owner and captain. Ah, so *this* was who all the effort was for. He wondered if the man even realised that a member of his crew had the hots for him. "Welcome to the *Comet*, Mr Drake," Pelquin said, evidently oblivious. "Bren, Monkey, bring our guest's luggage aboard."

For a second it looked as if Bearman would challenge the order, but then she shrugged and moved to pick up the trunk, offering Drake a curious stare as she did so. Monkey slouched across to help, muttering, "Thought I was supposed to be the mechanic around here, not the friggin' porter."

Drake went to follow them into the ship, at which point Mudball chose to put in an appearance, poking his head up from the papoose-like pouch that supported him.

Pelquin, who still stood at the top of the ramp and was now no more than a dozen paces away, froze and stabbed a finger towards the furry face as soon as it peered from behind Drake's shoulder. "What the hell is *that*?"

"Just my genpet," Drake replied, the familiar lie tripping freely from his tongue.

"Nobody said anything about any *genpet*." Pelquin made the last sound like a swear word.

"I don't suppose anyone saw the need. Mudball goes everywhere with me."

"Not aboard the *Comet* it doesn't."

Bren and Monkey had stopped halfway up the ramp and were watching the exchange with interest. Drake felt the grip on his cane grow firmer, matching the tightness of his smile. "This is your ship and of course it's your choice, Captain Pelquin. But without Mudball, I don't come aboard. Without me on board, you don't go anywhere."

Their gazes locked. Drake could sense the man's anger, but he also knew that he had the upper hand – one which rested firmly on the purse strings. The *Comet* wasn't ready to leave yet, and Drake could freeze the flow of funds in an instant. Excerting his authority this early wasn't something he would have chosen to do, especially not in front of the crew, but Pelquin hadn't given him much option.

"Ah, come on, Pel," Brenda Bearman said, surprising the banker. "I think Mudball is kind of sweet,"

Her words broke the tension. Pelquin's gaze flickered between the woman and Drake. He drew a deep breath, as if sucking in air might somehow cool his temper. "All right, but that damned thing is confined to your quarters at all times. Is that clear?"

"Perfectly."

"If I catch a glimpse of its hairy hide anywhere else during the course of the trip it goes straight out the airlock."

I'll kick his ugly face straight out the airlock if he says much more, Mudball's affronted voice muttered in Drake's head.

Behave yourself. "You won't even know he's on board," he assured Pelquin. *Will he!*

Of course not. Soul of discretion, you know me.

Only too well, Drake reflected, while pondering Pelquin's extreme reaction and wondering what exactly the *Comet*'s captain had against genpets in any case.

Monkey interrupted his thoughts, calling out, "Hey, does the T *really* stand for Thadeus?"

"It does," Drake confirmed. "Still, it could have been worse. People might call me 'Monkey'."

Bren guffawed. The mechanic merely looked puzzled, as if trying to decide whether or not he'd just been insulted. Drake smiled to rob the words of any malice, and followed Pelquin inside.

They were joined by a waiflike, ebony-skinned girl who was presumably older than she looked. "Hi, I'm Anna," the newcomer said. "I'm the *Comet's* pilot... at least I am when the captain's hands can be prised off the helm."

Drake didn't recognise her from the infofiles, which meant that either she was a comparatively new addition to the crew or the bank's records were incomplete. Both possibilities struck him as equally plausible. He didn't especially like this sort of variable, but with the way the crew rosters shifted and changed aboard fringe traders it was inevitable. He smiled and gave a curt nod in greeting.

Anna tagged along as the captain showed him to his quarters – a recessed alcove just deep enough to contain the width of a bed and just long enough to squeeze in a small cabinet and table at the foot of a crewcot. Quite where Bren and Monkey were going to stow his trunk was anyone's guess. Drake was glad his suits were crease resistant, since any hanging space was going to have to be well and truly improvised.

"You can leave the furball here," Pelquin said, "and I'll show you the bridge."

It's Mudball, a voice seethed in Drake's head.

"I will if you insist, but I wouldn't advise it," Drake said, pulling at the flimsy curtain which was the booth's token gesture towards privacy. "There's no way of securing anything in here. Mudball's obedient enough, but I can't guarantee he won't wander off if left alone for too long. Now, if he were to stay with me, I could ensure he behaves himself."

"Ooh, he's cute!" Anna said, evidently spotting Mudball for the first time.

I like her, said the voice in Drake's head.

Pelquin scowled. "We agreed you were going to keep him in your quarters."

"True, but I was assuming I could lock him in."

If he suggests putting me in a cupboard...!

For a split second the captain looked as if he might indeed suggest something along those lines, but in the end his need to keep First Solar's representative happy must have won out. "Very well, but this is the *last* concession you get. He stays put in that little papoose thing of yours at all times. No exceptions. Give me any excuse to lock him away somewhere and I will."

Drake nodded his acceptance. "That's fair. Thank you." He suppressed a smile, noting that already Pelquin had inadvertently slipped from referring to Mudball as an 'it' to 'him'. The alien had a way of winning folk round, but this was swifter progress than he'd anticipated.

Internally, the *Comet* held few surprises, conforming to standard layout for the class, with fitments better maintained than on a few ships Drake had seen, though here and there they showed their age – handholds worn smooth with use, lettering partially rubbed away. Nothing critical, just an indication of how worn a few elements of the ship's interior had become. On the whole décor was functional and neutral, as he'd expect; which was why the 3D image fixed to the wall beside the final gantry leading to the bridge came as such a surprise: it served no practical purpose whatsoever – at least none that the banker could fathom.

He paused to study the picture, taking in the image of a ship which looked to be racing out of the wall and about to shoot over the observer's left shoulder. Both the ship and the dramatic starscape behind it were vividly depicted, and the observer in question might have been forgiven for thinking that this was the very vessel they were standing in, *Pelquin's Comet*, but they would have been wrong. It was the same class, certainly, but a very different ship.

"That's the *Ion Raider*," Pelquin supplied without being asked. "The greatest freebooter ever to have roamed the stars."

"Apart from *Pelquin's Comet*, of course," Anna added.

"Including *Pelquin's Comet*," her captain corrected.

The captain moved on but Drake delayed for a second, lingering over the image. It was a long enough pause for Anna to whisper, "Pel sees himself as the natural successor to Captain Cornische, the *Ion Raider*'s commander, or at least that's what he'd like to be."

Did he now? Drake mulled that over as he followed after Pelquin. Aspirations were all well and good but he mistrusted the whole concept of hero worship, and this titbit of information made him uneasy. Trying to emulate anyone was a fool's pastime and an open invitation to poor decision making. Precious seconds spent wondering 'What would so-and-so do?' took attention away from the real question: 'What the hell should *I* do now?'

Not the most encouraging of starts; he'd barely stepped on board and already he'd aggravated the captain and found cause to question the man's competence.

On the brighter side, said a familiar voice, *things can only get better.*

He fervently hoped so.

Drake didn't get a chance to meet the two remaining members of the *Comet*'s crew until much later in the day. Neither was aboard when he arrived. Nathaniel 'Nate' Almont, who was the first to turn up, scowled at him in greeting. Almont was a seasoned spacer from a long line of spacers. No strong family ties.

Almont and Pelquin, though, went way back, their association predating the latter's acquisition of the *Comet*. They appeared to have been inseparable for many years, right up to the point where they had fallen out so spectacularly and Almont had left, disappearing for over a year. The bank had no information at all on that missing period, which worried Drake, since Almont and the knowledge he carried were so pivotal to this expedition. Cache hunts could be divisive; greed putting a strain on even the strongest of friendships.

Drake had no idea what Almont had been up to while at large in New Sparta either, but nothing pleasant judging by the sight of him. The man looked shabby, grimy – as if he had been sleeping rough – which suggested some subterfuge or other and instantly piqued Drake's curiosity.

Pelquin seemed equally in the dark regarding his friend's recent whereabouts, at least to judge by the heated exchange which Drake caught the start of when Almont appeared. They quickly moved out of earshot, but the exchange suggested that some degree of tension still lingered between them.

The final crewmember, Ahmed Bariha, was in town somewhere replenishing the ship's medical supplies, or so Drake was told. Judging by the dilated state of the man's pupils and the distracted air he displayed on his return, the good doctor had been extremely diligent in his duties, to the extent of sampling a few of the products before buying. The bank's files had less to say about Bariha than anyone else – apart from Anna, about whom they said nothing at all. Having a medic on a ship this size struck Drake as something of a luxury, but Bren put him straight on that score.

"He only calls himself the medic because it makes him feel superior," she explained. "The doc likes to think he's a cut above the rest of us,"

"He's not a real doctor, then?"

"Oh sure, he's a doctor all right, qualified and everything, but that doesn't count for beans around here. Unless somebody gets ill or injured, of course. Other than that, he's just regular crew like the rest of us, whatever he likes to pretend."

None of which explained why a qualified doctor would be working as crew aboard a small independent trader like this.

Bren clearly guessed the nature of his thoughts. "Everyone's got a history," she said. "While they're on the *Comet*, a person can talk about it or keep things tight, whichever they choose. Long as they do their job, we're happy to let whatever happened in the past remain in the past; their business and no one else's."

This was perhaps as polite a way of telling him to keep his nose out of things as he'd ever heard.

Drake spent the next couple of days on the *Comet*, doing his best to stay in the background and determined not to get in anyone's way, as he monitored the equipment being brought on board and did his own discreet calculations. The front of the ship's voluminous cargo hold – the area furthest from the main hatch – swiftly filled up, with departure fast approaching. He wasn't privy to the actual purchase negotiations Pelquin had conducted, but he did know how much the bank had lent the man and had a pretty good idea of what most of the equipment arriving ought to have cost, and by his estimate there ought to be a good chunk of the bank's money left over… which was curious given most folk's aversion to accruing interest.

One thing these early days provided was a chance to assess the crew's reaction to him, and he wasn't displeased on the whole. Pelquin didn't like his being aboard but accepted the necessity and had settled on being polite. Monkey felt much the same but seemed incapable of being polite to anyone. Doctor Bariha occupied his own cocoon of space aboard the ship and, since Drake didn't impinge on this, largely ignored him. Bren was happy to treat him as a fellow human being and give him the benefit of the doubt, while Anna was positively friendly. Out of all of them, only Nate Almont gave him any real cause for concern. The big man clearly didn't like him and displayed the sort of resentment that might fester unless Drake could bring it into the open sooner rather than later.

He tried the reasoned approach first. "Mr Almont, I appreciate you might not like my being on board but I'm here for the duration, so we might as well make the best of it." Almont had grunted and walked away.

Things came to a head one time in the hold, where Drake was busy doing another quick tot-up. The last of the equipment had finally arrived and Nate and Monkey were busy stowing it in preparation for departure. Despite his attempts at discretion, Drake's habit of running his eye over each new delivery irritated the hell out of Nate, who seemed on a particularly short fuse that day, but Drake felt it essential that the crew should get used to his presence as soon as possible.

He's taking something, Mudball concluded.

Something provided by Bariha?

Probably. Performance rather than recreational, judging by his vitals.

If Nate was taking stimulants, that might explain his being so tense.

Just how tense soon became apparent. With a growl of frustration, Nate yanked tight a final strap and then abandoned what he was doing to turn and face the banker. "You don't have to come down here every friggin' time there's a delivery, you know."

"Merely doing my job, Mr Almont."

"Leave it, Nate," Bren advised.

"No, I want to know what it's like to spend your life looking over other people's shoulders? Get a kick out of it, do you?"

Drake smiled, watching Nate closely, waiting for the narrowing of eyes, the tensing of muscles that would telegraph the lunge or the swipe of a fist that he felt certain was imminent. "Oh, you'd be amazed at what I learn."

The screech of tyres from outside distracted him. Just beyond the foot of the cargo ramp a car had pulled up and doors sprang open. As a result, Drake missed the tell-tales he'd been looking for.

Nate's fist came powering forward before he realised it, giving him little chance to react. He was only just beginning to jerk his head out of the way when the clenched ridge of bone and knuckle flew narrowly past his nose to smash into the wooden crate beside him.

A deliberate miss, a bluff, he realised belatedly.

"Nate!" Bren yelled. And was that someone laughing? Monkey, he was sure of it.

"There's a lot of heavy machinery down here," Nate said. "Accidents can happen when inexperienced people start nosing around and getting under our feet. It would be better for all our sakes if you stayed well out the fucking way from now on."

Drake barely heard him. He was trying to look past the crates and the others, to see what was happening at the loading ramp.

The car had disgorged half a dozen men. They weren't uniformed in the strictest sense of the word, though they might as well have been. All were clad from head to toe in black clothing of various sorts and all wore tight-fitting hoods and tinted visors – guaranteeing anonymity should they be picked up on any security cameras. The ensemble seemed unlikely to win any fashion awards but as a statement of intent it was pretty hard to fault. And if their get-up didn't give the game away, the guns they were sporting did the job nicely.

"Look out!" Drake yelled to the trio of *Comet* crew, who were so focused on the confrontation before them that they hadn't noticed what was happening behind them.

"Oh shit!" was Bren's take on the situation when she spun around.

The black-clad figures had spread out. There was no subtlety here, no attempt to negotiate or to board the *Comet*. Two of the men were kneeling, while the others brazenly planted their feet, forming a crescent-shaped cordon across the ship's entrance.

Monkey darted to the left, towards the controls that would retract the ramp and close the hatch, just as the men raised their guns and opened up, spraying the *Comet*'s hold with automatic fire.

Drake took cover behind the nearest group of crates, getting safely behind them even as the first slugs thudded into the opposite side. Bren joined him an instant later and in the corner of his eye he saw Nate dive for another crate. He didn't see where Monkey had gone, but presumed he'd found his own refuge.

The stream of lethal munitions continued. Bullets slammed into walls and ricocheted off the metal steps way above Drake's head, with no attempt at accuracy. Equipment and fittings shattered and fell to the floor and splinters were thrown in all direction as whole sections of wooden crating were chewed to pulp, while a heavy chain that hung from a gantry danced to the bullets' refrain. Beside him, Bren squatted down, head bowed, arms across the back of her neck. Belatedly, Drake followed suit, realising that they were more at risk from rebounds and shrapnel than they were from a direct hit, and such secondary threats could come from any angle.

The sound was deafening. It had to be reverberating throughout the length of the ship, and the rest of the crew couldn't fail to hear it. Drake only hoped this didn't bring them charging in to investigate, straight into the hail of fire.

Still there were no demands and no attempt to actually board.

Drake suddenly realised that they weren't serious. No, that wasn't right. Of course anything that involved bullets being sprayed around with complete abandon was serious, but they weren't intent on seizing control of the ship or even killing anyone, not really. This was a warning, or perhaps a gesture; a sharp, violent gesture. So what were they after? What was the point of such a brutal display?

The three crewmembers weren't armed – why would they be? This was New Sparta, the heart of civilised space. Drake, however, was. He'd held back up to this point, not wanting the situation to escalate, but he was beginning to reconsider when the shooting stopped. The sound echoed around the cavernous room, or perhaps within the confines of his head, for several seconds before he could be certain that it had indeed ended.

Car doors slammed, the sound penetrating in a distant, muffled fashion. He risked peering around the corner of the crates and was just in time to see the vehicle pulling rapidly away. At the same instant the metal staircase above him rang to the tread of heavy footfalls. Pelquin appeared, with Anna and the doc a little behind him. The captain was carrying a hefty-looking energy gun. The cavalry, arriving too late.

Drake heard a gasp from beside him. "Monkey!" It was Bren's voice.

Only then did he register the form of the diminutive mechanic, curled up in a foetal position behind a cluster of crates far smaller than their own. Monkey wasn't moving.

Drake's respect for Pelquin grew in the moments immediately after the one-sided fire fight. The *Comet's* owner checked on his crewmember first, ensuring Monkey was still alive, before standing aside and letting the doc examine him. Only then did he turn his attention to discovering exactly what had happened here, inviting Drake, Nate and Bren to describe in turn what they had seen and heard. Next it was the welfare of the cargo and equipment. He tasked Nate, Bren and Anna with checking every item and every crate for bullet holes and other damage. Nate had suffered a flesh wound where a bullet had grazed his left arm but he was otherwise unhurt. The doc sprayed the resultant gash with something and slapped an antibiotic skin patch over it, then left Nate to get on with things.

Monkey was another matter entirely.

Pelquin turned to the banker and said, "And that was it? Really? They simply shot the place up and then left, without attempting to board or take anything."

"Yes," Drake replied, realising that the captain was merely looking to reaffirm what he already knew and that the question was all but rhetorical. Pelquin nodded, as if he now understood fully what had just happened.

Drake suspected that he did too, now that he'd had a chance to analyse events. He just hoped the captain was as sharp as his reputation suggested.

"Anna," Pelquin called. "Forget the damage inventory for now, get up to the controls and start the engines. We can finish this off once we're underway. Nate, shut the bay doors and prepare for lift off."

"*Lift off?*" the doc looked up sharply from where he knelt beside the wounded mechanic. "You can't. We need to get this man to a hospital."

"Out of the question. We're leaving. Now."

"But he'll…"

"Put him in stasis."

"In *his* condition?" Bren said, staring at the captain. "It'll kill him."

"Maybe, but I doubt it. He's stronger than he looks."

"Pel, this is *Monkey.*"

The captain ignored Bren and addressed the doc. "What'll happen if we don't put him into stasis and don't get him to a hospital?"

Doc hesitated for an instant and then said, "He'll die."

"So he *will* die if we don't put him in stasis and *might* die if we do, yes?"

The doc nodded.

"Did you follow that, Bren?"

"Yeah, you made your point. I'm angry, not deaf."

"Then quit yapping and get on with it. The sooner Monkey's in a cryochamber the better his chances of surviving."

Bren's glare looked hot enough to melt steel. The two of them locked gazes. The woman broke first. "You'd better be right about this, Pel."

She crouched down, scooping Monkey's deceptively frail form up in her arms.

"Be careful with him," Doc said.

The anger hadn't fully left her eyes as she straightened up, but evidently her trust in the captain had won out. She left without saying anything further, the doc hurrying in her wake.

Pelquin watched them go and then looked across to Drake, perhaps expecting the banker – such an acknowledged symbol of officialdom – to object, but Drake had no intention of doing so. He sensed that the *Comet's* captain had reached the same conclusion he had. Logically, the raid could only have had one purpose: to delay them. This was New Sparta, where order was paramount and any disruption stamped down on mercilessly. Local security would already be on the way. The first thing they'd do was impound the ship and lock everything down until the situation was clarified. The *Comet* and her crew would be stuck here for a long time while red tape coiled around them and questions and suspicion crystallised in the blink of an eye. Extricating ship and crew from the resultant quagmire of bureaucracy could take months.

So it was now or never. And yet... *and yet*, wouldn't this be exactly how a shrewd enemy might expect Pelquin to react? Was Drake missing something here?

He dismissed the thought; there was too little evidence from which to draw a conclusion. Getting the ship off world was his priority here, or First Solar would never see a return on their investment.

"You were a witness," Pelquin said. "If questions are asked later, you can confirm that we were attacked and I took us up for the safety of the ship and crew."

Drake hesitated. First Solar couldn't be seen to be involved in anything illegal, but up to this point he could claim to have been no more than an innocent bystander swept up in events beyond his control. Letting things continue meant stretching his remit to the limit, but the alternative was to close things down now and lose the chance of securing a significant Elder cache. The potential reward more than justified the risk.

None the less, he chose his words carefully when replying. "I'm only here to safeguard the bank's investment, Captain, but I'll do what I can should it ever prove necessary."

An empty promise, one which sounded supportive without committing him to anything, but it was evidently enough to satisfy Pelquin, who acknowledged the comment with a curt nod.

Falyn de Souza stared out the window as the world sped past. All those insignificant people scurrying around in pursuit of whatever their inconsequential lives demanded. They were no more than blurs at this speed, an impression of outline, a smudge of colour – a surrealist's painting that suggested shape rather than defining it and left imagination to fill in the rest – though in this instance each was replaced by the next before his mind could begin to fill in any detail, even had he felt inclined to do so.

The buildings though, they were a different breed entirely. Solid, resolute, meant to last, housing corporate entities which the scurrying folk were slaved to feed and serve. Here beat the financial heart of humanity's star-spanning society, and within these towering edifices dwelt the minds responsible for shaping and redefining humankind's destiny.

De Souza relished these visits to New Sparta, loved the decadence of the hotel suites his position afforded him and loved rubbing shoulders with the corporate bigwigs even more, as if some of their glitter and success might inadvertently rub off on him. Oh, he knew that Jossyren were just one of many corporations here on New Sparta, whatever standing the company commanded out in the fringe worlds, but he felt an affinity with the movers and shakers, with the whole ethos of the place. He didn't doubt that one day he would have an office in one of the ostentatious buildings that flashed past him as the car sped through the city centre. Perhaps with Jossyren perhaps with somebody else – loyalty to an employer only stretched so far – but, one way or another, he would be here. It was his destiny.

He'd been neglecting his guest, ignoring the man sitting beside him in the car's plush upholstery for long enough. Deliberately so, but he judged the moment now right to turn his attention away from the wider world.

"Well?" he asked.

"I told you, there was nothing I could do."

If de Souza had expected the man to feel discomfited by being ignored for such a protracted length of time, he was disappointed. Archer seemed completely at ease, as if it were only natural for a visiting businessman to stare out the window as New Sparta flashed past. Perhaps it was.

"It's just our bad luck he booked in to see Terry Reese," the banker continued. "The old bat had Drake assigned to the case before Pelquin had even left the building. No way I could get involved after that."

De Souza grunted. Excuses. They were all he kept hearing. It was enough to make him wonder why he'd gone to the trouble and expense of securing an insider at First Solar in the first place.

"Let's just hope there are no further slip-ups, for all our sakes."

"There won't be," Archer assured him. "Drake's record is exemplary. His presence actually works in our favour. This way we get what we want without taking any of the risks."

"Indeed," said de Souza, who hadn't been planning on taking any risks in any case.

A ping in his left ear distracted him. An incoming communiqué, the caller ID unavailable. He turned his head away from Archer as he answered.

"Speak" he said, knowing who this had to be.

"Job done," a male voice said.

"Our visitors have left, then?"

"Yes, and in something of a hurry."

"Good, good. It was so nice of you to see them off."

De Souza cut the connection, confident that the signal was untraceable and that the voices involved had been automatically scrubbed to remove all identifiers, but he was cautious by nature and so had kept things as brief as possible.

He was already tiring of Archer's company and asked Gant, his driver and bodyguard, to take the car off the AI controlled grid and find a discreet side street where they could pull over and deposit the banker. Having done so the interior of the vehicle was his own once more.With Gant at the front and isolated behind tinted glass, he could relax. He even managed the shadow of a smile. The game was afoot, or a-spaceship in this particular instance. Pelquin was currently rushing across the stars to claim the ancients' cache, doing all de Souza's dirty work for him.

His gaze returned to the buildings that again rushed past. If all went to plan, he might yet be occupying one of them a lot sooner than expected. Now there was a pleasant prospect.

Five

Taking off without clearance was reckless in the extreme, Pelquin knew that. He'd jeopardised the lives of not only his own crew but countless unknown others. New Sparta was one of the busiest of all the human worlds with ships coming and going constantly. The skies were clogged with freighters, passenger ships, exec craft – all manner of vessels – and it required a delicate balancing act to keep all of them in secure orbit and at safe trajectories; an intricately choreographed ballet of constantly shifting performers, which the manoeuvre they'd just pulled would have ripped apart. A rogue ship taking flight without permission on an unsanctioned flight path had to be the port authorities' worst nightmare. He'd occasionally heard about such things and had shaken his head in bemusement, astonished at the stupidity of those involved. He'd never expected to actually be responsible for something like this, but needs must.

There would be all hell to pay should *Pelquin's Comet* ever want to return to New Sparta; which it did, very much. Nor would it stop there. The repercussions would ripple outwards as quickly as ships and gossip could carry news, and events would doubtless be embellished with each fresh telling. A year hence, Pelquin wouldn't be surprised to hear in some portside bar of how *Pelquin's Comet* had lifted from New Sparta one step ahead of the law and leaving a flotilla of police cruisers floundering in its wake.

"Skip, we're being hailed," Anna said from the seat beside him.

"Yeah, I can see that. Who is it?"

"A police patrol unit. They're demanding we stop accelerating and stand down."

Damn! So much for fanciful embellishments. "Can they intercept us before we're at a safe jump distance?" Gravity was the key here. Too close to a gravity well and a jump would be impossible, but there was a grey area between that and a definable 'safe distance' in which a jump *might* be possible… or a ship could get ripped apart trying.

"Maybe. It'll be touch and go."

"How about an *almost* safe jump distance?"

"No. Not unless they're willing to really chance their arm. They could always take a shot at us but I don't see them risking it, not with this much traffic around."

"Thanks." Exactly what he needed to hear. The day he'd decided to hire Anna had been one of his better days. This, clearly, was not. "Let me know, by your best estimate, when we can risk it."

Pelquin knew full well what he was asking and resisted the temptation to look around at his pilot; no pressure on the young woman at all.

"Yes, skip," she acknowledged, calm as you like.

He opened a channel to the approaching ship. "This is *Pelquin's Comet* to New Spartan Patrol Ship SG 731," he read the designation from the incoming call tag. "We acknowledge your message but must respectfully decline. We've come under armed assault and our lives are endangered. It is imperative we leave New Spartan space immediately, for the safety of this ship and its crew. We will explain matters more fully on our return." He was tempted to say something about making reparations but stopped himself. Once that sort of a commitment was on record it was hard to wriggle out of.

Anna gave him a wry look. "Is that really going to help?"

"Probably not," he admitted, "but it might buy us a few extra seconds and simply by replying I've avoided breaking yet another law, which saves us from at least one writ."

A trivial consideration when set against the charges already accrued against them. He was gambling everything on claiming Nate's cache. At this rate, they'd need most of it just to meet the fines. If for any reason they failed to come back with a hold brimming full of Elder artefacts, the *Comet* was finished. It would be seized by the authorities and auctioned off – something he couldn't bear to contemplate. But that would be it: the end of the line.

A single decision forced upon him by circumstance and suddenly his whole life was in the balance, not to mention the livelihood of everyone aboard.

"We're coming up to the first realistic jump point," Anna told him.

"Take it," he said, without hesitation.

"All crew, brace for jump," Anna announced on the open circuit. "Enjoy the ride!"

The two of them – Pelquin and Anna – were already buckled into their seats, but others throughout the ship weren't so privileged. They'd be grabbing handholds, pressing cling-patches to panels in traditional belt-to-wall bonding, or strapping themselves into their bunks – it would all depend on where they were at the time.

Without any further ceremony, Anna started to really pour on the V. Given that they had a police cruiser closing in on them, she wasn't holding back. The discomfort experienced on leaving New Sparta's atmosphere had been little more than an appetiser for what hit them now. Pelquin found himself pressed into the upholstery of a seat deliberately designed to minimise the effects of exactly this sort of rapid acceleration. For everyone other than himself and Anna, this had to be hurting a hell of a lot more – except perhaps for the doc, who had his own methods for sidestepping the discomforts of a jump. Come to think of it, if all jumps were like this Pelquin might have made sedatives mandatory for the whole crew.

Was this what it felt like to die? The thought flashed through his mind as he waited for the ship to fly apart around him. *Will it be quick? Will I have time to realise…?*

Joints ached, his chest felt as if someone were pressing down on it relentlessly with both hands, but worst of all was his jaw, which felt as if it wanted to dislocate at any second. Just when he thought he couldn't take any more, it was over. There was a moment of euphoric expansion, as if his mind was dimly aware of his soul spreading outward to fill the whole cosmos, then a jolt as consciousness snapped back into its proper place and a degree of normality resumed. The pressure had disappeared as if someone had flicked a switch. They were through; into the strangely clinical, oddly detached state that was RzSpace – which Monkey had always insisted on calling 'Arsie-space' – the mathematically defined shortcut that enabled mankind and presumably Xters to cheat on the speed of light.

As Pelquin understood it, they'd just punched their way through into another plane of existence, one with its own set of laws defining time and space that differed radically from those he was used to. A non-place, some even suggested that RzSpace was a limbo that existed *between* realities, since it was essentially empty, possessing no permanent physical features that anyone had yet discovered. Defined by mathematics that Pelquin would never grasp, RzSpace was an enigma.

Pelquin didn't know the minutiae of how it worked any more than he knew the mechanics of a ship's engine; he just knew that it did. He'd even heard someone argue that RzSpace only came into being when a ship needed it to; that otherwise it didn't exist at all.

Even with RzSpace journeys were still far from instant, but by dipping in and out of this nebulous quasi-place stellar distances became manageable, negotiated in a matter of days rather than lifetimes. Navigation here required disciplines that were beyond a merely human mind, so they were at the mercy of the ship's computer systems until they dropped back into the normal universe. It was also impossible to track anyone in RzSpace, which had to count on the plus side given their current circumstances. Unfortunately, it was also impossible to stay in this strangely altered state for long. Protracted exposure did something to the human psyche, which meant that the majority of journeys had to be accomplished in a series of hops.

Anna raised her eyebrows and grinned – that infectious, gleaming smile of hers. "That was fun."

"If you say so." Pelquin unbuckled and eased himself upright. He needed to assess how much equipment they'd lost in the shootout, not to mention what might have torn loose and bounced around the hold in their precipitous escape. Fortunately, they were heading for a world that was tailor-made for picking up replacements, and now he even had a plausible reason for taking the ship there. Two, if you included Monkey's condition. Pelquin felt oddly satisfied with the situation. No matter how screwed up things were, you could always find a silver lining; it was all a matter of perspective.

"Realistically, it comes down to a choice between three: Newton Four, Pendle's World, and Babylon," Nate Almont said, turning from the screen to seek his captain's guidance.

Judging by the frown the comment elicited, none of the options sat too well with Pelquin.

Tensions aboard the *Comet* had shown little sign of easing since they escaped from New Spartan space, though Drake was willing to bet that Pelquin wished they had. The detachment that RzSpace inspired helped, blunting the edges of emotion. Bren in particular was far from happy, still smarting over the way Monkey had been treated, her resentment towards the captain almost palpable. Given the fact that she was clearly attracted to the captain, she must really have taken his treatment of the mechanic to heart.

Seeking medical aid for Monkey had become everyone's top priority. It *had* to be, given the prevailing mood.

Drake watched the exchange between Nate and the captain with interest. This was a tight-knit group used to living and working together, a micro-community. No question that the captain's word was law, but only for so long as the crew allowed. Pelquin liked to bluster and act the part of benevolent dictator, but under it all he knew the score and was careful to court the crew's approval on sensitive matters. Most of the time he had it by default, but right now the life of one of their own was in the balance and nothing could be taken for granted.

Everyone was clustered in and around the cramped control room – too basic a place to dignify with the name 'bridge'. Nate Almont and Anna had the two chairs, Pelquin fidgeting restlessly directly behind them. Speculation as to who had organised the little farewell party back on New Sparta had run its course, with the mining company Jossyren emerging as odds-on favourite. Though no one seemed inclined to explain why, Drake had filled in most of the gaps for himself. It was becoming increasingly clear that Pelquin had been less than fully open during his interview at the bank; something that wouldn't come as a surprise to anybody, particularly not Terry Reese.

Quite apart from Monkey, they needed to replace the equipment wrecked in the attack. Damage hadn't been as extensive as it might have been, but replacements would still have to be found. The problem came when they tried to prioritise the two imperatives: new equipment and Monkey. It seemed that the captain was at odds with the majority on that score. A compromise was needed and fast, which was where Nate Almont came in, narrowing down the possible choices of destination.

Pelquin shook his head. "There's no way I'm going back to Newton Four, not after what happened there last time."

"It is the nearest," Anna pointed out.

"Yeah, I can see that, but even so… Show us what you've got on the other two, Nate."

Leaning forward to look over Almont's shoulder, he stared intently at the screen and, after a few seconds, shook his head again. "It'll have to be Babylon. Pendle's World is too primitive."

Bren wandered off, presumably to escape Pelquin's company and to simmer in private – the captain still hadn't given any indication that he'd noticed her hostility. Drake stayed where he was, just within the doorway, ignored by everyone, while the doc was in a world of his own.

"You've got the list of everything damaged?" Pelquin asked.

"Yup," Nate confirmed. "None of it should be a problem, so long as you've got enough credits to buy the replacements."

"No problem there either, thanks to our friends at First Solar," and the captain finally deigned to glance in Drake's direction.

The words were barely spoken when the world shook violently; or at least theirs did, as the ship bucked and jolted, causing Drake to steady himself against the door jamb and Pelquin to stagger and grip the back of the pilot's chair to regain his balance.

"What the hell?" came Bren's voice from somewhere down the corridor.

"Nate?" Pelquin said.

"I'm working on it."

"We've been hit by something!" Doc blurted out; an indication of panic that didn't bode well for a medical man in Drake's opinion.

"No we haven't," Bren assured him as she squeezed past Drake and back into the room. "We're in RzSpace, remember; a *non*-place. There's nothing out there to hit us."

"Even now air is spewing into the vacuum of space from our ruptured hull…"

"Shut up, Doc." Pelquin snapped.

"The only vacuum around here is between his ears," Bren muttered, too quietly for the doc to hear.

The juddering stopped but at the same time a bright amber light started to flash directly in front of Anna on the pilot's console display.

Pelquin had obviously seen it too. He frowned. "Any idea what that's trying to tell us?"

"In general terms, something's up with the engines; specifically, not a clue; except that we need to check things over pretty damned quick."

"The ship's still running, though."

"For the moment," Anna confirmed.

"After the way the ship just rattled our bones we really need a *light* to tell us there's something wrong," Bren noted.

"Where are the diagnostics when you need them?" Pelquin

grumbled.

"Busted," Bren said. "Waiting for you to authorise repairs, same as they have been for the last two trips."

"Then why wasn't it sorted out at New Sparta now that we've got some credit behind us?"

"Maybe because nobody told anyone to sort it out!"

"Engine temperature's rising," Anna cut in. "Pel, I really need to take us out of Rz and down to sub-light."

"Can you bring us out near Babylon?"

"Probably."

"*Probably?*"

"Hey," Bren said sharply, "don't take it out on Anna. If we could give her some clue what's wrong with the engines she could probably give us a better idea." Her gaze flicked to the smaller woman. "Right?"

Anna flashed her a grateful smile.

Pelquin nodded. "Fair point," he said, so robbing Bren of the argument she seemed keen to engage in. The captain drew a deep breath. "Okay, so we keep heading for Babylon, dropping out of Rz as soon as we can."

Nobody argued. Tension still dominated the room, though it wasn't about Monkey any more. Instead it was as if everyone present was just waiting for a renewed bout of juddering to rattle through them, while wondering whether it would stop as abruptly the next time or continue until it shook the whole ship apart.

Pelquin looked around. "Has anyone been to this 'Babylon' before?"

Shakes of the head and a subdued "No" were his only response.

His gaze fell on Drake, but the banker couldn't offer anything either.

Nate continued to tap away at his keyboard, murmuring "Ba-by-lon" in almost rhythmic fashion. He seemed the only one totally at ease, as if being an acutely vulnerable organic entity reliant on a potentially faulty ship in the depths of space didn't faze him at all. Drake wondered again what he was taking.

Something about the recent exchange nagged at Drake. He couldn't escape the conviction that Pelquin was glad they were going to Babylon, as if that had been his intention from the outset and the rest had been a performance.

Can you tell me anything more about the world Babylon? he thought.

Only what's in the ship's database, came Mudball's response. *Which is a fair bit, actually, though nothing much to distinguish it from a hundred other worlds. If you like, I could list Babylon's top fifty tourist attractions for you.*

No thanks.

Or would you like me to detail the most highly rated red light districts?

Again, no.

Didn't think so. Okay, how's this: the capital, la Gossa, seems to be a thriving industrial centre.

What sort of industry?

All sorts. You want it, they'll make it.

Interesting. Did that explain why they were going to Babylon? Whatever the reason, Drake remained convinced that the choice of destination had been nowhere near as random as it had seemed.

Six

La Gossa, Babylon's principal city. Morning had already arrived, settled in, and made itself at home by the time Leesa crawled out from under her bedding and stumbled across to the vast ribbed door. She grasped the metal with both hands and pulled. It was a swine to budge initially, but once she got things moving the laws of momentum came to her aid and the great sheet of metal rolled out of the way in its own sweet time, settling with a clanging thud. Leesa squinted out at the day. The sky was low and dominated by heavy clouds, but then the sky was a tease. It wouldn't rain today; the air didn't taste of rain.

The back of her right hand felt raw and tender at the knuckles, as if she'd scraped it along a wall or something, though goodness only knew when. As yet, the events of the previous evening were pretty much a mystery; one more blank space in her mind to sit among the many.

She leant forward and spat the stale taste of sleep from her mouth, then eased herself down from the old carriage and started to shuffle leaden-footed across the deserted goods yard. The part of her that never slept started to fill in the gaps, feeding memories of her exploits the night before to the conscious areas of her mind. It did so by drip-feed, thank God, or she might have been tempted to retreat back to the carriage and bury herself beneath the voluminous sleeping blanket, putting off having to face the day for at least another couple of hours.

She saw herself dancing at one of her usual haunts, the Green Gecko – a cavernous dark and grungy space throbbing with sound and heaving with cavorting forms. She recognised some of the faces associated with the gyrating bodies around her but by no means all of them. There'd been one guy in particular: cute face and a fit body, well worth setting her sights on; but, to her considerable disappointment, he'd faded away pretty early on. The world had subsequently narrowed to a point where there was just one lithe form monopolising her attention: a stunningly beautiful black girl of indeterminate age, her hair teased into a flame-dyed crest which ran like a mane front-to-back along her otherwise shaven scalp. The jewelled nose stud that caught and glittered in the lights looked expensive but was probably fake.

Leesa had noticed this girl once or twice before, but only ever across the room – they'd never entered each other's orbits. Until now. And God, did she know how to move. Leesa wasn't into other women as a rule but life was there to be experienced, and this slinky temptress was pretty hard to ignore.

Their dancing swiftly developed into a grinding, sweaty clinch. She remembered being surprised by the other woman's strength as she found herself pressed back against a wall, with the other woman's mouth and hands seemingly everywhere. There was nothing cute or dainty about their kisses; they were urgent, hungry assaults, carried out as lights and music pulsed and fellow club-goers drifted around them. She'd scored something off Jamiel – couldn't recall what, she hadn't been able to analyse it; something synthetic certainly, though it had an ur-root base. Something new.Something which she and the ebony-skinned demoness had inhaled greedily from fractured capsules once they were alone in the other woman's apartment. Something which made flesh sing in soaring harmonics at the gentlest of caresses and amplified the body's response to more intimate intrusions a hundred-fold. Leesa had never felt so open to stimulus. Their love making had been wild, piquant, unfettered, and totally exhausting. Even now, memory of it sent a tingle of pleasure coursing down her spine, the merest echo of last night's rapture.

There had been a bedside table, draped in a grubby linen cloth and supporting a framed picture of the woman with a fresh-faced man – brother, lover, son; who knew? She was smiling, the sense of happiness and contentment it engendered jarringly at odds with the woman Leesa had just coupled with so aggressively.

Quite why Leesa remembered that detail and little else about the room she couldn't say, except that it made the demoness more human, somehow.

Despite the instant buzz, the lovemaking left her feeling empty in its aftermath, as did the drugs, as did everything. In those rare moments when she took the trouble to analyse her life, she saw herself as a hollow shell with nothing but need at its core.

She recalled returning to the club, sans demoness, scoring something else from Jamiel, who'd insisted on a good grope as down payment.

She was unsure what had happened after that, but whatever he'd given her hadn't been worth putting out for. It hadn't worked.

Some people took drugs to forget. Leesa took them to remember, and the dreams hadn't come that night.

She crossed the abandoned freight yard, picking her way over rusted rails and sleepers turned brittle as balsa wood by age and exposure to the elements. She felt as broken and discarded as her surroundings. A few other shambling figures were to be seen, testament that she wasn't the only unfortunate to claim this forgotten corner of the city as home. This was just temporary, though; she wasn't staying. This wasn't the dead-end of her life, merely a pause.

Traffic noise rumbled in from a distance, otherwise the whole world might have been this wasteland.

A small shack stood at the far edge of the yard, its door propped open. A plank had been nailed in place above the door, bearing the hand-scrawled legend 'CAFE' in bold red letters. Leesa had once overheard the owner, Sal, say, "Screw originality. I want a sign that's gonna tell folk what we do here. Reckon this does the job."

The logic was hard to fault.

Sal stood behind the counter, larger than life, his stained red and white candy-stripe apron looking to be no more than one deep breath away from bursting, as it struggled to encompass his corpulent girth. Sal greeted Leesa's arrival with his customary snaggle-toothed grin, thumping a mug of coffee down on the counter and saying, as he said every morning, "Mornin', hun'; black an' strong, just how you like it!"

Just how I like my women too, apparently, which wasn't what she thought every morning.

Somehow, Sal always managed to serve drinks piping hot, which was what Leesa most appreciated about his coffee. Otherwise, the brew was a little bitter for her taste and only moderately strong, despite Sal's proud boast.

She took a seat at an unoccupied table and sipped the drink immediately, savouring the sensation as liquid scalded the back of her throat to leave it raw and tingling.

The shack was a little more than half full. Leesa glanced discreetly at those around her, not wanting to make eye contact, not wanting to be snared into a conversation. Derelicts, one and all.People who had given up on society, on themselves.

I'm not like them, she told herself, while fearing all the while that she was. Leesa had a plan, though. She was going to get out. Soon. La Gossa was a trap. A sweet and seductive one baited with drugs and clubs and music and sex on tap, but it was a trap all the same. She'd given in to temptation and dallied here longer than intended. The more she stuck around the harder it was going to be to move on. Leaving required effort, and she'd been following the path of least resistance for far too long.

Molly shuffled in through the door. Her rounded shoulders always seemed even more rounded in the mornings, her steady gait all the more stiff and laboured. Leesa averted her eyes, not wanting the older woman to come across and join her, not today. Molly had been the first person to accept Leesa when she'd arrived here, making sure she found a place to sleep and teaching her how things worked in the yard. Even then Leesa had sensed that Molly wasn't quite right and soon made every effort to distance herself from the other woman.

She owed Molly, no question; but she'd repaid the debt by degree in a dozen little ways: ensuring that Molly didn't go hungry, making certain she had enough warm clothing when it turned cold. Little things, but they all added up.

Leesa needn't have worried; Molly didn't even seem to register her presence. Instead she took a seat at the far side of the café. As she sat down, her body undulated in an inhuman fashion. A small whiskered snout protruded from beneath her grubby sweater, and Molly was soon cooing at the rodent and feeding it cake crumbs.

This wasn't the same rat Molly had kept when Leesa first arrived. She knew that for a fact. She'd witnessed the old woman kill that particular rat and eat it raw.

Leesa looked away, disgusted with herself rather than Molly, ashamed that she had lingered here for so long. Babylon didn't hold any answers, only distractions. It was high time she resumed her quest to piece the fragments of her life back together.

Once the coffee mug had been drained, Leesa felt more alive and ready to wrestle with the world. She had resolved to move forward with her life; and this time she meant it.

Standing up, she waved a vague farewell in Sal's direction and left the shack, heading behind it to squeeze through the hole in the wire fence, ready to trot along the short alley that formed the yard's umbilical to the city proper.

Head bowed, hands stuck deep in pockets and her thoughts still firmly focused on the excesses of the night before, she stepped into the alley, just as another memory from the previous evening dripped into her consciousness. Leesa stopped dead in her tracks, horrified. It seemed she *hadn't* accepted Jamiel's groping as passively as usual, or at least she hadn't for long. Already high from the previous score and the fast-fading buzz of some glorious sex, her inhibitions must have been low enough to let her loathing come to the surface. She'd lost control, suffering his pawing for a while but then pulling away.

She recalled saying, "That's enough!" The words came to her now as if she'd heard them spoken by someone else, but it was her voice saying them all right.

Being Jamiel, the cocky little dealer hadn't taken her seriously, reaching out to slip his hand back inside her top, saying, "Hey, baby, *I'm* the one who decides when it's enough, not you." The smile never left his face.

Until she slapped his hand away and hit him. *Really* hit him. A straight jab to the jaw. No wonder the back of her hand had felt sore this morning. Jamiel had gone down without even crying out. *Shit!* She hadn't killed him, had she? No, even stoned she wouldn't be stupid enough to hit him that hard. Unconscious, that was all. Mind you, that was enough.

Gabon, the great bull of a minder who was never far from Jamiel's side, had lunged at her, trying to wrap his tree-trunk arms around her torso. A kick to the knee, punch to the stomach and chop to the back of his solid neck had sent the big man collapsing beside his boss.

And then she'd just gone on with her life as if nothing had happened!

Dear God. Why had memory waited until now to reveal this little gem? If she didn't set about some world-class grovelling immediately her life here was over whether she wanted it to be or not. It might not be much of a life but it was all she currently had.

Only then did Leesa sense the two figures emerging from the shadows.

One on either side, approaching together, faces artificially darkened to a near-grey hue by manipulation of the skin's melanin. Leesa wasn't impressed: she'd seen better skin scrubs on podium dancers at the Green Gecko – more imaginative ones, at any rate. A quick chemical wash and the melanin 'fix' would break down, the induced colour fading away to normality. She knew the significance of those grey faces, though, and of the stylised downward-pointing dagger currently emblazoned in gold on each of the pair's foreheads, the tip of the blade just bisecting the eyebrows. It marked them as Cellothan, a theoretically banned warrior-elite sect specialising in the sadistic; the source of many an urban legend and reputedly the nastiest bastards on the whole of Babylon.

Jamiel had turned to *them*? Damn! He wasn't messing around.

Leesa had one thing going for her. They were bound to underestimate her. Men always did. No matter if Jamiel *had* told them how she'd handled herself the previous evening. They would still see before them a scrawny no-hope girl and dismiss Jamiel's claims as either exaggeration or a reflection of his own ineptitude rather than of her skills. Or so she hoped. Right now the two were busy behaving like the professionals they were. As Leesa stepped carefully backward, one of the grey-faced men angled his approach to move behind her, the other circling so that he was in front, the pair always keeping her between them while edging ever closer.

What was their intent, murder or just a serious beating? No weapons in sight, so presumably the latter, which gave her a little more manoeuvring room.

When Leesa acted it was quick and decisive. She feinted to go forward and to her left – one step and a convincing shift of body weight, the merest suggestion of a sway which the two Cellothans instantly responded to. Her actual movement was in the opposite direction. She sprang backwards so that both of the bastards were in front of her. She didn't hesitate, didn't give them a chance to revise their perception of her and respond. A sweep of her hand as her foot landed and she grasped the concealed knife, drawing the weapon from its boot sheath and flinging it in one smooth motion. She aimed for the body; the head presented too uncertain a target for such an improvised throw. The whole move was concealed within the flail of limbs and jerk of body caused by her backward hop. The Cellothan she was aiming for couldn't have seen it coming, couldn't have anticipated the attack. Yet, impossibly, he somehow managed to react, twisting and turning out of the way in the split second the knife was in the air, so that the blade tore into his upper arm rather than his torso.

Leesa didn't pause to watch but was already taking the fight to the other man, swivelling to kick him hard in the solar plexus. The Cellothan wasn't wearing body armour. She'd heard they never did; too much *machismo*, presumably, too tough for such wimpish self-concern. Her kick found its mark, partially paralysing the man's diaphragm to leave him struggling for breath. She had no idea how she knew to do these things when so much else eluded her – evidently her body remembered how to fight even if her consciousness didn't, as if violence had seeped indelibly into the cells and synapses that formed her to become an integral part of her being. She didn't have to think about what she was doing, she simply *did*.

Despite being hampered, her opponent still managed to block the next blow, which had been aimed at his kidneys, but he was too slow to avoid the follow-up, a chop to the throat with the side of her hand. Something gave – larynx, trachea, she couldn't be sure, but it was enough to send him collapsing to the floor, clutching at his throat and gasping noisily for breath as if his very life depended on it, as indeed it might.

The other one had pulled the knife out of his arm, displaying reckless indifference to the damage that might be caused in the process. His right arm now hung awkwardly by his side and blood dripped from the dangling fingertips, but he adopted a fighter's wide stance, oblivious to the pain, her knife now brandished in his left hand. She closed in, conscious of the weapon but watching his eyes. When the attack came she was ready for it, dodging, swaying and arching her back so that her body was outside the reach of his thrust. The blade passed a hair's breadth from her midriff. She grabbed his arm with both hands as he started to bend the elbow and bring the weapon back. Putting all her body weight behind the action, she twisted his wrist and used the instinctive retraction, forcing the blade around to stab into his stomach.

For a frozen instant they stared into each other's eyes – his brown orbs flecked with gold. Leesa watched as the realisation of death dawned in those eyes and then the light of life drained from them. She stepped away, allowing his body to collapse to the ground.

She held the knife tightly clutched in her fist. Crouching, she wiped it clean on the dead man's clothing before quickly cleaning her hand.

Then she stood up, breathing hard as adrenaline receded enough for reason to put in an appearance.

Shit! She'd just killed one of the Cellothan. Only one, thank goodness; the second looked fit to survive. The man was now on all fours throwing up, but at least he was still breathing.

On impulse she strode across and crouched, holding the knife to his throat. The man froze.

"I could have killed you as well. Remember that," she hissed, before whipping the knife away and swivelling around to leave him there.

Not that it would make a scrap of difference. They'd still be after her and wouldn't rest until she was dead. After all, she'd just kicked them straight in their precious *machismo*.

She hurried along the alleyway, mind racing as the realisation of what she'd just done hit home. *Shit! Shit! Shit!* If she'd needed something to kick her arse into action, this ought to do the trick. Her old pal procrastination was going to have to find a new best friend, because she was getting the hell out of here while she still could.

Leesa ran a quick inventory in her head. Virtually all her possessions she carried with her. The two men, whether muggers or assassins, had been lying in wait at the mouth of the alley, and that meant they knew where she slept. The only things back in the carriage were the old sleeping blanket and a few changes of clothing; certainly nothing worth the risk of going back for.

Once word was out that the Cellothan were after her, she wouldn't have a friend in the world. She might have been able to smooth things out with Jamiel, though he would doubtless have demanded his pound of flesh, but *this*... This was something else entirely. Eye for an eye, life for a life; it was a maxim she understood only too well.

She headed for the spaceport, distracted, annoyed at herself for losing control like that and oblivious to the strident blare of horns as she dodged between taxis, bikes, and tin-topped vans, pausing as a tram glided across her path and swearing at the phut-phutting motorbikes that weaved through the traffic and always seemed to be in the way wherever she wanted to go next.

As she walked and dodged Leesa reflected on the irony of it – what the mind-wipe had taken from her and what the process had left her with. Fundamental things such as who she was or how she came to be on Babylon remained frustratingly elusive, but she knew that she liked steak – rare and not too much or it quickly filled her up – and she knew she liked fish and loved fruit but hated creamy desserts and loathed root vegetables. Most importantly, she remembered her skill sets, such as fighting and mechanics. And therein lay her hope.

Eventually she made it across the commercial district and into the quieter backstreets that bordered the landing field. Here, away from the bustle and commotion, she moved swiftly but cautiously, every sense straining, acutely aware of the shitstorm she had just stirred up, which would be coming her way sooner rather than later.

Leesa *had* to get off world. Head down but eyes now scanning every shadow, she made her way to the Rusty Rivet. Standing directly opposite the main entrance to the space port, the Rivet might not have been the most salubrious of the several bars that clustered around the area, but it was certainly the most obvious.

No flashing neon signs or fancy holo-displays to attract punters into the Rivet, just an open door, a homely atmosphere and cheap local beer; well, cheaper than any of its nearest competitors at any rate. Drinks still needed paying for, though, a realisation that caused Leesa to pause at the door, slipping fingers into tight pockets to fish around. Thankfully, her questing fingertips found enough coins to buy at least a couple of drinks, which could be eked out for a good few hours if she was careful.

It was nearly lunchtime and the place was already starting to fill up. Leesa nodded to a couple of familiar faces as she made her way to the bar. Being recognised had both an up and a down side. One or two of these acquaintances might be able to point her in the direction of a job if there were any going. On the other hand, some of them undoubtedly knew Jamiel and wouldn't hesitate to sell her out for the price of a beer.

Shipees – non-permanent crew – were constantly hired and fired, taken on for a single trip and subsequently released. It was just a question of being in the right place at the right time. Leesa could only pray that, on this occasion, she was.

This wasn't the first time she had staked out a portside bar in the hope of latching onto an outbound crew, but it *was* the first time she'd ever been this desperate.

SEVEN

Pelquin studied the monitors intently as the ship breached Babylon's upper atmosphere and dropped towards the planet's thick cloud layer. The hull – that thin shell of layered metal and insulation that surrounded and protected them – was increasingly buffeted by turbulence, but there had been no recurrence of the alarming stutter the ship had suffered in transit. He remained on edge, though, expecting one, and the orange warning light only stopped winking once Anna had deactivated it on his instruction. He knew there was a problem and didn't need to be constantly reminded of the fact.

As if that wasn't enough pressure for any man to handle, Drake had wandered back onto the bridge as they began their approach.

The banker's presence made him uneasy, so he did his best to ignore the grey-suited figure and get on with his job, concentrating on the monitors, watching intently as they passed through the clouds and the world of Babylon was unveiled. This really *was* his first time here and he always enjoyed the anticipation of a new world. It wouldn't be Nate's first time on Babylon, perhaps, but there was nothing in the ship's memory to betray that fact.

As they dropped lower, zeroing in on their destination and quickly reaching the point where individual features were visible, the thing that most drew Pelquin's eye was the broad river that wound its way through the centre of the city. This was La Gossa, the largest city on Babylon's only significant continent, and the river was flagged as the Kusbah, which meant in the local language 'brown artery'. The name couldn't have been more apt. The Kusbah's waters were dark with minerals and silt, while in places its surface was choked with enormous barges and cargo vessels, suggesting that the river was a major commercial thoroughfare.

Docks and factories clustered around the river's banks, hemming the water in at every turn as it wriggled a serpentine course through the heart of the city. Vast bridges spanned the Kusbah's expanse at irregular intervals – seeming from this vantage to be crude stitches across an open wound, holding the two halves of the city together.

As they dropped lower he lost sight of the river, which was replaced by the concrete sprawl of human habitation interspersed with an erratic grid of myriad roads.

Seconds later and they were over the landing field, buildings replaced by the metallic beetle-like forms of flitters and ships as Anna brought the *Comet* over the allotted berth and set her down.

They opened the cargo door almost at once – the most effective way to vent the staleness of recycled air, even if only to replace it with fresh urban pollution – and so had the opportunity to sample Babylon from an in-your-face perspective It wasn't the river that grabbed their attention now so much as the smell. La Gossa stank. Of too many people crammed for too long into too little space. The heat didn't help either. Humidity was so high that Pelquin half expected to see the air itself start to sweat.

Bren had been on the coms long before they hit atmosphere, tracking down and then hiring the medical help they would need for Monkey. It meant another chunk of Pelquin's money gobbled up – or rather the bank's money – but he had no choice, at least not if he wanted to avoid a mutiny. The little mechanic was popular, and the last thing he needed when heading off on the biggest caper of his life was dissent from a crew that wasn't fully committed to the cause.

Besides, the medical emergency would provide a convenient distraction while he and Nate saw to the business that had really brought them here.

Pelquin glanced to one side to find Drake staring at him. The intensity of the banker's gaze was discomforting, almost as if the bastard could read his mind. Pelquin resolved to be more guarded with his expressions. If anyone around here needed distracting, it was Drake.

An ambulance screeched up within minutes of their landing, which Pelquin thought pretty impressive, though Bren didn't seem to agree. "Bastards told me they'd be waiting here for us!" she growled. Monkey, still in his cryochamber, had been loaded onto a gravsled, though not without considerable effort and cursing. As soon as the back of the ambulance slid open, Bren and Nate manoeuvred the over-burdened sled through the loading bay and down the ramp, to where a pair of green liveried medics waited.

Bren wanted to go with Monkey, but Pelquin forestalled her. "What good is that going to do?"

"It'll reassure me he's being properly looked after, which will do me the power of good, I can promise you," she replied.

"The doc will see to that. I need you here."

"To do what, exactly?"

"Help me find a new mechanic."

"A new *what*? You're abandoning him?"

"Of course not! You know me better than that. But the doc reckons that," he hesitated, choosing his words carefully, "whatever happens, it'll be a while before Monkey is going to be fit enough to travel, and we can't afford to hang around. So we take someone on, temporary crew, this trip only. We bring them back here when the job's done and pick up Monkey. By then he'll be all fixed-up and as lecherous as new." Or so they could all hope.

"Really? A shipee, for one trip only?"

"My word on it."

She might not have liked it but Bren was professional enough to know he was right. She stayed and the doc went off in the ambulance. Shortly afterwards, Nate disappeared into town to start sourcing suppliers for the equipment that needed replacing.

"Anna, break out the hull scrubbers." The hiccup in RzSpace had unnerved him, and he wasn't about to take any chances. Despite the name, earned because the small beetle-like mechanoids *looked* as if they were cleaning the ship as they made their methodical way across its hull in tight formation, they had nothing to do with cleaning. Instead, they were designed to check the integrity of the hull in minute detail, noting any possible weakness. Hairline cracks in the heat laminate, fatigued plating, stressed cooling fins – scrubbers could spot a potential failure before one actually occurred, long before a ship's standard systems would pick up on a problem. They were, however, something of a luxury; hideously expensive and considered unnecessary by most. The look of surprise on Drake's face spoke volumes.

Evidently Anna had noted that look too. "The skip won them in a particularly intense hand of Black Hole," she explained.

"You don't think we'd have anything as extravagant as hull scrubbers otherwise, do you?" Bren added.

Pelquin chose to ignore her.

They were on a tight schedule, which gave him very little leeway. As soon as the formalities of their arrival had been dealt with, Pelquin went in search of Monkey's temporary replacement, with Bren in tow. Drake chose to tag along as well. Nobody objected, not even Pelquin. At least this way he could keep an eye on the banking bastard.

The saying goes that if you want to find a decent bar you should follow the spacers, because no one knew more about booze than they did. To Drake, the flaw in this frequently quoted maxim was obvious: when a spacer came into port, especially after a lengthy trip, proximity generally won out over quality. *Anywhere* serving alcohol would do. He therefore had low expectations of the bar Pelquin led them to, which was just as well because the place fully lived down to his every fear. The captain's own philosophy when it came to finding a new engineer seemed about as sophisticated as the spacers'. The Rusty Rivet was the nearest bar to the landing field – and Drake had to wonder if this was really the best that local knowledge could recommend.

The bar was busy. While it might not have been the worst establishment he had ever drunk in, Drake wouldn't be recommending it to anybody either. Dark, over-warm and smoky, those were his initial impressions.

Anna hadn't joined them, staying with the ship, Nate was off somewhere in La Gossa, purportedly to replace the equipment damaged at New Sparta, though why he couldn't have done so from the security of the *Comet* Drake wasn't entirely certain. Perhaps it was just an excuse to stretch his legs and see something of the place before they lit out again. Or perhaps he had his own reasons.

The doc had yet to return from the hospital; which left the three of them: Drake, Pelquin, and Bren. They attracted a few stares as they came in, though probably due to the banker's grey pinstripe suit rather than anything else.

Pelquin got the first round in. Drake carried his and Bren's drinks across to the booth she'd managed to secure. Pelquin lingered at the bar, chatting, asking after any ships' engineers who might be looking for a job. The place was packed with spacers; word should spread quickly enough.

Please tell me we're not going to be staying here for long, Mudball said. *The stench of stale tobacco will be sticking to my fur for days.* Drake ignored him, though he harboured similar concerns regarding his own suit.

He held his glass to the light and studied the unappetisingly pale amber-brown liquid within; the colour reminded him of rotting fruit, or urine. He sipped at the drink tentatively, finding a flat, sour brew that tasted as tired as the atmosphere. He was beginning to think that accompanying Pelquin and Bren had been a mistake.

By the look of things, the two of them were intent on spending a sizeable portion of the day sitting in this bar simply waiting for would-be mechanics to wonder over. They were welcome to, he certainly wouldn't be.

He still didn't believe that their arrival at Babylon had been as random as it was meant to appear. The captain's expression as they came in to land had been one of satisfaction. The man was up to something and Drake was determined to find out what.

He gulped his beer down, finishing it more out of politeness than for any other reason, and then made his excuses.

"What?" said Pelquin, feigning surprise. "You're not going to hang around to second guess my decision?"

Drake paused in the process of leaving and glanced around at the motley crew of spacers that surrounded them. "Oh I'm sure you'll cope without any input from me. It looks as if you'll be spoilt for choice."

Pelquin raised his eyebrows but said nothing.

As soon as Drake had departed, Pelquin's expression slipped towards a scowl. "Typical banker," he muttered.

"What do you mean?" Bren asked.

"He didn't even get a round in."

"And that's a bad thing?" She lifted her glass and squinted at its contents. "I mean, have you tasted this rat's piss?"

"Yeah, I know, but it's the principle."

"Heads up. We've got company."

The figure approaching them didn't exactly inspire confidence. Dishevelled, unshaven, bleary-eyed, looking as if he'd been out on the mother of all benders the previous night which had only wound down a short while ago. However, Pelquin knew better than to judge by appearances.

The man stopped in front of their table. "Hear you're looking for an engineer." He gazed at them from beneath heavily lidded eyes, swaying slightly like a tree responding to the whim of changeable winds, and Pelquin feared he was about to topple onto them like so much felled timber. The man looked barely capable of standing on his own two feet, let alone wielding any tools.

Pelquin glanced across at Bren, whose sour expression suggested she was about as impressed by their first candidate as he was. He was saved from the need to respond by the intervention of a new voice, a woman's. "No they're not, 'cos they've already found one."

At least she sounded sober.

The tottering man jerked his head around as if stung. He stared at the speaker with a vaguely baffled expression, clearly trying to sift meaning from the string of words. "Wa... waddya mean? Who?"

"Me, obviously."

It would have been easy to underestimate the girl's age. Her build was the culprit there, though there was nothing soft about her; instead her slenderness suggested the toughness of taut wire. Her body was almost androgynous, with no real widening of the hips and the merest hint of breasts beneath clothes that had surely been chosen for their neutrality. Only her face bore unambiguous testament to her femininity. Despite being framed by hair cut short into a ragged crop and the absence of makeup, the combination of high cheekbones and large eyes conspired to make her undeniably attractive. Pelquin liked her at once, without being able to articulate why. Perhaps it was the eyes, in which he read intelligence, fierce defiance, and, most intriguingly, desperation, perhaps even fear. This girl was running away from something, whether inner demons or more tangible ones he couldn't say, but it meant that she might need them just as much as they needed her.

"Who the fuck are you?" asked their first would-be mechanic, who still hadn't grasped the fact that he was already redundant.

"The right woman for the job," she replied.

She certainly talked a good fight. Pelquin just hoped her competence matched her attitude. If so, they might just be in business.

Her attention then switched fully to Pelquin and Bren, effectively dismissing the swaying man. "You came in on an old comet transport, right? Twin thrusters and mobile landing jets."

So, she'd had the sense to ask a few question of the barman before coming over. Clearly not stupid, this one.

Their drunken friend continued to ignore the inevitable. He snorted and said, "Anyone could have said that."

The girl favoured him with a cold smile. "Perhaps, but you didn't. And you'll know, of course, what type of engines she's heftin'."

"Well, it depends…" the man said, brow furrowed as if trying to remember something just beyond the reach of his recall.

"Yeah, you're right, it *does* depend. So what are the options?"

As job interviews went, this was an interesting twist – one applicant interviewing the other. Pelquin sat back, enjoying the show.

"Ehm…" The man was clearly floundering.

"Come on," the girl pressed, "none of us have got all day."

"Well, that is… I'd have to see…"

She put him out of his misery, turning back to face Pelquin. "Most likely it's the seven point twos, unless she's a really old 'un, in which case it might be the six point eights. Either way you've got a lot of grunt for a comparatively small ship, though she handles like a pig in atmosphere – except when it comes to landing, when you can drop her gently onto a dinner plate, if your pilot's good enough."

Pelquin was aware of Bren beside him giving an appreciative nod and didn't see the point in wasting any more time. It wasn't as if the Rusty Rivet was the sort of place anyone would *want* to waste time in unless they had to. "Okay," he said, "you've just earned yourself a trial." He rose to his feet, glad to abandon the half-drunk beer.

"Hey, what about me?" asked the tottering man.

"You, my friend, have just earned yourself some more time at the bar." Reaching into a pocket, Pelquin flipped him a coin – enough to cover the cost of a beer.

The coin dropped to the table. The man stared at it and then turned to glare at his conqueror, who grinned and shooed him away with a contemptuous flick of her hand. For a moment he hesitated, but then he snatched up the coin and stumbled off muttering, "Fucking freak."

The girl clearly heard him and jerked around, but the offender was no longer paying attention. The words had obviously stung, as if this wasn't the first time she'd heard them.

As they left the bar and headed back towards the ship, Pelquin fell into step beside Bren, slowing down slightly and letting the girl walk a few paces ahead.

He said quietly, "She was right about the engine models, I take it?"

"Haven't got a clue," Bren replied equally sotto voce.

He grunted. "I suppose we both ought to know, but…"

"I know; that's always been Monkey's department," she finished for him.

"Exactly."

Pelquin studied the girl's back as she walked ahead of them. One thing she'd definitely been right about was the way the ship handled in atmosphere – a real pig – and he had to admit that the kid had balls; metaphorically speaking at any rate.

"What did you say your name was again?" he asked.

"I didn't," the girl replied without breaking stride. "But you can call me Leesa."

They'd taken Leesa straight to the engines. She wasted no time in sliding aside the cowlings and getting to work. He left Bren to keep an eye on her and headed to the bridge. Anna was there, lounging in the padded pilot's chair and watching something on the screen as she sucked on a carton of goodness knew what through a striped straw.

"Not interrupting anything, am I?"

She relaxed her vacuum-like sucking long enough to say, "No," oblivious to any sarcasm. "Just catching up on a space rom."

"Don't know how you can watch that garbage," he grumbled. "Any word from Nate or Doc?"

"Nope, not yet."

"Let me know when you do."

She looked at him as if he'd said something stupid, but then smiled and said sweetly, "I will."

Pelquin resisted the temptation to say 'carry on' as he left, realising that she already had; the straw firmly back between her lips, gaze glued to the screen. He shook his head and left, stopping off at the galley for some chilled water – anything to wash away the taste of that wretched local beer – trying to find things to do so that he wouldn't return to engineering too quickly. Futile effort, as it turned out, since Bren appeared even as he swallowed the last of the water.

"She's finished already?" he said, while thinking: *And you've left a complete stranger alone with our engines?*

"Well... you need to come and hear this."

What the hell does that mean? Nothing good, he'd warrant. He followed her along the gantry and down the steps.

The girl, Leesa, was still fiddling with something under the cowling.

"Have you fixed it?" he demanded as they strode in to join her.

"No," she replied, taking her arms out of the engine and looking round.

Pelquin felt disappointed. "Well, good luck on finding a berth on another ship, then."

"I *could* fixit," she continued, "but I wouldn't be doing you any favours if I did."

Ah, good, perhaps not the disaster he'd feared after all. Pelquin had to fight back a smile. "And that would be because…?"

"Because if I *did* sort out the immediate fault I wouldn't be dealing with the source of the problem, just patching up a symptom. You've got a dodgy inductor sheath fitted, completely the wrong model. I don't know who's responsible, but it's been jimmied into a space that it really doesn't want to go into and that's putting the whole system under pressure. 'Cos of that, you've ended up with a ruptured feeder pipe. If I fix the pipe without swapping the sheath, the pipe or something else will only blow again sometime, somewhere… and soon."

Pelquin shrugged. "Then put a new inductor sheath in."

"Now why didn't I think of that?" Sarcasm too; she had spirit, no denying that. "I'd love to; and the new one would be… where exactly?"

"No idea." Monkey always dealt with that sort of thing.

"Isn't there anything in the store room that would do?" Bren indicated the closed door behind which lay the small cupboard-like space that was Monkey's private domain.

"Ah, yes, the store room. You've got a few bits and spares knocking around in there, sure," and the girl glanced towards the door with disdain, "but I don't see no inductor sheath."

"So how come we've managed to get along fine for so long with the wrong part, then?"

"Oh, it'll work for a while… A day, a month, a year maybe, but at some point it'll go, most likely when you'd least want it to, stranding you. No telling when. You've been lucky so far, but do you really wanna count on that sort of luck forever?"

Bren snorted. "Not with the way Lady Luck's been treating us of late, no."

Leesa shrugged. "It's up to you. I can patch things up so that your engines will work but they'd be an accident waiting to happen – and it might not be anything as simple as a busted pipe the next time – or I can do the job properly and squeeze some extra performance out of the system at the same time."

This was more like it. "Extra? How much extra?"

"It's hard to say; maybe as much as ten percent, maybe a little less."

*Ten percent?*Monkey had better watch out. He might find himself out of a job when and if he eventually woke up. This girl was good, assuming she could deliver.

"All right, fix the leak and then see about finding us a new sheath. There must be one somewhere on this godforsaken planet."

"Yeah, sure, I can find a new inductor sheath for you…"

Pelquin stared at her. "But…?"

"Well, it's the sort of thing a mechanic would do without hesitation for a ship she was crew on, but why would I want to go to all the trouble of ferreting out a new part for a captain who hasn't even said he'll hire me yet?"

Pelquin felt almost offended. "Listen, I won't be held to ransom, not by anyone, least of all by some slip of a girl who thinks she knows how to tinker with engines."

"Fair enough. On the other hand, I'll be hanged if I'm gonna be taken advantage of by the captain of some…"

"I'm sure no one intends to take advantage of anyone," Bren cut in quickly before the girl said something Pelquin wouldn't overlook. "Or insult anyone," and Bren glared at Pelquin in a manner that just dared him to gainsay her. "The original task was to fix the leak, and you can do that with what we have on board, yes?"

"Sure, but, like I say, the leak's the least of your problems." Leesa's reply earned her another of Bren's patented looks, the older woman clearly urging the newcomer to work with her.

Interesting, so Bren liked her too. That sealed it as far as Pelquin was concerned. They'd found their new mechanic.

"Well, if you can prove yourself by doing *that*," Bren continued, "then you've passed the test that the Captain set you, and he'll have no reason *not* to hire you, right Captain?"

Pelquin raised his eyebrows, as if the idea hadn't occurred to him.

"*Right?*" Bren repeated with feeling.

Pelquin looked from one woman to the other, then, deciding he'd probably milked the situation as much as he dared, said, "*If* she can fix it, and if she's capable of taking orders, then yes, she's hired."

He didn't miss the flicker of relief on the girl's face; quickly masked, but it had been there.

Bren turned back to the girl. "Will that satisfy you? Fix the leak, join the crew, and then go and find us the right part."

"She's on the crew *provided* she can fix the engines properly," Pelquin said, backtracking slightly but still reckoning he was being more than reasonable. "Guaranteed,"

"Sounds good to me," their new mechanic replied, pushing herself to her feet. "I'll have this patched up in no time."

"Good." Pelquin considered her for a second.

Whatever had inspired that quick display of vulnerability it was hidden again, supplanted by her absorption in a task she seemed to relish. He lingered for a few more seconds. Then he caught Bren's eye and the two of them left, heading towards the rec room and leaving the girl to her work.

"You know," Bren said as they walked, "I think she's going to work out."

"Yeah," he said. "So do I as it happens, so do I."

EIGHT

There was a time when Pelquin would have been itching to rush off and explore La Gossa. Too many responsibilities limited his opportunity for such excursions these days, so he welcomed an excuse to leave the ship and meet up with Nate.

Drake had conveniently vanished off with the new mechanic into parts of the city unknown, and Pelquin had done nothing to discourage him. Supposedly the banker was keeping tabs on their new engineer as she looked for the replacement engine part, but Pelquin never took anything for granted where Drake was concerned.

The banker's absence came as blessed relief; only once he'd gone did Pelquin realise how heavily his constant presence had weighed upon him in recent days. The timing was perfect, enabling Pelquin to leave the ship with just a quick, "Keep an eye on things for me," to Bren and without the need to explain himself further.

Taxis crowded into a pick-up point just outside the port entrance – uniformly liveried in a jarring combination of yellow and pink, nose pressed to tail as if desperate to reach the front of the queue but not so desperate that they'd risk breaking rank. Nate had recommended he take one, saying it would be easier. Pelquin, however, preferred to stretch his legs. So he walked straight past the waiting vehicles despite a hopeful shifting of feet from drivers lounging by their cabs.

Pelquin trusted his wrist perminal for guidance. Sat Nav was as reliable here as on any world with a satellite network.

According to Nate, the restaurant was 'only five minutes' away' from the port. The perminal quoted thirteen, and in the event it took Pelquin nearer twenty, but then he wasn't in any great hurry. The first ten found him negotiating streets crammed with shops and clogged with traffic, the latter ten had him walking along narrow side streets. He emerged from one such to find his goal directly in front of him.

Describing the place as a 'restaurant' was pushing it; the tired-looking café could never hope to live up to such a lofty ambition. Twin glass doors had been pulled open, sliding back behind full-length plate windows to leave the interior exposed to the street. No air conditioning, then. The garish yellow façade stretched across the full width of the frontage had bold black and red lettering plastered across it. The effect was cheap and tacky; though Nate would doubtless describe this as 'shabby chic'. Not that Pelquin minded – he'd eaten in places far less inviting than this, and eaten well for that matter.

This sort of experience came with the territory if you were a friend of Nate Almont's – a man who delighted in discovering what the local cuisine had to offer wherever the ship landed and who took pride in ferreting out 'hidden gems' that were so far off the beaten track, they didn't even know a track existed. Pelquin had to admit that most of the time Almont's instincts were good. *Most* of the time… He just hoped this wasn't one of the occasions when the odds ganged up to claim a bit of retribution.

More a noodle bar than either restaurant or café, he realised as he stepped inside, and perhaps his initial assessment had been a little harsh. Twin decorative pillars stood just inside the doors, one to either side. The décor was basic but everything looked clean enough, and the whole place was open plan, with the busy kitchen at the back fully exposed to patrons' scrutiny. Pelquin's gaze was immediately drawn by a sudden flare of bright orange flame, as one of the white-vested chefs flipped the contents of a large black iron wok over a gas burner, the oil or liquor within it briefly catching alight.

A large propeller-like fan hung from the ceiling, turning lazily with a perpetual muted whirring to mark its presence.

A shortish man of indeterminate age with slicked-back hair and sporting a broad smile came up to greet him. "Good day, sir. Your friend is waiting over here." Which suggested they entertained few off worlders here; hardly a surprise – this place didn't strike him as the sort to feature the tourist guides; a typical Nate 'find'.

He had already spotted Nate, who raised a hand to make sure of the fact. He took the seat opposite his friend, who grinned in greeting. Trying his damnedest not to think of Julia, Pelquin smiled in return.

The little man hovered at his shoulder, asking, "More drinks?"

"Thank you, Henry," Nate said. "Two more beers."

Pelquin mouthed 'Henry?' as the waiter scurried away.

Nate shrugged. "It's what he said to call him, and I'm not about to argue."

Slipping away to some out of the way eatery when time allowed – just the two of them – had once been an established tradition, but this was the first time they'd done so since Nate's return. It resonated with a whole stack of good memories and made this outing almost like old times, but that was a pretty weighty 'almost'. Pelquin *wanted* to trust Nate, wanted to relax and simply enjoy himself, but Julia's intangible presence still came between them.

"You found the place all right then?" So Nate could sense the tension too. He was overcompensating, trying just a little too hard.

Pelquin was happy to play along. "Of course," and he tapped the diminutive perminal strapped to his wrist.

Nate tutted in feigned disgust. "Typical. It's a wonder you manage to wipe your own arse without a gadget to explain how to do it."

"That much I *can* do. Besides, you were the one who wanted me to take a taxi."

"Pampered mechanist!"

Pelquin found the corners of his mouth curling into the suggestion of a grin. This was a well-gnawed bone of contention between them, mostly an excuse to tease one other. The hypocrisy of a man who spent most of his life flitting through RzSpace at the mercy of hi-tech guidance systems disdaining a SatNav within the environs of a city continued to bemuse Pelquin.

Two pale, chilled beers arrived. The interruption came as a welcome relief. No menus were offered or asked for, and Pelquin guessed that Nate had already ordered for both of them.

"How's the hunt for Monkey's replacement going?" Nate asked, and Pelquin told him briefly about Leesa, before asking, "Has everything gone smoothly your end?"

Nate nodded. "No problem at all. Everything we need should be delivered to the ship by late tomorrow."

"Good, good. And the... ah, more *sensitive* items?"

"First thing tomorrow morning."

"A shame they couldn't arrive today."

"While that interfering son-of-a-banker Drake's off the ship, you mean?"

"Yeah, that's exactly what I mean."

"All right, leave it with me. I'll see what I can sort out."

Pelquin nodded. He was subconsciously using this lunch as a test, he realised; perhaps they both were. If they could make it to the end of the meal without mentioning *He* mame, maybe a few bridges would have been repaired... But there was a long way to go yet.

The first course arrived, Henry bringing over an oval platter which he placed between them on the table. It held a small pile of what proved to be lightly battered seafood; among them a prawn variant which was superb – very succulent and packed with flavour. Nate didn't hesitate but reached out to take one in his fingers.

"Careful, these are piping hot," he warned.

Pelquin followed suit, fascinated by the way the pink flesh of the cooked fish was visible through the thin, almost translucent coating of batter. They proved crisp to the bite and had been dusted with a hint of chilli or some equivalent; not too much, just enough to lift the flavour.

While they were finishing off this local take on tempura, Henry reappeared with a plate for each of them, piled high with noodles interlaced with vegetables and dark strips of meat, all of which glistened with a coating of sticky dark sauce. Pelquin breathed in the exotic fragrances appreciatively – aromatic, almost woody, with overtones of sweetness and undeniably mouth-watering.

Following Nate's example, he picked up the chopsticks and tucked in. The meat was beef, or near enough. Given a choice, Pelquin would have preferred a plain grilled steak with a pile of fried onions on the side, but he had to admit that this noodle dish was a delight.

"Good?" Nate asked, looking up.

"Mmm," Pelquin confirmed.

Nate drew the edge of his hand across his lips and grinned. He knew full well what Pelquin's culinary preferences were. "Well, I like it in any case."

"Have you heard me complaining?"

"No, can't say that I have."

This struck Pelquin as the first truly relaxed moment of the meal, which shouldn't surprise him: if it was common ground they were searching for, their shared love of food was as reliable a starting place as any.

"This is a hell of a lot better than the *last* place you took me to..."

Nate laughed. "God, yes! That enclosed fire pit on Cannelos Three; what was it called...?"

"The Salamander Garden."

"That's the one. Now that really *was* awful. Hot as hell; claustrophobic as a giant's codpiece and almost as sweaty, benches for seats, the surliest waiter in the known universe, and so many flies buzzing about they might as well have been a side dish."

For a moment, the spectre of Julia receded.

"Had to be tried, though," Nate said.

"No it didn't," Pelquin replied. "Trust me, it really didn't."

"But it came so highly recommended!"

The meal continued in similar vein. As the last of the noodles were polished off, Nate said quietly, seriously, "We needed this."

Pelquin stared for a second and then nodded. It was as close to an admission of what still lay between them as either was likely to make.

After a pause, Nate said, "Do you really think we're going to pull this off?"

"Yes. Why, don't you?"

"Yes, of course I do, but... God, Pel..."

"I know."

They had been through so much together over the years, him and Nate, but Julia had wiped all that away at a stroke. And now they were involved in a venture beyond anything either of them had ever dreamed of. Would it be enough to expunge her shade once and for all, or was this to be their last hurrah, a parting of the ways?

Pelquin didn't want to consider that.

Despite the fragility of their current bonhomie, he wanted to discuss something. "The shootout back at New Sparta..."

"Yeah, what about it?"

"I think we're agreed that Jossyren were behind it."

"I don't see who else."

"Nor do I, but what do you reckon they were hoping to achieve?"

"Delay us, I suppose; get us tangled up in red tape and law suits."

"That's what I thought at the time, but now I've had a chance to think about it I'm not so sure. It had the opposite effect, after all. What if that's what they were trying to do from the outset – spook us into acting before we were ready?"

"Why would they?"

"Perhaps to keep us off-balance, to make sure we went into this before we were fully prepared..." Pelquin shook his head. "I'm not sure; still trying to figure that bit out. I just don't trust that attack; it doesn't feel right."

"Good luck with that one. I gave up trying to understand those bastards a long time ago."

Pelquin didn't comment. Nate was the one who had brought Jossyren into all this, after all. Come to that, Nate had brought *all* of them in.

Pelquin paid for the meal; he had a feeling it was his turn anyway. Along with the bill, Henry also brought them a small brown paper carrier bag, which bore a single bold black glyph emblazoned on both sides.

"I didn't order..." he started to say, but Nate shushed him and then spoke to Henry in a dialect that Pelquin couldn't understand a word of. He played along though, smiling and thanking the grinning man, and even picking the bag up as they stood and left the building.

Only once they were out in the street did he ask, "What's with the takeaway?"

"Thought you might like some noodles for later, when we're back on the ship."

"Right. And...?"

"To be honest, while I'll happily eat the noodles if you don't want them, I'm more interested in the bag, or at least the squiggle on it."

Really? Pelquin glanced down at the bold, stylised mark. "I assumed this was just the noodle bar's name or something."

"Not quite. It's the emblem of the Red Tigers; a local street gang – 'disberos' they call them here. Henry's noodle bar is one of their places. Carrying something with that emblem on puts us under the Tigers' protection and ought to keep us safe until we reach the ship."

"I made it here without any hassle," Pelquin pointed out.

"Yeah, but do you really want to count on that sort of luck twice? I thought you'd come by taxi, not *walk* here. Look, if I'm wrong, what's the harm? But, if I'm right, this will keep us from being mugged, even by any chancers who might have spotted a gormless tourist wandering around with something as classy as a miniaturised perminal strapped to their wrist. Sure you don't want to consult it for directions, by the way? I'll wait, no problem."

"No, that's fine. I'll be happy to let you be my guide," Pelquin assured him. "I'll even carry your noodles, okay?"

They made it back to the ship without challenge, though Pelquin still had his doubts about how much of that was due to Nate's symbol-emblazoned bag.

"Are you going to keep that, then?" Nate asked, indicating the takeaway.

"Might as well," Pelquin replied. "I paid for it, after all."

Nate grunted. "Well, just don't eat it all."

"Why not?"

"I want to feed some of the noodles to the autochef, just to see if it can replicate the dish."

Pelquin had to laugh. "Really? I remember what happened the last time you tried something like that." All that had emerged was a gloopy brown textureless mush, a million light years away from the delicately spiced casserole Nate had been hoping for.

"Yeah, but that was different," Nate said. "We were low on supplies then. This time, with the protein banks, spices, and food reserves fully restocked at New Sparta, it ought to work fine."

"If you say so. You can try whatever emerges first, though."

"Wouldn't have it any other way."

Pelquin took his leave and went to his cabin, the takeaway bag still in hand and the smile still in place. It had been good, this lunch with his oldest friend.

The captain had been surprised when Drake chose to tag along with the new girl, that much was obvious. Pelquin's expression suggested that he'd never understand what motivated the banker's choices; which was just as well. Drake had no desire for *anyone* to understand.

Seeing Leesa again had been one of the biggest shocks of his life – her sudden reappearance throwing him so off-kilter that even Mudball was concerned. *Is this woman turning up really such a big deal?*

Yes. But he refused to explain why, clamping down on his thoughts while wondering how much the little alien was aware of in any case.

After leaving the Rusty Rivet Drake had returned to the *Comet*, where he'd chatted briefly with Anna, whose normally effervescent mood was subdued, probably because she had been left to mind the ship while everyone else went off exploring the new world. After that, he retreated to his crewcot and set about breaking into the captain's private files while no one else was around to monitor and notice his efforts. Or, to be more accurate, Mudball's efforts.

It hadn't taken the little alien long to crack the relevant encryptions, allowing Drake access. He began with the most recent updates and worked backwards, examining everything and uncovering hints along the way that Pelquin's activities had on occasion strayed beyond the limits of the law, which hardly came as a shock, but nothing relating to the current situation. Past misdemeanours were of no interest to Drake and whatever the *Comet's* captain might be up to now, he was keeping it to himself. Satisfied there was little worthwhile to find here, Drake had Mudball withdraw and cover all trace of their intrusion. He was just contemplating what to do next when Bren and the captain returned with the potential new recruit, curtailing any further efforts.

Drake didn't bother going to meet the new arrival at once – why hurry when she was merely a trialist? So it wasn't until a little later that curiosity caused him to stroll down to the engine room.

Sight of her stopped him in his tracks.

Drake had never been one to panic. He'd always believed that rational thought was the best counter to any problem and that succumbing to the body's instinctive emotional response was the surest way of making a bad situation worse. He reminded himself of this as he stood there, very deliberately drawing a deep breath as he watched this woman at work. She didn't seem aware of him as yet.

You know this chick?

Oh yes, he replied to his diminutive companion's query. *From way, way back.* "Leesa?" he said out loud at last.

"Yup, that's me," she said, briefly glancing round at him. "But this isn't a spectator sport. I'm busy here, so move along, okay? Feel free to come back and say 'hi' when I'm finished."

He stared at her, astonished by her response, or rather lack of it.

Are you certain you know her? 'Cos she sure as hell doesn't seem to know you, Mudball said.

So I noticed.

Drake walked away, deep in thought. Did Leesa genuinely not recognise him, or was she merely feigning it? How could she *not* know him? Of course, his problems would really begin when and if she did. He preferred his past to stay where it was: a long way back, not reaching out to touch upon his present.

The sooner he could determine whether this was all part of some elaborate game Leesa was playing the better.

NINE

Drake didn't hesitate in volunteering to accompany Leesa on her trip into La Gossa. She gave every indication of complete indifference, apparently accepting that *someone* would accompany her, if only to handle the financial side of things.

The urge to say 'it's me' as soon as they were alone was a temptation he firmly resisted. Until he could fathom what she was up to, or whether indeed she was up to anything at all, he settled on a watching brief; without, hopefully, being too obvious about it.

The first thing he noted was anxiety bordering on fear. Going back into La Gossa was the last thing she wanted to do. He waited for her to let her guard down, just for a second, to show some sign of recognition. It never came. If this was acting, then it was a consummate performance.

"We don't hang around, right?" she said. She was setting a quick pace, forcing him to take long strides to keep up. "We find what we want, you buy it, and then we head straight back to the ship so that I can get on with the repairs."

Or so that she could avoid bumping into whoever or whatever was making her so jumpy.

Leesa led the way through bustling streets that skirted the busy commercial quarter and into quieter, less frantic ones. In the face of her silence Drake divided his time between studying his surroundings and studying her. It had been years since they'd known each other. She'd changed, growing leaner and, in appearance at least, harder. Leesa had always been as tough as they came on the inside but now that toughness was starting to show through, in the set of her jaw, the gaunter look to her face. Her body seemed more angular and wiry. She still managed to look younger than she actually was but he sensed that even her apparent youth was fading. He felt a pang of guilt at the way they'd parted, not that he'd had much choice.

Doubtless he had changed too. A business suit was the last thing he would have worn when they knew each other, but he hadn't changed that much; certainly not enough to fool the part of her that never slept. Yet she showed not a flicker of recognition, and he was increasingly confident that her ignorance was genuine. What had happened?

There was something oddly out of synch about her, as if she'd been damaged and not healed properly, like a fractured bone that had knitted incorrectly. She was functioning but not quite as she should be. Despite the evidence, he remembered all too well who she was and what she was capable of, and he couldn't entirely rule out the possibility that she was faking it, but the possibility seemed less and less likely.

Babylon wasn't a world he'd visited before and new places always held a fascination for Drake, so he didn't have to pretend interest in the surroundings. Judging by the squalid streets she was now taking him through, Leesa had no compunction about showing him La Gossa in the raw. She clearly felt no strong affinity to the place, no desire to impress a stranger. Either that, or she didn't consider him worth the trouble of impressing.

The fault that had forced them out of RzSpace was genuine; Mudball had been able to confirm that. The *Comet* wouldn't be going anywhere until the engines were fixed, which gave Drake a rare opportunity to step away from his responsibilities for a while. Besides, he was still convinced that Pelquin had an ulterior motive for being here, and Drake's need to analyse Leesa outweighed any slight residual risk of his being abandoned.

He had to admit, too, that being out and about in La Gossa was infinitely more appealing than the prospect of sitting around on a grounded ship or whiling away the afternoon in a bar with random members of the *Comet's* crew.

His companion's obvious discomfort continued to intrigue him. He sensed that her hostility towards him was rooted in more than just the casual concern that he'd cramp her style or slow her down. She really didn't want him around. Something had her spooked, a fact she was trying hard not to show, perhaps believing it might jeopardise her position on the crew. His presence was providing a convenient focus for her displaced anxiety. Fine, he could live with that.

One thing was certain: wherever she intended to conduct her business, it wasn't going to be anywhere in the city's more salubrious districts. They stepped from an alleyway, pushing aside a drape that might have been leather, and a vista of extreme poverty unfolded around them; a shantytown Drake would never have suspected existed given the thriving city he'd been in just a few streets before. Ad hoc homes surrounded them, built of canvas walls draped over foraged wooden frames, plastic crates, and the occasional sheet of corrugated metal for the lucky ones. Bright coloured rugs or blankets hung down the sides of several, though it wasn't clear if they were intended to provide privacy or simply put out to dry. Rubbish was everywhere, great drifts of crushed cartons and abandoned tins, screwed up packaging and torn cellophane, all heaped together, piled up against flimsy walls. And the stink was appalling.

Two tatter-clad children chased each other, clambering into the skeleton of a car which stood by the roadside, its windows as absent as its wheels while one door was missing completely. The children's shrill laughter was the first remotely happy sound Drake had heard since entering the shantytown. Gaunt-framed men and women with flat, dead eyes squatted outside many of the shacks and suspicious gazes followed their progress. The smell of urine and decay permeated everything, while the incessant buzzing of flies surrounded them.

Nobody challenged them, even to beg. Drake suspected that most here simply lacked the energy to do so.

As they'd almost completed their passage across this depressing place they encountered three youths, loitering with attitude; not doing anything overtly threatening, just hanging around. The tallest stood out because he was too well dressed and looked to be a mean son-of-a-bitch: all black leather and piercings. The other two, a boy and a girl, were almost insignificant in comparison. Drake sensed Leesa grow tense under the youths' scrutiny.

"Trouble?" he asked quietly.

"Maybe," she replied, equally softly, her eyes staring straight ahead. "Don't look at them!" Drake quickly averted his eyes. "They're disberos – district boys – small time hoodlums but worth staying on the right side of, if only because there are so many of the bastards."

This was the most she'd said to him since they set out and he decided to push his luck. "Shakedowns, extortion, that sort of thing?"

"Yeah, plus drug peddling, smash and grabs in broad daylight, muggings, knifings simply for the fun of it when they're in the mood, which is generally when they're high on yanyel or cheap liquor." She quickened her pace. "They've got half the city – the poorer half –

divided up into territories and their influence is too ingrained for the authorities to do much about it. Just keep walking and keep your eyes front. With a bit of luck they'll ignore us."

Thankfully, they did, and Drake and Leesa walked past without being troubled. Soon after, the great swath of shacks ended, giving way to the solid reassurance of brick-built permanence once more. The great wash of makeshift homes crashed up against the brickwork like sea at high tide against a cliff face, the nearest shacks leaning against the walls, taking advantage of their stability. Drake imagined for a moment that if you were to remove the support of those walls the nearest dwellings would instantly tumble down, bringing with them the next row and the next in an irresistible domino effect, a collapse that would spread out across the district until the whole shantytown was flattened.

He was forced to pause as two battered bikes chugged past, heading into the slum. The short sleeves and back of the first rider's brightly coloured shirt billowed in the slight breeze stirred by his own passage. Neither man showed any sign that they'd even noticed Drake and Leesa. As the second bike drew level, Drake saw a small child hugging the rider's back, precariously perched on a seat intended for one. Even the kid's desultory gaze slipped over him as if he wasn't there.

Drake soon realised that although the buildings around them might have changed the sense of poverty remained, as did the air of hopelessness. Boarded windows stared down at them from concrete walls whose only decoration was a mosaic of cracks that emanated haphazardly from sill corners. The banker continued to trust that his reticent guide knew where she was going, taking reassurance in the conviction that Leesa wanted to get off this world as much as anyone.

She walked straight up to a slatted wooden door in the side of a building. Beyond it Drake could hear the thrum of machinery. Leesa didn't hesitate, pulling the door open and stepping inside. Drake followed, into a world of throbbing heat and bass vibration.

Ahead of him stretched long workbenches and longer conveyor belts, around which were clustered native workers, most of whom couldn't yet be out of their teens. A sweat shop, with the emphasis very much on the 'sweat'; no doubt drawing on workers from the nearby shantytown.

Pale grey suits had been Drake's uniform of choice since he first started working for the bank, but rarely had he regretted wearing one more than he did at that moment. He could feel the perspiration gathering beneath his clothes and running in ticklish drops down the side of his face. Even Mudball's familiar weight had become an uncomfortable burden, the alien's small body an unwelcome source of heat at his shoulder.

Not that the locals were immune. The small man who came to greet them bore testament to that, his forehead beaded with sweat. Only Leesa seemed completely unaffected. Acclimatised, obviously, but it went beyond that. There was something remarkable about her body's absolute lack of reaction to the extreme heat and humidity, something which reassured Drake enormously. So complete was her indifference to him that he'd begun to wonder whether this really was the same person he'd known.

The enigma remained, but at least he felt more confident that she really was Leesa and not some doppelganger.

The small man greeted them with a broad smile and addressed them in a language Drake didn't recognise. Leesa responded in the same tongue.

Mudball?

She's just explaining what you're doing here. The old man's nervous at the presence of a stranger.

Drake felt a sense of amusement in the alien's thoughts. *What?*

Nothing... It's just that her explanation of who you are has proved quite... shall I say, colourful.

I'll bet.

She eventually turned to Drake. "This is Wai Lun." The man clicked his heels together and performed a shallow bow. "He's the manager here, and thinks he might have an inductor sheath that would do us."

Her speech had improved noticeably since they left the *Comet*, as if she'd been putting on the local accent and inflection solely for Pelquin's benefit, giving the captain what she thought he'd want to hear in order to secure a berth. Drake knew she wasn't local, but she'd sounded it at outset.

Wai Lun led them through the long factory towards a small door at the far end. *What are they actually making here?* Drake asked, confident that Mudball would have hacked the factory's systems by now.

Machine parts, components of all sorts.

Knock-offs.

Indeed.

Drake did his best to turn a blind eye to the sight of so many children – and most of them were little more than that – working so hard around him, and to ignore the stench, which was even worse than it had been in the shantytown. Not his world, not anything he could influence, but the prospect of doing business with this man made his skin crawl. He knew such places existed, but knowing at a cerebral level and having his nose rubbed in the fact were entirely different.

Leesa's half-smile as they stopped suggested she had a fair idea of what he was thinking and was enjoying his discomfort.

Wai Lun pushed open the door, which led into semi-darkness until the flick of a switch brought a neon tube light stuttering to life. The room's opposite wall held another door, the view through that obscured by the heavy mobile strips of an industrial style plastic fly curtain hanging from its top, though Drake could make out what looked to be a serving counter and perhaps a small shop beyond. Two men's voices in animated discussion reached them through the doorway. They were speaking the same language Wai Lun and the girl had used, exchanging phrases with machine gun rapidity.

Around them, the walls of what could only be a stock room were lined with shelves that bulged with a bewildering variety of machine parts, many of them jammed in tightly or balanced so precariously that the removal of one looked likely to bring others crashing to the floor. The room was comparatively narrow but opened up to right and left, the shelving disappearing into the gloom in both directions.

After a few more unintelligible words and a smile to the girl, Wai Lun scurried off to their left before clambering up a short set of mobile steps and starting to rummage through the parts that rested on one of the higher shelves.

"Is this our only option?" Drake asked, keeping his voice quiet despite the likelihood that Wai Lun wouldn't understand in any case.

"How do you mean?"

He glanced across at Wai Lunn, making sure the smaller man was still busy. "Is there anywhere else we could get this sleeve of yours? Perhaps even an officially manufactured one."

"Wai Lun produces good quality work. You're not on New Sparta now, banker man. Copies or reconditioned jobs are as good as it gets around here. Live with it."

"Then perhaps we could look at getting a reconditioned one...?" He suggested.

She'd turned away to answer a shouted question from Wai Lun, but shook her head vigorously, saying without looking back at Drake, "That would mean trawling through dozens of junk shops and stalls, going from street to street; and even once we found the right sized sleeve there'd be no telling how good a recon it was, how long it would last. Besides... The captain said to get this done quickly. So swallow your scruples and let me do what we came here for."

Wai Lun had returned to ground level. He came over to them smiling broadly and clutching a part which he thrust towards the girl. It was a gleaming cylinder of silvered metal, a little longer than Drake's forearm, slightly flattened so that it was ovoid in shape rather than circular. It was sobering to realise that a component of this size, something he could comfortably carry in his arms, was capable of grounding a starship.

Leesa examined the cylinder critically, frowned, and shook her head, passing it back to the older man with a curt comment.

He said something plaintive and gesticulated dramatically, but then turned and hurried back to the steps, pushing them noisily across the concrete floor before climbing up them again, complaining all the while.

"That would probably have done us," Leesa said to Drake, "but it still wasn't quite right, not if I'm going to get the extra performance out of the engines I promised the captain."

He was surprised she took the trouble to explain herself, particularly given her earlier reserve. Perhaps having something to concentrate on had enabled her to forget for the moment whatever it was that had her spooked.

This time when Wai Lun scampered down the ladder and presented Leesa with his prize, she nodded her approval, though the proffered part looked no different to Drake than the previous one. "Yup," she said, "that's our boy. Pay up, banker man."

He did. And then found himself carrying the thinly-wrapped cylinder as they left the building, moving his cane to his left hand so that he could cradle the engine part in the crook of his right arm.

If anything, Leesa seemed even more agitated as they made their way back towards the ship. She relapsed into silence and stalked through the shantytown with all the wariness of a predator that has strayed onto a rival pack's turf.

This time, their passage wasn't as untroubled as it might have been.

"Shit!" Leesa said.

Drake had seen them too. The same youths they'd passed on the way in, except that now there were more of them, and they made no attempt to hide their interest in the pair of outsiders. Drake saw the nudge that one gave to another, saw too the nod in their direction.

"Head down, eyes front," Leesa murmured.

Despite Leesa's instruction, Drake watched the cluster of youths from the corner of his eye and so saw the pack start towards them. If not for the nudge and the nod it would have been easy to assume this was a random attack – bored street kids spoiling for some action, but those gestures and the purpose with which they advanced told him otherwise. The gang had been waiting for them. Since he was new to the whole planet, they had to be after Leesa.

"Hope you can handle yourself," she said quietly. "Because I'm gonna have my hands full and won't be looking out for anyone else."

"Don't worry, I'll cope," he assured her, adjusting the grip on his cane and taking a few paces sideways so that they both had room to fight. He shifted the precious induction sleeve so that it rested in the crook of his left arm, conscious of its weight but confident he could hold it there in the short term without hampering his movements too much.

The disberos came on. The biggest of them, the one who'd been nudged, led the way, approaching with the sort of swagger that suggested he owned these streets. A shaved head and plenty of metalwork around the face; in fact, facial piercings seemed to be the tribal badge. This one, evidently the leader, sported several earrings, a spiked stud through his right cheek, and a pair of silver hoops which emerged from just below his bottom lip and circled downwards to disappear beneath his chin. Hardly the most practical of embellishments to take into a fight, Drake would have thought, but each to their own. Those advancing behind Hoopface all bore their own variations – studs, spikes, rings, bars, cones, and jewels thrust and displayed through cheeks, brows, lips, ears and even foreheads. Half a dozen in total; no, scratch that; another pair had appeared from the opposite side of the street and were clearly intent on joining the party. That made it eight against two. Doubtless the eight expected this to be easy. They were in for a shock, assuming Leesa hadn't forgotten everything she used to know about fighting and he wasn't compromised too much by the inductor sheath.

Without breaking stride, Hoopface reached with both hands to his chin, clasped the two hoops, and jerked them free of his face, before flinging them in a backhanded throw, all in one fluid movement. The nature of the attack was so unexpected it almost caught Drake by surprise, but at the last moment he raised his cane, swatting one of the two curved missiles aside and intercepting the other. For an instant, that second ring clung to his cane, three-quarters of a circle wrapped there and jangling, threatening to slide towards his hand until the missing quarter came into play and it dropped to the ground. Drake had expected sharp points or blades but in the split second that almost-ring had rattled on his cane energy had played across the cane's smooth surface. He didn't feel it – the cane was too well insulated for that – but it caused him to upgrade his initial assessment of the gang's threat; they were evidently more sophisticated than they appeared. Suddenly the prospect of fighting them while holding an awkward object didn't appeal. Drake crouched, to put the sheath on the ground and push it away behind him, before straightening and preparing to meet Hoopface, his cane held to the fore.

As the far larger man came within grappling range Drake lunged forward and jabbed him quickly with the stick, like a fencer with the tip of a foil. Hoopface laughed and let the blow land, which was a mistake. As the tip of the cane made contact, Drake activated its repellor field, magnifying the force of impact exponentially. What had been a simple prod was converted into a hammer blow; one which flung Hoopface backward, to crash into and then through the crowd of thugs behind him. The big man landed heavily several metres away, where he stayed: on his back unmoving.

Drake didn't hesitate but waded into the stunned disberos before they had a chance to react. He kicked, punched, elbowed and swatted, knocking down two more of them before the rest could recover and muster a response. He was vaguely aware of Leesa fighting beside him but was too focused on his own battle to note more than that.

To his surprise, Drake found he was actually enjoying himself. It had been years since he was involved in a street brawl like this, and he'd forgotten how much satisfaction could be gained from kicking the life out of someone who was intent on doing the same to you.

He lost track of how many he was fighting, suspecting that others had joined the fray. Four or five lay unconscious on the ground, including Hoopface, but plenty were still on their feet.

He ducked beneath a roundhouse punch, sweeping his cane at ankle level to trip one opponent before standing and cracking another around the ear. Then they were on him, a solid body barrelling into him, arms wrapping around his torso, squeezing. He lost hold of his cane and was carried backward, stumbling to the ground.

Hey, watch it! Mind who you're falling on, afamiliarvoicesaid as he went over.

He'd almost forgotten about Mudball but couldn't afford to spare the alien a second thought. Impact with the ground had loosened the bear-hug a fraction. He kicked, writhed, bucked, twisted, and landed a solid blow with his elbow, feeling it smash against his opponent's cheek and nose. Suddenly free, he rolled to his knees.

His ribs were bruised, his left arm was cut, his knee sore, his teeth hurt and he tasted blood in his mouth... And he was loving every ache of it.

He scrabbled to his feet, spotting the cane as he did so and stooping to retrieve it; which was when disaster struck. Mudball must have been dislodged by the recent tumble, and was clearly taken by surprise at Drake's instinctively bending down to pick up the cane. Even as Drake straightened, he heard a dismayed yelp inside his head, felt Mudball fall free, and caught a glimpse of a brown-green tumble of fur go sailing past his ear.

He tried to grab his falling companion, missed, and the distraction cost him dearly. He looked up to find a club of some sort whistling towards his head, too close to avoid. Even as the realisation sank in and he tried to turn away, pain exploded in his right temple. He was abruptly aware of the ground rushing towards him at alarming speed, and then oblivion claimed him.

Ten

Falyn de Souza's mood was even darker than the oppressive sky. He stared out of the window at the rain, which had been falling incessantly all morning and showed no sign of relenting any time soon, and wished fervently that he was somewhere else. The weather had been much the same since they landed and he had yet to find anywhere decent to eat in this miserable excuse for a town.

He left the window and moved further into the hotel's spacious lobby, taking a seat at an empty table that was still in sight of the main door. After brief indecision he placed an order via the table tender; opting for a white wine – both label and grape variety were unfamiliar to him, but the menu promised a wine 'crisp and dry with light citrus overtones'. The 'citrus' gave slight cause for concern – it was so often code for 'overly acidic' – but nothing else on offer appealed to him.

De Souza never had been the most patient of men. It was a failing, one that he recognised and had learned to accommodate in the course of his life. In fact, his tolerance of fools and their incompetence seemed to lessen with each passing year. From the moment they first met, De Souza had sensed in Archer a prime candidate for failure. So few individuals *ever* managed to live up to expectations.

However, he was willing to be proven wrong, so had given the banker the benefit of the doubt and granted him considerable leeway; a privilege that was fast disappearing. To date, Archer had shown few signs of exceeding that initial damning assessment, despite the man coming highly recommended, which just went to prove how low some people's standards must be.

It was Archer, for example, who had brought them to Newton Four, where, contrary to his confident predictions, they had found neither hint nor rumour of the *Comet* and its crew.

The wine arrived. Another disappointment. The very first sip told him that it lacked the promised crispness and, as feared, was too acidic. He took a second taste from the delicate crystal glass – the vessel being of far higher quality than its content – which confirmed the assessment.

He placed the glass down, in no hurry to pick it up again.

On the surface, de Souza was calmness personified, but inwardly he was seething. Evidently this was the finest hotel in town, which said much about the town. He doubted this establishment would have made the top one hundred on New Sparta… or indeed the top thousand.

At that moment Archer arrived, accompanied by a gust of wind and a flurry of rain as he paused to collapse the energy shield of his umbrella. De Souza didn't acknowledge him, not at once, watching from the corner of his eye as the banker paused to stow the stubby handle of the umbrella in his jacket pocket.

He was wearing a suit, for goodness' sake; even on a God-forsaken planet like this and in the incessant rain. That said it all, really.

Archer spotted him and headed over. De Souza glanced across to the next table, where his bodyguard, Gant – a solid, shaven-headed powerhouse of a man – waited with two other slabs of hired muscle, and gave him a subtle nod. Gant knew Archer and probably wouldn't have intervened, but it never hurt to be certain. De Souza didn't get up as the banker arrived – that would have shown too much respect. Instead he simply raised his eyebrows and said, "Well?"

"They definitely haven't been here." Archer said. "I don't understand it. This is the obvious choice. Newton Four is by far the most industrialised option available to them. Logic says they *had* to come here."

De Souza dropped his gaze to avoid craning his neck. The banker's trousers were darker at the bottom, he noted, presumably soaked through courtesy of water splashed up from puddles by hurrying feet. Shame. "Perhaps they fixed the work of your saboteur themselves and didn't need to stop off in order to effect repairs," he said.

"No," and Archer shook his head. "I studied the crew files. With the mechanic, Palmer, out of the way, they don't have anyone capable of diagnosing a drive problem let alone fixing it. They'd have to set down or risk being stranded, and Drake would never countenance a gamble of that sort."

"Then clearly they must have gone somewhere *else*." De Souza didn't care how much irritation showed in his voice.

Archer nodded, apparently oblivious to any hint of criticism. "Babylon," he said. "That's where they've gone. It's the only plausible alternative. Still doesn't make much sense them passing over Newton

Four, but it *has* to be Babylon."

At last, an excuse to leave this inferior hotel with its pretentions of grandeur. The single night's stay he'd been forced to endure had been more than enough for one lifetime. It reminded de Souza of how precarious a word 'hotel' was: never more than a single letter away from 'hovel'.

"Babylon..." He nodded, having heard of the place but never been. "Very well, Babylon it is. Let's hope you're right this time."

"I am, don't worry."

De Souza made no comment. It wouldn't be a disaster if they failed to pick up the *Comet*'s trail, but he'd feel a lot happier once they managed to. If Babylon didn't pan out, he would have to consider cutting Archer loose. A pity, since the man represented a considerable investment in time and money – cultivating an insider within First Solar Bank didn't come cheap – but there was little point in pouring good money after bad.

Consciousness returned to Drake in stages. To begin with his head felt so fragile that moving didn't seem a particularly good idea, but at least he managed to open his eyes and take stock, realising that he was in a room, on a bed. Not the softest of beds perhaps, but it beat the ground any day. To his right, pushed to one side as if to keep it out of the way but on hand if needed, was a bulky, cumbersome unit that might have been a Medidoc, albeit an old and outdated model. Associations tumbled into place one after the other. He was in an infirmary, on a ship, comet class: *Pelquin's Comet*, it had to be. He felt remarkably unconcerned about how he came to be here and benefited from a general sense of well-being; nothing as strong as euphoria, but he was definitely a few steps along the road to that joyous state. Drugs, obviously. Evidently the good doctor hadn't managed to consume *all* the supplies, retaining enough to use on a patient or two at least.

He started to sit up and his head protested; a detached, almost muffled stab of pain. His questing fingers felt the smooth tightness of a plaskin patch on his right temple, just below the hairline, and he found another on his left arm.

Welcome back, said a familiar presence. Mudball squatted on the pillow beside an indentation that presumably marked where his head had been.

You're lucky I didn't squash you.

Trust me, there was no luck involved, the diminutive alien assured him.

The pain was still there, but it remained a dull and distant thing, squatting somewhere towards the front of his head and, on the whole, perfectly manageable.

How did I get back here?

You've got Leesa to thank for that. She beat off the rest of the street louts and then called the ship. Doc and Bren came to fetch you.

The doc's back from the hospital, then?

Obviously.

Drake was a little surprised that Leesa had enough foresight even to know *how* to contact the ship, but perhaps he shouldn't have been.

What didn't surprise him was the speed with which the good doctor appeared at his bedside, Pelquin at his heels. After all, it would have been remiss not to have some sort of monitor or alarm set up to alert them when the patient regained consciousness.

Doc fussed. "You shouldn't be sitting up." But the protest was at best half-hearted, spoken from a sense of duty rather than concern. Doc was the one crewmember Drake had yet to get a handle on, perhaps because this was the person he had spent the least amount of time with, but there was something very private about Ahmed Bariha. Here was a man who didn't court attention or company. That in itself made him a rarity aboard this ship.

"How's Monkey doing?"

The doc looked surprised at the question, presumably expecting his patient to be focused entirely on his own health. "He'll live," he said; good news – it might at least brighten Bren's mood. "Though he'll need some time to recuperate," the doc added.

The *Comet*'s proprietor appraised the banker thoughtfully. "So, you couldn't stay out of trouble, huh?"

"I didn't have much say in the matter."

"The local pols have sent a PoD over to interview you."

Drake closed his eyes. "Really?" This was all too tedious. He'd gained the impression that gang violence was hardly a novelty in La Gossa and was surprised that a scuffle like this even warranted the assignment of a drone. Unless the incident had been reported by someone, of course, in which case he supposed they'd have to react. Surely Leesa hadn't... No, of course not; he dismissed the thought immediately. There was no way she would risk drawing that sort of attention to herself.

"Yeah," Pelquin said. "I guess they have to be seen to react, what with you being from off world. The thing is, if they insist on going through the motions, so must we."

Drake could hardly argue. "Doc, can you give me something to help clear my head?" Whatever painkillers and sedatives the doc had dosed him with had left his head stuffed with the mental equivalent of cotton wool – fine for cosseting against pain but not so helpful for alert responses when questioned by the police.

"You ought to rest, give your body a chance to recover," Doc said.

"No doubt, but it appears that's not an option right now."

Bariha sighed. "Very well."

The doc produced a white hypo-pen, touched a control on its side and pressed it against Drake's neck. "That should give you an hour or so," he said. "After that, the effects will fade rapidly and the sedative will take over once more."

"An hour should be fine," Drake assured him, hoping the interview wouldn't last that long.

"The PoD's in the galley," Pelquin said as Drake got up. "It was busy taking the new engineer's statement when I left. Should be ready for you any time now, I'd reckon."

PoDs, or Police Drones, came in all shapes and sizes, their level of sophistication equally as varied. Drake was guessing La Gossa's law enforcers wouldn't have top of the range models at their disposal. He'd fooled PoDs before, though not lately. Still, it was only a *little* lie he would have to tell; for the most part he could be as honest as the day was long. Assuming, that is, the PoD didn't ask him if he had any reason to suspect the attack was anything other than random. He saw again that exchange between the two kids – the nudge and the nod; the very things he now had to forget all about.

Don't worry, you'll be fine, Mudball assured him.

You can influence a PoD then?

No idea.

Great, thanks for the reassurance.

Despite sharing so much with the alien, he had never discovered the limits of Mudball's abilities. Proximity was certainly a factor, but defining parameters was another matter entirely. Still, he was learning all the time. Did he trust Mudball? As much as he trusted anybody; but that was hardly a glowing commendation.

Leesa was just leaving the galley as he arrived. She looked a little flustered, and favoured him with a thin smile as he stood aside to let her past, as if to indicate she was glad to see him back on his feet. It was the closest to a friendly gesture he'd yet received from her. Presumably the fight had brought them closer in her eyes, even if he had spent the closing stages unconscious.

The PoD waited by one of the tables, hovering a little above the floor. A squat and irregular elongated bubble of a drone, like a giant bullet; it bore blue and silver livery to denote its allegiance to local law enforcement. If ever a machine could be said to look tired, this one did. Its shell was scratched and tarnished, showing several small dents and at least one scorch mark. Here was a unit due an overhaul.

"Ah, Mr Drake, please sit down." At least the voice, a woman's, sounded bright and clear.

"I should warn you that I've been dosed with sedatives and painkillers," he said, "so apologies if my answers are a little... woolly."

"Duly noted. This won't take long."

Nor did it. The questions were direct and few in number, dealing with factual matters without asking him to conjecture on the motive for the attack. This wasn't an interview conducted in the hope of actually identifying any perpetrators but merely for the sake of form.

As he left the galley, Drake couldn't help ask, *was that your doing?*

No, Mudball replied. *I didn't need to interfere at all. Not sure I could have done without being obvious in any case.*

Another useful titbit to be filed away. He had grown to accept the bond between Mudball and himself. At first he'd been far from comfortable with another presence inside his own head, but he soon discovered how adaptable humankind can be; a case of familiarity breeding contempt, perhaps. It meant that he never fully relaxed – never completely let his guard down. But even this was something he'd grown used to, to the extent where he began to think of the situation as 'normal'; though, deep down, he knew it was anything but.

The most disturbing aspect of this strange symbiosis was that he didn't really know what Mudball *was*. A leftover, the survivor of a client species that had been tasked with watching over the Elder cache where Drake first encountered him; the lingering afterthought of a long-vanished civilisation; that was how Mudball tended to explain himself. Yet there were so many topics about which the alien was unfailingly evasive: what the Elder civilisation had been like, the nature of the Elders themselves, what had become of them, even how old he was: *how the hell should I know? I've been sealed up in a crypt for God knows how many centuries – you really think time has any significance for me?*

If life was passing you by while you were stuck in there, then yes, I'd have thought that would *be significant.*

Humans! Mudball had become adept at conveying contempt when he wanted to.

One thing Drake did know was that he would have died in that cache if not for Mudball, which earned the little alien considerable leeway. If the chirpy little being that had just saved his life wanted to see the universe, why not? It made sense that a newly liberated intelligence would want to experience the civilisation that had sprung up in the wake of the one he'd known, and Drake sympathised with his saviour not wanting to become a test subject, a lab rat, an imprisoned zoo exhibit, which would have been Mudball's inevitable fate if his existence became known. So Drake agreed to become his host, to hide him, pass him off as a pet, and in the process take him to see the stars.

He owed the little alien that much and, besides, he was an expert at keeping secrets. None of this prevented him from having reservations or from suspecting, on occasion, that Mudball wasn't being entirely straight with him; that things were going on just beyond the reach of his knowledge and understanding. Drake had made it his personal mission to discover what.

*While you were sleeping...*Mudball said.

I was unconscious, he corrected.

Whatever. Anyway, to keep myself busy, I did some snooping and discovered an interesting little anomaly.

Anomaly?Of what sort?

The sort created when the ship's records are tampered with to hide something that came aboard while we were off searching for engine parts.

Now that is interesting. I don't suppose there were any clues as to what it might be?

No, none whatsoever. You can't expect me to do all the work.

The interview with the PoD had taken a scant twenty minutes, which meant he still had a little time before the stimulant faded to leave his body wide open to the Doc's sedatives again. *A quick visit to the hold would seem to be in order, then, don't you think?*

Oh goody, you really do take me to all the best places.

Just be grateful I take you anywhere.

He needed to know exactly what had been sneaked aboard. Did it indicate that Pelquin was involved in some sort of elaborate scam and merely using the rest of the crew to get to the cache, with the intention of double-crossing both them and First Solar along the way…?

Before he could act on this determination, however, his reveries were interrupted by Pelquin. "Drake, a quiet word. I'd like your opinion on something. You've spent more time with our new mechanic than anyone else has; what do you think of her?"

Gods, why was the man asking him?

Perhaps because he knows you have a vested interest in the welfare of the crew and the mission, Mudball suggested.

"She seems competent enough…" he said.

"Do I sense a 'but'?"

Now was his chance. If he really thought Leesa was a threat and wanted to get her removed from the ship, he just had to say as much. "Nothing specific," he temporised, "but I'm pretty certain she comes with a considerable amount of baggage."

"We *all* come with baggage, Mr Drake."

"True, but hers strikes me as the sort that's not easily ignored."

"The fight, you mean? You think she was the cause?"

"Maybe, yes. It wasn't a random attack; we were targeted."

Pelquin shrugged. "We all have issues, Drake. So long as she leaves hers behind when we depart Babylon, I'm not concerned. Unless you're suggesting hers are more than that?"

The pivotal moment. The last thing he wanted to do was let Leesa down again, but at the same time he had a job to do, one that Leesa's secrets could endanger. "It's hard to be sure," he found himself saying, "but no, I haven't seen anything to suggest this is any more than a local problem."

"Well, in that case, I'll take my chances. We need an active engineer, and it's not as if I'm spoilt for choice right now. I appreciate your candour, but there's not a man or woman aboard the *Comet* that doesn't have their secrets, Mr Drake. Even you, I'll warrant."

Drake smiled. "Not me, Captain. I'm as straightforward as a man could be. First Solar wouldn't employ me otherwise."

"In that case, Mr Drake, I pity you. We should all have our secrets, each and every one of us. They help define who we are."

"You may well be right, Captain, you may well be right." With that, Drake nodded farewell and took his leave.

Very cryptic, and despite your misgivings you chose not to say anything about her, Mudball said. *I never will understand the way you humans think.*

Don't worry, much of the time nor do we.

So, this Leesa,she really is an auganic?

Yes. And therein lay the problem. Drake was *almost* ready to accept that Leesa's amnesia was genuine – she certainly hadn't given herself away during their time together in La Gossa – but whereas he might still be in the dark about some aspects of Mudball's capabilities, he knew full well what an auganic could do. So he couldn't be certain she wasn't faking it, and that lingering doubt was going to irritate the hell out of him until he could put it properly to rest.

Cool, Mudball said. *Thought I'd never get the chance to meet one of those. This is all tremendously exciting.*

No it wasn't, not from where Drake was standing.

The hold was deserted, with deliveries made and the big cargo door shut for the night. There was a security camera, but Mudball ensured the image was recycled in a loop so that anyone who might happen to be watching would merely see continuous, undisturbed stillness.

Identifying the recently arrived crates proved easy enough. With all that had happened in the past few days the equipment taken on at New Sparta had yet to be unpacked; nobody had paid it much attention beyond checking for bullet holes and damage. Crates that didn't show any sign of either had been pushed to the back of the hold. The later additions – those brought aboard that day at La Gossa – had simply been stacked in front of the New Spartan ones. There weren't many, either; certainly not as many as Drake would have anticipated.

Using his perminal, he scanned each container's coded label, which Mudball then compared to the official inventory.

In a matter of minutes they'd accounted for all of them.

They all match, Mudball observed. *I don't get it, why bother tampering with the loading records in that case?*

Patience, Pelquin advised, *patience.* There had to be something else, and, aware of his penchant for inspecting things, it wouldn't surprise him in the slightest if Pelquin had made at least a superficial attempt to hide whatever it was.

Useful tool, a perminal; his was also primed with a number of apps specific to his job.

By common practice, packing crates for anything less than corporate scale commercial shipping were manufactured from genetically strengthened wood: a cheap, renewable, bio-degradable resource. Drake held the perminal steady, close to one of the crates they had already checked. A barchart of chemical components appeared. Next, he walked over and repeated the process with one of the crates taken on at New Sparta. The results were very satisfying.

Different, Mudball observed.

Exactly. Different trees grown on different worlds; their chemical composition varies in a few key indicators.

Clever, Mudball allowed. *Now you just hope that one of the shipping companies isn't recycling crates that originated on the other world.*

There is that, he conceded, *but if so we'll try something else. For now, though…*

It didn't take long. Nate, and presumably Pelquin, must have been in a hurry; Drake found what he was looking for immediately behind the foremost crates: wood that had originated on Babylon rather than New Sparta.

No shipping labels of any sort, Mudball pointed out.

It wasn't a large crate – by no means the largest there – but, lacking a gravsled or a powerlifter to help move some of the other containers aside, opening it took a while longer than Drake would have liked. By the time he succeeded and could see what was in there, pain and wooziness were creeping in again. Drake ignored them, determined to discover what Pelquin was up to before succumbing to the doc's drugs.

His perseverance was eventually rewarded, though sight of the crate's contents made him wonder whether the drugs weren't kicking in after all. Using the torch facility on his perminal at widest setting, he stared at the compact curved unit and twin stacks of metal plates, eight in total.

"Well I'll be…"

You know what this is? Mudball said.

Yes. It came as a relief, in a way. Yes, the captain might be keeping tight-lipped about things, but this didn't smack of a double cross, merely of caution.

Drake centred the beam on the lettering, depicted in flowing script on the side of this innocuous looking engine: PTARMIGAN. The counterfeiters had even mimicked the proper logo. *It's called a Ptarmigan, after a mountain dwelling bird of Old Earth which changed its plumage to white in winter as camouflage against the snow.*

Presumably it's an acronym; the letters stand for something, right?

Not that I know of.

Oh come on, they must do… Phase Tension And Resonance… Ehm… Okay, maybe not.

The cute little name they've given it doesn't really matter, Drake said.

Right. It's what the thing does that's important.

Exactly. He'd seen pictures of something like this, though he never expected to actually encounter one. *It's a dissonance field generator. Or, if you prefer, a cloaking device.*

Drake fought the onset of fatigue as he made his way back from the hold, his feet dragging at every step. The last person he wanted to bump into was Nate Almont, so inevitably he did, in a very literal sense. The broader man turned his shoulder, clearly intent on catching Drake in passing. Drake saw the move coming and was able to twist out of the way, avoiding all but the lightest of brushes, but conversation was a little harder to evade.

"Now I wonder where you've been," Almont said. "Snooping around as usual?"

"Merely taking my daily constitutional," Drake assured him. "There's so little room to exercise on a ship, don't you find?"

Almont grunted, and Drake took that as his cue to walk on, ending the encounter before it could develop into anything more significant and before he fell asleep on his feet.

"I'm keeping an eye on you, banker, you remember that," Almont called after him.

It was all Drake could do to keep his legs moving, so he ignored Almont's parting shot and continued to his alcove – that little corner of *Pelquin's Comet* that was his, however temporarily. Once there, he stretched out on the bed, lying on his back and trying to organise his thoughts before sleep claimed him. Mudball hopped down to squat on the pillow beside his head.

Events were mounting up, an accumulation that invariably created patterns. All Drake had to do was recognise and interpret those patterns. He started reviewing what he knew. A superficially senseless raid had come close to killing the *Comet*'s engineer. During the ship's next jump a fault had developed which nobody still conscious was capable of diagnosing. The ship had landed on Babylon to seek medical and technical assistance. Pelquin, possibly in collusion with Nate Almont, had ulterior motives for coming to Babylon. As a result of landing there, Leesa came on board: somebody who knew Drake in another life, though she didn't appear to know him now. While on Babylon, the ship had taken delivery of specialist equipment which the captain had hoped to slip aboard unnoticed...

Was all of that mere chance? Of course not; but that didn't mean that *all* these disparate factors were directly related. It was easy to jump to false conclusions, to sweep up associated but quite separate occurrences and assume they were part of one unified pattern, warping the shape of the real pattern in the process.

The challenge was determining which facts were linked to which others and to recognise those that merely *appeared* to be. Nor could he afford to be wrong. But then this was one of his primary skills, and he did so enjoy a challenge.

Nate Almont sat at the heart of things. He was the catalyst that had set events in motion. It was Almont who had left the ship on acrimonious terms; Almont who returned after a year of doing goodness knew what professing knowledge of an Elder cache, and Almont who brought with him an artefact; the same Almont who disappeared for protracted periods whenever the ship was in dock.

Drake closed his eyes and set about pairing facts in his mind, testing them to see how they fitted and where they led. He knew sleep was imminent no matter how hard he tried to stave it off, and could only hope that come morning his subconscious would have unpicked the various threads and identified the true nature of the pattern. Only then would he know the best way to proceed.

He was dead to the world by the time the *Comet* took off and left Babylon's atmosphere behind.

ELEVEN

As a child, Leesa had always loved the name her community had adopted, believing it to be the most romantic name in the universe: Liaise. She imagined the settlement had chosen this in honour of some ancient city of Old Earth and, to her childhood self, the word conjured up images of exotic wonder; of darkly handsome chisel-jawed princes guiding elegant swan-necked boats beneath dramatic skies, slipping silently along mist-wreathed waterways propelled by nothing more than a pole of burnished wood, while the whole world held its breath awaiting the outcome of their noble quests. The glint of steel in the depths of their eyes told you at once that these were not men to be messed with: strong, silent, and determined to be reunited with their one true loves. The women in question would of course be spirited and beautiful maidens, oppressed by the dictates of misguided parents and denied their heart's desire; all for their own good, or so they were told. Pennants fluttered from flagpoles while water lapped against quaysides with ominous portent and cobbled, torch-lit courtyards stood ready for the long shadows and purposeful footsteps of determined suitors. Glittering masks were optional, but clothes were invariably long, flowing, and fashioned from finest silk, while love would overcome every obstacle.

Her dreams withered the day she learnt what 'liaise' actually meant and realised that the word was as unglamorous and utilitarian as every other aspect of her life. It was a label, not a name; no more than an apt indicator of the colony's purpose. They were a human enclave on an alien world, scientists and sociologists bent on building bridges between the cultures of two very different sentient races, and she was merely a biological by-product of the length of time they had been there. So much for romantic fancy.

To an extent, then, she'd grown up among the aliens; though that wasn't right, as her mum kept telling her, because on this world she and her family were the XTs – the aliens – while the Xters were the natives. Except that they weren't, which was something her mum's work later confirmed. The Xters were colonists just like them; they'd merely arrived a bit earlier – by a handful of centuries or so. The *real* natives had died out even longer ago than that.

The Xters weren't hostile, though there had been a lot of posturing and brandishing of military hardware when the two cultures first encountered each other. Somehow, out and out warfare had been avoided, which was a shame by Leesa's reckoning. She enjoyed nothing more than a good Warvie and the real thing would have been so absolute.

The prevailing peace was even more impressive given the one factor that, above everything else, had defined relationships between the two species ever since First Contact: namely that each was deeply repugnant to the other. Not for any profound ideological, religious or political reason, it was far more fundamental than that. The many-limbed, quick-moving Xters, with their multi-faceted eyes and cloying odour that sat somewhere between rotting melon and overripe corpse, awoke in the human heart a primordial fear that seemed universal. They weren't really *that* much like spiders – only six limbs to start with – and even spiders didn't inspire revulsion in everyone… But the Xters did.

The loathing was entirely mutual. Evidently Xters found the bipedal, constantly tottering form of humans alarming and counter-intuitive to a degree that unsettled them profoundly. They thought the near-absence of bodily hair obscene, while human odour was even more repulsive to them than theirs was to us.

Given all this, the avoidance of war seemed little short of a miracle, but, having benefited from a largely pragmatic upbringing, Leesa didn't believe in miracles. There had to be more practical explanations; they were merely less obvious. Economics doubtless played a part, for example. Wars were expensive. Then, of course, there was the lack of competition.

Theirs was a small community, the settlers on Dinares IV. Leesa wouldn't claim that she knew everyone her own age in the town, but she'd have bet she knew most of them. The atmosphere and environment were a fraction beyond the limit of natural human tolerance – the shortage of free oxygen being merely the most immediate problem – and towards the bottom end of the Xters'. Leesa remembered an elderly offter with a big smile and very white teeth – she didn't recall his name, just the contrast of those teeth against his tanned skin – addressing an assembly of the colonists once and going on about 'patient diplomacy' and 'the triumph of civilised co-operation', claiming that the lasting peace with the Xters was proof positive that mankind had finally outgrown the aggressive tendencies of its youth. Everyone had clapped enthusiastically. Her mum had been impressed – she suspected more because such an apparently eminent off-worlder had visited them at all than by anything the man had actually said – but Leesa wasn't buying any of it, even then. She still reckoned that the real reason humans and Xters hadn't ended up at each other's throats was because they weren't in direct competition; or not so's you'd notice.

Worlds compatible to human habitation would have required a great deal of adapting – gruelling, complex, time-consuming and expensive modification to the atmosphere and the whole ecosystem – before they became suitable for the Xters, and vice-versa. Tackling the issue from the opposite end – the genetic engineering and physical adaptation of populations to suit a given environment – would likewise have been a delicate, time-consuming, and prohibitively expensive procedure; a fact those on Dinaries IV knew all too well.

Why would either race bother, unless population pressures became too great to be relieved by the usual safety valve of expansion into new, suitable worlds? It was only on the borderline planets such as this one that the two species' interests came close to overlapping. This particular world, on the fringe of Xter space, was marginally more suitable for the aliens while others were closer to human requirements, or so Leesa had heard. If both races had been just a little more similar in physiology and metabolism, she'd be willing to bet that every world would have become a potential target and likely battleground.

What she couldn't understand was: if she, a mere kid, had worked this out, why couldn't any of the adults? It wasn't until she was much older that she realised it was because they didn't really want to.

Leesa came fully awake, the organic majority rapidly catching up and falling into synch with the part of her that never slept. The dreams were growing more vivid, the memories more distinct, which had to be a good thing, she supposed. She just wished they didn't dwell so much on her early life. It was the more recent past she craved to reclaim. Only then could she hope to figure out what had happened to her – exactly who had put the blocks in place and so clinically wiped away her identity. Just as importantly, she might then hope to discover *why*.

One thing the dreams were bringing home to her was what a pain she'd been as a kid; so confident of her own assertions, so convinced that she was an expert on subjects about which she knew next to nothing. She had no idea how Kegé and her other fathers had put up with her. She supposed an attitude like that hardly made her unique, but few people had the opportunity or the inclination to revisit their childhood self with the sort of clarity she was experiencing.

Such memories were welcome, of course. They were comforting, providing her with a centre, an emotional and psychological anchor that she'd been lacking and had so desperately needed. Until *something* began to seep back she'd been a disorientated mess, cast adrift and rootless, even entertaining the conviction at one point that she wasn't a real person at all but a construct of some kind; which was when the first echoes of childhood began to seep through into her dreams. Leesa had wept that night, allowing herself a moment of self-indulgence before she set about clawing her way back towards mental stability, clinging to those slender threads of returning memory. She'd killed someone, though, during that recovery. She couldn't remember the full details: who it was or why she'd done it – this had been during the very worst period – but she knew she had. Even that had served a purpose, providing her with the impetus to move to La Gossa and begin the search for her true identity.

No question that these returning memories had helped her reclaim her sanity, but she was now impatient to rediscover something more contemporary and, for the most part, those times continued to elude her. It was frustrating, her inability to exercise control. She had to, if she was ever going to learn who had stolen her life.

The hum of the ship's engines intruded on her thoughts. Their murmur suffused everything. A subtle sound, which probably went unnoticed by most, but not by her; especially when she was lying in her crewcot with the vibration whispering through every solid surface. In order to dream, Leesa needed to sleep, and she wasn't doing a great job of that just then.

She rolled onto her front and reached into the compartment provided for personal effects. Despite the space being insultingly small, her few possessions would have rattled around in there if shaken. She took out the slumberpoule, thumbed up the dosage and held the snub end against her throat, squeezing it to activate. If this didn't work, she could always try hitting her head against the bulkhead.

Tossing the ampoule back into the cubbyhole, she settled back and determined to think only dull thoughts.

Memories arrived as disjointed fragments, variously sized shards of a life that had been snapped apart like brittle chocolate.

She was livid and boiling over with frustration. This was soon after the Tull incident, which had subsequently overshadowed so much of her childhood, and she was railing against the unfairness of existence. "It's my life and I'll do whatever I fucking want to!" she had screamed.

"Leesa! Mind your language!"

"Sorry, Noon-father. It's my life and I'll do whatever I fucking *wish* to."

A petty victory, but the look of shock on Liat's face had been a joy to behold.

Frustratingly, the memory slipped away without leading to anything. Once upon a time all these chunks of mental flotsam had combined to form a seamless whole. She just needed to find the missing pieces and work out how.

Next she was having a conversation with her eve-father Kegé, always her favourite from among her paternal quad. She was talking to him about the future, or rather *at* him, and had doubtless sounded foolish, saying far more than she should in the naïve belief that the conversation wouldn't be repeated to her other parents. She trusted Kegé, confided in him, and he invariably offered sound advice, but of course he was going to discuss such things with the others, especially Liat, his lover. It was his duty to do so, but she hadn't seen it that way.

"Nobody can stop you from leaving, little one," he had said after hearing her out. "You're free to fly the coop whenever you choose, but don't underestimate what we have here. The family protects and nurtures. Out there…" and he waved vaguely towards the heavens, "life can be harsh, with jagged edges that tear at your spirit and wound your heart. Down here we smooth out those rough edges so that any bumps you feel are gentle ones."

She had giggled at the image painted by his words, picturing the corridors of their home bulging with pink fluffiness and smelling of marshmallow and candy, but the laughter had been short lived. "I know," she'd said; though of course she hadn't really, and would only come to realise the truth of his words when she eventually escaped Dinares IV. "But I can't stay here, Kegé, not forever." To be stifled, to be bored to death, to be driven mad by the inescapable almost-presence of the Xters, whom she imagined in her nightmares filling the world beyond the immediate confines of their small 'town'.

Even so, many years passed before she eventually left. There were any number of reasons, the warmth and love Kegé provided chief amongst them. She'd thought herself prepared for the universe at large, but the sheer spite and meanness of spirit that awaited her proved a shock beyond her imagining. Somehow, she survived. After a fashion.

The sense of being stifled wasn't the only reason she had been so desperate to leave Dinares IV. There was also Tull.

Tull had a different mother to her but they shared the same paternal quad. This didn't automatically make them bosom buddies or anything but they did tend to hang out together. He never had been her best friend – too big, too loud, too brash, too keen to impress – but he was part of 'the gang'; the four or five or seven or eight of them who gravitated together. The exact number and composition varied, though the central core remained the same: her, Meg, Cally, and Zané. Others drifted in and out of their orbit at the dictate of circumstance and whim. Tull was there more often than not, but she refused to acknowledge him as part of the 'core'. He was the one who always took things a step too far, as if to compensate for not quite being accepted to the same extent she was. If any of them were going to break something or fall off anything, you could bet it would be Tull.

No, he was never her *best* friend, but the day he died it felt as if he was.

They'd been playing in the Gully – the shallow defile that ran in a ragged line to the south of the plateau on which Liaise stood. Parents would have disapproved of their being there but generally turned a blind eye. After all, this was familiar ground only a stone's throw from home, and even the parents realised that kids couldn't be kept cooped up forever and needed to let off steam occasionally.

It should have been safe enough. They'd all had the modifications by then – the implants that enabled their bodies to draw sufficient oxygen from the planet's frugal air and filter out the toxins and pollens and microbes that human metabolism couldn't cope with. The programme of modification didn't stop there, either. The parents were constantly tinkering with genetics, tweaking what it meant to be 'human', so that in a generation or so the implants wouldn't be needed at all – the type of slow and costly adaptation that became untenable on a macro scale being made to work for a small, dedicated group.

Already their modifications were far less extensive than their parents'. Leesa couldn't help wonder whether it was her familiarity with the Dinares IV implants that made her susceptible to the idea of techorg in later life. Techorg was a completely different level of modification, of course, but once you've taken that first step, contemplating the next and the one after that becomes a little less daunting.

Leesa might not have been able to recall when or why she'd acquired the invasive augmentations that transformed her from organic to auganic, but she *could* understand and even sympathise with the underlying motivations that might have led her there.

"You great sassinbat! You'll get your kuccle caught on something if you're not careful." Leesa could hear Meg's voice as clear as day – shrill, excited and full of laughter. Meg always had been more impressed by Tull's antics than Leesa would have liked.

"It would serve him right if he did," Leesa had said; words that would come back to haunt her later, or rather the sentiment behind them would. "Not that he's got a kuccle big enough to catch on anything in any case."

"Oh yeah, really? And how would you know?" More laughter.

Tull was showing off by doing a series of split-jumps over a row of low, knobbly rock formations, which resembled the gnarled stubs of half-burned candles made irregular by the flow of congealed wax.

The final one looked a little different – something which afterwards everyone claimed to have noticed but no one had commented on at the time. It seemed newer, fresher. By the time Tull reached it he was overbalancing a little and losing momentum. If he'd had any sense he would have pulled out and given up on that last one, but no chance: this was Tull, after all.

The jump was an ungainly one, lacking any real height, and his crotch caught on the tip of that final mound. He was laughing and doubtless anticipated a painful blow, as did the onlookers, but instead the irregular top of the pile crumbled away. Not rock, then, at least not solidly so. Instead it was formed of dust and earth and stuck together with goodness knew what. A nest, as Leesa would subsequently learn, a hive, deliberately fashioned to mimic the prevailing rock formations as camouflage.

Unprepared for the comparative lack of resistance, Tull did overbalance then, sprawling onto his hands and knees amidst a cloud of reddish dust, still laughing.

The laughter choked off in an "Ow" of surprise and pain. At first Leesa assumed Tull's knees or hands were stinging following the fall, but there was something odd about the dust he'd kicked up. Most of it had settled, but some still seemed to be moving, and not as she would have expected. It took her a moment to realise what was happening. What she had taken to be dust was boiling out of the decapitated 'rock' and flowing with apparent purpose directly towards Tull. Already his lower legs were covered in a red, writhing, stain. Not a stain; this wasn't one single thing but a multitude, a living carpet of tiny creatures moving with common purpose.

Tull started to scream. Whether from fear or pain, Leesa wasn't sure. He leapt to his feet and jumped into the air but still the mites found him, clung to him, bit him.

Meg started towards him as if to help, but Zané grabbed her, thank goodness. Tull was cavorting around as if in a macabre, disjointed dance; an undignified, hot-footed jerk, body convulsing, arms shaking vigorously in an attempt to dislodge the mites. And the screams – definitely pain now – took on an air of desperation. They were unrelenting and the most chilling thing Leesa had ever heard.

"Help me!" he yelled amidst them. No one did; no one could. Even Meg had stopped trying to. Part of Leesa wanted to look away, felt that she *should* look away, but she couldn't.

The mites continued to boil from the nest, rising in a red tide to engulf Tull's body. Someone else had joined in with the screaming. It was herself, Leesa realised.

Tull's struggles lessened and then stopped all together. He sank to the ground and, with only occasional glimpses of his skin or clothing visible beneath the writhing mass of ruddiness, it seemed as if his very body were melting.

Zané still gripped Meg by the shoulders, though by then Leesa suspected more for his own comfort than to restrain her. Meg had begun to cry in fitful wails, her face contorted as tears spilled down her cheeks. Zané simply stared, ashen-faced.

As she glanced across, Leesa saw movement beyond her two friends and instantly froze. As if things couldn't get any worse. An Xter stood there, presumably drawn by the screams. Neither Zané nor Meg had noticed it as yet. Once they had, its presence did nothing to calm the situation. Meg's crying turned to hysteria. Her screams replaced Leesa's, who had lost the ability to give voice to anything. Meg scurried around the far side of Zané for protection. As if puny little Zané could protect anyone from a falling leaf let alone this adult Xter. The alien was all quick-legged movement. It didn't dart, but somehow Leesa had the impression that it was about to, all the time. It ignored them, scuttling towards where Tull lay cloaked in a blanket of crimson mites. One of the creature's forelimbs held a broad-nozzled object which looked to be a cross between a gun and the business end of a hose. The alien pointed it towards Tull and a jet of white liquid shot forth, directly at where the red mites were the thickest. The effect was immediate. The mites disappeared wherever the liquid touched – either dying or recoiling, Leesa couldn't be sure which. Within seconds, Tull was wholly visible again, the flat crimson limb of mites that had covered him withdrawing back into the mound that spawned it.

Tull lay twitching and spasming. Where exposed, his skin was puffed up and blotchy, his face almost unrecognisable. Without hesitation, the alien scooped up the boy's form in its forearms, lifting Tull as if he weighed nothing, and then started towards Liaise. Leesa did her best to keep up but the Xter's four-footed gait was far too swift for her. This was the first time she'd been so close to one of the aliens, and, despite the way it moved sending shivers up her spine, she was fascinated. The body wasn't segmented like an insect's but the way it carried itself almost horizontal to the ground and the arrangement of limbs suggested one. The face was dominated by multi-faceted eyes, far more sensitive than a human's, and it was impossible to tell what it was wearing – she couldn't distinguish between clothing and skin. Xters normally walked using all six limbs, though analysis showed that even then most of the body's weight was carried by the thicker middle and rear limbs, but they could swap seamlessly to a four-footed gait when carrying something; such as now. Leesa knew all this from lessons, but witnessing the real thing in motion was something else entirely.

Making light of its burden, the Xter negotiated inclines that the humans could never have attempted, and the alien was soon lost to sight despite their best efforts. By the time Leesa and her friends reached Liaise, the whole settlement was alerted and on the case.

She never saw Tull again. None of them did. Leesa learnt from Liat, her noon-father, that despite the alien's haste Tull had been dead on arrival, and there had been nothing anyone could do to revive him. She further learnt that the Xters called the mites that had killed him 'red dust', a name that needed no explanation. Red dust was evidently a hive creature, aggressively territorial. Individually, each bite was relatively harmless, the implants carried by all of Liaise's citizens would have nullified the toxin as a matter of course, but the mites attacked in the tens of thousands, biting all the while, and in Tull's case the protection afforded by his implants was simply overwhelmed.

Red dust had been eradicated from the area decades ago, but recent signs suggested that a colony had re-established itself. The Xter that helped them had been one of a number tasked with hunting down the infestation, but evidently it hadn't occurred to them to inform the human colony of a possible threat.

Liat did his best to put a positive spin on events, telling Leesa that Tull hadn't died in vain, that he'd discovered the red dust nest and so helped to remove a serious threat. He went on to say that Tull should be considered a hero, but she wasn't buying it. Tull was simply a buffoon who had tried to show off once too often. That was the problem with Liat: he always treated her as if she were still a kid and overestimated her gullibility. A mistake Kegé would never have made.

When she came awake this time, Leesa was aware of being not quite cold but on the cooler side of comfortable. Her bed sheets lay strewn on the floor and she guessed she must have been tossing and turning in her sleep. Again. This wasn't the first time she'd relived Tull's death – it wasn't a memory she enjoyed but presumably the incident had affected her deeply, or why else would she keep returning to it?

Leesa sat up, dangling her feet off the side of the bed, and rubbed her eyes. She didn't need a clock to tell her the time, her aug took care of that. She knew it was early hours of the morning, ship's time. This particular dream always disturbed her. Besides, her throat was dry and she reckoned sleep had been given enough chances for one night. She slipped out of bed and, after making a token effort at tidying things by picking up the sheets and dumping them back where they belonged, she padded to the galley on soft feet, conscious that no one else was likely to be awake yet. Shifts weren't split aboard the ship. The captain claimed there was no point in keeping a night watch when they were in transit; alarms would soon rouse anyone who needed rousing if anything interesting happened. She supposed he had a point, but she'd have kept one anyway.

Leesa didn't bother with lights. Her aug could pick up and amplify the slightest hint of illumination, enabling her to see in just about any conditions short of complete darkness, and when that occurred she could always fall back on the infrared.

For company, all she had was the ambient hum of the engines, but she was enjoying the near-quiet, the sense of solitude.

A light flickered on automatically as she entered the galley – the sensor working fine, the light itself less so, stabilising at the third or fourth attempt. The *Comet* had a lived-in charm which somehow failed to extend to the galley. This place, which should have been the heart of the vessel, struck her as cold and functional – all grey plastic and metal, no sense of any time or effort spent here. Perhaps none of them were cooks. She'd soon change that. Leesa smiled at the thought, pleased to have hit upon a possible way of ingratiating herself with the crew.

She made a beeline for the large cool cabinet squeezed in between the far wall and ceiling, pausing before its double doors. A dilemma: chilled water or juice?

A slight noise from behind sent her spinning around, automatically dropping into a fighter's crouch as she did so.

The banker, Drake, stood in the entrance. How the hell did he get there without her hearing him? Bastard must move as daintily as a cat.

He smiled and said in a subdued voice, as if to emphasise the intimacy of their situation with everyone else still in bed, "Couldn't you sleep either?"

"Something like that." He'd done all right in the fight against the disberos, but something about the man still made her uneasy, and she couldn't quite put her finger on why. Perhaps it was his air of supreme confidence, the sense that he was always in control of a given situation no matter what. "How's your head?" she asked because she felt she ought to.

"Not so bad, thanks. Suffering more from the effects of the doc's sedatives than from any lingering effects of the blow, I think."

She smiled and then turned her attention back to the juices. The cabinet door slid open at her touch and she took out an orange bulb. The slight weight of the chilled flexible carton felt somehow reassuring in her hand as she lifted it to squirt a stream of juice into her open mouth. Cold and tart, with just enough sweetness to dull the citrus sting. Part of her noted that she was tossing acid straight onto an empty stomach; Night-father would have been horrified.

"Just from curiosity," Drake said quietly from behind her, "are you ever able to sleep, I mean *really* sleep?"

She froze on the verge of squeezing a second mouthful of juice, and turned to stare at him. *He knew.* That carefully phrased question cut to the very heart of what it meant to be her, to be auganic. The words might have sounded innocent to any eavesdropper but they conveyed a wealth of meaning to her. *He knew.* She read the truth of it in his eyes.

Drake smiled. Not a gloating or malicious expression, in fact it was almost... *friendly*, but Leesa felt no inclination to respond in kind. Giving a slight nod in the face of her silence, he said, "Well, might as well try to grab a few more hours' shut-eye if I can. I'll see you in the morning." And with that, he turned and strolled away.

Leesa stared after him, her thoughts in turmoil. Without meaning to, she clenched her fist, squeezing the fruit bulb and sending a cold eruption of juice bubbling out to run down her fingers. She barely noticed.

Somehow, that enigmatic smooth-talking bastard knew what she was. So where the hell did that leave her now?

"She really doesn't recognise me." Drake was finally able to accept the truth of it. The look on Leesa's face when she turned around had been unguarded and far too raw to be faked.

No, Mudball agreed. *There were no physiological indications of recognition at all, not even a glimmer. Her reaction was one of unmitigated astonishment.*

"So, I'm a stranger to her." He still found the concept an oddly novel one, not to mention intriguing. What could have happened to her memory?

So it would seem. Do you intend to enlighten her?

"No, not immediately at any rate; stranger is good for now."

Even one she now knows is privy to her true nature? Perhaps tonight's little scene wasn't the wisest choice of action.

"I had to be certain…"

Quite. Even so, it's just as well that one of us doesn't need to sleep at night.

They'd arrived at Drake's crewcot. He lifted the flimsy cover and slipped inside. "Leesa would never harm me."

Of course not; if she knew who you are. I believe we've effectively established that at present she doesn't have a clue. So as things stand you're merely a stranger who has alerted her to the fact that you know her darkest secret. Congratulations, Drake, you've just managed to make an enemy of the most dangerous person on board. Sleep well.

Twelve

Mornings aboard ship always seemed much the same to Leesa: grey and sombre, with the first few breaths of the day tasting of metal, industry, and recycled air. She was the first up, which was threatening to become a habit. She headed straight to the galley and fixed herself a hot, glucose-rich and vitamin-laden fruit drink. The dreams hadn't helped her that night, dwelling on a part of her life she already knew well – events that had happened since she'd woken on Babylon, confused and stripped of her past. These immediate memories all started and ended on that world, whereas those she sought lay far beyond. She'd known instinctively that Babylon wasn't her home. From the outset she had been 'other' – someone who didn't belong, even on the farm where her life had restarted. A small community, miles from anywhere – all swaying crops and hedgerows, with trees on the skyline and wind and birds and insects… as different from life on the *Comet* as anything could be. She hadn't stayed there long; couldn't afford to linger anywhere until she knew who she was. Her name was all they'd been able to tell her – the farmer who ran the place and his stout and sombre no-nonsense wife. Leesa had considered the name and it seemed to fit, but beyond that no one could or would tell her anything. The couple were middle aged and they struck her as decent, honest folk; hard working but far from wealthy. They were quite open about the fact that they'd been paid to care for her until she woke. When she asked who by, they insisted, "You did."

Everyone seemed terrified of her, and once she began to discover her body's capabilities she couldn't really blame them. Nor could she take issue with the way the farmer and his wife had discharged their duties. She was still alive, after all.

They left her to her own devices for the most part, to wallow in her angst, her confusion and her despair. She had left soon after waking and getting her bearings. She needed answers that clearly weren't to be found on the farm, and so had set out for the 'big city': La Gossa, travelling cross country and by back roads, avoiding people where she could and stealing food when necessary.

This was a dark, dark period. She'd been frightened, confused, and angry; most of all angry. Somewhere between the farm and La Gossa she had killed someone, in circumstances that still weren't entirely clear. In retrospect, she hadn't been entirely sane during that period, but she remembered hands on her body, more than one man's – two, perhaps three of them. Vagrants, she thought; an attempted rape – a young woman travelling alone along a quiet road. There'd been a knife, and at one point her arms had been pinned behind her back, though not for long. She'd broken his neck, she thought; could remember her hands clasping his throat, fingers digging into the tendons while the other hand reached up to fasten onto the side of his head. She shied away from examining what happened after that, and tried to avoid thinking about the incident at all. Not with complete success.

Somehow, she made it to La Gossa. If anyone had helped her along the way she failed to remember them. All she knew was that this was where the space port waited. If she truly had come from off world, La Gossa was the place to start looking. She had a vague hope of finding some record of how she had arrived here, aboard which ship; anything that would give her some clue. No such records existed, it transpired.

La Gossa was intended to be the first step on her journey, but the city proved to be quite an education. Looking back, she'd been lucky to survive those early, fear-driven, memory-blinded days in the capital, relying on her wits and augmented abilities to get by. She had already learned by then to hide the latter.

In La Gossa she fell in with the wrong people and allowed herself to become distracted. She had immersed herself in the city's seedy underbelly, which enabled her to lose herself, to put off the need to uncover whatever dark secrets her past might conceal.

She shuddered at the memory of that so-recent past, of the lifestyle she'd spiralled into. Not that she regretted the drugs and the fun, or even the sex – well, not the majority of it – but that whole period had been nothing more than wilful evasion of her responsibilities to herself.

If asked, she would have denied ever being a prostitute, but there had been a *lot* of sex, and if money was on offer, well, how could a girl refuse?

Leesa looked up as somebody entered the galley, glad of the distraction. Anna, the pilot; not that the *Comet* needed much piloting as far as Leesa could see, but that was how the ebony-skinned woman had introduced herself. Dazzling smile. Leesa was reminded for an instant of another dark-skinned beauty back on Babylon, but suppressed the recollection.

"Hiya, sleep okay?" Anna asked.

"Fine," Leesa lied. She was still getting used to life on board ship and felt a little wary of how the established crew might react to her, but Anna's greeting seemed warm enough.

"Hear you've got the engines running better than ever," Anna said, as she poured herself a coffee, programmed some breakfast and then dropped into a seat opposite Leesa. "Thanks."

The 'thanks' likewise sounded genuine, without any obvious guile or sarcasm. "It's nothing," Leesa said, unused to compliments and feeling as awkward as she doubtless sounded.

Anna's breakfast duly arrived. Scrambled eggs, dotted with flakes of something that might have been crisped bacon. Anna ate it daintily though with little attention, while asking Leesa about life on Babylon, questions which she danced around with banalities and half-truths while trying not to sound evasive. She liked Anna.

Eggs finished and plate recycled, Anna stretched and lifted first one bare foot and then the other to rest on an empty seat, flexing her toes. *Nice legs*, Leesa couldn't help but notice.

"We're due to make planet fall early tomorrow," Anna said, which was news to Leesa. "Can't say I'm sorry. There's nothing much for me to do out here once the course has been laid in, except stare at the monitor screens. Which reminds me, I haven't said good morning to them yet." She dropped both feet to the floor and stood up.

The comment puzzled Leesa. "Wouldn't an alarm have sounded if there was any kind of a problem?"

"Oh, sure, but I always like to check in person first thing. Wouldn't want the controls to get lonely now, would we? I'll be back in a bit."

With that Anna bounced from the room with the sort of carefree vigour that Leesa could only envy. No sooner had she left than Drake entered. Leesa froze, but the banker merely smiled and said, "Morning."

Even when he had his back to her, the brown saucer-like eyes of his genpet stared at Leesa from the creature's perch near the man's shoulders. She did her best not to squirm, while reckoning that in one respect mornings on the *Comet* were much the same as mornings everywhere: they started out greyly and went downhill from there.

During the night things had become a little clearer for Drake, but not as much as he'd hoped; the possibilities hadn't yet narrowed down to a single irrefutable certainty. He did, however, now know where the Elder cache had to be located and why the captain was being so coy on the subject, but even that realisation opened the door to more questions than it answered. He needed more information, which meant it was time for a bit of deliberate agitation to stimulate a response.

He chose his moment carefully, waiting until there was nobody else in obvious earshot before stopping the captain and asking, with studied casualness, "Just from curiosity, when do you intend telling the crew that you're taking us all into Xter space?"

Pelquin stared at him for a startled second but recovered quickly, asking, "What makes you think I am?"

"A number of things. To start with, there's your continued refusal to disclose our destination."

Pelquin waved a dismissive hand. "A precaution. I wouldn't want anyone getting drunk in some portside tavern and letting slip something they shouldn't. Once we're on the final leg of the journey, I'll make everything clear enough."

Final leg? So we're stopping off somewhere else? "Then, of course, there's the equipment we took on at Babylon. Some of it is replacement for what was damaged in the attack, granted, but by no means all of it."

Pelquin tutted. "Mr Drake, I do believe you've been snooping again."

"I prefer to think of it as keeping an eye on things, Captain; which, after all, *is* what my employer pays me to do."

"All right then, so what exactly *did* we take on that has so aroused your suspicions?"

"A Ptarmigan; a dissonance field generator."

Pelquin feigned a puzzled frown. "A what?"

"A device that supposedly works by putting an object marginally out of synch with the rest of the universe, making anything within the field it generates very difficult to find. A cloaking system, if you will."

"Really? I wonder how that got to be there."

"With a great deal of planning, I would imagine. That's military grade tech, supposedly classified; a system that isn't legally available and could only be obtained in a haven of knock-off enterprise such as Babylon. Even then, it's not the sort of thing you can just walk up and buy on spec. It would have to be ordered well in advance."

"Would it indeed? My, my, Drake, you're a positive mine of information today."

Drake smiled without any hint of humour. "Massaging the estimates presented to First Solar to include enough slack for such an expensive piece of equipment must have taken some doing. I applaud your enterprise."

Pelquin scratched his chin, keeping up the charade. "So, let's assume for the moment that you're right. What if I *did* commission a cloaking system? Doesn't mean we're headed into Xter space. There are a lot of people itching to get their hands on what we know. You've seen first-hand how far they're willing to go. I don't want us being followed. I'm just being cautious, that's all."

Drake shook his head. "No you're not, and we both know it."

Pelquin shrugged. "Have it your own way."

"You're going to have to tell the crew at some point, Captain. I'd recommend doing so sooner rather than later."

"Thank you. Your advice is duly noted."

"You do realise that I can't condone an illegal incursion into Xter space, don't you?"

"Trust me, Mr Drake, you won't have to. Now, if you'll excuse me..." With that, Pelquin continued on his way.

That went well, Mudball commented. *Anyone else on board you'd care to antagonise? Not that there are too many left to choose from.*

Mudball...

Yes?

Shut up.

Will do.

Drake didn't really believe that the captain was stupid enough to blithely fly into Xter space without a stratagem; which meant that he was missing something, and it irritated the hell out of him that he couldn't figure out what.

Everybody bar Anna and the captain spent the morning in the hold, unpacking the equipment that had come aboard at New Sparta and

Babylon.

Nate and Bren were doing most of the heavy work, of which there was plenty despite the presence of a compact but solid powerlifter with its claw-like crane functions, easy-lift netting, and forklift appendages. The doc was largely peripheral, as he tended to be in most things. He was there and he contributed, helping when instructed, but he was rarely proactive.

"Feel free to muck in anytime you want to," Bren said at one point, looking across to where Drake stood and watched.

"No chance," Nate said immediately. "You don't really think he's going to risk getting his precious suit dirty, do you?"

Drake refused to be baited and declined the invite to help, though not without a twinge of guilt. That changed when a crate was knocked by the powerlifter and began to topple towards Leesa, who was squatting down examining an already unpacked item and oblivious to the danger. Drake was there immediately to half hold and half steady the tottering carton.

"Thanks," Bren said, stepping in to join him. Between them they managed to manoeuvre the heavy container back into position. Leesa glanced up, stared at him blankly, and then went back to work without saying a word. Once he was there, with his hands dirtied, it seemed churlish to step back and simply observe again, so Drake took off his jacket, setting it neatly aside and ensuring Mudball was sitting comfortably on top of its folds.

Aren't you afraid I'll go running off and causing trouble?

Behave.

If you insist.

Drake then rolled up his sleeves and joined in the unloading, contributing at least as much as the doc did. In fact, that worthy seemed to take the banker's arrival as an excuse to do even less, smiling at Drake as if he were an ally come specifically to relieve him of this burdensome chore.

"My, my," Nate commented on seeing Drake beside him. "Wonders will never cease."

Drake reckoned that if this was the worst Almont was going to throw at him then he was doing okay.

The biggest crate of all sat firmly in the centre of the floor with the other crates surrounding it. Nate levered the front open and it moved as one piece, hitting the floor like a felled tree, to reveal what waited within. Bren let out a whistle of appreciation.

A haulage buggy. Drake knew the type – a broad, flat-backed vehicle designed to handle rough terrain. Two sets of big wheels with fat tyres that were almost impossible to puncture and could be automatically pumped up with extra pressure when the buggy was loaded. Predictive suspension ensured a smooth ride for fragile cargo— dedicated sensors monitored the ground in minute detail and enabled each wheel to react to conditions a fraction before they were reached rather than a fraction after – while a powerful engine meant that the buggy could really shift when empty and haul an impressive amount when loaded. All in all, a handy vehicle to be taking on a cache hunt.

"I'll bet these beauties don't come cheap," Bren said, stepping inside to run an appreciative hand over the fender.

"They don't," Nate confirmed, "which is one of the reasons we have to put up with our grey-suited friend's company."

Even Leesa put aside what she'd been doing to come and stare as Bren and Nate pulled away protective packaging material to reveal the buggy more clearly. It was a bizarre contraption, little more than a rimmed platform with an open two-seater driver's cabin at the front and multi-spindled wheel braces and axles projecting from the four corners, but that didn't seem to bother Bren.

"Bags I get to drive it," she said,

"Not likely," Nate replied. "That'll be Anna's job, while you get your hands dirty with the rest of us fetching and loading things onto it."

Although there were still a few crates to unpack, including the one housing the dissonance field generator – a fact that Drake suspected was far from coincidental – the unveiling of the buggy signalled an end to the morning's work. Nate disappeared to report to Pelquin, Leesa went off frowning to run some tests on the pumping system of one of the big drills, which evidently she wasn't happy with, and the doc used the departure of those two as an excuse to make his own. Bren lingered, sitting down on the steps leading to the rest of the ship and staring wistfully at the buggy, which still sat in its crate, facing outward like a dog in a kennel.

"Are you all right?" Drake asked her.

"Yeah, fine. I was just thinking."

"About Monkey?"

She nodded. "About Monkey." She studied him, quizzically. "How do you do that? How do you know what people are thinking without being told?"

"I notice things; that's all. It's just a matter of being observant." She grunted and seemed about to say more, but he pre-empted her, changing the subject back to where they'd started. "So, what brought Monkey to mind?"

"The buggy. If he was here he would have had that thing out of the crate the minute Nate's back was turned. By now he'd be racing around the hold, seeing what it could do. Probably lose control, probably skid into a crate, probably damage something, and *definitely* get a bawling out from the skipper."

Drake chuckled. For a moment, their smiles matched, then hers faded into something more wistful.

"You really miss him, don't you?" he said.

"Is this you doing that 'observing' thing of yours?" Her smile returned. "Yeah, I miss him. More than I ever thought I would, but don't you dare go telling the skinny runt I said so when we pick him up on the way back."

"My lips are sealed," he promised. They sat in silence for a few seconds. His pitching in with the unpacking had earned him a little tacit approval, perhaps even respect. Enough that he dared push it a little. "Bren, mind if I ask you something?"

"What?" she asked sharply.

"This big falling out between Nate and the captain, what exactly caused it?"

Bren gave him a hard stare, and he sensed she was tempted to tell him to mind his own business, so he got in first, saying quickly, "Sorry; I don't mean to pry, but the more I know about what's gone on, the better I can understand people and the easier it is for me to do my job without treading on anyone's toes."

"I don't see how raking up the past is going to help."

"Because whatever happened then is relevant to what's going on between them *now*," he said.

"Okay," and she glanced around, as if to confirm they were the only ones in the hold. "Just don't go asking either of those two about it, not unless you fancy getting your ear chewed out."

"I *haven't*, and I don't want to have to. That's why I was hoping you might fill me in."

Bren was quiet for a second. Eventually she said one word: "Julia."

"Who?"

"Julia; real easy on the eye and almost as easy to get on with – she was a good listener; someone you felt you could trust, you know? She used to be one of us, part of the crew I mean, before Anna joined."

"You liked her, then?"

Bren shrugged. "Some. Quite a bit at first, to be honest, until she started to get above herself and stirred things up."

"The men…?"

"Yeah, the men." Bren gave a sour smile. "She hadn't been with us all that long herself, but, like I say, she was friendly and she was pretty. Pel took a real shine to her."

Bren must have loved that, Drake reflected. No wonder she quickly cooled towards this Julia.

"There was a connection between them," Bren continued. "Nothing heavy, just a sort of closeness that was obvious to all of us. I don't think the captain thought too seriously about it really, not until Nate started to take an interest in her. Julia enjoyed that – the attention she was getting – and suddenly Pel began to get all competitive and jealous, like Nate was trespassing on his territory. Julia *really* liked that. Started to play one off against the other. Neither of the dunderheads could see it, but I could."

Bren paused, shaking her head. Drake waited for her to resume. "Never thought I'd see the two of them fall out – Nate and the captain, I mean – but I guess jealousy can do that. Things on board got uncomfortable, and one day it all boiled over. There was a scene – a lot of things were said that shouldn't have been, a punch was thrown… and Nate stormed off; left the ship saying that he wasn't coming back.

"What happened to Julia, did she leave as well?"

Bren shook her head. "Not at first. She stayed on the crew, but I reckon deep down she regretted not going with Nate, and she never forgave Pel. Things weren't the same between them after that and life on board sucked. The captain can be a real surly bastard at times. Something had to give or we'd all have quit. I think Julia recognised that, and at least she had the decency to do something about it. A couple of months after Nate left, so did she, saying that she couldn't stick Pel and his moods any longer. So she just upped and joined another ship. Good riddance, if you ask me."

"And that was when Anna came aboard?"

"Yeah, thank goodness. She might be a bit kookie but she ain't trouble, and kookie gets my vote every time."

So the argument had been about a woman, which shouldn't have surprised him; that argument had led to Almont disappearing for a year, and in that time he stumbled upon a significant Elder cache. Something about the scenario still didn't feel right to Drake, and he couldn't help but wonder what else Almont had been up to in that year, who else he'd met and how much resentment he still harboured towards Pelquin.

Interesting questions, all of them.

"And don't you think of trying to ask me anything else about this," Bren said, "because I've said all I'm going to on the subject. Clear?"

"Perfectly," he assured her. "And thanks. I appreciate you filling me in."

She nodded and climbed to her feet. "I'm going to get something from the galley. See you later."

She seems to be in a good mood today, Mudball observed. *Do you think she had sex last night?*

Sex isn't the only thing that puts humans in a good mood, Drake assured him.

Really? You do surprise me.

THIRTEEN

Leesa held her position effortlessly, confident that all was as it should be and that they couldn't possibly fail. They moved like ghosts across a blasted landscape, mottled suits shifting colour and pattern constantly as they adapted to background and surroundings, dampener fields minimising heat signatures to fool infrared sensors, decoy beacons would be causing 'ghost' units to flicker to life and disappear at strategic points, further confusing the enemy. Their radios were silent. They didn't need anything as archaic as radios, not these soldiers. Her brothers' and sisters' voices sang out clearly, joyously, in her head.

This was Tyson Five. Federal forces had the temerity to come *here*, to beard the Auganics Corporation in its own lair, and the authorities were about to be taught a lesson they would never forget. A bold move, a magnificent move, to strike at the opposition's very heart; she applauded them for that, but it was also a desperate move; a do or die gambit which would likely decide the outcome of the war; for war it was, there could be no escaping the fact. This might have started out as a philosophical disagreement but it had escalated far beyond that, and the coalition oligarchs knew themselves truly challenged. If government forces failed here, their strength would be broken, their cause severely damaged if not lost. Of course, if they won…

But they wouldn't. They *couldn't*. The planners and schemers who sat spider-like at the corrupt heart of the bureaucratic behemoth had no idea what it was they faced on Tyson Five, or the mayhem that was about to be visited on their military, the backbone of their authority. This day the coalition would be humbled, swept aside by the full flexing of auganic might, which, for once, could be brought to bear at the same place at the same time. Human destiny was about to be rewritten.

There was no consideration of failure in any of their minds as the technologically augmented host swept into battle. The day could end only one way: in resounding victory.

So they sang their silent song, her brothers and sisters, as battle-lust coursed through their veins and excitement coloured their every thought with dreams of imminent triumph.

What the auganics shared wasn't complete gestalt; it wasn't the total sublimation of self to create a shared consciousness, a combined whole, but it was the closest thing to that state that humanity had yet achieved. Much of what made them individuals was moulded and channelled to produce unified thought, response and purpose. Leesa had come to yearn for such moments and now felt complete only when acting in concert. Yet she was still herself; immersed but not wholly subsumed.

This tight-knit sharing of thought and emotion enabled an auganic unit to react far more cohesively and effectively than even the most elite of organic troops. This cohesion combined with their other attributes made them the most formidable soldiers mankind had ever committed to the field. And they knew it. And they were reviled for it.

The authorities outlawed techorg, declaring it an abomination, and two philosophies clashed. The corporations accused the authorities of being anti-technology and anti-progress; recidivist suppressors of human evolution. The government painted the techorg companies as inhuman monsters, dispassionate meddlers in what it meant to be human. The government controlled the media and the propaganda war was lost before it had begun, but the coalition had underestimated its foe. When the authorities tried to treat this as a mere policing action their collective noses were bloodied in a dozen disastrous operations across human space. So began what amounted to civil war, though those in power preferred to use less inflammatory terms.

And now they chose to go for overkill. They had committed their full strength, to stamp out the unrest once and for all, wary lest public sympathy swung behind the auganics and their sponsors, who were being cast in the role of underdogs – ever a seductive lure for the public's conscience. Coalition forces attacked with overwhelming force, their intent obvious: to win by sheer weight of numbers if all else failed.

Leesa and her fellow auganics stood ready to welcome them.

Even so, even at the very height of the combined euphoria that swept through auganic ranks, a part of Leesa recognised that this wasn't *her* euphoria, her fanaticism; rather it arose from the pooling of all of them and represented the majority emotion of the many, not the one. An emotion magnified to the nth degree by the fact that it *was* shared. She wasn't swept away by the moment, however, not entirely. Afterwards, she would wonder whether it was this small corner of reserve that saved her.

At first everything went to plan. She remembered a heavy fire fight in which the enemy outnumbered them but didn't stand a chance. Distantly she sensed similar upwellings of triumph from other auganic units around her and in the jet fighters, singleships, and heavy ships stacked in layers above her. Not her cadre, not part of her bond group, but still her brothers and sisters. The heavens were lit by a stuttering dance of pyrotechnics, lightnings never destined to reach the ground as squadrons of nimble fighters duelled for supremacy of the air and, higher still, dreadnought pounded dreadnought with lethal energies beyond the planet's atmosphere. The whole world growled with rolling thunder and the frequent report of lethal munitions.

It was night in the part of the world she fought in; a fact that made little difference to either side but less to Leesa and hers. It meant that the skyborne conflict was all the more spectacular. She and her unit were now enjoying a rare respite after coming through several vicious skirmishes in which they had suffered light losses – a brother or sister dropping away from their communion, to be mourned properly later when time allowed. Around them stood the ruin of a recently abandoned village; ahead the village's central square. The setting made all of them uneasy, though they couldn't pinpoint why.

Without hesitation they sent in decoy drones – basic humanoid robots in battle suits, containing enough viable organic elements to register on enemy sensors, designed to imitate poorly shielded soldiers. The ploy worked. As the drones crossed the square they were caught in the crossfire of lethal energies from concealed positions and obliterated in a few spectacular seconds.

The realisation that the enemy was able to hide so effectively from their auganic senses came as a shock but they didn't hesitate, she and her fellows, falling upon the would-be ambushers without mercy. They wiped them out, suffering no further losses themselves. Only then did they pause to consider the implications. What other surprises might the coalition have in store for them? For the first time, a seed of doubt entered the collective consciousness.

The next skirmish went much the same as previous ones had, but were her brothers and sisters a little less wholehearted in their celebration? Was their subsequent advance a fraction less enthusiastic? It seemed so to Leesa. Prescience, perhaps; an inexplicable foreboding of what was to come.

And come it did.

Noise. Leesa had grown used to the external sounds of combat, from far and near, and to the internal sounds of her brethren – as comforting and constant as the love of her paternal quad – but this was something else. It started somewhere in the background, a shrill discordant whine, distant but at the same time internal. Before she had time to analyse its presence the whine had grown to become a roar, a piercing, agonising gale of almost-sound that clawed at her thoughts and shredded the fabric of auganic communion.

This was no gentle dissolution such as might occur when the unit stepped down at the end of the day and her kin became no more than a comforting background presence, but rather a violent, agonising rending; trauma as opposed to relaxation. One instant they were whole, the next torn apart. She heard her brothers' and sisters' screams and caught a hint of their suffering as they were carried away from her, before she was consumed. Fire raced through her head like molten lava, washing into every corner of thought and obliterating reason,

She was on the ground, kicking, writhing, screaming, helmet discarded as she tore at her head, her hair, trying to make the agony stop. Consciousness deserted her with the fading realisation: *so this is death.*

She came to in daylight, amazed to be waking at all. Sunlight bathed her face and the constant drone of flies welcomed the return to awareness. Something large flapped upward on black wings as she moved – a carrion bird. It didn't fly far, settling nearby atop a stunted tree, neck bobbing as it inspected her suspiciously.

Aside from the flies, the world seemed draped in an unnerving blanket of silence.

Leesa allowed herself to see then what she'd been trying so hard not to. She was surrounded by the dead; her slaughtered brothers and sisters, mown down by an awful and wholly unsuspected weapon of the coalition. Many of the bodies were contorted at odd angles, testament to their perishing in the throes of intense suffering. Some appeared to have clawed at their own faces, cutting open fleshy cheeks. The caked white of dried spittle and the yellower stain of vomit crusted open mouths. She took one hard long look and then averted her eyes. She strode from the scene with her gaze fixed firmly on the horizon. A cloud of black flies and blacker birds surrounded her, disturbed by her passage; her own dark bow wave as she traversed the sea of the dead.

Leesa came awake suddenly, eyes wide, breathing hard, momentarily overwhelmed by the pure emotion of her dreams. It took her several ragged breaths to regain full composure. She sat up slowly, rubbing at her forehead. She'd revisited snippets of the battle before and experienced tantalising snatches of that wonderful communion of auganic minds, but never in such a coherent sequence, and this was the first time she'd relived the battle's finale. A shudder coursed through her body. Gods, she hoped her dreams didn't ever take her back there again. Yet she suspected they would, given that her subconscious mind appeared to have a penchant for revisiting significant moments of her past; and this counted as one, no question about that.

She'd had no idea... Could *this* be the reason her memory was wiped – because she was an auganic who had somehow survived the genocide of her kind? No, that made no sense. Why not kill her as well, or imprison her, or pull her mind apart under the guise of research? Why would the authorities wipe her mind and cast her adrift on some random planet with no idea of who she was?

Leesa reached for the compartment where her drugs were stored but hesitated, reckoning that she'd had enough dreams for one night. She wasn't sure she could handle any more revelations, not right now. Nor did she fancy another encounter with the banker, so she didn't get up. *How* had he worked out what she was? What had given her away? Instead of moving she simply settled back, stared at the bland off-white ceiling of her cubbyhole, and considered this newly reclaimed segment of her past, examining it tentatively as she might an unexploded bomb.

One aspect of the harrowing experience stayed with her, resonating with her current self: the sense of being adrift and alone in the universe that had overwhelmed her as she trudged from the killing field. That was a feeling she knew all too well.

Balanced against that was the intoxicating joy of union. That melding of minds, that sharing of so much with her auganic brethren, had been seductive and so very, very special, but at the same time so utterly terrifying. A part of her mourned the fact that she would never experience that again while part of her felt relieved.

FOURTEEN

Pelquin had summoned him to the bridge, which was a first. Drake wondered whether the venue was meant to emphasise who was boss or if the tiny cockpit was merely the closest thing to privacy available on the ship. Probably a bit of both. There was no sign of Anna, who tended to hang around here much of the time, so they had the place to themselves.

The *Comet*'s captain sat comfortably – Drake was almost tempted to think 'lounged' – in the pilot's chair, while the banker was left to stand.

"Ah, Drake, thank you for coming."

The man really could be a pompous ass at times. "I'm always at your disposal, Captain."

Pelquin smiled but let that pass without comment, saying instead, "I was wondering, are all those suits of yours the same, or do you keep one for special occasions?"

Momentarily nonplussed, Drake temporised with the obvious, "Why do you ask?"

Pelquin shrugged. "No reason. It's just that there's this function I have to attend once we make planet fall; a formal affair, you know the sort – circulating waiters and fussy canapés, chilled wine and stilted conversation. The invite includes a 'plus one' and I thought you might like to be that one."

Drake stared at the other man, knowing that no such invitation could have reached Pelquin while they were in transit, so this must have been another pre-planned, not to mention carefully timed, commitment. None of which explained why the captain should extend the invite to him. "I take it you're not asking me out on a date, so presumably there's a specific reason you want me to go along rather than anyone else aboard – one of the women, say."

Pelquin smiled. "There might be. For a start you're just about the only person on board I can trust not to show me up in polite company, then there's the small matter of the man I'm going to meet; someone I've done business with in the past. He's going to ensure, you see, that

143

should we happen to stray into Xter space through some unfortunate miscalculation – as you seem convinced we're about to – it'll be all nice and legal... Well, mostly legal at any rate."

"Is that so?" *Legal?* Now that would be a trick worth seeing. "In that case I'd be delighted to accept. I wouldn't miss this for the world. And yes, I do indeed have a suit for formal occasions."

"Excellent, excellent. That's settled then. We'll be dropping to sublight shortly and will make planet fall late this morning, ship's time; so dust down your glad rags, for tonight we party!"

"And precisely which planet will we be falling into, dare I ask?"

"A place called Brannan's World. It's a bit colonial but pleasant enough."

Brannan's? Drake made sure his expression never faltered. He was becoming adept at hiding dismay. First Leesa and now Brannan's World; it was as if somebody had deliberately plotted a course through the dark and dusty recesses of his past.

Don't go getting all paranoid on me, Mudball said. *This is the area you used to operate in, isn't it?*

You know it is.

Well what do you expect, then?

He supposed the alien had a point. It was almost inevitable when coming to this sector of space that a ghost or two would be waiting in the wings, but that didn't make their appearance any more palatable.

Dropping out of RzSpace was the reverse of entering it but less so, in that the sensations were gentler; the folding-in upon itself that the mind experienced – that return from a higher level of awareness which the brain didn't even realise had been there until it was gone – came with a good dollop of stability, of sensing that all was right with the universe once more. Part and parcel of that experience was a sharpening of mental focus and a return of emotional intensity. Scientists claimed that all these sensations – the feeling of rapid mental expansion when crossing into RzSpace and the impression of returning limits when departing it – were entirely psychosomatic, that people felt these things only because they expected to. Pelquin knew otherwise. Let the boffins dismiss whatever they wanted too. Spacers knew from experience the difference between what was and what was supposed to be.

"We'll reach Brannan's World's upper atmosphere in a little under an hour," Anna informed him.

"Good work." He sensed there was something she wanted to add. "And...?"

"Well, I was just checking the register of ships in port at the moment. "I know this is probably nothing, but one of them – a flash exec number called *The Star Dancer* – is listed as belonging to the Jossyren Mining Corporation."

Pelquin digested that. "Thanks for letting me know but it's a coincidence; has to be. Jossyren must own a whole fleet of ships and we're bound to come across one or more of them from time to time. There's no way whoever was messing with us back at New Sparta could have got here ahead of us." *Not unless they knew where we were going*, but that was impossible. The only person privy to his plans was Nate, and Nate was as tight-lipped as a vacuum seal. Unless he had good reason... No, Pelquin had to believe in Nate, or they were all in trouble.

It wouldn't hurt to do a little snooping, mind, to see if they could learn what the Jossyren ship was doing here. "Anna, let's keep this to ourselves for the time being, shall we? No point in worrying the others over nothing."

"Okay. You're the captain."

He let Anna take them in to Victoria – Brannan's main port. She was a good pilot. Better than Julia. Better than him, truth be told, though he'd never admit as much to her face. Initially everything was automated in any case, their course dictated by local traffic control, the ship responding to data packages squirted to them from the ground.

"*Pelquin's Comet*, you're cleared for final approach," a calm voice announced right on cue. "We're set to guide you down."

"Thank you, Victoria Control," Anna responded. "Your signal received and locked in."

That didn't mean that the pilot was redundant, though; far from it. No system was foolproof, and any pilot worth their salt would sit glued to their station during landing; monitoring, checking and rechecking trajectory, entry speed, hull temperature, along with every scrap of data that groundside fed them.

Take-off and landing were where pilots earned their keep.

During the approach, Brannan's World looked very different to Babylon. More greenery for one thing; and even from here the city looked less crowded. Victoria always gave Pelquin the impression that buildings here were granted the room to breathe.

He liked Brannan's, always had. It was the sort of place where a man might consider settling down one day, if he were that way inclined; which, of course, he wasn't.

Once above the landing field Anna resumed control and brought the *Comet* in for a cotton wool landing. Bay 133: the designated slab of concrete that was theirs for the duration of their stay. Which wouldn't be long if everything went to plan. While docking fees at Victoria were by no means the steepest Pelquin had encountered, they accumulated by the hour, and First Solar's money was running pretty thin – the damage inflicted by the gun fight had eaten up most of the reserves.

There was one other thing he needed to sort out: his old friend Mokhtar. Mokhy had his sticky fingers in everything, and he was bound to catch wind that *Pelquin's Comet* was back in port. In fact, he'd probably been told about their arrival before they'd even touched down. Mokhy termed himself a 'facilitator'; the kingpin among local fixers, he knew everyone and everything worth knowing, and the last time the *Comet* was here, Pelquin had left something with him for safe keeping, something he hadn't dared carry with him on the ship given the amount of heat focused on them at the time, and which he swore faithfully he'd collect at the first opportunity. He'd called in a big favour that day, and Mokhy would expect him to collect as soon as.

Mokhy had always had a soft spot for Bren. She was the ideal person for the job, particularly given the nature of the item in question. He might even suggest she pick up a bottle of Tarkhillan brandy on the way. If there was one thing Mokhtar was even more partial to than Bren, it was Tarkhillan brandy.

Leesa liked the feel of Victoria immediately. Whereas La Gossa had been all bustle and crowds and heat, Victoria was more laid back. If anything the port was even busier than La Gossa's, but it was more efficiently organised, lacking the haphazard attitude that had typified Babylon and its culture. Conversely, this greater degree of organisation led to a calmer ambience, possibly because people were less worried about what might happen next.

The climate here was described as 'temperate', which Leesa took to mean cool, since it was certainly a lot milder than La Gossa had been.

At the same time the air wasn't as oppressive, and it tasted fresher, cleaner. She imagined that rainfall here would be light and refreshing, a definite boon, whereas in La Gossa rain tended to fall with such intensity that it resembled an assault.

Nate slipped off the ship almost as soon as they touched down, and Bren looked set to follow soon after.

"Where are you off to?" Leesa asked, reckoning that, as the new girl, she could get away with a degree of directness.

"Oh, nowhere special," Bren said.

"Great! Is it okay if I tag along to nowhere special with you?"

"Well, I'm not sure..."

"Oh please, Bren. I don't want to stay here on the ship kicking my heels and I've never been off world before, so I'd rather not go out there on my own." A cocktail of truths, half-truths and fabrication – always the best policy when spinning a line. Her real motive was to put some distance between her and the banker for a while, and she didn't trust herself to wander around a new city on her own. Judging by recent experience, she had too great a knack of finding the urban underbelly.

"The thing is," Bren said, "I've got an errand to run..."

"That's fine. I won't get in the way. I'll just stay in the background and you won't even know I'm there. Promise."

Bren didn't look convinced this was a good idea, but she said, "All right, you can come, but you do what I say *when* I say. Clear?"

"Perfectly. You're the boss; and thanks, Bren."

Victoria differed from the city she was used to in more than just climate. On leaving the spaceport they walked down a broad multi-laned street called something-or-other Boulevard, which had a line of tall healthy-looking trees growing from a long island that ran down its centre. There were cars, yes, and taxis and other vehicles, but they all moved at a sedate, patient pace, without the frantic darting and changing of lanes and constant traffic snarl-ups she was used to in La Gossa. This all seemed so much more *civilised* somehow.

The shops here, too, were different. She noted immediately an absence of outlets selling gizmos and gadgets, while the only jewellery store she saw had a sparse, tasteful window showcasing a few expensive looking items as opposed to a plethora of dazzling gold spilling out in every direction. Clothes shops predominated, their windows full of sweeping, elegant dresses and immaculately tailored suits. While colourful, they lacked the dazzling vibrancy she was used to.

She paused before the jeweller's, which, with its dark marble shop front, struck her as far too daunting to venture into. Not that this stopped her from staring in at the gorgeous pieces on display. Taking centre stage was a wonderfully crafted ring featuring an imposing solitaire diamond. As she watched, the ring disappeared, and she realised this was a holographic projection showcasing choice items that were doubtless held safely in the shop's interior. The projection had been faultless, and she would never have known she wasn't seeing the ring itself. A teardrop pendant, the like of which she'd never seen before, replaced the ring. The stone rippled with red, orange and yellow, like a drop of condensed flame.

Even Bren was impressed enough to comment, "Yeah, I know; a firestone. Gorgeous isn't it? After we've come back from this job you'll be able to afford everything in that window and more."

Leesa knew by this stage that they were on a cache hunt. The way Pelquin had sold it to her, she was to get half a share – half of whatever the regular crew got. In effect, one share was to be split between her and Monkey Palmer, the injured mechanic she'd replaced. That way, none of the others lost out through her coming aboard, she could still walk away a wealthy woman, and Monkey was compensated despite missing the trip. As compromises went, it worked for her.

"This is the second fanciest shopping street in Victoria," Bren was explaining.

"The fanciest would be...?"

"The one we're going to be turning into shortly: the Row," and Bren gestured ahead to where the street they were on ended in a T-junction. "Home to the swankiest, most exclusive shops – sorry, boutiques – this side of New Sparta."

"And the shop we're going to, that's on this Row, is it?"

"Good Lord, no," and Bren laughed. "Mokhy's got his faults but he's not *that* much up himself. They wouldn't let him set foot in most of the shops on the Row, let alone own one of them. Mokhtar's place is sort of off-off-Row. See, the Row contains the crème-de-la-crème; off-Row you'll find places which can claim to be almost as good as the Row but not quite; off-off-Row are the ones that would like to be. Though, in Mokhy's case, he doesn't try too hard. You'll see what I mean when we get there."

They turned left into the street that Bren had called the Row. Despite lacking the trees down its centre, the Row seemed similar to the boulevard they'd just left but even more so. The facades of the shops were magnificent, the window displays works of art in their own right, yet Leesa would have hesitated to enter any of them. She was used to shops' windows that were designed to entice you in, whereas these all seemed to do the opposite; they were more intimidating than inviting – presumably because she wasn't their target audience – and she wasn't sure whether to feel fascinated or appalled.

The store fronts slipped past – a sparsely chic boutique decked out entirely in white, the shop's name spelled out in what might have been diamonds, a designer outlet, another boutique, and then an art gallery. This one she granted a little more attention. Although the artist's name meant nothing to her, there was something about the large, bold abstract piece claiming centre stage – a cascading collision of brightly coloured geometric shapes which seemed to leap out of the frame – that appealed to her. Reluctantly, she moved on. Bren had kept walking, forcing her to catch up.

They were only on the Row for a mercifully brief time. Shortly after the gallery they took a turning to the right, giving her senses a much needed break; though at first the stores here seemed indistinguishable from those on the broader street they'd just left. That soon changed, and Leesa realised it only applied to those at the very top, the ones clinging to the Row's grandeur. Beyond these first few the shops became more approachable and less likely to inspire sensory overload. Leesa found them all the more appealing as a result.

Bren stopped at one of them and darted inside, saying, "Wait here a sec." The shop was a vintners of considerable distinction to judge by the window display and the prices. Bren soon emerged with a bottle wrapped in paper.

Another minute's walk and Bren took them right again, this time into a narrow street which lacked any of the pizzazz of the Row. Shops had been largely replaced by cafés and eateries, and the stores they now encountered reminded Leesa of those back in La Gossa. The window displays were busy and crowded, presumably adhering to the principles of scattershot marketing: throw enough temptation at the customers and something's bound to stick; while pulsing lights thrust the latest bargain discount at browsers' consciousness like a blade; a pretty blunted and ineffectual one perhaps, but the intent was there.

Leesa assumed their destination was one of these stores, but instead it was tucked just around another corner. She had a fleeting opportunity to take in the crowded window before Bren led the way inside. The window displayed a bizarrely varied selection of goods, from items of clothing – the rugged, outdoors variety – to ornaments and knick-knacks, stopping off at hunting knives and camping equipment – self-erecting tents, water purifiers, instant-light fires etc – and kitchen gadgets. The confused impression only intensified once she stepped through the door. The shop was far bigger than it appeared on the outside and she found herself in a bursting-at-the-seams wonderland of wildly varying goods, which inhabited front-to-back aisles to her left, stood in haphazardly piled stacks at the end of each aisle, and even climbed up the wall to her right.

Immediately in front of her stood a counter, behind which leaned a tall, slender man. He was handing across a wrapped parcel to an affluent-looking couple who smiled and thanked him, clearly delighted at their purchase. His return smile as he said, "Do call again," was warm and friendly, though Leesa wasn't so sure about the gold tooth which glinted in the process.

She stood aside to let the couple pass. As soon as they had exited, the man came out from behind the counter, his arms spread wide. "Brenda, my dear friend! What a lovely surprise. I had no idea the *Comet* was back in port." He hugged the object of his greeting, who didn't look entirely comfortable with the embrace but endured it stoically.

"Hi, Mokhy, it's good to see you, too," she said. "We just landed."

"And who is this delightful creature?" he asked, releasing Bren.

"This is Leesa. She's standing in for Monkey on this trip. Leesa, meet Mokhy."

"Enchanted," and the tall man stooped into a half bow, taking and kissing Leesa's right hand. The gesture, which would have irritated the hell out of her from most people, struck her as charming coming from him. He had kind eyes, she decided, and found herself smiling.

"So, it's just you two? Pelquin too busy to call on an old friend, is he?"

"He sends his apologies – we're not stopping long – but he did ask me to give you this." Bren held out the bottle.

He took it eagerly, pulling aside the paper wrapping. His smile broadened. "Ah, Tarkhillan brandy! What a gentleman Captain Pelquin is. Come, come, you must sample this with me."

"That's very kind, but I'm not sure…"

"I'll not take no for an answer, Bren! Tarkhillan should never be drunk alone. It requires the appreciation of friends! Now, come on through, please." He beckoned them behind the counter and into a cluttered back room. Bren hadn't resisted too hard, Leesa noted.

A boy was asleep, or feigning sleep, in one of the two chairs that stood by a small dining table, his head slumped on his chest, feet up on the table itself.

"Get your shoes off there!" Mokhtar snapped, physically pushing them off at the same time. The boy – in his early or mid-teens by the look of him – jumped to his feet, startled. The lad was scrawny and a little gangly, having yet to fully grow into his frame.

"Now go and make yourself useful by minding the shop, eh?" Mokhtar said. "Can't you see I have visitors?"

The lad scurried out without speaking, though casting an inquisitive look in their direction. Mokhtar watched him go and shook his head. "My sister's boy," he explained apologetically, turning back to his guests. "About as much use as an unperforated sieve, but he's family; what's a man to do? Sit, sit!" He gestured towards the two dining chairs.

Following Bren's example, Leesa sat as instructed; she wouldn't have dared do otherwise in the face of Mokhtar's earnest imploring. The man himself hastily removed a biscuit tin and a small pile of folded sheets from an armchair, placing them on the floor before pulling the chair forward. He then took three small tumblers from a head-height cupboard, holding each up in turn and examining it critically against the room's single light. He then plonked the three glasses down on the table and himself into the armchair, which he shuffled forward a few steps in order to reach the table.

Having done that, he picked up the bottle of Tarkhillan, broke the seal, and pulled out what looked to be a genuine cork stopper, which he sniffed with great dignity, declaring, "Nectar!"

Three generous measures of caramel-brown brandy were then poured into the glasses. They each took one. Mokhtar held his up in salute, saying, "To the crew of *Pelquin's Comet*. May her stardrive never falter and her shower units never pack up mid-journey."

"I'll drink to that!" Bren agreed.

Cold fire hit the back of Leesa's throat as she joined in, while her mouth filled with the tastes of caramel and alcohol. The whole experience was powerful but inexplicably smooth; there was fire here, but it was fire that had been tamed. "Wow!" she said, holding up her glass to look at the brandy that remained within. "That's fantastic."

Mokhtar grinned. "Isn't it?" He turned to Bren. "I see why you let this one on board, Bren. We have here a lady of discerning taste. You should carry a bottle of Tarkhillan with you and use it, sparingly of course, as part of the interview process for new crew."

"Not a bad idea. I might recommend it to the captain."

He laughed, and topped up their glasses.

After another refill, Mokhtar's demeanour turned more serious. "So, you've come here just to catch up with an old friend, or is there something I can do for you?"

"Actually, there is something..."

"I thought so," and he wagged a mischievous finger at Bren. "What is it you're after, Brenda? Something difficult to get hold of, something not available over the counter, something a little... illicit, perhaps?"

"Sorry, Mokhy, I'm not looking to *buy* anything as such. Pel sent me to collect an item he left with you for safe keeping; told me to say that he'd given it to you against future need and that the need is now."

Mokhtar's expression turned even more serious. "Did he now? And what exactly is this object you've been sent to retrieve?"

"No idea. I was assuming you'd know."

He nodded, slowly, his gaze never leaving her. Then he stood up, walked across to a sink unit which occupied the wall behind him, and knelt down to open the door of the cupboard beneath. Various tins and cartons were pulled out and left haphazardly on the floor so that Mokhtar could reach all the way to the back. He then took out a large white tile, presumably from the wall itself, which he placed down with greater care, and, seconds later, drew out a long leather box, which he brought across and placed on the table. It reminded Leesa of the fancy case a piece of expensive jewellery might be presented in, but larger.

Mokhtar stood there, both hands resting on the table, leaning forward and staring first at Leesa and then at Bren.

"Do you have any idea what this is?"

"No," Bren said, "and I don't need to know."

"Oh, but I think you should," he said. "Nobody should deliver something like this without knowing what it is they carry." With that, he opened the hinged lid of the case and, taking almost reverent care, lifted away the cloth beneath to reveal the most beautiful weapon Leesa had ever seen. It resembled an old-style pistol, though with a greatly elongated barrel – half a metre and then some. Three quarters of the way along that barrel a small ridge of metal disfigured its underside: the stand, for resting on a wall or table or other convenient surface to steady the gun and ensure maximum accuracy. Another difference was that the gun's two sights, both front and rear, were clustered just above the handle, close to where the rear sight would be on a standard pistol; in this instance they were merely the frame for the virtual sighting system that would appear when the gun was activated.

"*Now* do you know what this is?"

"I was in the army for five years, Mokhy," Bren said. "Of course I know what it is."

So did Leesa, though she couldn't have said how: it was a needler. Not the type of thing you'd necessarily wanted to carry into battle – too specific, too tightly focused, too limited – but a formidable weapon all the same. This was a specialist piece of kit; an assassin's gun.

"Best sighting system ever invented," Mokhtar said. "You can see through solid walls with this thing, and shoot through them as well, of course. It allows you to set up multiple targets and take them out in quick succession without the need to adjust or recalibrate. A beautiful tool, isn't she?"

"And you're sure this is what Pel wanted me to collect?"

"I'm certain. This is the only thing your captain has ever left with me, along with instructions to safeguard the gun on pain of death, torture, and the ruining of my good name – though perhaps not in that specific order."

"Makes sense, I suppose." Bren still didn't look certain, as if she was trying to convince herself. "He wouldn't want to keep this on the *Comet*, that's for sure; couldn't risk it being found in a customs search. It'd be an instant prison sentence for anyone caught holding one of these and, as I recall, we were the subject of some pretty intense attention from the local pols last time we were here."

"Precisely," Mokhtar said, spreading his hands. "So *I* have taken that risk, on behalf of my good friend Captain Pelquin."

Leesa couldn't begin to imagine what Mokhtar had demanded from Pelquin in return. On reflection, she probably didn't want to know.

"A needler..." Bren shook her head. "Cheeky bastard – no wonder he sent me to collect this rather than Nate. I wonder why he wants it back now."

"That, my dear Brenda, I cannot help you with," Mokhtar said as he replaced the cloth and closed the case. "I can only suggest you ask him."

"Don't worry, I intend to." Bren picked up the gun case and frowned. "Have you got a rucksack or something I can use to carry this in?"

"Why certainly! We offer an extensive range of hardy bags of every description. You'll find them at the far end of aisle two, on the left. Feel free to buy whichever you prefer."

Bren scowled at him.

"...at a substantial discount, of course."

Fifteen

Archer took a cab from the space port, grateful to escape de Souza's presence for a while. The delicate balancing act he was attempting was proving to be more tiresome than he'd anticipated. The aim was to appear just competent enough to remain useful but stupid enough for the Jossyren executive to underestimate him. So far so good.

The cab carried him beyond the glitz and crowds and into the blandness of the city's Eastside. As they ventured deeper into a district of tired tenements and seedy cafés, Archer had the driver pull over and drop him off, despite being well short of his destination. In part this was because he was in no great hurry but mostly it was a precaution, to make certain that no one was following him. For a moment he simply stood and observed the passing traffic, watching for any vehicles that threatened to slow down. He didn't think de Souza was bothered enough to have him tailed or that Pelquin and his crew were alert enough, but it never harmed to be careful.

After a few seconds he walked on. A man loitering in the doorway opposite took casual interest and stared after him, but this was just a curious local and of no consequence.

There were a few other people about but not enough to muster a crowd – this was not the sort of district that tourists were likely to venture into let alone linger. Those folk he did pass were too wrapped up in their own concerns to pay him any mind. After several minutes' stroll he turned left, and then left again, walking without any apparent haste. He paused to scrutinise a shop window, though he couldn't have said afterwards what was displayed there; his attention focused more on the reflection of the street behind him. Then he strolled across the road and continued, eventually turning into a narrow alleyway of dirty brickwork and rusted fire escapes. Music reached him from somewhere – the tune muffled and leached of tone and passion by the intervening walls, so that what he heard sounded like a dirge.

He stopped before a door, its peeling paintwork indistinguishable from any of the others. The choice of unfashionable address was deliberate: all part of a front. No bell or knocker, so he simply rapped on the wood with his fist.

He couldn't see a camera but knew that someone would be watching, so he lifted his head to ensure his face was clearly visible. The door swung open immediately and apparently of its own accord. Beyond lay a dark and empty corridor which led to a narrow stairway. So far, everything was in keeping with the squalid, run-down surroundings, an impression dispelled as soon as he reached the top of the stairs. He entered a bright and open living space of polished floorboards and remarkably little clutter.

Further observation was curtailed as a great bald-headed bear of a man engulfed him in a full-on hug, blocking out the room. "Archer! It's been too long, brother."

"Far too long, Max," the banker agreed, going with the flow and suffering the hug – there was little point in trying to extricate himself until those massive arms relaxed.

Once they had, he stepped back and was able to take in the rest of his surroundings. The three other occupants – two men and a woman – were all seated and were all new to him. They were also busy and only one even deigned to look up and acknowledge his presence. Data fields flickered into life before them, to hang suspended in the air for a few seconds – figures and code scrolling across them – before winking out to be replaced by the next. The operators' fingers wove an intricate dance on virtual controls invisible to the observer and the trio kept up steady conversation in muted tones.

"Three of the best dealers in the whole of Victoria," Max said proudly, his voice barely above a whisper.

Archer nodded. He knew this was how the operation was funded but had never seen the dealers in action before. Long gone were the days of executives and politicians rendezvousing with shady characters on street corners to get their fix. No need for them to sully their sharp suits and designer heels by venturing into the rougher end of town these days – life was far more civilised, and chemical narcotics were as passé as dinosaurs. Every aspect of a deal now took place online, with e-hits sold in batches: data-squirts that, when triggered, delivered stimulation directly to specifically targeted areas of the brain. Swift, clean, no-nonsense transactions. And business was clearly booming.

Max ushered Archer to the far end of the room, where the

murmuring voices of the dealers faded to barely audible. "We've been busy since you were last here," he said.

"So I gather."

Max waved a hand to activate dormant systems and a translucent wall flickered to life before them. Thirteen figures, first among them the unmistakeable form of Captain Cornische, commander of the *Ion Raider* and leader of the Dark Angels. As ever, the captain's face was obscured by a privacy screen, which created a patch of ever-shifting static above the collar of his familiar blue-black uniform. This was typical of how Cornische presented himself to the world, which explained how his identity had remained hidden for so long. There were no known photographs of the man's face and no credible witnesses. What little they did know, gleaned from detailed analysis of thousands of images, was displayed beside the figure. Height: 1.94 metres; weight: 85 – 100 kilos; hair: dark brown; and that was about it. Archer was unfailingly dismayed by just how little information existed about the man – evidence, should any be needed, of Cornische's excessive paranoia or commendable caution, depending on your perspective. There was some conjecture, based on analysis of his posture at various times, that the captain had worn inserts in his shoes to disguise his true height, but that was uncorroborated.

Less open to debate was the variance in height of Hel N, one of the most prominent Angels. She relied on a very different method of anonymity, her skin coated from head to toe in what appeared to be a layer of silvered liquid metal, like mercury. Analysis of her height produced two distinct results, varying by about 7cm. Either two different women had been hidden beneath the Hel N identity, or she too had deliberately disguised her height for a period. As with so much else about the Angels, this was open to debate, since it was based on informed conjecture extrapolated from frustratingly little data.

Hel N's second skin was undoubtedly the product of elder tech, and therein lay the reason for Archer and his colleagues' interest in the Dark Angels. They called their organisation the Saflik – 'Purity' – and were bound by the conviction that plundering elder tech for personal gain constituted violation at a sacrilegious level. No one had abused elder tech more brazenly than Cornische and his Dark Angels. The Angels had always fiercely guarded their true identities, which presented a challenge the Saflik were determined to rise to. Their agents were dedicated to tracking down the Angels and meting out retribution.

Archer surveyed the display of figures, which represented all the Angels thought to be still alive. Thirteen.

"Unlucky for some," he murmured. "Which are the two we've found?"

A pair leapt forward to take centre stage: Gabriel and Spirit, one male, one female.

"And you don't have any doubts?"

"Nah," and Max grinned. "They're Angels all right. We've people in place, just been waiting for you to give the word; thought you'd like to be here when the termination order went out."

Archer appreciated the sentiment. It was something he could have done from a distance, but, since fate had conspired to bring him here to Brannan's, where Cornische was known to have operated and where the Saflik were based, it had seemed fitting to wait.

At length he nodded. "Do it!"

"All right!" Max bellowed, startling the three dealers into momentary silence and causing them to look round. Not that Max noticed. He grinned broadly. "Scratch two Angels."

This time when Drake went down to the cargo hold it wasn't to search for suspiciously smuggled crates, but rather to find a suit. The hold was where his trunk had ended up – the only place on board large enough to store it apart from the captain's quarters and the galley. He rifled through the selection of clothing until he found the allsuit. At least Pelquin's unexpected and intriguing invitation justified his decision to bring this remarkable garment along. He'd been tempted to leave it behind, but the allsuit had proved too useful on too many occasions in the past.

Most of the time between planet fall and leaving for the reception he spent scouring the Brannan's World infonet, checking on local fashions and the degree of formality expected at the evening's event. The event was global news and there was plenty of online gossip and speculation about which celebrity guest would be wearing which designer's creation, enabling him to glean more than sufficient indicators from the abundant chatter. As a result, he configured the allsuit to mimic a traditional black dinner suit. No bow tie though; in fact, open-necked was the current vogue, even when wearing a tux.

This wouldn't have been his preferred choice, but who was he to argue with the dictates of fashion? Especially on Brannan's, where celebrity was king and fashion its doting courtier.

One of his enduring memories of this place was its preoccupation with glamour, fame, and all things celeb. The two worlds of politics and the gossip columns had become strangely entwined on Brannan's, as the politicians sought to curry favour with younger voters by courting the friendship, in effect the patronage, of celebrities. One-upmanship in terms of who could attract the biggest names to which functions had become an accepted feature of the political landscape, and the media loved it. Fortunes were spent on securing an hour's flying visit by this prominent A-lister or that, with constant escalation; careers had been made and wrecked by such choices. Brannan's was a decent place, all in all, but this global fixation with celebrity was one aspect of the society that had always bemused Drake, and it was clear within the first few minutes of his surfing the infonet that little had changed in that regard.

The closer the evening's event drew the more intrigued Drake became by Pelquin's decision to invite him. He did wonder whether this might simply be another ploy to keep him off the ship and he had even entertained the thought of crying off all together, but in the end curiosity won out. If Pelquin's sole intent *was* to get him out of the way, the *Comet*'s captain was destined to be disappointed. It had been made abundantly clear that the evening's invite did not extend to Mudball, which meant that the alien would be left aboard the *Comet*, perfectly placed to witness and report on any goings on.

Shortly before it was time to leave, he sought out Anna, who was going to be staying aboard the ship.

"Would you mind looking after him for me?" he asked her, holding the little alien out to her.

"Of course not; I'd love to. We'll have lots of fun while you're away, won't we?" and she stroked Mudball as if he were a cat.

Be nice! Drake warned, knowing how much the alien hated to be stroked.

I am, trust me. This is *me being nice.*

"Don't worry," he said out loud, "he won't be any trouble." *Will you!*

"Of course he won't," she said, stroking Mudball again.

Stop fretting. I'll be as good as gold, the alien assured him.

Good. While you're at it, see if you can determine why we're here on Brannan's.

I have been, but there's nothing to report. Besides, I thought that's what you were hoping to do at this swanky party.

It never hurts to tackle a problem from two directions.

"You look nice, by the way."

"Pardon?" He'd been so caught up in his internal dialogue with Mudball that Anna's comment caught him by surprise.

"A tux really suits you." She reached out to lightly grip the suit's lapel between finger and thumb, running both downward.

Was Anna *flirting* with him?

"Ehm… thank you."

I think she fancies you, Mudball opined.

Shut it.

Oh, go on, it's been an age since I've watched you copulate with anyone.

Drake clamped down hard on his thoughts, which were anything but charitable.

Anna's hand withdrew and she presented her customary dazzling smile.

By the time he entered the taxi and took his seat beside Pelquin, all thoughts of Anna had receded to the hinterlands of his mind. The car was electrically powered, as were all vehicles on Brannan's by law, and its interior smelt of polish. While being far from the most luxurious chariot Drake had ever travelled in, he couldn't fault its cleanliness.

The driver proved to be of the friendly, chatty variety, and Drake was soon wishing they operated automated cabs here on Brannan's.

"So, you're going to the big shindig at the Settlement Hall. Famous then, are you?" the driver asked.

"No," Drake said quickly and not entirely honestly.

"We're… visiting dignitaries," Pelquin elaborated, playing equally loose and free with the truth.

The driver grunted. "Pity, but I suppose you'll be meeting plenty of famous people, eh? I understand Laurena Cole is gonna be there, *and* Tabitha Gabon. Now there's a couple of girls I wouldn't mind giving a ride to, if you know what I mean!"

"Never heard of either of them, to be honest" Pelquin said, echoing Drake's thoughts and cutting short the driver's throaty chuckle.

"Typical! Opportunity like that completely wasted. Now if *I* was going to this thing, 'stead of just ferrying folk to and from the door..."

Drake did his best to filter out the driver's gabbling. The trip didn't take long – no more than fifteen minutes – and it passed largely in silence once their cabby took the hint.

They avoided the busy urban centre, heading into leafier suburbs – all substantial houses with neat front gardens. The taxi climbed a steep hill stacked with smart residences before turning into a sweeping crescent drive, giving Drake his first view of the evening's venue – the Settlement Hall. It was an imposing edifice; one of those mock classical buildings designed to evoke the impression of a bygone age. For once, the designers had paid attention to proportion. Here was a structure that actually managed to accommodate the columns guarding its entranceway without making them look wholly ridiculous. With its elaborate portico and ornate bay window bulging out at first floor level, the building managed to convey a sense of grandeur.

As they exited the taxi – the vehicle glaringly incongruous among so many sleek and expensive cars – Drake paused to grasp the lapels of his black tuxedo and adjust the fit of his jacket, just a fraction. Pelquin was already several paces ahead but Drake refused to be hurried, forcing the captain to pause and wait for him.

The tell-tale translucent shimmer of a caress curtain stretched across the building's entranceway. Drake hated the things, considering the curtain a cheap and tacky gimmick, but he knew that he was in the minority. As you passed through the veil, your face and any other exposed areas of skin felt as if they received a feather-light fingertip caress – hence the name. The effect was intended to be sensual but Drake had always found the idea of being stroked by unseen hands discomforting, even a little creepy.

Beside him, Pelquin gave a small shudder and said, "Lovely."

Both he and Pelquin accepted flutes of pale champagne from one of several waiters standing sentry on the far side of the curtain and paused to take stock of the room. What awaited them was glitzy, opulent, and entirely predictable. The cavernous room was already filling up with black suits, glittering dresses and gleaming smiles, and more people were arriving all the time. The room itself boasted a high vaulted ceiling and panelled walls – each panel featuring a heavy-framed portrait. Marching down the length of the ceiling was a series of ostentatious crystal chandeliers, which were merely the most obvious lighting system; variously sized spots and doubtless other devices were hidden artfully in the vaulting, offering hosts a choice of mood and effect. For now, the chandeliers blazed gloriously. The carpet was a rich, patterned red, and here and there around the perimeter of the room clusters of comfortable chairs had been sprinkled; by no means a sufficient number for all the guests but enough to provide some with temporary respite from the merry-go-round of circulating.

There were five doors other than the one they'd entered by, Drake noted. All were of dark wood and decoratively panelled. The two in the left hand wall were fairly close together and constantly swinging open and shut as waiting staff came and went with trays of glasses, full as they emerged from the door nearest him, empty as they retreated through the other. The three doors in the right hand wall were evenly spaced and presumably led to anterooms of some sort or, conceivably, may even have been mere dummies, there to provide the illusion of the hall being part of a far more substantial residence.

Initially, Drake stayed close to Pelquin, but quickly tired of the sheer banality of the ensuing conversations. He was out of touch with the celebrity culture here and had no interest in hearing about it. Pelquin, by contrast, was clearly in his element. Drake could only admire the deftness with which the *Comet*'s captain played the room. He clearly took to socialising like a solar sail to sunlight. Where Drake tended to stand back and observe, Pelquin dived straight in and immersed himself in the ebb and flow of interaction, switching with apparent ease between serious discourse and light-hearted frivolity as circumstance required. Not that Drake was in any way envious. Social finesse on this scale was a skill he'd never valued enough to cultivate, but that didn't prevent him from appreciating it in another.

Pelquin had a certain charm, no question, which he played to shamelessly. The women in particular appeared susceptible. Most of the people in this room doubtless encountered each other at similar high-profile events throughout the year, whereas Pelquin represented that most valued of rarities: something *new*. He was an off worlder, a space captain, a charismatic adventurer whose flamboyance invited comparison to the rakish rogues so beloved of Trivies and popular space roms.

Despite his best efforts to keep at the fringes of things, Drake wasn't completely immune to attention himself. The most persistent culprit was an eye-catching redhead who wore a figure-hugging diaphanous gown that danced with oranges and reds in mimicry of living flame, apparently taking its cue from the wearer's hair, which tumbled to her shoulders in a cascade of curls that might have looked over the top in any other setting, but here suited her perfectly. All her features were artfully highlighted by subtle and well-chosen make-up, while her skin showed the flush of true youth – the product of nature rather than rejuve, he felt certain. She was quick to smile and, under other circumstances and on a different day, Drake might have been flattered and even interested, but as things were...

"So, you work for a bank?"

"Yes," he said, his attention focused largely on Pelquin, who now stood at a slight remove behind the woman's left shoulder. A rather lovely shoulder, he couldn't help but note, left bare by the strapless design of her dress. "The First Solar Bank."

Pelquin had just approached a ruddy-cheeked but distinguished looking gentleman who for once seemed immune to the captain's charms. In fact, the stranger looked anything but pleased to see him. There was also something different about Pelquin: a hint of tension in his posture which suggested that this mattered more than the evening's previous frivolities. Drake suspected this encounter was the reason for their being here; at this event and, indeed, on this planet.

"Laurena, by the way; in case you missed my name earlier." She held out a slender, porcelain-skinned hand for him to kiss. Only then did Drake make the connection between the woman before him and the two celebs that the taxi driver had been fantasising about on the way here. Assuming this *was* the same Laurena, the man had better taste than Drake would have credited. There followed a frozen second in which Drake merely stared at the proffered hand with its chunky diamond cluster ring. He relented a split second before the woman could take offence, reaching out to take her hand in his own, bending forward to press his lips to its back. "Enchanted," he said, drinking in her pheromone-laced perfume.

As he straightened, his smile was all for her, but his gaze met her own for just an instant before sliding sideways to where Pelquin still conversed with the same man.

Drake was an able lip reader but neither of the two subjects was ideally positioned and, besides, effective lip reading required a degree of concentration.

"So, what do you do at this bank of yours? Something very high powered, I would imagine."

"Hardly," he replied. "I'm a field agent." He was able to make out occasional snatches of Pelquin's conversation, but without context they meant nothing.

"Really? I wasn't even aware that banks *had* field agents."

"Well, I can't speak for all banks but First Solar does; obviously – otherwise I wouldn't be here." Pelquin and the other man were moving away, and every step made it more difficult for him to join their conversation in any smooth and natural fashion.

"Touché. So what exactly does a banking agent do – spy on other banks? Fight opposing agents to the death?"

"Nothing so dramatic, I'm afraid. We do all manner of things: visit customers, promote the bank's services, discuss options with potential clients, remind errant borrowers of their responsibilities..."

"Sounds riveting."

"It has its moments."

"I'm sure... And you say this bank of yours is based on New Sparta? So what brings you all the way to Brannan's World?"

"It's a small universe. First Solar has interests and customers on any number of worlds."

"Even so, this is a hell of a long way to come just to remind someone they're late with a repayment..."

"Ah, but that depends on how much and how late the payment is. Besides, I don't make policy decisions. I just go where I'm sent."

"Right, I see. So your presence all the way out here wouldn't have a more... exotic explanation then? Only I hear New Sparta is the place to go if you're looking to fund an expedition... Cache hunting, for example."

Not stupid, this one; not stupid at all. "Well it would be, I suppose," he acknowledged. "After all, that's where the banks are."

She laughed. "True."

"Sorry to disappoint you, but I don't get involved in anything as exciting as that. I'm just a functionary: a tiny cog in the machine."

"Hmm..." She leant closer, so that he caught an intoxicating whiff of her perfume as she whispered in his ear, "Now why don't I believe that?"

Her hand brushed his elbow in an apparently innocent manner. He was acutely aware of that touch, even through his jacket and shirt. She really was gorgeous, and was proving impressively astute as well.

She stepped back, the half-smile suggesting that she was fully aware of the effect she'd had on him. Perhaps his earlier thought hadn't been entirely honest; he *was* interested, and flattered, despite circumstances.

None the less, he forced himself to say, "Look, much as I hate to tear myself away from your delightful presence, there's someone I really must go and talk to."

Pelquin and the other man were most of the way across the room now and were clearly making for one of the doors on the far side.

"Oh, I'm sorry..." She looked offended. He imagined she wasn't used to being rebuffed, no matter how gently.

"This isn't a brush-off," he assured her quickly, surprising himself. "I really *am* here on business and have to pursue this, whatever I might prefer to be doing."

His words were evidently enough to assuage her wounded pride. She even smiled. "All right, then, I'll let you off. If you mean that, how about I send you my perminal id?"

"Thank you. I'd be flattered."

She touched her bracelet, which he hadn't even realised *was* a perminal until then – far more elegant than the unit Pelquin habitually wore. He felt a small vibration from the inside of his jacket and knew she'd just pinged her contact details to him. It would be up to him to accept or reject the data package later.

"Thank you," he said. Politeness should have prompted him to reciprocate with his own details, but he refrained. If his reticence offended her further she gave no indication of the fact. "I live locally in Victoria. Get in touch when this... 'business' of yours is concluded. I'd love to hear all the boring details."

He hesitated, searching for a suitable response, knowing that the *Comet*'s stay on Brannan's was set to be a short one and that he had no plans to come back this way. "I'll see what I can do," he temporised.

"Good." With that, she leant forward and kissed him on the cheek. "Don't forget to call."

He could still feel the ghost of her lips as he went after Pelquin, who was in the process of entering the right-hand door with his new friend. So, the trio of doors were definitely not dummies, or at least not all of them were. In a way this made it easier. Knocking and entering with an apology for being late dispensed with any pretext and made it very difficult for Pelquin to deny him.

The door wasn't far, but crossing the now crowded room without bulldozing through conversational knots, bumping into people's backs or colliding with liveried waiters bearing platters of canapés required more patience than he cared to spare. To make matters worse, he was halfway to the door when a voice said, "Mr Drake, isn't it?"

Drake knew at once that he had never previously met the speaker – a man somewhat shorter than him, his head barely reaching Drake's shoulder – though he was able to deduce several things immediately. This was an individual of some considerable means – the suit was handmade and expensive, though over-elaborate for Drake's taste, with stitching forming an intricate filigree pattern on the lapels. Here was somebody who didn't shirk ostentation. And he wasn't a native of Brannan's either, at least not a sedentary one – accent and dusky skin tone gave that much away – while he had recently been on New Sparta; his shoes bore the subtle but distinctive emblem of a fashionista designer Drake knew well, a woman who was very much 'this season'. In addition, his naturally tanned complexion was washed with the indefinable pastiness bestowed by a good deal of time spent away from the natural light of any sun, while it also showed the smooth tightness of multiple rejuves, so he was by no means a young man.

All of which led Drake to conclude that their bumping into one other was anything but a coincidence. Since he had been a last minute addition to the guest list, very few people would know the banker's identity and even fewer would be interested; only someone paying keen attention to Pelquin's presence was likely to have noted such a detail. Recent events narrowed the field down to just one likely candidate.

"Allow me to introduce myself. My name is Falyn de Souza…"

"And you work for the Jossyren Mining Corporation," Drake finished for him. "Clearly in an executive capacity, so perhaps it would be more appropriate to say that a good portion of Jossyren Mining works for you."

De Souza blinked several times, obviously taken aback, but to his credit he recovered quickly, giving an appreciative chuckle. "My, my… That *is* impressive."

Drake said nothing, but he'd stopped walking. He felt torn between the need to find out what was going on between Pelquin and the stranger and a desire to discover what this de Souza wanted with him. In the end, expediency dictated the latter take priority.

"It's a pleasure to discover that at least *some* of First Solar's representatives live up to their reputation."

"I wasn't aware that any of us had a reputation to live up to." At the same time, he couldn't help but wonder which of his colleagues had failed in that regard.

"You do, Mr Drake, you very much do. Should you ever tire of living off the scraps First Solar pay you and want to earn some real money, come and talk to me."

Drake smiled. "I'll bear that in mind. In the meantime, flattering though all this might be, I very much doubt you've engineered this meeting merely to bolster my ego."

"Indeed not. And I do so appreciate directness."

Though generally, Drake suspected, only when de Souza himself was the one being direct.

"I know why you're here, Mr Drake."

If so, it would be interesting to hear, since Drake didn't yet know himself.

"And I know where you're going," de Souza continued.

Again Drake said nothing, though de Souza paused as if waiting for a response. "My point is that Captain Pelquin intends to double cross you," he said. "That won't come as a shock, I'm sure. You've had ample opportunity by now to see that he's not to be trusted. I'm sure you've already discovered that the good captain has been less than honest in his submissions to your employers, withholding vital, *pertinent* information. First Solar would never condone such an operation if they knew all the facts, not officially. But then that's where you come in, isn't it, Mr Drake? I understand that you representatives are granted sufficient... shall we say 'discretion'... to bend the rules a little when in the field, to sanction things that First Solar can later deny all knowledge of. Am I right, Mr Drake? Of course I am."

Drake sipped his champagne and remained quiet; he'd realised a while ago that he didn't need to contribute much to the conversation. De Souza was perfectly content to speak for both of them.

"I won't detain you any longer, Mr Drake, but I do hope you'll think on what I've said before you find yourself in too deep. My ship is in port for another couple of days, berth 56. Why not drop by so that we can continue this conversation in private? I'm confident it would prove beneficial to both of us."

As de Souza moved away, Drake saw the door that had been his intended destination open, to admit first Pelquin and then the other man back into the main room. Damn! He would now be forced to rely on whatever Pelquin chose to tell him about the brief meeting, and then decide how much of the captain's account to believe.

The old maxim about keeping your enemies close had never seemed more appropriate. Pelquin might easily have brought Bren along to tonight's reception – in fact that had been his original intention – but he'd decided to invite Drake instead and was now glad that he had.

Drake seemed a little uncomfortable in this social setting, which surprised Pelquin. He would have expected the banker to feel perfectly at home here, given his position with First Solar, but apparently not. Pelquin, on the other hand, was having a ball. He took quiet pleasure in seeing the banker marginalised by the flow of conversation. Drake drifted away towards the edge of the room like flotsam discarded on the beach by a discerning tide. More than one bright young pretty thing seemed impressed by Pelquin's colourfully embellished anecdotes and having the dour banker at his elbow would only have cramped his style. He could even hope that, with Drake at a slight remove, he might yet manage to arrange alternative sleeping arrangements that would force him to send his 'plus one' back to the ship alone.

Throughout all the flirtatious chatter, however, he kept half an eye on the slightly portly, mutton-jowled figure of Olly Webster. He had moved mountains to secure an invite to this shindig, calling in favours from people who would never talk to him again, and he was determined not to waste the opportunity. Pelquin was probably the last person Olly would expect to see here, and as yet he didn't appear to have noticed him. Which was fine: it would make the surprise all the more enjoyable. Finally he saw his chance as Webster stepped away from two men he'd been deep in conversation with. Breaking off in mid-story and excusing himself, Pelquin abandoned his own small audience and moved across to intercept Webster.

"Hello, Olly."

For an instant Olly looked puzzled, as if trying to place who this was, but the look of shock that followed was a pleasure to witness. "Pelquin!" He spat the word out, as if he couldn't wait to eject its foul taste from his mouth. "What the fuck are you doing here?"

A distinguished-looking woman in sequinned gown turned round sharply, clearly shocked to hear such language.

"Olly, it's good to see you too," Pelquin said, all smiles. "Is that any way to greet an old friend?"

"That's Senator Webster to you; and we were *never* friends."

"Olly, how can you say that, after all that we've been through...? Successful business partners, at the very least."

"That's enough! I've no idea how you blagged your way in here, Pelquin, but whatever you're after I'm not interested."

"Oh I think you are, Olly. Trust me, you can't afford not to be." He dropped the smile. "Is there somewhere a little more... private we can talk?"

Pelquin watched panic, anger, and calculation play across the man's face. For a moment he feared that Olly might yet have him thrown out and damn the consequences, which would be unfortunate; especially for Olly. In the event, though, common sense prevailed. "Five minutes," Olly said. "Then you leave."

"Five minutes will do just fine."

Senator Webster produced a broad smile of his own, flashing it to all and sundry. At the same time he muttered, "Come with me."

It was too early to feel triumphant – the hard part was still to come – but Pelquin was enjoying himself; not least because he knew Drake was a little behind him, chatting to that red-headed starlet. A striking looking woman, one he wouldn't have minded knowing better himself. He resisted the temptation to look round as he followed the senator, not wanting to give the banker an excuse to join them. He suppressed a smile, knowing full well how vexed Drake would be.

Olly led the way to the rightmost of the three doors in the far wall, opening it and ushering Pelquin inside. Only once the door shut firmly behind them did Olly turn to face him.

"That's your first minute gone crossing the room," he said. "You've got four left."

The noise from the party had dropped away instantly the door closed; all that now reached them was a muted murmur. Unruffled, Pelquin smiled and stepped past Olly, to glance around at the room, which was clearly modelled on the drawing room of some old colonial manse. "Nice place," he said. "Who'd have thought you and I would ever be allowed into somewhere like this, hey, Olly? But then you're a senator, now, aren't you? I was delighted to hear how well you're doing for yourself these days, by the way."

"I'll bet. Three and a half minutes."

"So very different from when you and I knew each other..."

"Get to the point, Pel. It's your own time you're wasting."

"We're both businessmen, Olly. Let's face it, you wouldn't be where you are now without the profit made from our former ventures."

"That's all in the past. I'm a changed man now."

"No argument from me; I'm sure you are... Which is why it would be such a pity if any of those dirty little dealings came to light, don't you think?"

"I wondered how long it would take you. So, it's blackmail."

"Such an ugly word; I'd like to think of this more as a business arrangement, one that we can both benefit from."

"Both?"

"Of course 'both'. You enjoy the benefits of my silence. The last thing I want to do is undermine all the good work you're doing with the Xters and everything... which brings us, of course, to your side of the deal. I want a permit."

"What? You're joking."

Pelquin smiled. "No. I really admire the way you've championed detente between us and the Xters – it's been your road to success, eh, Olly? I need to go into Xter space and you're the man who can ensure that I do so legally. So... a permit."

"It's called a Sanction, not a permit. And no fucking way!"

"Do you remember that old warehouse you used to have in the industrial sector over on the Eastside, what I used to deliver there?"

"That was all a long time ago. I was young... The foolishness of youth..."

"Of course, Olly, I know that. Let's just hope your colleagues and those nice people in the media see it the same way. Everything's documented, of course; photos, recordings..."

"You really are a complete bastard, aren't you, Pelquin."

"So they tell me. Here are the details of what I need." He handed across a scrap of paper – old style, the one system of messaging guaranteed to leave no electronic footprints. "We'll meet again tomorrow, midday, outside the warehouse – for old time's sake."

"You're mad; that's impossible. I can't organise a Sanction that quickly, even if I wanted to."

"Of course you can, Olly, if you put your mind to it. I've got every faith in you."

"There are procedures in place, protocols to follow..."

"Circumvent them, Olly, circumvent them. Now, perhaps we should get back to the party before someone misses us; well, you, no one's going to miss me." Pelquin gestured towards the door. "Don't let me down, Olly."

"You bastard!"

"I'll see you tomorrow."

Sixteen

Alexis Chapel felt that she had finally found her niche. Oh, she knew she was nothing special. That particular facet of reality had been drummed into her from an early age. If you were to take all her education reports and ask a computer to assess the contents and produce a one line summary, the result would most likely have been those very words: Nothing Special.

This wasn't something she felt any great bitterness about. Alexis was a realist who entertained few illusions regarding herself, either flattering or derogatory. She accepted who she was and knew it to be better than many: not *bad* looking – face a little too angular, nose a little too prominent to be considered 'beautiful' perhaps, but she could pull off 'cute' when she wanted to and she'd never lacked for male attention; she wasn't stupid, either – though she could never claim to have been a high flyer academically. She'd landed a good, solid job – which was more than some of her old school friends could say – even if she'd had to sit and watch on more than one occasion as other, brighter prospects were promoted over her head. She was a decent enough person as well, though sainthood was definitely beyond her reach. Alexis had never stolen anything in her life – apart from a friend's boyfriend in an isolated incident which had been fully merited retribution for a particularly catty insult. She had now been married for nearly four years and had only cheated on him once; well, half a dozen times but with the same man, so that still counted as once in her book. And in any case, she'd ended it months ago. Her marriage was a *happy* one. There were no children as yet, but all in good time. Maybe.

No, Alexis knew full well that in many ways she was doing okay; it was just that she'd never *excelled* at anything... Except perhaps at art, and her mother had put paid to any ambitions in that department. Not deliberately, of course – far from it. Her mother, Emalia Chapel, had always been encouraging, in that reserved, aloof manner which had always been her default setting when dealing with her daughter. Emalia's attention was invariably focused elsewhere: on her *own* art.

And *that* was the problem. Alexis' mother had been an outstanding artist, celebrated in fact; the single most famous artist on the whole of Brannan's World, or so it had seemed to her daughter. How could Alexis ever compete with that? Her mother painted, too. Really painted, using oils, watercolours and acrylics, rarely dabbling in the digital forms that had opened art to so many. Emalia could create more emotion with a single stroke of a brush than any of her contemporaries could with a glut of pixels.

The teenage Alexis had felt awed, humbled, embarrassed by her own efforts, and so her burgeoning talent had gone unrealised, and she backed away from art entirely, despite the encouragement of others. To her mind, the prospect of being forever dubbed 'The Daughter of' was far worse than not being known at all.

She hadn't attempted anything artistic in years.

And then of course there was her husband, Joe. He'd never been remotely interested in art; maybe that was one of the things that first attracted her to him – he represented an escape. Between them they made a comfortable living. Joe was in haulage, while the security services provided her with an adequate income; and Alexis knew that her superiors valued her – they had told her so more than once. 'Dependable'; that was the praise most often heaped upon her. It was why she was chosen for this particular operation, ensuring the safety of a roomful of government ministers and VIPs at a swanky function. It was also the reason she was stuck inside a dimly-lit, claustrophobic cubbyhole of a room staring at a bank of screens depicting the input from assorted micro-cameras rather than out there on the floor mingling. Still, as Alexis had told Luke, one of her colleagues who *had* been tasked with working the room that evening, in her opinion chef-devised canapés and chilled champagne were highly overrated. Particularly when she was denied the chance to sample them.

Alexis had devised various means of entertaining herself – an essential undertaking, otherwise monitor duty made her feel like a voyeur at the most unexciting orgy in history. Initially it wasn't too bad – she occupied the time by zooming in on the gorgeous dresses and fabulous jewellery worn by the assembled women and no few of the men, trying to work out which celeb was wearing which designer, and how many years' worth of her own salary a given outfit was likely to have cost. Once she tired of that she turned her attention to spotting who was having a surreptitious word with whom and predicting which exchanges were likely to be political, which commercial, and which were of a more intimate nature.

She smiled at seeing one particular minister, who had narrowly survived a recent scandal that saw the media daub him 'Randy Reggie', whisper a few brief words to a strikingly pretty starlet half his age. Whatever it was he said – his face was at the wrong angle for the lip-reading software to be of any use and there was too much background hubbub for sound enhancement to help – earned him a quick smile and a shallow nod of response, after which he moved away to rejoin his wife, who was laughing with forced enthusiasm at some comment made by the Aleuthian ambassador.

Next she saw two notoriously bitter political rivals talking and smiling like the very best of buddies, and a supposedly gay actor clearly hitting on the same starlet the minister had whispered to a short time before. Alexis shook her head. There was a fortune's worth of potential revelation and scandal unfolding before her very eyes. It was almost a pity she valued her job so much.

The door behind her opened, startling her, but it was only Luke. He edged into the room, balancing a flute of what had to be champagne and a plate of half a dozen mouth-watering canapés.

"I thought you might appreciate these."

He was right. "Thanks."

He put glass and plate down and craned forward, leaning over her, ostensibly to stare at the screens but in the process getting close, his cheek almost touching hers. She didn't pull away, enjoying the attention. Luke was one of her more personable colleagues. A year or two younger than her but not bad looking by any means, and he made no secret of fancying her. If she ever decided to embark on a second extra-marital dalliance, Luke would be a prime candidate.

"Anything of interest?" he said, almost breathing the words into her ear.

"Not really," She still hadn't turned away but nor did she move closer. They were alone, completely unobserved and unlikely to be interrupted. She was tempted to look round, to tilt her head, to accept the kiss she felt certain would come, but she didn't; in part because she hadn't yet committed in her own mind to an affair with Luke, but also because she was enjoying his pursuit and didn't want that phase of the game to end just yet.

"Just the usual schmoozing, networking and flirting." Alexis felt proud of how calm her voice sounded.

Despite her earlier resolve, Alexis was almost disappointed when she felt Luke stand up and step away. "Well, I'd best be getting back to the floor before I'm missed," he said. "You can bring me up to speed on all the juicy gossip later."

"Will do." She looked around. "And, Luke…"

"Yes?"

"Thank you." On impulse, she blew him a kiss. He left, grinning.

After he'd gone she sipped at the champagne, her gaze resting on the screens but her attention elsewhere, as she imagined Luke standing bare-chested before her.

It took a conscious effort of will to dispel the image and focus on what she was supposed to be doing.

Second guessing the nature of people's private conversations had lost its appeal, so she moved onto her next standard mechanism for staving off boredom and activated the monitors' facial recognition software – this particular distraction pretty much fell within the job description anyway.

For the next half hour she took a visual tour of the room, focusing on one individual after another, allowing the software to examine the structure and specific features of each subject's face using sophisticated isometrics, analysing minutiae that were supposedly impossible to mimic effectively. In this way she was able to confirm the identity of most of those present – no doubles in attendance tonight. The software even highlighted a couple of celebs who'd had a little surgery on the sly.

Growing bored of checking over those she already knew, Alexis turned her attention to the waiting staff and the visiting dignitaries who were unfamiliar to her. One or two, usually the more handsome males, piqued her curiosity sufficiently for her to summon up their profiles.

Then her camera focused on one face in particular and she froze. The software did its job, identifying the man as a visiting off worlder; Corbin Thadeus Drake, registered as an employee of First Solar Bank. The problem was that she knew him by a different name entirely.

At least she thought she did… But it couldn't be. Surely he was *dead*. She kept the camera trained on Drake's face and dredged up memories she hadn't revisited in years. He looked a little older, and the face might have benefited from some cursory restructuring – though perhaps that was no more than faulty memory; she'd been little more than a child then, after all. The eyes, though, they were the same: so dark, and with a quality that suggested they understood the nature of the universe and mocked it at the same time. It was him. It *had* to be him. And yet...

Then she remembered her mother's paintings. Emalia Chapel had withdrawn from society years ago, establishing a new and doubtless pampered life with a man Alexis loathed. Mother and daughter had never been close and Emalia had rarely been generous with the considerable wealth her paintings had generated, but that was okay; Alexis was content to make her own way in the world.

The only real concession Alexis ever made to being Emalia's daughter was stored on her perminal: a digitised library of her mother's paintings. As far as Alexis knew, Emalia didn't even know she had these.

Taking the perminal out, she flicked the display to broadest setting, which brought a selection of icons floating in the air before her. She accessed the appropriate library and then riffled through the obliquely presented close-packed images, swiftly finding the one she was after.

A deft stab of the finger and that image emerged to take centre stage. She found herself staring at a portrait of the man she'd known as 'Uncle Frank'. The three years he and her mother had been together were by far the happiest of her childhood, if not her entire life to date. For that brief period Emalia Chapel had found the time to notice things beyond her work, had even, for a while, made Alexis feel *wanted*...

The moment Uncle Frank left, though, everything changed, and her mother became colder than ever.

This portrait, painted from memory after Uncle Frank had gone – he would never have posed for anything like that – was all that Alexis had left of him. There were no photographs – she'd searched, thoroughly and desperately in the weeks immediately following his disappearance – none at all.

Alexis both loved and hated that painting. She'd known, even then, why he had to go, but that hadn't made it any easier to forgive him, or to ever stop missing him.

She froze the camera image, choosing a moment when 'Drake' was facing her, almost straight on. She then magnified her mother's painting and compared the two. As she studied them, trying to convince herself that this was just some form of deeply hidden wishful thinking on her part, inspiration struck.

Alexis uploaded the image from her perminal into the monitoring equipment and then used the face recognition software to run a comparison. She had no idea if this would work; after all, one of the subjects was only a painting, but it was her *mother's* painting, and Emalia Chapel's eye for detail and perspective was legendary.

Even so, she half expected the comparison to draw a blank, for the system to report an error, an inability to complete the requested task... But it didn't. Instead it highlighted correlations and concluded a 59% probability that both images were of the same person.

Alexis drew a deep breath and exhaled it slowly. Damn! There it was. The rest was up to her. 59% still left plenty of room for doubt, but under the circumstances it was more than she'd dared hope for.

She stared at the four words displayed beneath her mother's painting – the tag giving Uncle Frank's full name – and wondered what the hell she was going to do next.

Did she hate this man, or love him? By rights, she should immediately contact Luke or one of the more senior officers and report this. Career-wise, it would be the making of her. *But this is Uncle Frank.*

Alexis had never been one for soul-searching but right now her thoughts were in turmoil. For some reason she kept coming back to all the promotions that had slipped past without coming within reach, of all those others whose careers were progressing along faster, slicker tracks than hers. It had never really bothered her, not until now, but her loyalty had never before faced a stiffer test than this.

One thing was certain: the next few seconds would determine once and for all just how dedicated to this career she was.

Alexis came to her senses abruptly. Whatever her personal feelings, not reporting this would be an inconceivable dereliction of duty. There was only one thing to do, no matter how unpalatable it might be. She took a deep breath, preparatory to issuing the call signal... And yet... *and yet...* Still she hesitated, staring at the image one final time, as if to imprint those features indelibly on her mind. Could this *really* be him?

Pelquin and the stranger separated as soon as they re-entered the room, as if they couldn't wait to get away from each other. The captain didn't give the other man another glance but instead made a beeline for Drake. The banker tried to read his expression and body language as he approached, seeing there excitement, perhaps even triumph, but also a degree of anxiety.

"Everything go as planned?" he asked as Pelquin reached him.

"More or less, but we have to leave."

"So soon? I was just beginning to enjoy myself."

"Be that as it may, my friend Olly has suggested we make ourselves scarce and I don't want to push our luck."

Drake had kept half an eye on the other man – Olly – and noticed that he was now talking to a suit that just had to be security and looking in their direction. "Maybe you've got a point."

They began to make their way towards the door. It was then that Drake saw her: a woman whose eyes were focused on them, specifically on *him*, and there was no question she was headed in their direction. Yet something wasn't right. The manner of her approach didn't suggest determination to fulfil a mission; there was nothing resolute or assured in her body language, rather she appeared ill at ease, almost furtive.

He realised they weren't going to reach the door before she intercepted them. He stopped walking, wanting to see how she'd react. She adjusted course, coming directly towards him. That settled it.

"What's wrong?" Pelquin asked, pausing and looking back.

"Nothing, I hope. But whatever it is seems to be about me and not you. You'd best keep walking. I'll meet you outside."

Pelquin followed the line of his gaze, finally spotting the woman. After another quick glance in Drake's direction, he nodded and then continued on towards the door, not looking back.

Drake tensed as the woman came up, looking quickly around to see if there was anyone else trying to outflank him.

"Mr Drake, relax, look natural," she intoned by way of greeting. "Smile as if we're old friends. I had to catch you here, close to the door. It's the one area I could arrange not to be covered by security cameras."

So, she was part of the security set up, which was far from reassuring. She looked nervous and upset, though, conflicted even.

"Mr Dra…" she paused. After a shaky breath she continued, and what she said stunned him. "Uncle Frank… *Don't you know me?*"

And he did; of course he did. "Alex, is it really you?" There was no chance at subterfuge, no possibility of pretending she'd made a mistake.

His expression would have given him away even had he tried.

"Look, I understand…" she said. "Why you had to leave. I don't blame you."

Blame him? Didn't she know what her mother had done, how she betrayed him? Probably not.

"Take this," and he found something thrust into his hand. "My card. Call me, when you can; please."

"I will," he said, with no idea whether he meant it or not.

She smiled, almost shyly. "I've got to get back. Don't forget, call me." With that she turned and was gone, hurrying off the way she had come. He swallowed on a suddenly dry throat and took a few seconds to compose himself before strolling across to the door and out to where Pelquin waited, clearly anxious.

"Well, what was it?" the *Comet's* captain wanted to know.

"Nothing," Drake assured him. "Nothing at all."

"Really? Who was she then?"

"Just someone I used to know a long time ago. I hadn't expected to meet her here, that's all. Just goes to show how small a universe this is." *Too small*, he added silently, *too small by half.*

Alexis returned to her cubicle to find it still empty and with everything exactly as she'd left it. She breathed a sigh of relief, only then daring to admit to herself how big a risk she'd just taken. She seemed to have got away with it, though, which meant that no one would ever know about her abandoning her station or the reason why. The thrill of a risk taken and gamble won surged through her. Clearly this was a night for such things. She adjusted the cameras covering the wide entrance hall to a more normal configuration and then simply sat there for a moment, breathing deeply and battling to recover her composure.

Would he call her? There was so much she wanted to say; so much she needed to know. She'd always felt that her mother blamed her for his leaving, as if whatever had gone wrong between them was somehow her fault. She would never forget the day, years later, when Emalia informed her – very formally, as if mentioning newly prepared travel arrangements – that her Uncle Frank was dead.

Yet here he was.

"Pull yourself together, Alex," she muttered. There were still some things she needed to do: expunging her mother's painting from the security systems for one. After that she'd have to cover her tracks by removing all record that it had ever been there.

She hesitated for a split second, gazing at the magnified picture one more time; her mother really had managed to capture those eyes… Then she erased the image and, with it, the four identifying words printed beneath: *Captain Francis Hilary Cornische.*

SEVENTEEN

The highlight of Leesa's morning was a leisurely wander around Victoria's Westside shopping district, which proved far more extensive than anticipated. She went there on impulse. The *Comet* had been allocated a launch slot for later that afternoon, which meant that, having already checked and double checked the ship's engines and systems, she had some time to kill. Bren had mentioned Westside in passing, saying that it was worth a visit; and the prospect of a little retail therapy sure as hell beat sitting around kicking her heels on the ship. The vague notion of picking up a souvenir or two soon evaporated. After all, she didn't really need any herself and had no one else to buy them for.

The *Comet* was quiet when she returned, with only Nate, Anna, and the doc on board. Presumably Pelquin, Bren and Drake were off making the most of what little time remained planetside, much as she had. Anna was all right, but the other two were hardly Leesa's ideal choice of companions; not that she'd yet worked out who was.

Nate Almont was in a tetchy mood, even by his usual standards, so she quickly decided to forego the galley and the pleasure of his company in favour of the bridge.

She carried a drink up to Anna, who smiled in thanks.

"What's up with Nate?"

"Oh, ignore him," Anna advised. "He's just sulking. He and Pel were going off somewhere when Drake intervened. Not sure what was said exactly, but it ended up with Nate staying behind and the banker going in his place. He's been in a foul mood ever since."

"Where were they going?"

"No idea. We'll be the last to know, as usual." Anna suddenly sat up, staring at her monitor. "Hello... What's this?"

Leesa leaned forward for a better view of the screen. It showed three uniformed figures, presumably approaching the ship.

"Nate, you'd better get up here," Anna said. "We've got company."

"Who is it?" Nate replied over the intercom.

"Port authorities by the look of it, with cops…"

"I'm on my way."

Pelquin drove a hired car. He had barely spoken to Drake since they left the ship. Clearly he was far from happy. Tough. The banker had worked out in a general sense where they were going but that was the point: he shouldn't have *needed* to deduce that. As First Solar's representative he ought to have been kept in the loop and was fast losing patience with the captain's continued failure to do so.

Pelquin had proved evasive the previous evening when Drake asked him about the stranger, and Drake had decided enough was enough. He wasn't in the least surprised to catch Pelquin and Nate trying to slip off the ship unnoticed that morning. Pelquin had even looked surprised when he said, "I take it this has something to do with Senator Oliver Webster," as if it hadn't dawned on him that the banker might cross reference last night's guest list to identify the stranger. "Based on his current responsibilities," he continued, "I'm assuming you're after a Sanction to legitimise a trip into Xter space. By all means correct me if I'm wrong."

Their reaction told him that he wasn't.

The argument was won and everyone present knew it. Drake couldn't pretend he was disappointed when Nate said, "We can't go in mob-handed. If he's going with you, I'll stay here."

Pelquin was left with little choice but to agree; which didn't mean he had to like the situation. On the plus side, Pelquin hadn't once thought to complain about Mudball, who rode in his accustomed position at the banker's shoulder.

"Now that I'm here," Drake said at length, "you might at least give me some idea of what I've talked myself into."

"A meeting, much as you guessed," Pelquin said after slight hesitation. "When we get there, I want you to stick close to me at all times. If I move, make sure you follow, understood?"

"Understood." Why, though?

"Knowing 'Oily' Olly Webster as I do, things won't be straight forward," Pelquin added.

"You don't think he'll have the Sanction ready?"

"Oh, he'll have it. He could probably have signed off on one last night at the reception – he has the authority. No, Oily wouldn't risk *not* having a Sanction prepared. It's just that handing it over will be his Plan B. Plan A will be to try and bully me out of it first.

"So this is likely to get physical?"

"Why do you think I was taking Nate along?"

They arrived at an extensive industrial site, though the lack of activity suggested it was currently disused – long buildings with shuttered doorways and empty forecourts providing a downbeat setting. Not quite deserted. A single black limo stood before one and, as they approached, three men got out. Drake recognised one as Senator Olly Webster – the stranger from the previous evening – while the other two gave every impression of being hired muscle.

"Right, game on," Pelquin said as he stopped the car. "And remember, follow my lead." He was all smiles as he climbed out. "Olly, good to see you."

The senator scowled. "Who's this?" and he gestured towards Drake.

"My associate, Mr Drake."

"And these are *my* associates, Mr Terrivel and Mr Feliz." The two men wore matching smart suits and might almost have been twins.

"Three of you? This Sanction must be heavier than I'd realised."

As Pelquin spoke, he stepped away from the hire car. It was a casual movement but took him unnecessarily wide. Drake followed.

"Ah yes, about the Sanction… It turns out that both Mr Terrivel and Mr Feliz have strong reservations on that front, Pel. I spoke to them after our little chat last night. Well, of course I did. They have a vested interest, you see, having provided considerable support to my political career – money, influence… You know the sort of thing."

"I can guess."

Webster smiled. "So I'm sure you can understand why the prospect of someone from my past appearing out of nowhere and threatening to *undermine* that career is of concern to them." He held his hands out, as if to display his helplessness. "They'd like a little chat, Pel, to explain their take on the situation and why it would be best for all concerned if you were to simply forget that you ever knew me."

"That's not going to happen, Olly."

Drake had been watching the senator's companions throughout, waiting for them to make their move. When it came, however, he was still caught off-guard by the sheer speed of attack. Instead of the forward movement he had anticipated, the one on the right – Feliz – simply raised his left arm, as if to scratch his ear, and there was a weapon in his hand. Without hesitation, he fired, straight at Drake, who whipped his cane up, barely in time. It was an instinctive reaction rather than a deliberate attempt at defence, but it proved at least partially successful. Much of the energy spent itself on the staff's non-conductive surface. Unfortunately some of the blast still got through to strike his arm. Pain screamed from every fibre. He felt as if the skin were being flayed from his limb, despite what his eyes told him – that the arm had suffered no physical damage.

The cane tumbled from fingers that would no longer obey him, and the arm twitched as his muscles spasmed. A stun blast, and a nasty one. He was just grateful that he hadn't taken the full blast.

Can't you do something about the twitching? he asked silently.

I am. Why do you think you're not a quivering wreck already?

Olly's two associates were converging on Pelquin, and there was nothing Drake could do about it. He tried, crouching down to reach for the fallen cane with his left hand, but the twitching and his own haste turned the effort into a fumbling and clumsy one.

"I'm sorry, Pel, but what can I do?" he heard Olly say.

Then one of the twin-like pair – Drake had lost track of which was which – spun round and dropped to the ground, crying out. The other followed a split second later, and this time Drake could see the blossoming wound near the man's shoulder.

A sniper. Drake had assumed Pelquin was being so particular about where they stood to allow clear line of sight for photographs or a recording, perhaps for the purpose of further insurance, but the captain was evidently playing hardball. It had to be Bren. She was the one on the crew with military training and had disappeared from the ship ahead of them that morning.

"What the fuck have you done?" a horrified senator asked. "They weren't going to *kill* you."

"And I haven't killed them, though that can soon be rectified. If you like, we can make it three bodies as easily as two…"

"Now, come on, Pel, this was nothing personal, you know that."

"I know, Olly, just business. As is this: the Sanction?"

"Yeah, of course. I've got it here, all ready. Given a choice, I would have preferred to just give it to you in the first place, but…" Olly reached into his jacket and produced his perminal. "Everything's ready, all drawn up. Just needs your retinal scan to confirm acceptance."

Pelquin gave the details no more than a cursory glance before staring directly into the screen for the scan.

Drake heard the captain's wrist-worn perminal give a muted chime to indicate an incoming message. Pelquin opened up the document, studied it for a moment and then smiled.

"It's exactly what you asked for," the senator said, his attitude transformed into the epitome of obsequiousness.

"So it would seem. Thanks, Olly; it's been a pleasure doing business with you, as ever."

"You do realise this is a one use only Sanction? You go into Xter space and you come out again; there's no going back."

"One trip is all I'll need."

"And, sorry, but I have to say this… Please, don't screw up. In effect, you'll be an ambassador for humanity while the Sanction is evoked. If you mess up in any way the potential repercussions don't bear thinking about."

An odd time for the senator to get conscientious by Drake's reckoning, but better late than never.

"Olly," Pelquin said, "you know you can trust me."

Following Pelquin's lead, Drake climbed back into the car, the twitching steadily subsiding and the pain reduced to a widespread ache.

"What do you expect me to do about these two?" Webster called after them. Terrivel was sitting up, one hand clasped to his shoulder, but Feliz appeared to be badly hurt and had hardly moved.

"Not my problem, Olly," Pelquin replied. "I wasn't the one who brought them into this." And with that they drove away.

"You might have warned me," Drake said.

"Of what? I didn't know for certain how things would play out. Bren was just there as back-up."

Like hell said a silent voice in Drake's head. He couldn't have agreed more.

They stopped round the corner to let Bren in. She scampered across to the car, clutching a holdall, and Pelquin gunned the engine as soon as she was safely inside.

"Where's Nate?" she asked.

"He decided to sit this one out."

She raised an eyebrow but made no further comment.

They were halfway back to the ship when Pelquin received the call. "Shit!" he said in its aftermath.

"What's happened?"

"Our launch slot has been cancelled. The port authorities have impounded the *Comet.*"

They parked in front of a large, oblong redbrick block of a building. The legend above the door declared its purpose candidly: Port Authority Police. Bren had already been dropped off, not wanting whatever she had in the bag to be inspected, so just the two of them marched into an over-bright, over-bland reception area, where Pelquin announced himself to the receptionist.

Their arrival brought an immediate response.

Five uniformed figures appeared – four men and a woman. Five seemed a little heavy-handed to Drake, bearing in mind there were only two of them and they had walked in here of their own volition. A deliberate display on the authorities' part, to demonstrate they meant business. The officer in charge – slightly older than his fellows and, conversely, the only one who *didn't* resemble a nightclub bouncer – said, "Captain Pelquin?"

"That's me," Pelquin confirmed. "And you would be...?"

"Sergeant Willis, of the Port Authority Police. Captain, I'd appreciate it if you would instruct your crew to open up your ship and make all records available for inspection. They are currently being... less than helpful."

"With all due respect, sergeant, like hell I will."

Willis smiled. "Don't be an arse. We're going to gain remote access to your systems eventually, with or without your permission. Things will go better for you if you co-operate."

"What exactly do we stand accused of, Sergeant?"

"The way I hear it, you made an unauthorised departure from New Sparta, recklessly endangering lives and ignoring instructions to abort."

"That's bullshit," Pelquin said, looking suitably outraged.

"Be that as it may, I'm duty bound to investigate the allegations."

"Sergeant," Drake spoke up for the first time. "I'd advise a degree of care here. My employers have a considerable investment in Captain Pelquin's current venture and will be concerned by any unnecessary delay."

"Is that so? And you are?"

"Corbin Thaddeus Drake; senior representative of First Solar Bank."

I like that 'senior' bit, Mudball said.

"First Solar, huh? Then I'll interview you too, Mr Senior Representative, and you can explain to me what your employers' part is in all this."

Drake remained deadpan, though the previous evening's encounter with Alexis had rattled him more than he cared to admit. He'd been circumspect when living on Brannan's, as was his habit, but he hadn't been a complete hermit, and last night had proved that the odds should never be taken for granted, no matter how much you thought them stacked in your favour. It only took one person at the wrong place at the wrong time…

Logically, he ought to be safe. He'd declared an officially sanctioned identity to this Sergeant Willis, one that could be confirmed readily enough. There was no need for anyone to look beyond that. And yet, what if they did? What if there was the ghost of an image somewhere on a forgotten system that might be dredged up? He'd been careful in that former life, but had he been careful enough?

The sergeant spoke to his men, indicating Pelquin. "Throw him in a cell, and put this one in the waiting room. Oh, and, Gav, *don't* leave him alone in there; okay?"

Drake found himself ushered to a windowless oblong box of a room, totally in keeping with expectations. He settled onto one of a line of moulded, hard plastic chairs set against a wall; each indistinguishable from the next. The hapless officer, Gav, sat down opposite him.

Feeble lighting from a low-energy ceiling strip completed the picture. Drake would have been hard pressed to imagine a more cheerless room had he deliberately set out to design one. If the cells were a step down from this, then God help Pelquin.

Not that Drake minded the sparse surroundings. He was too busy to worry about comfort. He slipped his perminal from his pocket, linked into the local infonet and started to manipulate the touch screen.

He paused at the sound of a chair leg scraping and glanced up to find his guard looking far from comfortable, as if caught in two minds.

"Gavin, isn't it?" he said quickly and smiled. "Look, Gavin, the

187

sergeant told you to keep me here. He said nothing about my having to sit still and stare at these bare walls all the while, did he?"

"Well, I…"

"So I might as well get some work done while I'm waiting. That's if you've no objection. You have my word that I won't kick up a fuss or give you any trouble. I'll just sit here quietly and work."

"I suppose there's no harm."

"Exactly, none at all. Thank you." With that, Drake bowed his head and went to work, not knowing how much time he had.

The First Solar name had kept him out of a cell for now, but he needed it to do a lot more than that; he needed Sergeant Willis to see both the bank and the representative of that bank standing before him as a significant threat.

"What's that thing on your shoulder?" Gavin asked, before he could properly begin.

"That? That's just my genpet, Mudball."

"Your *what*?"

"Genpet: genetically engineered pet. They're all the rage on New Sparta."

"Oh, right."

Drake smiled and then bowed over his perminal once more. *Can you access this Willis' personal files?* he asked without speaking.

Already done. For a policeman, friend Willis could do with learning a thing or two about personal security.

Drake studied the sergeant's details and an idea began to take shape. Working feverishly, he spawned search after search, questing for answers both on the web and in the sergeant's own personal records. As information gathered and a picture began to emerge, Drake was able to refine his initial plan and set about constructing the means of Sergeant Willis' downfall.

When he was eventually summoned, he strode from the waiting room confident and prepared.

He was taken to a prefab office with windows overlooking the central workspace. The room was slightly on the messy side of neat without quite teetering into the untidy; coffee stains on the desk edge, dust on screens and a generally lived-in feel.

"Drake," the sergeant greeted with no inflection of either warmth or hostility. "Take a seat."

After brief hesitation, the banker did so. A 3D picture stood on the man's desk, double-sided so that the image was visible to the sergeant and his visitors. The picture changed every eight seconds, through a sequence of what were clearly family photos.

"I'm delighted to say that you check out," though he sounded anything but delighted. "It seems you genuinely are an officer of First Solar Bank and, while they're not so big around here, we of course wouldn't want to piss off such an upstanding organisation. So, you won't be joining your friend in the cells. You're free to go."

"Back to the ship?"

"No, not that," and the sergeant chuckled. "The ship's off limits. She's staying right where she is, same as her captain; and if you can do anything to persuade those on board to open up and let us in, so much the better. These are serious charges, and the longer we're denied lawful access the worse this is gonna be for everyone concerned. And we will get access, even if we have to burn our way through her hull to do so."

"Ah, then I'm afraid you *will* be pissing off my employers, very much so. The ship in question *and* its captain are currently engaged in a business venture directly sponsored by First Solar Bank..."

"Yeah, I heard all about what you're up to from your pal, Pelquin. Cache hunting, isn't it? If you ask me, that's no better than stealing – just grave robbing with a fancy name."

Drake drew a deep breath. *One of those.* "I think you're being a little harsh, sergeant," he countered, flashing his most disarming smile. "I would say it's more akin to respectful exploration and recovery, comparable to the uncovering of the Egyptian pyramids back on ancient Earth. At the time, that process greatly improved mankind's understanding of a once mighty and highly advanced culture. How much more do we stand to gain from increased understanding of the Elders? By reclaiming and examining..."

"Yeah, yeah, whatever," Willis interrupted, "but it's still grave robbing in my book, and I'm not sorry to be putting the kibosh on this little venture of yours, wherever you might be bound. First Solar evidently value you, and while that's good enough to keep you out of a cell for now, it doesn't mean I have to like the fact."

Drake allowed himself a cold smile. The sergeant's attitude made what was coming all the easier. "While I was waiting in your... charming waiting room, I was able to compose a message..."

"Well, I'm glad your time wasn't completely wasted. Now, if you'll excuse me," and Willis waved a hand towards the door. Drake ignored him. He had been watching as the 3D images in the desk frame slipped one to another, waiting for the picture he felt sure must be there to come around, as it now had.

"Is that your home, sergeant?" he asked, indicating the picture.

"What?"

"It's a lovely place, I must say. I can quite understand why you would be willing to take on such a hefty mortgage to buy it. That must be a worry though, I would have thought – all the money you owe."

"What? What the fuck business is that of yours? How dare you..."

"The Bulman Welfare Bank; that's who the mortgage is with, isn't it? A fine institution, no question. Did you know, by the way, that they're a wholly owned subsidiary of First Solar Bank? It's been that way for the best part of, oh, half a century or so. That's why the First Solar name isn't especially prominent here on Brannan's World. Second largest financial institution on the planet, the BWB; why go to all the trouble of establishing our own organisation on Brannan's when all we had to do was take over an existing one?"

"I don't know what..."

"Fascinating things, mortgages – complex financial instruments. Did you read the small print when you signed up for yours? No? I'm not surprised; few people do; there's so much of it, isn't there? All that legal jargon and niggling details – not worth bothering with, are they? Or perhaps they are. A clause that perhaps you *should* have read is the one that allows the lender – BWB in this instance – to call in a loan at any time without justification. Not a clause that's often activated, of course, but you know how banks like to cover all the bases."

"Now just hang on a minute..." An indignant Willis was craning forward and looked set to stand up, but Drake hadn't finished and the policeman froze as if pinned to the spot as the banker renewed his verbal assault.

"I gather your wife was working when you applied for the mortgage – very useful, having a double income like that. How many years is it now since she gave up work? Two, or is it closer to three? Of course, you could always try for a replacement mortgage with another bank, but you'd never be able to borrow anywhere near as much based on your salary alone, even with the pay rises. Still," and Drake smiled, "you could always move to somewhere smaller. A lot smaller."

"You bastard. How dare you threaten me!" Willis *was* on his feet now, pointing dramatically at the door. "Get out of my office *now* or I'll have you thrown in the cells no matter who you work for."

Pelquin, however, was just warming up. "I'm glad you raised the matter of offices," he said, easing back into the chair and crossing his right leg nonchalantly over his left. "It's interesting, isn't it, that every single building around here, from the warehouses and distribution centres to the headquarters of all the various port authorities, even this impressive edifice we're sitting in right now, is owned by the same company: the Victoria Port Property Management Company, to be precise. Very smart move that, keeping hold of all the land around the port when it was first established – worth a fortune now, of course. So, everyone, from commercial interests to civil departments, rents from the VPPMC; who, incidentally, are a subsidiary of the Corkhill Property Assets Association, who themselves are a subsidiary of the Brannan Property Company, which are owned by an outfit called Lassiter Holdings, which is part of the Hoffman Group, which, it might surprise you to learn, is owned by... First Solar Bank. Are you sensing a pattern here?

"The message I mentioned, the one I composed while waiting to see you, is addressed to one Kenneth Brockheimer, the man who oversees First Solar's interests here on Brannan's World. If sent, it will set in motion a most unfortunate chain of events, resulting in a demand for instant repayment of your mortgage reaching you tomorrow morning and notice being served on the lease for this property, making it clear that your continued employment within this department is the reason for said notice."

Willis said nothing for a protracted second, before managing, "You're bluffing."

"No I'm not, Sergeant Willis. I never bluff. You can verify everything I've said in minutes. The ownership of the Bulman Welfare Bank and the Hoffman Group are matters of public record and I'm sure you can call up your own mortgage contract. Oh, and one more thing while we're having this little chat. This is your son, Jai Pol, isn't it?" He indicated the latest image displayed on the photo cube. "Sweet looking boy, by the way – clearly takes after his mother. He goes to a rather exclusive school, I understand."

"What's that got to do with anything?" Dismay had replaced indignation in the sergeant's voice and the rising note of alarm was unmistakable.

"The Calbreith School for Technical Excellence – a very impressive title. It's a shame they didn't include excellence in financial management as part of the curriculum. You're aware, I take it, that the school's former Treasurer, a Miss Emilia Pershaw, absconded some ten months ago with a considerable sum of the money that had been entrusted to her care? No? Well, I suppose it's not the sort of thing that such a prestigious institution would wish to make public. Your colleagues in the police haven't found her yet, by the way, and nor have they recovered the funds. The school came close to financial collapse. No need to worry, though. Thankfully, a company called Bulman Investments stepped in and provided a substantial loan to prop up the tottering edifice. Recognise the name? Yes, you're quite right, Bulman Investments is a subsidiary of the Bulman Welfare Bank, which is owned by... But you know that part by now.

"The situation is only temporary, of course. I'm sure the school will recover and endure in the long run; but, in the *short* term, they're dependent on that loan and, need I say, deeply, *deeply* grateful.

"Now, let's be candid here. Your grounds for holding the ship *Pelquin's Comet* are spurious and clearly motivated by malice. I don't know whether you are the person directly responsible for this outrage or somebody higher up in the chain of command, and frankly I don't care. Whoever's getting the payback on this, *you* are the man I'm dealing with and *you* are the man who will suffer as a consequence. If you do not give immediate clearance for *Pelquin's Comet* to leave port, I will send this message, and by tomorrow morning you will have no home, no job, and your son will have been expelled from his highly prestigious school.

"Tell me, Sergeant Willis, is your wife an understanding woman?"

Ten minutes later Drake walked out of the port authority police building with Pelquin at his side. Neither looked back and for the first few moments neither spoke, as if by doing so they might risk fracturing the spell and bring events tumbling down upon their heads once more. They simply walked at a smart pace towards where they knew the *Comet* to be waiting.

"Not sure what the hell sort of magic you worked back there, Drake, but I owe you one," Pelquin said at last.

Too true he does, Mudball concurred.

Drake just kept walking, his thoughts troubled. Being a bank representative in the field often required quick thinking and the use of initiative. His employers expected as much and were happy to turn a blind eye to a certain degree, so long as it got the job done. However, Drake knew there was a point beyond which the bank would refuse to condone his actions and disown him if things turned sour. He had a feeling he might just have crossed that line.

"Hell of a job. Well done." De Souza stared at Archer approvingly, impressed despite himself; though it was past time the man started to pull his weight. A few hours ago, all his plans had threatened to collapse into rack and ruin. Pelquin and Drake were languishing in custody and the *Comet* impounded. In a fit of rage, de Souza had demanded that Archer *do something about it...* And, wonder of wonders, he had. De Souza wasn't sure *how* Archer had managed it, but all concerned were now free as birds. He was forced to admit that the banker had surprised him this time.

Not that Archer looked particularly triumphant... "I wish I could take the credit," he said, "but the truth is I had nothing to do with it."

"Oh?"

"I told you Drake was good. He managed to talk his way out of jail himself, somehow."

Dear Lord, the idiot didn't even have enough intelligence to claim glory when de Souza was trying to thrust it upon him. "Lucky for us that he did, then."

"Yeah."

"Did you at least manage to discover who tipped off the authorities to the *Comet*'s stunt at New Sparta?"

Archer shook his head. "Could have been any of the ships that arrived here in the past few days; without backtracking each and every one of them there's no way of knowing."

So he hadn't succeeded in *any* of the tasks de Souza had set him; what a surprise.

"You do realise that Pelquin's going to assume it was us, don't you?" Archer continued.

De Souza nodded distractedly. Of course he realised – and had done so the moment Pelquin was arrested. Did Archer really think that everyone's mental processes moved as sluggishly as his own? "That's no bad thing, overall. The hot breath of pursuit on the back of their necks can only make them run faster."

Archer smiled and nodded, as if the two of them were colluding as equals. The idiot.

EIGHTEEN

The ship was cleared for departure within minutes of Pelquin and the banker returning. Bren had made it back on board just ahead of them.

Pelquin was feeling *good*. This was due in no small part to the excitement of what lay ahead, but it was more than that. He felt secure. An odd thing to claim perhaps when the dice were rolling on the biggest gamble of his life, but it was true none the less. Ever since New Sparta and the decision he'd been forced to make regarding Monkey, Pelquin felt that his authority had been slipping and that he no longer commanded the full support of his crew, particularly Bren. Bit by bit, though, he'd won them back, and that was important to him; more important than he'd realised. With his ship and this crew once more at his back, he felt whole again, cocksure even, ready to defy the universe and deal with whatever obstacles life tossed at him.

He finally released the coordinates of the cache world to Anna. Until now they had been secreted away in a bubble file isolated from everything else and accessible only via his own perminal; he wasn't taking any chances, not with this.

The cache was located on an Earth type world which was not so very far inside Xter space. There were pluses and minuses to this. On the plus side, the fact that this wasn't natural territory for the Xters doubtless accounted for the cache going undiscovered for so long, and this being a human-friendly world meant that Pelquin could tap Oily up for the Sanction that lent the trip a thin veneer of legality. On the minus side, the same factors made the host world a natural target for the integration programme, which meant that a genuine survey team would be dispatched there sooner rather than later.

He and Nate knew they had to act quickly but also that they had to do so effectively. Rather than dashing straight to First Solar with the gonk, they'd set things up properly: ensuring the brief recording of the cache shown to Terry Reese was professionally scrubbed of any locational indicators, commissioning a cloaking system from Babylon, setting up the opportunity to confront Oily on Brannan's World...

Only once everything was in place did they approach the bank.

The one fly in the ointment was Jossyren. He'd expected interference at New Sparta; he and Nate knew the mining corporation had a strong presence there, but how had they turned up on Brannan's World? Despite his assurances to Anna before they landed, he was in no doubt that the attempt to have him arrested and the ship impounded could only have one source. Oily wouldn't have dared a tactic like that. Thanks to Anna's vigilance he knew that the Jossyren ship was there *ahead* of them... which meant they'd known in advance where the *Comet* was going. But how was that possible, when the only person he'd discussed things with was Nate?

He shook his head, refusing to accept where that train of thought was leading. He had too much riding on this to start doubting Nate at this point.

Jossyren aside, everything was going more or less to plan. The need to replace damaged equipment and find a new mechanic had delayed them at Babylon and left things tight but they'd still made it to Brannan's in time for the reception, and the nonsense with Sergeant Willis and the Victoria Port Authority had delayed them a little, but not significantly.

Bren seemed to have forgiven him for his treatment of Monkey. She had backed him all the way with Oily Webster, and she and Nate were currently setting up the Ptarmigan, deploying the cloaking device's relays at strategic parts of the ship as if she'd been doing things like this all her life. The Ptarmigan might be overkill in some folk's eyes but he felt better for having it, and between that and Oily's Sanction, he reckoned things were pretty well covered.

As the *Comet* left Brannan's World behind and prepared to enter RzSpace, Pelquin decided it was time to take Drake's advice and confide in the crew.

This ought to be fun.

Drake noted that the brief sojourn in a police cell had done nothing to dampen Pelquin's spirits. In fact, quite the opposite; Pelquin seemed in ebullient mood now that they were close to their goal and his irrepressible good humour was proving infectious. Even Nate Almont managed to crack a smile in Drake's presence, while whatever resentment Bren might have felt towards her captain had clearly melted away. He seemed fully reinstated as the apple of her eye.

Many politicians and talented performers struggled to compensate for a lack of natural 'presence'. Pelquin had no such problem. At the reception Drake had seen that Pelquin had charisma in bucket loads; more than enough to keep audiences attentive and ensure that his opinion was heard and listened to. It was at times like this, as the captain stood in front of his assembled crew and prepared to address them, that Drake could almost see what so attracted Bren. In this sort of mood Pelquin could charm the fish from the sea and the stars from the skies, so selling the crew on an illegal excursion into Xter space should be simplicity itself.

"All right, you'll be glad to hear that as of now we're heading straight for the cache," Pelquin announced to a smattering of cheers. "So from here on in I want everyone to be on their mettle. This is the Big One, boys and girls, the once in a lifetime opportunity, so let's not mess it up. We're about to pull off a raid that even Cornische and his Dark Angels would have been proud of!"

The knowledge that they were now directly en route to the Elder cache put everyone in a party mood. Even Drake, if he were honest. He would be glad when this one was over. Mudball sensed his unease. *Say the word and I can seize control of the ship,* his silent companion assured him.

Thanks, that's very reassuring.

If the alien caught the sarcasm he didn't show it. *Don't worry, I'm raring to go; just give me the green light and I'll be all over these systems like a rash. They won't know what's hit them.*

And where exactly would that get us? Drake asked.

In control, of course. You don't really trust Pelquin and you sure as hell don't trust Almont. Seize control. Let them dance to our pattern for a change.

Tune, Drake told him. *It's dance to our tune.* He corrected Mudball by long-established reflex, though the little alien rarely made such idiomatic errors these days. *You really think you could control and navigate a starship with just me for help?*

Probably.Maybe.

And what would we do with Pelquin and the rest of the crew? There are no secure facilities on board, don't forget, and not enough cryochambers for everyone, before you suggest that.

We could always toss them out the airlock.

Thanks but no thanks.

Well, just remember I offered.

Pelquin was still talking. "Now, as seems fitting for such a bountiful trove of glorious goodies, things haven't exactly been easy up to this point, as we're all aware, and they aren't likely to get any more comfortable from here on in. You know what it's like on this ship – we never do anything the easy way."

"You can say that again."

From the moment he'd allowed *Pelquin's Comet* to blast off from New Sparta without challenge Drake was complicit in that act and in everything else that followed. When he stood by and watched as the ship entered RzSpace in the face of direct police instruction to stand down, he was complicit; and again, when he was less than fully open with the PoD back on Babylon and had subsequently bullied the Brannan's World authorities into releasing Pelquin and his ship... he was complicit. The thing was, taken individually each decision had been logical and even justifiable. It was only when you added them all together that it became apparent just how many boundaries he was stretching on this trip.

The discretion afforded him by First Solar only stretched so far. It had happened by increments, with his condoning one minor indiscretion after another, but he now had as much invested in the success of this venture as anyone. Return with a hold bulging full of Elder artefacts and it was astonishing what could be forgiven: all hail the healing qualities of wealth! Generous reparation presented in proper fashion could dampen the most righteous of civic indignation.

Nice of Mudball to let him know that he was in a position to take control of the *Comet*, but, with all due respect to the alien, *so what?*

Pelquin's next pronouncement dragged Drake's attention fully back to the meeting. "So, there are a few things you need to be aware of," he said. "For starters, the cache we're about to claim is in Xter space."

After a moment's stunned silence, Bren said, "And you didn't think this little detail worth mentioning to us before now?"

"Worth mentioning, certainly; *wise* to mention, no I didn't; not with Jossyren snapping at our heels and trying to sabotage us at every turn. Not until we *couldn't* be stopped. And that's not meant as a slight on anyone; just hear me out, okay? I realise we're playing a little fast and loose with the legal side of things here, but it won't be the first time we've done that and we're not pushing things as much as you might think." A quick glance in Drake's direction at this point. "That was why we stopped over at Brannan's. As we all know, we've got our section of space and the Xters have theirs, but a lot of folk – humans and Xters alike – want to see that change."

Bren snorted. "Fat chance."

"That's as maybe, but the hope is that before long we'll be allowed to settle human-friendly worlds inside the limits of Xter space which they've ignored as being more hassle than they're worth, and the Xters will settle on worlds in human space which are ideal for them and not so for us. Eventually, no more borders, just one big happy human and Xter universe."

"Would that work, though?" Anna piped up. "I mean, aren't we already colonising the marginal worlds here in our own sector?"

"That's not entirely true," Drake said. "You'd be surprised at how many marginals have been abandoned in the last century as folk get tired of working their backsides off merely to survive and realise there's a much easier way of life to be had elsewhere. A new world opens up offering fresh opportunity and suddenly scratching around trying to eke out a living on a planet that doesn't really want you there loses its appeal. There are still colonies on a few of the marginal worlds, but a lot less than you'd think, and people can always be relocated if needed."

The situation was more complex than that, of course. Most of the settlements that still remained on the marginals were mining communities. They weren't so much interested in claiming another planet for the greater good of humanity as they were in plundering its natural resources for the good of their own pockets. Such folk were hardly likely to welcome Xter settlers with open arms. This, in Drake's view, was why the 'greater sharing' idea was doomed to fail: if humanity couldn't find one use for a world it could always find another; but it suited him at that moment to support Pelquin.

"Still sounds like wishful thinking to me," Bren said. "I bet you half a cache share that a hundred years from now the Xters are still sitting on their side of the fence and we're still stuck on ours, glaring at each other with mistrust and menace."

"Maybe you're right," Pelquin said, "but who cares? That's not the point. The point is that the groundwork for this 'greater sharing' is already underway. Low key, and out of the public eye because nobody wants to start a panic, but at this very moment expeditions from both races are being authorised to slip quietly across the border and into each other's space to carry out feasibility studies on potential worlds with a view to future settlement; and, as of now… we're one of them."

"No fucking way!" Bren looked both stunned and amused.

Pelquin grinned, clearly enjoying himself. "*That* was what our recent altercation with Olly Webster was all about."

"You mean *Oily* Webster," Bren said.

"One and the same, though these days he prefers to be addressed as Senator Oliver Webster and is a highly respected pillar of the community; the sort that can't afford the faintest whiff of scandal."

"Such as the fact that he used to bankroll a large scale smuggling operation bringing contraband goods onto Brannan's, you mean."

"That's exactly what I mean. Old Oily is now one of the big noises in the 'greater sharing' integration programme, and he has been persuaded…" Bren snorted. "… to arrange for the *Comet* to be officially registered as one of the ships involved."

"You mean that, as of now, we're all on official government business."

"To an extent… yes."

"Good Lord," the doc muttered.

"I know," Pelquin said. "It just goes to prove that there really *is* a first time for everything."

This time they were in RzSpace for a while, and it showed. It wasn't that passion and urgency deserted you at the flick of a switch, more that it seeped away bit by bit, as if by osmosis; compulsion and the ability to feel anything strongly leaked away, like colour draining from an old photograph left exposed to the full glare of sunlight. Drake tended to look back on extended visits to RzSpace as time spent in a sepia world.

Had he been a religious man, he might even have suggested that when you entered RzSpace you were stripped of your soul, only reconnecting with that most intangible facet of self on returning to normal space. RzSpace possessed an implacable sense of dispassion which seeped into a person to replace all the intensity that bled away.

Scientists insisted that this much-reported phenomenon had no substance in fact, but Drake wasn't so sure. He believed himself a rational man capable of telling the difference between delusion and perception, and he had experienced the effects of RzSpace too often to discount it so glibly.

RzSpace was a mathematical construct that demonstrably worked but which continued to defy physical definition. Turn a ship's monitors on in RzSpace and all they reported was static. The same was true of every type of sensor, receiver, collection device or monitor, in fact for *anything* that mankind had yet thought to try. All produced the same result: nothing. Abstract formulae remained the *only* quantifiable definition available.

On this trip to date, *Pelquin's Comet* had done little more than dip in and out of RzSpace in short bursts, giving few opportunities for the malaise to take hold. This final stretch, however, was a little longer, and Drake was treated to one of the most blatant examples of the phenomenon he had yet seen.

When he might otherwise have expected to see excitement among the crew ratchet upwards, the opposite held true. Within moments of emerging into normal space, however, all that changed. Enthusiasm that had been suppressed in Rz rekindled. Bren in particular seized upon this return of spirit. Drake heard her laughing, quickly joined by somebody else – Nate, he thought.

Drake was one of the first to the bridge following the return to normal space, Bren and Nate close behind. Pelquin had announced in advance that as soon as they came out of Rz he was going to activate the Ptarmigan, and everyone was curious to see the cloaking device in action. They needn't have bothered; it proved to be something of an anti-climax, in that there was no discernible sign of it working at all.

"Is that it?" Bren asked. "No fireworks, no sizzle of energy, no strange new vibration in the air, not even a tingle?"

Ignoring her, Pelquin told Anna to activate the viewing screens.

Drake had been on ships where the entire front-facing wall would turn virtual-transparent and display a magnified image of what lay ahead; but an old comet class cargo hauler enjoyed no such luxuries. Instead, screens in front of the pilot seats blinked to life – three virtual windows, all currently showing the same section of space dominated by a blue and white orb, still too distant to discern much beyond that.

"At least in Rz the monitors go blank so you know that *something's* happening," Bren muttered. "I reckon they've sold you a dud, Pel. I mean, how do you even tell when this Ptarmigan is on or off?"

"Have a little faith, Bren. The systems say it's on line, so let's go with that, okay?"

"If you insist. When somebody takes a shot at us the first time we try to sneak past them, it'll be too late for me to say 'I told you so'."

"Magnify," Pelquin instructed Anna, again ignoring Bren. The image jumped closer, gaining definition. It now looked like a dark blue ball over which somebody had melted a candle, the melted wax congealing to form a tattered and irregular white coating.

"And again." The image leapt closer still, now filling the majority of all three screens. Brown and green could now be seen amongst the blue; land masses glimpsed in the cloud breaks.

"Wow," Anna said.

Most there were hardened spacers who had approached dozens if not hundreds of worlds before, but this was a little different: a virgin Earth-type planet. No ships coming and going, no orbital stations, no satellites to clutter the approaches, no radio chatter or electronic pollution bleeding out into the vastness of space, no cities clustered around its rivers and coasts, no industry, no traffic control to identify incoming ships and guide them in, and no infonet. An unblemished world, with none of the trappings of civilisation, good or bad, just a great big blue globe swathed in a mantle of clouds, serenely following its predestined course around the sun.

Even Nate, who had been here before, seemed a little awed. All of them knew they were unlikely to encounter anything quite like this again.

"It's almost spooky," Anna said quietly.

"But at the same time majestic and quite, quite beautiful," Bren added. "It's like a new Eden."

Drake had a feeling the name might stick, at least for those aboard the *Comet*.

Pelquin clapped his hands, just the once but loudly, which caused Anna to jump in her seat and effectively broke the mood. He then rubbed palms and fingers together, saying, "And it will all become even *more* beautiful once we reach the cache. Focus, people, focus!"

Suddenly Anna was all business again, reeling off length of time before they hit the planet's outer atmosphere, expected time until landing, and confirming systems' status. The screens returned to normal magnification and others started to drift away, doubtless to make their own preparations for planet fall.

Drake stayed at the back of the cramped cockpit, mesmerised by this marbled jewel suspended in space. He was a little surprised when, after disappearing with the others, Leesa returned to nudge him and hold out a bulb of chilled water.

What was this, a peace offering? He accepted with a quiet 'thank you', to which she nodded before turning her attention to the screens.

Careful it isn't poisoned, Mudball cautioned.

Leesa stayed to watch. He sipped at the water, making a conscious effort not to stare at her, determined not to turn her fetching him a drink into a big deal.

The world – Eden – drew rapidly closer, and it wasn't long before they'd established a low orbit while Anna and Pelquin pinpointed the cache location based on Nate's coordinates. Once that was done the ship began its descent. Although she could operate in atmosphere when required, the *Comet* was most at home in the far rarer medium of space. As with most interstellar ships, aerodynamics had been a low priority in her design, which left her with a high sink rate, especially in lower atmosphere. Descent was therefore far more rapid than it would have been with a purpose-built atmosphere-loving aeroplane. Drake should probably have gone and strapped himself in somewhere, but he stayed where he was, keen to watch this new world reveal itself as the veils of cloud drew apart. Leesa stayed too, possibly out of 'anything you can do' determination, though in fairness she seemed as absorbed by the images on the screen as he was.

Watching the ocean and then the vast landmass rush towards them, and considering all that this world represented, Drake's thoughts wandered a little, revisiting the enigma of intelligent life and its scarcity.

Studies of human and Xter DNA had shown no correlation of any significance between the two – nothing that couldn't be explained by chance and parallel evolution. It was a blow to those who had predicted a traceable common root, confident that the comparison would support their view that man's development was something other than entirely natural. Loudest among these was a sizeable minority lobby group who insisted that humans were merely one of several races seeded across the stars by the Elders before their departure. The DNA results proved to be far from a fatal blow to them, though, as they rallied behind the argument that such omnipotent beings would of course ensure the races they seeded were as genetically diverse as possible.

None of which prevented those who maintained that man's evolution was a purely natural Darwinian process from feeling a little smug.

Drake had always favoured the Darwinian view, but seeing this pristine world caused him to wonder. A complex macro ecology teeming with life: highly developed flora and fauna, forests, abundant oceans, jungles, herds of grazers supported by vast plains of grasses, doubtless carnivores as well... yet no sign of intelligence beyond basic hunter-killer levels. Why had advanced intelligence developed on Earth but not here?

Was it simply that they had arrived here too early in this world's development? If left untouched for a few thousand years would a species with technologically capable intelligence emerge to shape the raw material of Eden to its will? Or had the denizens of Earth been beneficiaries in the greatest of all cosmic lotteries; had they simply been *lucky*? Another option, of course, was that mankind had received a gentle but crucial nudge in the right direction from benefactors unknown.

"Are you still with us, Drake?"

Drake looked up to find Pelquin staring at him. "Yes," he assured the captain. "I was just admiring the view."

It fell to Anna to bring everyone's eager anticipation crashing down. "Ehm, skip," she said. "I don't know how to tell you this, but it looks like someone has beaten us to it."

"What?"

"There's another ship down there, parked right on top of the cache site."

Nineteen

"The ship's systems are still active and judging by the residual heat around her drive she's a recent arrival – been down a couple of hours at most," Anna said. "But I'm not picking up any life signs."

The *Comet*'s crew had crowded back onto the bridge. Nate had pushed forward to position himself behind and between the two chairs, studying the displays intently, and Pelquin was conscious of the weight of expectation from those behind him. They *couldn't* be thwarted, not this close to their goal.

"I wonder who this other lot are," Bren said. "Jossyren?"

They didn't have a visual as yet.

Pelquin shook his head. "Doubt it. They'd have no way of knowing where the cache is." He resisted the urge to look at Nate. "More likely to be local action."

"Xters, you mean?" Bren said.

"Yeah, that would be my guess."

"Shit!"

"That'd be my guess too, given these readings," Anna chipped in.

Nobody seemed inclined to expand on that. All present knew that the legality of their presence in Xter space was flimsy at best. Explaining how they just happened to pitch up at a previously undiscovered Elder cache site would bend credibility to breaking point.

"Might whoever they are still be inside the chamber?" Pelquin wondered. "Would that shield them from our sensors?"

"Maybe," Nate said. "Anything's possible given Elder technology, and I know from experience how difficult it is to get a signal through the walls of a chamber – but I doubt it, not completely,"

"Which means that either the crew of that ship aren't here anymore…" Bren said.

"…or they're not alive anymore," Pelquin finished for her.

"Pretty much," Nate said. "And since the ship is very obviously still here, I reckon we can downplay the likelihood of option one."

Pelquin agreed. It seemed unlikely that anyone would park a ship next to an Elder cache and then simply wander off somewhere else. "Looks as if those cache defences you came up against last time have been reset and rebuilt."

"Yeah.Hardly a surprise."

A cheery thought, all the same.

Any doubts regarding the origins of the other ship disappeared as soon as they saw it.

The cache was buried within the steep slope of a hill, the mouth of the access tunnel gaping like a recently excavated cave; which, in a sense, it was. A ship, perhaps twice as long as the *Comet*, nestled on the ground a short distance away from the entrance.

Pelquin had seen images of Xter ships, so what confronted them didn't come as a total surprise. Unlike human ships, which boasted any number of variations dependent on model, manufacturer, place of origin, purpose, Xter vessels all seemed to follow the same basic design, differing only in scale. Very utilitarian, displaying a homogeneity that only helped emphasise their alienness.

At the prow, a bulbous, tapering nose, pitted and layered as if by scales – access vents, sensor arrays, weapons systems: the layering could house all of those – the result made the front section resemble a squat pine cone resting on its side. From the 'base' of this cone a series of identical cylinders emerged – three in this instance, though Pelquin knew that these could run into the dozens in larger vessels. The three tubes were apparently fused together to form the ship's fuselage – two currently in parallel closest to the ground, one resting above them – but in truth they were modular: detachable, transferable, replaceable; and, despite appearances, each served a different purpose. He guessed that in this instance one probably housed the engines, a second would serve as the hold and the third most likely crew quarters.

This was the secret of Xter design – the modules were interchangeable. One ship, no matter which world it had been had built on, could be hybridised with any other to serve whatever purpose; all dictated by the selection of modules incorporated into its hull. There were people who didn't accept this, who insisted that the aliens had to be holding something back. Surely somewhere deep inside Xter space, safe from any prying human sensors, they must be hiding specialist warships if nothing else. But, if so, no human had ever seen or caught a hint of one.

Pelquin stared at the monitors as they approached, taking in the contours of the strange vessel.

"Still no answer, I take it," he asked Anna, who had been hailing the other ship continuously as they approached.

She shook her head. "Not even an automated response. It's as if they just popped out, intending to be back in a minute or two."

He grunted; that probably wasn't far from the truth.

"When we land," Nate murmured, "I want to scoot over and take a look at that thing."

"No," Pelquin said. "We need you here. You're the only one who's been inside the cache chamber."

"Well someone ought to go across and check it out."

"I'll go, if anyone does," Bren said immediately.

Pelquin didn't reply. His attention shifted from the Xter ship to the gaping maw of the cache chamber's tunnel. It beckoned like the open trap it was, as Nate and his mining buddies had found to their cost.

Quite what they'd been doing in this sector of space was another matter entirely. "Exploring new opportunities away from the clutches of the big corporates," had been Nate's explanation when asked. Pelquin wanted to accept that, wanted to trust his old buddy without reservation, and yet...

As if on cue, Bren said, "Remind me, how the hell did you find this place again?"

"A little out-of-bounds prospecting," Nate admitted. "You know how it is: the big cartels like Jossyren have all the rich pickings sewn up, leaving us independents to feed on scraps, scratching around the fringes of the asteroid belts hoping to strike it lucky."

"So you came all the way out *here*? There must have been easier options, surely; safer ones at least." Good old Bren; where Pelquin might ponder a question, she just came right out and asked.

"We were desperate. We'd had a run of bad luck; one trip after another which yielded sod all. Debts were mounting and morale was lower than Monkey's IQ... We knew the next one had to produce, big time, and the chances of finding anything rich enough in human space was pretty close to zero, so..."

"Yeah, but *Xter space*?"

"Yeah, Xter space. Live with it," Nate said, evidently tiring of the questions.

"It's not as outrageous as it sounds," Drake said. "It's a big frontier out here. Slipping across unnoticed would be a lot easier than you might think, especially since RzSpace doesn't recognise the arbitrary boundaries we've created."

What, the banker coming to Nate's defence?

"Right," Nate said, clearly as surprised at this unexpected support as Pelquin was. "It was an all or nothing gamble, but we didn't go in blind, we'd done our homework. Human-friendly worlds, just inside Xter space, uncolonised and with no record of mining or other activity; that's what we were looking for. This one came out top of the list."

"Still sounds like a hell of a risk to me."

"Which is why we've taken a few more precautions than Nate's crew did this time around," Pelquin felt obliged to point out.

"And when you arrived at this world, you just happened to stumble on the cache?" Bren prompted.

"Pretty much. We were carrying out preliminary remote scans – surveying a number of potential sites for minerals etc – when we came across an anomaly, buried just beneath the surface, at the foot of a hill."

"The Elder cache."

"Lucky bastard."

"You think? Nate said. "I'm the only one left alive from that whole crew… You call that lucky?

"You're alive, aren't you?"

"Yeah… There is that."

Bren looked as if she were about to add something but evidently thought better of it. Instead she looked at Pelquin and said, "So what do we do now, skip, with another ship in situ and all? Tip-toe meekly away and give up on this whole thing?"

"Like hell," Pelquin said. "We wait."

"For what?More Xters to show up?"

"No, to see if these ones do. If they *are* inside the chamber collecting artefacts and somehow our sensors have missed them, they'll have to come out eventually. And don't forget that if that *is* what they're doing, the chances are they're just as illegal as we are. The Xter authorities prefer to leave elder caches undisturbed from what I hear. And this lot have brought just one small ship with them. Does that sound like an official operation to you? Where's all the support staff, the bureaucracy, the warnings for us to stay away as soon as we came anywhere close to Eden's atmosphere? No, these are privateers like us. If they're bringing stuff up then they're doing so to sell. So, we're much the same, them and us, and we're the ones with the tactical advantage; our ship's in the air while theirs is a sitting duck on the ground."

"Why, Captain, you're not seriously suggesting we rob them, are you?" Bren asked, feigning shock.

"No, actually I'm not." *Not yet, at any rate.* "We're not pirates." At least they weren't when they had a representative from First Solar Bank on board. "I'm just saying that tactically we've got the higher ground so to speak; we're mobile while they're just squatting there, which puts us in a strong bargaining position, that's all."

"If there's anyone left alive to bargain with," Nate said.

"Do Xters really go in for that sort of thing – robbing caches, I mean?" Bren said.

"Sure they do."

"Since when did you become such an expert on alien behaviour, anyhow?"

"What if they don't come up?" Anna asked.

"Sorry?"

"What if they never emerge from the chamber?"

"Then we can assume the cache defences got them, which means there's one less source of competition for us to worry about."

"Oh, right, of course. We just have to worry about whatever it was that killed them," Bren said.

"That's where we came in, boys and girls." Pelquin pointed out. "So let's just sit tight for the moment and see what happens, shall we?"

No one had anything more to add. They waited for a little over half an hour without any sign of activity, the *Comet* circling in as tight a holding pattern as she could manage in atmosphere.

At length, Anna said, "We're burning up a lot of fuel, skip."

Pelquin was aware of that.

"I don't think there's anyone left alive in there," Bren opined.

"I reckon you're right," he agreed. "Anna, set us down close to the other ship, but keep the engines warm and be ready for a quick dust off." He then turned to Bren, saying, "Let's get one of those new probes programmed and set to fly, shall we?"

"Now we're talking!"

New tech; always guaranteed to float Bren's boat. She was on her way in an instant.

"I'll give her a hand," Nate said.

"Okay, but don't use being down in the cargo hold as an excuse to slope off and take a peek at the Xter ship." Nate had a stubborn streak; he'd always been a bit of a maverick, but in the past Pelquin had thought of him as *his* maverick; now he wasn't so sure. "We'll have a look at her *after* we've claimed the contents of the cache. Understood?"

"I hear you."

The ground was uneven and dotted with sparse vegetation. Even so, Anna brought the *Comet* down with enough of a bump to jog the froth off a cappuccino but little more. Pelquin rated that as pretty impressive given the lack of a landing area.

"Are we still trying to contact the Xter ship, Anna?"

"Yup; I'm running standard greeting on a continuous loop. Reckon it's a waste of time, though. Still no one over there who wants to talk to us."

"The probe's ready to go," Bren reported within minutes of the ship having settled.

"Send it out, then," he told her.

Considerably larger than the spyflies that had dogged his footsteps on New Sparta, the probes were still wonders of miniaturised tech. Torpedo-like and around the size of a chunky pen, they provided better images than a spyfly ever could and cost a good deal less – though that was purely relative. The damned things were still far from cheap.

With the probe's systems slaved to the *Comet*'s control board, Anna was able to fly the tiny drone out of the ship's hold. She and Pelquin had the best view – the triple screen in front of them showing a panoramic 3D representation of all that the probe encountered. Leesa, Drake and the doc were crowded in behind them, watching over their shoulders. They were soon joined by Nate and Bren.

The native terrain leapt into abrupt focus as the drone set out. This was the same rugged scrubland they'd witnessed on the ship's monitor screen but it had now been brought vividly to life; the uneven ground, which was festooned with tussocks of grass and small spiky bushes, took on contour and gained substance as a result. A series of digits winked into being at the bottom left hand corner of the central image, detailing such things as temperature, barometric pressure, atmospheric composition – Pelquin barely noticed, his attention focused on the hole in the approaching cliff face. Seen from this perspective it didn't resemble a cave at all; more a wound. The opening was too stark and too fresh to be mistaken for anything natural.

As the drone drew closer, the central image zoomed in, while the two side images remained at a more natural definition.

"Residual energy readings," Bren murmured. She was evidently paying more attention to the numbers than he'd been. "A weapon's been discharged here recently." At times like this he was glad to have an ex-soldier on the team.

The first evidence of the party that had preceded them waited at the entrance. Leaning against the left hand wall, apparently abandoned, was a piece of equipment – small, light, and unfathomable.

"We ought to collect that on the way in," Bren said. "Xter stuff can be valuable in its own right."

He murmured acknowledgement.

Under Anna's expert guidance the probe slipped slowly inside the tunnel. Pelquin was pleased by the way its systems automatically compensated for the change in lighting conditions, ensuring that the quality of the images remained pretty much constant despite the drop in illumination. A little further in they came across what looked at first to be another piece of abandoned equipment, but this one proved to be different. Because of the way it rested, slumped against the wall, it took Pelquin a few seconds to realise that this was an Xter spacesuit, and it hadn't been abandoned; except by life itself. The body of the suit's occupant remained firmly in place.

"That's one bulky suit for an Xter," Drake commented.

"Yeah, I agree," Bren replied. "Armoured, I reckon."

Pelquin nodded. "Looks as if they went in there expecting trouble."

"If so, I think they found it. See the wound where the suit's been breached? And that has to be blood. Drying but not yet dried; so this is all very recent." Bren leaned forward and pointed at a position towards the bottom of the left hand screen. "Anna, can you focus there for a sec."

Their perspective pivoted as Anna complied, so that the indicated spot took centre stage, and then they zoomed in.

"Thought so," Bren said. "See where the rock's scorched? And it looks as if something's melted there. The temperature readings are still high as well. Rock retains heat. This area's taken some concentrated energy fire, and not too long ago."

"Nate, what do you reckon?"

"Looks like the smashed remains of the laser trap we hit when I was here before, except that we took it out that time around."

"Then someone rebuilt it."

"Seems so."

The probe continued and two more Xter corpses appeared. They were lying close to each other in the centre of the tunnel floor. Again Anna paused so that they could try to determine what had killed them.

"I don't think it was lasers this time," Bren remarked. "No sign of injuries or damage to the suits."

"Could be sonics," Drake said. "I've encountered that sort of defence before at Elder caches."

"Whatever this was, it looks as if the Xters managed to neutralise it," Anna said, highlighting four points on the tunnel walls where *something* had been destroyed, presumably by weapons' fire.

"These Xters are doing our job for us," the doc murmured. "Two of the cache defences destroyed already."

"Yeah, but it looks as if the defences did for them in the end," Bren reminded him.

"Bren's right," Pelquin said. "Let's not get too smug just yet."

Next they came to a part where the tunnel had partially collapsed – the left hand wall and ceiling having evidently come down.

"Will there be enough room to get the buggy through?" Pelquin wondered.

"I think so, hang on," Anna replied. Some deft repositioning of the drone produced a further scroll of digits. "Just, if I drive carefully and pull the shielding in. We'll have to move that Xter body out of the way first, though."

Two more fallen Xter suits marked the spot; one of them half-buried beneath the rubble. The other was lying prone and blocking the still-open right hand side. A line of fused circuitry – resembling crystal more than anything else – was embedded in a vertical groove in the tunnel wall, exposed by the collapse.

"What do you reckon this was?"

Nate shook his head. "No idea. That wasn't there last time."

"Do you think this is the last of the defences?" Bren asked.

"Only one way to find out." Pelquin signalled Anna to continue advancing the probe.

"We're not that far from the cache chamber itself," Anna murmured. "There can't be too many more…"

The words were no sooner out of her mouth than the screens abruptly went blank. There was a suggestion of rapid movement in the left hand screen and, before anyone could comment let alone react, all three winked out simultaneously.

"Whoa!" Anna said, giving a startled jump.

"One more defence at least, I'd say," Bren quipped.

"Shit!" summed up Pelquin's feelings on the matter. Scrub one expensive piece of kit. Fortunately, he had two equally costly replacements, but no point in committing either of those just yet.

Anna sat forward again, her fingers dancing frantically over the control board, but after a few seconds she shook her head. "Sorry Pel, it's completely dead; nothing's responding."

"Can we replay the last few seconds?" Pelquin asked.

They did, first at normal speed, and then slowed down, and then a third time grossly slowed down. Even at that exaggerated pace, the speed with which the line of pointed metal bars shot out of the wall was frightening. One of them headed straight towards the watcher – the probe – far too swiftly to register let alone evade. Even so, it was pure luck that any of the spikes had caught the probe. They were at least three times its circumference and there was more than enough space for the tiny drone to pass between them. Had it been ten centimetres above or below its actual elevation the probe would likely have survived, disturbed only by the wind of the bars' passage. As it was, one of the spikes had scored a direct hit.

"Let's wind things back a bit and examine the patches of wall those spikes emerged from," Pelquin said. The images played in reverse, the spears retracting to be swallowed by the wall, leaving no apparent trace. "Is there anything to tell us that the spears are there? Anything at all to say that this isn't just another ordinary stretch of tunnel wall?"

Anna shook her head. "No, not as far as the probe's sensors are concerned at any rate."

"Great," Bren muttered. "So we could all end up skewered at any moment. At least it would be quick – at that speed you'd be dead before you even registered the threat."

"The buggy has a more sophisticated sensor system than the probe, so we might be able to spot them," Anna said, sounding far from convinced. "Plus we now know where these ones are. If they're the only set of spikes, problem solved."

"You reckon? Knowing where they are doesn't mean we know how to get past them," the doc said.

Anna summoned up a diagram: a 3D representation of the tunnel. "Okay, judging by the images from the probe, this is what we're dealing with."

The image displayed twin sets of eight spears pushing out from either wall, their tips interweaving at the tunnel's centre.

"Both sides?" Pelquin asked. He had only spotted movement from the left.

"Yeah, if you check the final few frames the spikes release simultaneously from right and left. You just focus on the left ones because they're nearer and that's the direction the probe-killer comes from; it's the most obvious thing there and sort of grabs your attention."

"And once we're in the tunnel, we can pinpoint the exact spots where the stakes emerged?"

"Sure."

"Good. We'll use bonding foam on the placements."

"And if that doesn't work we'll come up with something else," Bren said; showing the sort of support he'd once taken for granted. Hearing it now came as a relief.

"Exactly."

"We're intending to go in through the entrance, I take it?" Nate said.

That brought a sharp look from Bren, as if it had never occurred to her they'd be doing anything else.

"Yeah, looks to be the best option. The Xters have already done at least half our work for us. Trying to open a new tunnel is going to take too long, and this way we avoid any risk of a cave-in."

"We hope," Anna murmured.

"Fair enough."

"You were seriously considering opening a new tunnel into a cache chamber?" Bren asked.

"Considering it, yes; to avoid the defences. Now we're actually here, I'm not so sure it was ever a good idea, but…"

The guardian knows we're here, Mudball told Drake.

You can sense it?

Oh yes, and I hope your friends don't expect to simply stroll in there and help themselves to the contents. They're in for a fight.

This wasn't like Mudball. Normally the little alien was all cocky swagger, boasting about how he could wipe the floor with any guardian of any cache. This time around he sounded almost... worried. *Is this guardian different in some way?* Drake asked.

Strong; very strong.

And does it know you're with us?

No, it's not looking for anything like me and I'm keeping my head down, so to speak.

But you know what it's got planned?

Not the specifics, no. Trying to find out would reveal my presence, but, trust me, that's one seriously pissed off guardian who isn't about to stand by and do nothing.

Duly noted.

No one had yet come up with a wholly satisfactory explanation for the guardian entities. When they were first encountered, in the very early days of cache hunting, it was assumed that these were automated defences which had remained active despite the passing aeons. Not impossible; in theory mankind could readily devise mechanisms of comparable durability. Then it became clear that there was something more going on, that the defences were reactive and in a few cases even proactive. That meant a whole different level of threat, a programmed, guiding intelligence, and slowly the reality of guardian entities dawned on humankind. They weren't always present, tending to occur at the larger caches rather than the smaller ones – though that was far from a universal truth – and they varied in capability and viciousness. It was assumed that these inconsistencies were explained by the passage of time, that some of the guardians had failed to survive while others had deteriorated over the years and were now less than fully functional.

Even the assumption that these were sophisticated systems left in place by the Elders to safeguard the caches was hotly debated: safeguard the caches against what? And why leave the caches behind at all if you were then going to guard against them being accessed?

Nobody had yet found the physical housing for these guardians – the systems they inhabited – and many had looked. Some believed that the Elders had found a way of utilising the very rocks around the caches for this. So many bizarre forms of unexplained tech had been discovered in the caches that nothing could be ruled out.

Drake had his own opinions and his own questions about the guardians. You would think that having Mudball riding on his shoulder and in his thoughts would make him an expert on the subject, but you'd be wrong. If Mudball wasn't a guardian entity, what was he? And if he was, then the guardian entities were not programming at all, at least not in any conventional sense.

On this subject as with so many others Mudball remained evasive to the point of reticence. Of course there were reasons; it wasn't that he didn't want to be helpful, it was just that his memory was impaired... that he had only vague recollections of events so long ago... that the Elders had excised all knowledge of such things from his mind... that it wouldn't be helpful to either Drake as an individual or humanity as a whole to know too much... Drake suspected that this last might at least hold some grain of truth.

One thing Mudball had stipulated at the start of their arrangement was that he wouldn't comment on the nature of the Elders, claiming a similar argument. Drake had agreed at the time – his life had just been saved and he would have agreed to anything – but it wasn't always an easy undertaking to abide by.

They were going in armed. The weapons locker was the only compartment on the ship routinely secured, to the best of Leesa's knowledge. Voice activated, it opened at Pelquin's command; a section of wall sliding away and a double-sided rack emerging from the resultant slot. The arsenal was hardly extensive but it was enough to ensure that everyone would at least be packing something. The stock weapon seemed to be machine pistols – matt black compact weapons with truncated nozzles. Leesa recognised the type: comparatively light, easy to handle, ideal for the enclosed conditions of the cache chamber. They fired slender bullets at high velocity, each slug packing an explosive tip. Two hundred and fifty rounds to a magazine, which was built into the weapon's handle. The captain handed one of the guns each to Anna, Bren, Nate, and Doc.

He hesitated in reaching to unclip a fifth from the rack, looking at Drake and asking, "You ever handled one of these before?"

"Once or twice," the banker replied.

Evidently satisfied, Pelquin handed the gun across. Everyone got a spare magazine as well, before Pelquin took a machine pistol for himself and also a longer-barrelled energy weapon. He then instructed the locker to close.

"Nothing for me?" Leesa asked.

"Nope. No need for you to be armed. You're staying on the ship to monitor us and handle the drones. We're counting on you to warn us if anything starts to go wrong."

"What? But…"

"No buts." Pelquin held up a restraining hand. "I know these people," he indicated the rest of the crew. "I've worked with them many times before, and that sort of familiarity could prove vital in a tight spot. *Somebody* has to stay on the ship. Anna's going to be driving the buggy so she can't do it, and we need someone here to control the other two drones, monitor the overall situation when the rest of us might be too close to see the wood for the trees and, perhaps most importantly of all, keep an eye out to ensure that another shipful of Xters doesn't turn up and catch us with our pants down. That someone is you."

Leesa pursed her lips and glared. What she wanted to say was: *but you're squandering your most effective resource. Let the doc sit back here monitoring the screens. I'm the best fighter you've got on board and you can bet your Elder artefacts you're going to need me out there!* What she actually said was… nothing. She could understand Pelquin's reasoning; it was wrong but she could understand it. He had no way of knowing how good she was in a scrap – the incident at La Gossa with the disberos aside, and he only had her word and the banker's for that. He was going with what he knew. Logical, conservative, and wrong; but nothing she might say was likely to change his mind.

So instead of arguing she simply watched, feeling very much the outsider. She'd almost begun to feel a part of this crew, but had now been reminded very forcefully that she wasn't. So she stood on the fringe of things and observed the others interact, as adrenaline took hold of her companions and jokes and banter flourished. The sense of mounting excitement seasoned with a touch of nerves was almost palpable.

The others trooped out, heading towards the loading bay and the planet's surface. Leesa watched them go. Anna at least glanced back to smile and give her a small wave. Once they'd gone, she didn't quite kick the cabinets but she thought about it.

Leesa wasn't entirely sure why she felt so strongly about being excluded. Yes, it would have been great to see inside an Elder cache chamber but, as the Xter dead confirmed, it would also have been dangerous. These weren't her people and this wasn't her fight. It wasn't even as if she would have been paid any more for putting her life on the line. A share was a share – or in her case a half of one – whether she went in there or merely sat out here and watched.

She made her way to the bridge. At least she got to sit in the pilot's seat for once. High-backed, well-padded and responsive; the material of the seat reconfigured to support her as she made herself comfortable. She sat up and wriggled, settling back to enjoy the sensation as the seat adjusted around her. She looked around and tried to convince herself that being left behind wasn't so bad after all. The bridge, which was always so cramped when the crew gathered here en masse, now seemed positively spacious. She squirmed in her seat, causing the chair to readjust again just for the hell of it.

As they arrived at the loading bay the doc handed out slap masks to everyone. Drake was impressed; these things weren't cheap. Further evidence that Doctor Bariha didn't squander his *entire* budget on drugs. Drake held the mask in the palm of his right hand and eyed it dubiously. He'd worn one of these before and didn't much relish a rematch. It resembled a standard oxygen mask though flimsier. Once the edges were pressed firmly to the face the mask formed a vacuum-tight bond with the skin, sealing in mouth and nose. The most uncomfortable part about wearing a slap mask was that it got hot in there, particularly if you were performing any exercise. Oh, and they could be buggers to get off again; he'd had masks that came away with an appropriate tug and others that clung stubbornly to the face even after the application of solvent. He felt sure that someone's facial skin would be sacrificed before the day was out.

Slap masks were made of a permeable membrane. They let air in but were said to scrub that air of harmful viruses, bacteria, or any other malicious mites that an alien ecosystem might have whipped up. Far more than mere filters, the masks employed an active agent capable of identifying, isolating and destroying invading microbes; nanotechnology in all its glory.

After only the briefest of hesitations he slapped the mask on. They all did, except for Nate Almont.

"No thanks, Doc," he said, handing his mask back.

"In that case, you really ought to wear a suit with an isolated air supply."

Almont snorted. "Doc, if you honestly think I'm going to totter around in an EVA suit on an Earth-normal world with an Earth-normal atmosphere, you've sniffed one tube of happy vapours too many."

"The risk of you picking up…"

"I'll take my chances. I've already been here once and, see," he spread his arms, "I'm perfectly okay."

"For now," the doc muttered.

Drake was opening and closing his mouth, keeping his cheeks and jaw as mobile as possible while the mask settled in place, hoping to minimize the discomfort. He found himself sympathising with Almont.

They piled onto the buggy, Pelquin and Anna in the front, the rest of them sitting two to a side on the flatbed behind, legs dangling over the edge. Drake found himself sitting next to Bren, with Almont and the Doc at their backs. A small powerlifter and a few other pieces of equipment – hastily but securely loaded – separated them. Drake held his cane across his lap, its end poking away from Bren and towards the back of the buggy, where a storage tank had been fastened.

It wasn't the most comfortable ride he'd ever experienced, as the buggy raced across the uneven ground, for all of Anna's skill and the buggy's supposed technology.

"Hey, take it easy, Anna," Bren yelled, "or are you trying to shake us loose back here?"

"Be grateful," Pelquin said. "This is the model *with* suspension."

Things were a lot easier once they reached the tunnel. Apart from anything else, Anna slowed down.

They left a small comms relay at the entrance, knowing how tricky it was to get a signal through cache-chamber walls and not wanting to take any chances with Leesa's monitoring them and her control of the probes. The tunnel leading in was straight, so the relay should provide a clear link no matter what. That was the theory, at any rate. They also collected the long handled piece of Xter kit left resting against the rock face. Bren seemed particularly pleased with this, examining the object as if it were some treasured bargain picked up cheaply at an auction.

Before starting forward into the tunnel itself they launched the two remaining drones, Leesa confirming she had control.

In no time at all they reached the first Xter body. There was no mistaking this for a human spacesuit. Everything about it was wrong; not just the configuration of limbs and the elongated body but the styling, the shape of the helmet, *everything*. It all screamed 'other' more forcefully than anything Drake had previously seen, despite his experience with Elder artefacts. Perhaps it was because this suit represented a living, thriving alien culture, whereas the cache chambers were mere echoes of a civilisation long gone, no matter how impressive those echoes might be.

They took things cautiously, with the two drones acting as scouts, bobbing around like wingless dragonflies a short distance in front of the buggy. They had to stop to move the next two Xter corpses out of the way, Nate and Bren jumping down to do the honours, though not without difficulty to judge by Bren's, "Stars, these things weigh at ton!"

To Drake's relief, nobody suggested taking all or part of the Xter suits as bounty or salvage.

They passed through the first two defences without incident, thanks to the unwitting sacrifice of the Xters.

Next up was the collapsed section of tunnel, which was somehow smaller and less dramatic than it had appeared on the drone's cam. They all got down and were forced to move another Xter corpse but the rubble itself proved no real obstacle for the buggy under Anna's deft guidance. A short distance beyond lay the shattered wreckage of the original drone, and their first fully active defence. Drake could almost sense the guardian entity watching them and willing them to fail.

Progress slowed to a crawl as they approached the spot, the two drones pulling back to either side of the vehicle.

Nate and Bren were in motion before the buggy came to a halt, jumping down and hurrying to the rear, where the boxlike oblong tank had been fastened. They each grabbed one of two nozzles, holstered on either side of the tank, and walked back to the buggy's front. Flexible hoses unravelled, linking them to the buggy like umbilical cords.

Anna was busy, staring intently at the screen in front of her while her fingers danced over unseen keys. Two pencil thin beams of bright red light stabbed out from the buggy's front, one to either side, indicating opposing sections of the tunnel wall.

"That's where we need to hit," she said.

"Well, here goes nothing." Bren planted her feet and trained the nozzle on the highlighted patch of wall.

Nate was a fraction ahead of her, but soon both were spraying a continuous stream of frothy, gungy foam. They started at ground level and worked their way upward. Anna continued to shine her indicators, raising them as required, but the light was soon lost in the foam. Not that either Bren or Nate needed much guidance once they'd started.

It looked as if they were spraying the walls with thick, bubbling scum, while the smell – which came through strongly despite the slap masks – was an unholy alliance between brick dust and detergent.

Little more than a minute after they'd started, Bren and Nate completed their work. The foam hardened in seconds, leaving the tunnel bracketed by two thick, lumpy and uneven columns.

"All right, Leesa," Pelquin said. "Send one of the probes through and let's see what happens."

Everyone was quiet as the right hand drone eased forward. It reached the space between the two grotesque pillars, hovering there... and nothing happened.

Anna let out a held breath with an exaggerated "phew!"

Just to make sure, Leesa moved the drone backwards and forwards and had it bob up and down above its mangled predecessor. Still no reaction.

"Looks as if the foam *has* done the trick," Bren said.

"Maybe," Nate said. "Unless the guardian is playing clever and holding back on the trap until we all wander through it."

"Thanks for that cheerful thought."

"Only one way to find out," Pelquin said.

He was out of the buggy in an instant and walking forward.

"Pel, no!" Bren cried out, but it was too late to stop him. They'd halted just short of the trap and a few long strides brought Pelquin level with where the drone continued to hover.

There he stood. Arms stretched wide. Drake could visualise the metal spears bursting free of their bonds in a shower of hardened foam shards to skewer the captain in half a dozen places; but, even when the man turned sideways to face the wall, arms still spread as if in willing sacrifice, there was no response.

"Looks good to me," Pelquin said, dropping his arms and walking back to them. He was grinning from ear to ear. Bren looked furious, as if now that the trap had failed to kill him she just might.

The buggy shot forward with all of them back on board. Anna had backed up a little before gunning the engines. No one wanted to be between those pillars any longer than they had to be. Drake felt a degree of sympathy for Anna, their pilot and driver, who would have to pass between the columns again and again, ferrying artefacts back to the ship.

Anna slowed down as soon as they were past the pillars. The cache chamber itself now lay only a short distance ahead. The buggy's headlights offered tantalising glimpses of its crowded interior through the shattered inner door.

"Did the Xters do that?" Pelquin wondered, looking at the door.

"No, I don't think they made it this far," Nate said. "That looks to be pretty much how we left it. A shaped charge, very tightly focused."

"What happened to the bodies of the men you lost getting this far?" Bren asked.

"No idea."

And not a question Drake cared to dwell on. "If the traps were rebuilt, why not the door?" he wondered out loud.

"Too big a job?" Anna suggested.

Nate shook his head impatiently. "If the guardian can repair and rebuild a laser trap it can fix a door."

"Which means this is almost certainly another trap," Pelquin said. They had come to a halt again, just short of the door. "Leesa…"

She didn't need telling. One of the drones was already drifting forward. Anna wasn't the only one holding her breath as the probe moved with frustrating slowness through the broken door.

It paused, hovering in the doorway as if inviting trouble; but none came. After a couple of seconds it edged forward, entering the chamber itself. Just when Drake was tempted to start breathing normally again there came a blinding flash and a quick wash of heat.

"Anna?" Pelquin snapped.

"Hang on, I can't see a thing right now."

"A discharge of energy, and a big one at that," Leesa's voice said. "Looks to be an energy net positioned just the other side of the door.

Give me a second… Right, I've got it. I'm sending you through a map of the points that need to be taken out to cripple the net."

Drake, still blinking away the afterimage of the flash, craned his neck to look over Anna's shoulder at the dashboard display. It showed an image of the doorway and the chamber walls just beyond with a tracery of orange points overlaid – seven or eight in all.

"Anna," Pelquin said, "can you upload this to the gun?" He held out the energy weapon from the *Comet*'s arsenal.

"Yes, sure, wait a sec… Done."

Pelquin stepped down from the buggy once more and moved to stand in front of them, holding the gun in both hands. This brought him to the edge of the shattered doorway, and Drake felt Bren tense beside him, though she kept quiet.

Pelquin held the gun at waist height, shooting from the hip like some macho marine, but Drake knew that he was doing so in order to match the targeting screen with the overlaid image sent across by Anna. He fired – a brief burst of white-bright energy – then repositioned and fired again, repeating the process another half dozen times. Finally, he lowered the gun and asked, "That's all of them. How did I do?"

"Looks spot on to me," Leesa confirmed.

"Good, because there's not much juice left in this thing."

That was the problem with energy weapons: they packed a heck of a punch but they were also thirsty little beggars.

"Leesa," Pelquin continued, "if you'd do the honours…"

Their final probe moved forward, edging past the captain's position and into the chamber. It did so unhindered and unharmed.

Bren was moving even as Anna let loose a whoop of triumph and before anyone else could react. She stepped quickly forward to put a restraining arm across Pelquin's chest. "You stay there," she said. "This time, let someone else be the hero."

"Actually, I was going to suggest that you and Nate use up the rest of the foam, just to make sure that this 'net' doesn't reknit itself while we're inside the chamber."

"Sounds like a plan to me."

So they were all forced to wait impatiently for a few moments more – the cache chamber and its glittering contents a few tantalising steps away – while Bren and Nate repeated their performance with the hoses and the foam.

As soon as they'd finished, everyone climbed back aboard the buggy and the whole group of them entered the chamber together.

How's that guardian entity doing? Drake asked.

Still here, still angry, and still up to something, Mudball replied.

But you can't give me any idea what?

No, not yet. Watch this space.

Nate dropped off the left side of the cart, stretching up to slam a stickalamp against the uneven wall of the chamber, as high as he could reach. The sharp rap of contact brought the bulbous blister of illumination to life, while its malleable underside adapted to the rough surface of the wall and bonded. Bren was only a fraction behind him on the opposite side, jumping up with her left hand flat against the wall and stretching with her right, as if determined to get her lamp higher than Nate's.

The wash of fresh illumination exposed the chamber and its contents; what had previously been no more than glimpsed in the buggy's headlights now stood revealed in all its glory.

Anna gave a long 'ooh' of delight while Bren grinned from ear to ear, and even Pelquin glanced across at Nate and smiled. The big man looked insufferably pleased with himself.

"Well, was I right or was I right?" he asked.

"Not bad," Pelquin allowed. "Not bad at all."

"Gods, this is really something," Bren murmured, as she came back to stand by the buggy. "I can't believe I'm actually standing inside a cache chamber."

The reverence in her voice brought home to Drake just how privileged he was. He'd been inside a dozen or more cache chambers in recent years and, while each was thrilling and wondrous in its own right, it was easy to become a little blasé about the whole thing and forget the sense of awe that stepping inside one of these places for the first time could invoke. The majority of humankind would never have the pleasure of doing so, not even once; and this was an impressive cache, perhaps the largest he'd seen in all his years with First Solar.

Bren had every right to be impressed.

Mounds of artefacts surrounded them, heaped on top of each other like some mad pirate's haul. There was nothing neat and tidy about it; objects tilted, spilled over and leaned against one another, and they came in all shapes and sizes – from tiny trinkets that glittered and winked in the light cast by the stickalamps to solid-looking blocks. It was all overwhelming, too impressive to focus immediately on any single item. Drake knew from experience that some of these things would be no more than baubles – still intrinsically valuable because of their Elder origin but of little scientific value – while others would be gimmicky little novelties such as the 'gonk' Pelquin had given to Terry Reese. But hidden among them were likely to be a few true marvels – things that human science had never encountered before and, quite possibly, never even dreamed of. These were the real prize. Even one such item would be enough to turn a small fortune into a large one, and in a cache of this size there was every hope of uncovering several. If not, the trinkets alone would still amass a tidy sum, but everyone would be hoping for the rarer artefacts that might just qualify as 'priceless'.

They had all climbed out of the buggy now, except for Anna.

"It's going to take us all day to get this lot on board," Bren said.

"Just think of the money totting up while we work," Nate said.

"Then what are we standing around gawping for?" Pelquin asked. "First we need to get the powerlifter ready and then, Anna, turn this jalopy round and let's get on with it, shall we?"

Nate and Bren took charge, unloading the powerlifter and sliding a number of light but deceptively strong pallet bases from the back of the buggy, where they had sat flush with the floor.

Anna proceeded to do as instructed, manoeuvring the vehicle back and forth a few times in the confined space until she brought it around to face the way they'd come.

Pelquin had already started clearing some of the smaller items to clear one of the larger, bulkier ones. Drake went to help him.

"Is there any way of telling, just by looking, which the really valuable pieces are?" the captain asked.

"No, not usually," Drake told him. "You can sometimes tell by touch – some of them respond to organic contact..."

"Thanks for the warning."

"...but even that's not reliable. Often you don't know what you've got until you bring it back home for analysis. And don't worry; most of this stuff is bound to be dormant or inert."

"Thanks again. 'Most'... that's very reassuring."

Privately, Drake reckoned they had bigger things to worry about. Not that they were doing this entirely blind. Anna stayed in the buggy, her gaze glued to its screens, and there was also Leesa back on the *Comet*. Yet, for all their vigilance, Drake doubted whether the two women combined would be enough to cope with whatever was coming.

TWENTY

Leesa continued to feel as if she was the only sober person at a party. She watched, from the limited viewpoint provided by the buggy's camera, as the others efficiently loaded up first one pallet and then another with Elder artefacts, using stasis tethers to keep the teetering loads in place. Nate then stepped into the powerlifter and loaded the first full pallet onto the buggy's flatbed – and presumably the second, though by this point her view was obscured by looming artefacts. She could still hear them, though: laughing, joking, clearly having a ball. She could always switch one of the minicams built into the stickalamps if she felt the need to see more. She chose not to.

"Leesa," Pelquin's voice came through, "Anna's on her way back to the ship. Go to the hold and be ready with a powerlifter your end to help unload the buggy, so that she can get straight back here with a minimum of delay."

Unload the buggy? Wasn't she supposed to be the guardian angel watching over the intrepid explorers? And what happened to keeping an eye out for more Xters? What if another shipload of aliens came roaring down from the heavens while she was in the hold wrestling with the controls of a powerlifter? Of course, all she actually said was, "On my way, skip."

She got there a few minutes ahead of Anna and so had a chance to practice with the unfamiliar powerlifter before the heavily laden buggy dragged itself up the loading ramp.

Seeing the artefacts on the viewing screen was one thing, seeing them with her own eyes was a different matter entirely, but she didn't have time to gawp.

"You ever used one of those before?" Anna asked.

"Nope," Leesa admitted.

"You'll soon get the hang of it. It's easy."

It wasn't; at least not at first, not for somebody who'd never been behind a lifter's controls before.

She understood the principle: step forward into the lifter, legs and feet fitting snuggly into moulded indentations designed to accommodate them. The lifter clings to you like some grotesquely mutated suit of armour. You're then faced with a choice of controls for the machines various functions. She opted for the forklift, which seemed a reasonable place to start.

So far so good, but then things got a little more complicated. She raised the triple tines of the fork until her display indicated they were at the right height to slip between the pallet and the buggy's flatbed, and started to walk forward; the bulk of the lifter sat in front of her like a vending stand at a sports game, but one that moved. She found it fascinating the way her own alternating steps were absorbed by the lifter, which rolled forward at a steady, even pace.

Five steps and she reached the buggy; the tines of the lifter slid forward... and missed. Only by a fraction, but they were too high, digging into the stacked artefacts.

"Careful," Anna warned. "You really don't want to bring that lot down on our heads. It was the walking," she went on. "You need to stop and realign immediately before extending the tines."

Leesa shuffled back half a pace and followed Anna's advice. This time the three long metal tongues slid home.

"There, you see? Told you it was easy."

Leesa didn't reply, determined to get the pallet unloaded without making a fool of herself. The fork rose slowly upward on its sliding mounting, lifting the pallet free of the buggy. Leesa swivelled round and delivered her prize to the floor, if not as smoothly as she might have liked. Fortunately the stasis tethers kept everything in place.

The second pallet proved much easier than the first; so much so that Leesa dared hope she was beginning to get the hang of this. Anna didn't stand on ceremony, but spun the buggy around as soon as the pallet was clear and raced down the ramp with a shouted, "See ya!"

Stepping out of the lifter, Leesa took a few heartbeats to stare at the Elder artefacts stacked before her. They clung together as if vacuum packed, seemingly fused into two solid lumps thanks to the stasis tethers. Then she turned, hurrying up the stairs and back to the cockpit, to see what had been going on at the cache in her absence.

Quite a bit, as it turned out. A third pallet had been filled and tethered and the crew was starting work on a fourth. Anna would be on her way back with another load almost before she arrived; it was a proper little production line, with Leesa as the spare part. An exaggeration, perhaps, given her newfound skills with the powerlifter, but it still felt that way.

She switched briefly to the camera on the buggy but soon gave up and returned to the chamber. With no passengers, Anna wasn't holding back. The view from the buggy was a jolting, mind-boggling blur.

After a moment's thought she reconfigured the screens, so that the buggy's jarring confusion showed on her left and the view from one of the stickalamps took centre stage.

Anna charged through the tunnel without appearing to slow, Xter suits showing briefly in the headlights and then sweeping past. As soon as she'd arrived and turned the buggy around, Nate loaded the next pallet onto the flatbed. In no time at all Anna was racing back again.

The unloading went much more smoothly this time, with Leesa remembering to pause and adjust the tines before attempting to extend them. Anna had been right, this *was* easy. She even managed to lower both pallets to the floor smoothly, without any danger of tipping them all over the deck.

By the time the buggy returned with its third load she was almost beginning to feel a part of things. Her disappointment about being left behind had receded, while concern about the guardian entity and any sense of imminent danger had all but disappeared.

Until she arrived back at the bridge. With no warning and no obvious source, Leesa was struck by a growing sense of foreboding. The auganic part of her mind stirred in a way that was both uncomfortable and unfamiliar. She was tempted to think that she'd never experienced anything like this before, but she didn't yet know herself well enough to make such a sweeping assertion. It was as if something fumbled to commune with the techorg inside her head but lacked the proper connection through which to do so. The result was an ephemeral suggestion of a meld which never threatened to really take hold and an irritation like a mental itch. She wanted to reach inside her skull to give it a good scratch. She had no idea what was going on or who was doing this to her, but as an aid to concentration it sucked, and she was felt sure it was linked in some way to the cache chamber.

The intrusive mental fumbling, whatever its source, triggered an unexpected reaction in her. Without any warning her consciousness shifted and the world slipped away.

Dr Augustine Bruckheimer, preeminent cyberneticist, acknowledged genius, and the father of the techorg project, smiled at Leesa as the nurse ushered her into the room. If the nurse's striking looks were intended to put new recruits at ease the ploy failed dismally on this occasion. Perhaps it worked on the male of the species but with Leesa it just made her starkly conscious of her own deficiencies.

"Ah, Leesa," Bruckheimer said, displaying a broad smile and the sort of sincerity that suggested he actually remembered her and hadn't merely checked her file a moment ago. "A pleasure to see you again."

They had in truth met once before, but she was just one among a score of others and didn't flatter herself that she'd made any lasting impression. The doctor was a consummate professional though, giving every indication that she had. "Now, there's no rush. It's important that you're fully at ease with everything before we proceed."

Leesa glanced around her. The room was gleaming and white. Two svelte Medidocs stood to attention at the top of the operating couch, their slender arms currently retracted and upright above their gleaming white chassis, so that they resembled patient herons waiting for gullible fish to swim past. High above the couch and currently sunk into the ceiling was a grey pod loaded with an unfathomable array of further instruments; as if to emphasise that, in this room, they meant business.

Her mouth was suddenly dry. She hadn't been nervous up to this point, but now that she was here, now that she could see all the equipment gathered about her like scavengers around a corpse, the import of what she'd signed up for finally sank in.

"You can still back out if you wish to," Bruckheimer said.

"No, I'm fine; this is what I want."

"Good. Now, do you have any more questions before the nurse shows you to the prep room?

"Just one. Is all of this really reverse engineered from Elder tech?

Bruckheimer's smile took on a forced rigidity, and she felt sure he'd been asked this same question a hundred times before. "No, not at all. Don't believe everything you hear. The Elders were a fabulously advanced race and much of their technology still baffles us today, but humans are by no means idiots. We made it into space all on our own, after all. These days, though, it seems that every advance we make in whatever field is attributed to knowledge gained from Elder tech and that simply isn't the case."

"I'm sorry, I just…"

"That's quite all right. So many insist that we're incapable of doing anything unaided; your question hardly comes as a surprise. We've always been like this, you know: self-deprecating. Were you aware that when mankind first bullied their way out of Earth's atmosphere and made it as far as the moon there were those who believed the whole thing to have been faked?"

"No, no I wasn't." Though it surprised her she hadn't heard about it; this was just the sort of thing her fathers would have relished telling her.

"Well it's true. Computer science was advancing so rapidly in those days that within a decade the computing capacity available at the time of the first lunar missions seemed paltry; and there were those who simply refused to believe that mankind could have reached so far with such simple equipment." He shook his head. "These people were making the same fundamental error that so many make today regarding Elder tech. They assume that because a capability is there *now* it's essential and always has been. The truth is that man is a stubborn beast; and a resourceful one. Set him a challenge and he'll bend heaven and Earth to meet it. The fact that ten or twenty years later there's a far easier, more certain and a much *safer* way of doing things doesn't invalidate the initial achievement. The fact that Elder tech is irrefutably here doesn't mean that we're now devoid of inspiration and incapable of developing our own technology. Far from it. Techorg is a case in point: human inspiration and human science, free of any taint of Elder influence, whatever the rumour mill might claim."

"I'm sorry," she said again. "I didn't mean to imply any insult."

"None taken, but I do believe in setting the record straight. Now, if there are no more questions…?"

"No, none at all." She wouldn't dare, and instead allowed herself to be led away by the unfeasibly gorgeous nurse.

Leesa shuddered back to the present. Well *that* was new. She had never before experienced such an intense recollection while wide awake. Not only that, she'd been concentrating at the time on the images from the cache chamber and was amazed that a memory could distract her so thoroughly. Presumably this had been triggered by that attempt to stimulate her aug.

Pelquin, Drake and the others must have disturbed something, presumable the cache guardian, and it was reacting – reaching out to defend itself. Somehow, that had extended into her head, however marginally. The thing that worried her was what else it might be doing. Was there something in the cache chamber itself that would respond to such a call? Presumably so, or why initiate such a powerful summons in the first place?

Again she felt that clumsy, insistent almost-touch, and she was instantly somewhere else...

Leesa was standing inside the cache chamber, or at least in *a* cache chamber. She was surrounded by objects that her perceptions struggled to identify. A dazzling array of glittering, beguiling things were heaped around her. Wood that wasn't really wood at all but equally wasn't metal or glass or polymer or plastic either, and wood was the closest thing she could come up with; slender wands of the stuff, shot through with glittering veins that might have been silver if silver contained ground-up diamond dust. The material fooled you into thinking it was natural and might once have been alive, while deep down a part of you suspected that it was purely the product of artifice. There were hundreds, perhaps thousands of these rods, stacked up, spilling over, leaning haphazardly against things or just lying around willy-nilly as if discarded. And they were merely one of the treasures that surrounded her. Feathers of filigree beauty that glowed with inner light; dots of iridescent colour that drifted on unfelt breezes and swirled in kaleidoscope eddies, one moment gathering to create a recognisable form and the next dispersing into nebulous beauty, all summoned back into a small matt-black box via a simple twist of its base; multi-faceted blocks that looked like mathematicians' playthings, their faces decorated with molten inlays; small bronzed spheres that sprouted dragonfly wings and soared across the room leaving glittering rainbows in their wake; incredibly fine filaments that, when gathered together, pulsed with cohesive colour that shifted and melded to form images: one moment a mirror that reflected her face, the next a window onto an exotic alien world; innocuous seeming cubes that collapsed and turned liquid when you picked them up, slipping through your gloved fingers only to regain their original form wherever they landed –

becoming solid, edged and sharp cornered once more.

All of these things and more she noted only in passing, for they weren't what drew her; they weren't what reached out to strum the chords of her soul… and something here did exactly that. It called to her, wooed her, singled her out and demanded that she respond. She found it at last, at the back of the chamber, folded and draped over the lid of a burnished not-wood trunk. A bolt of impossibly silver cloth. She didn't think, didn't hesitate, simply reached out and grasped it.

Afterwards, she could have sworn that the cloth stirred a fraction before her hand touched it, that it moved in anticipation and rose to meet her questing fingers. Whatever the truth, the instant her fingertips made contact the material flowed up her arm, as dammed water might flow through a suddenly cleared channel. And she could *feel* it. Even through her gloves and her suit she could feel the soft, cool touch of its passage. Swift and true, the cloth advanced, suffusing her suit and disregarding all barriers intended to keep her safe from invasion.

Invade her it did.

"Leesa!"

She didn't turn, didn't look towards the source of that call of alarm, that so familiar yet simultaneously anonymous voice. Her awareness was too focused on the progress of this liquid cloth to encompass anything else. It clung to her like a second skin. She felt it slide over her lips and teeth to coat the roof of her mouth, tasting metal and strangeness on her tongue, while at the same time conscious of it entering her ears and nostrils. She clenched her buttocks involuntarily as it slid across her anus. She couldn't speak, couldn't breathe; she was drowning in liquid chrome.

Leesa came back to herself once more, disorientated for a split second before organic and auganic components slipped smoothly into mesh and reasserted stability. She was frightened by this loss of control. Two vivid flashbacks in a row, could she prevent a third? It must have been the very thing she'd been studying – the images of the cache chamber – that stimulated the second. A brand new memory completely unlooked for. Did she *want* to resist another vision like that even if she could?

She had no idea where in her life this latest flashback fitted, couldn't relate it to any other memories at her disposal, but one thing Leesa was sure of: at least once before she'd been in a chamber much like the one on the monitors; a major find – enough to have made her and anyone else on that forgotten expedition wealthy beyond all reason. So why wasn't she? Why, instead, was she an incomplete mentally-crippled amnesiac?

Because things had ended badly, that was why. She shuddered at the mental echo of that silver skin as it spread over her and into her, as it invaded every orifice. This might just offer her the clue she'd been searching for; once she had the time to consider it properly. Right now there were more immediate concerns. She stared at the images of the *Comet*'s crew exploring the cache with an increasing sense of dread. Things were about to go badly wrong, she just knew it.

Leesa tried to analyse her feelings towards this crew. She wasn't one of them, not really – just a shipee as far as they were concerned, hired help along for the ride for this one trip only. From her perspective they were no more than a means to an end; her escape route from a bunch of killers hell bent on extracting revenge; not to mention a world where the search for her true identity had stalled badly. What did she owe any of these people? Nothing, not if you looked at it logically. And yet…

Anna had befriended her without hesitation, and Bren had always treated her decently enough, as had the captain, Pelquin. In fact, they all had. Even banker-man Drake, who seemed to have worked out far more about her than he had any right to; at least he had kept his mouth shut and hadn't broadcast her business to the whole ship.

Maybe she had more of an emotional investment in this motley crew than she realised; enough that she didn't fancy sitting around and watching them get smeared by some leftover alien tech, at any rate. With a sigh, and a silent question regarding her own sanity, she pushed herself out of the seat.

She was about to leave the bridge when she heard the scream.

Drake was beginning to think that Mudball's concerns were unfounded. After all, Anna had made three runs so far and they had almost finished loading another pallet ready for a fourth, without any sign of the guardian acting against them. Perhaps it couldn't. In the banker's experience, once you were past the cache defences there was little the entities could do.

Mind you, this one had evidently managed to clear away the human bodies from the first incursion by Nate and his crew, and it had managed to rebuild some fairly formidable defences as well. Therefore it had the ability to affect the physical world to a certain degree at least.

So why was it holding back? Mustering its resources?

So far, the only moment of mild alarm since they'd entered the chamber had been when Bren let out a yelp. For a moment Drake froze, thinking this was it, but drew breath again when a string of profanities followed.

It turned out that an object Bren had picked up – an orb of silvered metal – had started vibrating vigorously in her hand. She'd cried out, instantly tossing the ball away, and was more embarrassed by her own reaction than afraid. "It felt warm, almost alive," she said.

There were more of the gonks that Pelquin had presented to Terry Reese – a lot more – and Pelquin stumbled upon a bundle of wind sticks – a type of artefact Drake had encountered before. They didn't just make the sound of a strong gale, they created one, in miniature.

The doc made perhaps the first truly interesting discovery. An oblong sheet of glass, with no frame; it was simply propped up against a stack of other artefacts. It looked like a mirror that was waiting to be fitted somewhere. Except that when you looked into it what you saw was the room on the other side of the pile that it was leaning against. Drake went across to look when he heard the doc's initial exclamation.

"Cameras, mounted somewhere on the other side, do you think?" Doc asked as they both stood staring.

"Maybe," Drake said. "Let's see." Grasping it on either side – the edges were rounded and the whole thing was deceptively light – he picked the mirror up and carried it a quarter of the way around the pile before once more resting it against the other artefacts. The view had changed to show, dimly, the rough wall of the chamber, which sat in shadow on the mound's far side.

"Well I'll be..." the doc said from beside him.

Drake's favourite find, though, was a deceptively simple block of indefinable material, striped in caramel and cream and burnished like polished tortoise shell. It was small enough that he could grasp it in one hand. When he picked it up the block immediately started shedding bubbles; not from one or the other end but from all over – a cloud of tiny golden balls that rose leisurely into the air where they proceeded to burst. As each bubble popped it emitted a single clear sound; a different note for every bubble, it seemed, and, somehow, this didn't result in a discordant racket but rather in an eerie melody. Drake shook it, releasing a fresh flurry of bubbles and a new song.

Even Bren stopped working and stared for a second. "Now that's really something," she said.

Nate had just used the lifter to move the first items onto what would be their eighth pallet when a sound that could only have been a scream issued from the tunnel. Everyone froze, except for Nate who appeared not to have heard.

"Nate, hold it a second," Pelquin said, whilst Bren's call of "Anna!" mirrored Drake's instant thought.

A distant squeal of tyres followed by the screech of metal sliding along stone, and then nothing. Nate and Bren were the first to react, as the former abandoned the lifter and they both disappeared down the tunnel at a run, while Pelquin picked up the energy gun from where he'd left it while working. Drake would have been right behind Bren and Nate but a voice in his head stopped him.

Don't! Stay put. The captain's energy gun, you need to get rid of it; now!

Mudball had never sounded so insistent, so urgent. Drake didn't hesitate, and he didn't stop to argue with Pelquin, either. He snatched the gun from the startled captain's grasp and flung it towards the tunnel that Nate and Bren had just sprinted down.

"What the hell do you think...?" Pelquin began.

He was interrupted by a bright flash and an explosion as the gun's power pack detonated. The blast nearly knocked Drake off his feet.

"It's the guardian entity," he explained. "It's finally hitting back at us."

"How did you know..?"

But Drake was already past him, heading for the tunnel.

The blast from the depleted gun hadn't been enough to bring the place crashing down around their ears, though the air was clogged with dust which, worryingly, seemed to be trickling from the ceiling. Drake wouldn't have much fancied the chances of anyone holding the gun when it exploded, though.

I'd stop running towards the tunnel and find some cover, if I were you, Mudball advised.

The comment was emphasised by a burst of gunfire from somewhere ahead: the chatter of a machine pistol being fired. Drake stumbled to a halt and tried to peer through the dust and the darkness but couldn't make out anything. *What's going on up there?*

Before the alien had a chance to answer two figures burst through the murk, running at full pelt: Nate and Bren.

"Run!" Bren urged. "Take cover! We're being attacked by bloody ghosts."

On hearing the scream Leesa turned back to the screens, doing so just in time to see the wall of the tunnel loom ominously close on the buggy cam and then judder and spin alarmingly. Everything steadied for a second before the picture winked out altogether to leave a blank screen.

In that split second before the image disappeared, Leesa had seen something that made her blood run cold. A figure standing in the tunnel, caught in the beam from the headlights: an Xter.

Screw monitor duty! She turned and ran, going in search of a weapon.

Her thoughts raced as rapidly as her feet. The weapons locker would be sealed. She could try to force her way in using her aug but these were unfamiliar systems and that could take a while. Instead, she made for the captain's cabin.

This was the first time Leesa had set foot inside the compact room and she was surprised by its retro grandeur. She had somehow expected a degree of austerity, clean lines and modern touches, but found instead quite the opposite. The bed boasted a multi-coloured cover – deep red, blues and purples with gold tasselled trim – and next to it stood an antique wooden bedside table. The small desk looked to be equally antique; and there was a pair of black wrought iron wall sconces – *wall sconces* for crying out loud – bearing virtual candles that had sprung to life as soon as she entered, bathing the room in uneven, flickering light.

It was the desk that caught her attention. A double-winged affair, with a stack of three drawers either side of the central well that the chair was pushed into, and a longer drawer stretching across the length of the chairwell just below the desktop. A single item stood on the top itself: a static picture; predictably of the *Ion Raider*, though a different image to the one in the corridor by the bridge. This was a photograph rather than a graphic representation, and the ship was on the ground. Leesa glanced at it and moved on. You've seen one Comet class ship, you've seen them all. She was more interested in the desk's long drawer. By her reckoning it was the only one big enough. It wasn't locked, opening readily at her touch – the captain clearly trusted his crew. Inside she found exactly what she was hoping for: the case that she and Bren had fetched back from Mokhtar's shop on Brannan's World.

A nebulous sense of urgency caused her to hurry. She took out the case, opened it, and picked up the needler. The gun felt awkward in the hand, the elongated barrel ensuring it was hardly the best-balanced of weapons, but she knew all that would change as soon as the barrel stand rested on something; only then would the gun come into its own.

The one thing that worried her was how much charge the weapon still carried. It had obviously been stored at Mokhy's for an extended period of time – she had no idea exactly how long but presumably years. No telling whether it was even charged at all. She checked the display to find that it was; by no means fully, but hopefully enough.

Leesa was conscious of time slipping past, so, clutching the gun, she dashed from Pelquin's quarters and along the corridor to the loading bay, taking the stairs in a series of rapid pigeon steps. She held the gun in her right hand, making sure to keep her grip clear of the trigger. There didn't seem to be any holster and the barrel was too long for anything as casual as tucking it into her belt.

The loading bay doors stood open, ready for Anna's next trip, and Leesa was soon sprinting over the surface of this unfamiliar world, drawing ever nearer to the ominous tunnel mouth while hoping that she wasn't already too late.

There was shooting from somewhere ahead – presumably the cache chamber – the flicker-flash of gunfire starkly visible in the darkness.

Leesa found the buggy easily enough. It had ploughed into the tunnel wall, a glancing blow by the look of it and there seemed remarkably little damage. Anna still sat in the driver's seat, blood covering the side of her face, eyes staring blankly. Dead.

That realisation saddened Leesa more than she would have expected. She hadn't known the other woman long; perhaps that was half the problem: now she would never have the chance to.

Renewed gunfire drew her onward.

"Stop shooting!" Drake yelled from somewhere towards the far side of the chamber.

"Are you mad?" Pelquin countered, seriously wondering whether the banker had lost it under the pressure. Not that any of the rounds they'd poured into the Xters had made any difference as yet. The wretched things seemed to be impervious to injury.

"Shooting isn't going to stop them," Drake called again. "It's not the Xters we're up against. They're dead, we know that. It's the suits. The Xters were wearing powered suits and the guardian entity has taken control of them."

"You've got to be kidding me."

"Oh for God's sake," Bren muttered from beside Pelquin. She fired off another round. The two of them had taken shelter behind a pile of assorted artefacts. "Zombie alien fucking space suits?Gimme a break!"

"I told you," Drake called again, "shooting them isn't going to work."

"Yeah, well until someone figures out what *is* going to work, it's all I've got," Bren called back. For emphasis, she straightened and fired off another trio of shots.

This time, there was a response. Something slammed into their protective mound of artefacts. Pelquin felt the force of impact like a giant's slap where his right arm rested against a multi-segmented something or other. It knocked him from his feet, even as his ears rang with the report of an explosion and shards of metal and jewels and shattered gizmos went everywhere.

"All you're doing is forcing it to gain greater control in order to retaliate," Drake called.

"Yeah, thanks for the update, but we noticed," Bren assured him.

Pelquin felt his left arm grabbed, hauling him back to his feet. He and Bren stumbled in retreat, finding a bigger pile to hide behind. His slap mask was gone and blood oozed from a stinging cut on his left cheek, while his right arm felt numb, the dull ache of heavy bruising or worse just beginning to make itself known.

He stared at his open hand, only then realising that on top of everything else he'd dropped his gun. "Some swashbuckling marauder I am," he muttered.

"Cut it out, Pel. If you're looking for sympathy you've come to the wrong place. Stop feeling sorry for yourself and concentrate on figuring out how we survive this."

"That's easy; we don't."

"Well, if this really is it, there's one thing I've got to do before I go." In a sudden movement she wrenched off her own slap mask and leant forward, grabbed the back of his head and, without any further preamble, kissed him.

"Hell!" He stared at her in shock as she pulled away.

"It wasn't that awful, was it?"

"No, not at all, but, I mean... *really?*"

"Yeah, really. Now can we talk about this later?"

"Hell, Bren!"

"Stop saying that."

The strange shuffling sounds of the Xter suits were growing closer. Pelquin was almost glad of the distraction. Almost. Until that is, an Xter suit rounded their hiding place and raised its arm to shoot.

Mudball, where the hell are you?

I'm busy trying to save your ass from this over-excited guardian entity.

Drake had never been more pleased to sense the alien's mental presence. *Well try a little quicker, would you?*

That's easy for you to say. You just have to sit there and avoid getting killed. Me, I have to do all the hard work as usual.

A little swift evidence of that 'hard work' would be appreciated about now.

Give me a break, will you? This is his home turf after all.

So you're overmatched?

Of course not; I didn't say that. Now pipe down and let me concentrate.

Leesa wriggled and squeezed her way to the top of one of the artefact mounds, trying to find a decent vantage point without drawing attention.

She had grown up on an Xter world, born into a community dedicated to learning all they could about the aliens and their culture. She had quite literally forgotten more about the Xters than most people would ever know. Now, at this vital juncture, she *remembered*; remembered how their powered suits were built and how they worked. Most importantly, she remembered how they could be disabled. Of course, knowing and doing were two entirely different things, but in the needler she had a tool capable of managing the job. The rest was up to her.

She closed her mind to everything around her: the shooting, the shouting, the very real threat to those she was here to help. Success depended on focus, on not being distracted and not being rushed, on performing at her optimum.

That didn't mean dithering or wasting time, it merely meant taking the required seconds without feeling pressured into rushing. Smoothly, efficiently, she adjusted her body and positioned the gun, ensuring that the small support rested on a flat, stable surface. The needler, which had felt poorly balanced and awkward, was transformed into a perfectly designed killing tool. As soon as she activated the sighting mechanism a virtual screen leapt to life, hovering above the gun's chamber. A final shifting of her weight and she was able to stare through the screen and along the barrel. Without moving her hand she put slight pressure on a stud and the image leapt closer, centring on the Xter suit that menaced Pelquin and Bren. A red dot, visible only through the screen, indicated the precise target area. Another gentle squeeze and the section of the suit she was after dominated the screen – the middle of the back, encased in a bulge of armour. This was where the small motor that powered the suit was situated. It was well protected, but the beam from a needler could cut through all that like a monofilament blade through cream cheese. In fact, her chief concern was to avoid hitting either of the two humans on the suit's far side.

A minor adjustment to her aim and she was ready. She knew the gun was supposed to allow multiple targeting, but she was no expert with this particular weapon and didn't have time to figure out how. One slow deep breath and she gently closed her finger on the trigger. No recoil, no tremor of the handle to indicate that anything had happened. Just the flash of contact and the puff of a contained explosion on the suit she'd targeted, which stopped moving, becoming suddenly stiff and lifeless. Like a felled tree the Xter suit pitched forward, nearly toppling onto the two startled figures cowering in front of it.

The only other indication that the needler had done anything whatsoever was the alarming drop in the power level bar in the bottom left hand corner of the sighting screen. At this rate, she reckoned there were only one or two more shots in the gun, so she had better make them count.

One of the surviving suits turned and began to make its way towards her. She ignored it, centring instead on the one that was closing on Nate Almont and Drake – the pair looking to be in far more immediate danger than she was.

That proved to be a mistake. The suit advancing towards her raised a forelimb and fired.

The shot went low, slamming into the mound of artefacts and trinkets beneath her, which bucked and heaved like a giant turning over in its sleep. The pile, which had seemed so solid and stable before, was now transformed into a sliding and tumbling collection of individual components; Leesa among them.

She slid sideways, rolling over as things struck her and sharp edges scratched and cut. She landed on a bed of discomfort, with something heavy coming down on top of her and pinning her left leg. For the moment, the Xter suit was lost to sight behind a heap of fallen artefacts. That worried her more than anything. She kicked and squirmed, freeing her leg, though the ankle throbbed as if it was twisted or perhaps broken. The needler was still clutched firmly in her right fist. Something tickled her left cheek and she wiped at it absently with her free hand, the fingertips coming away smeared with blood. She hauled herself onto the top of this new, low configuration of tumbled artefacts, to see the suit much closer.

As she came into sight it raised its gun once more,

Leesa didn't hesitate, didn't have time to seek a flat surface for support. Still on her knees she straightened her back. She brought her left arm up, forearm horizontal and across her body at shoulder height, and this was where she rested the needler's barrel. The targeting display sprang to life. There was no time to think this through properly. She kept her left arm steady and let instinct dictate where on the front of the suit she should aim. With no room for doubt or time for hesitation, she pulled the trigger.

A bright flare as the needler's beam found its mark, burning through the front of the armoured suit and then on through the body to find its back. For a moment she thought she'd missed her mark, but then the suit stopped, its forelimb froze. In apparent slow motion the suit keeled over; toppling forward and to the right, where it lay unmoving.

No time to celebrate, no time to feel anything other than a fleeting sense of relief. Two of the suits were still active and the needler was spent. She discarded the gun, rolling and pushing herself to her feet, sharp pain radiating from the injured ankle as she tested it with just a little of her body weight.

"The motor and power supply are in the middle of the back, well protected but it's the only way to stop them," she yelled for the benefit of anyone who'd listen.

No one answered, but then they were sort of busy.

A hop, a limp, and she was back on her knees, scrabbling around in the fallen mound of artefacts, desperately searching for something to use as a weapon. She thought she had a few seconds, thought she knew where the danger was; until a shadow fell across her.

Leesa looked up to find the second Xter suit she'd shot standing over her with its gun levelled at her head.

Drake flung himself forward, trying to retrieve his cane, which had tumbled from his hand as he was sent flying by the Xter suit; the same suit that Nate Almont was currently grappling with.

They might not have been the best of buddies on the journey out here but Almont was a good man to have beside you in a fight, no question.

Even so, it was unnerving fighting a corpse.

Drake had heard Leesa's shouted advice about the suits having a possible weak spot at the back. God only knew where his gun had gone to, but, if he could get around behind their opponent while Nate kept it distracted, perhaps he could use his cane to disable the thing.

As his fingers finally closed around the cane, something went sailing over his head to land heavily. Nate Almont, he realised. So much for the distraction.

Almont groaned, rolled, and came to his feet, fragments of broken artefacts tinkling from his clothes. "Tough, bastard, isn't it?"

"Comes from having no pain receptors, I expect."

"Wish I didn't."

The suit was almost on top of them again.

"If you can keep the thing occupied, I'll attack its power source at the back," Drake said.

"Occupied, huh? I'll do my best."

With that, Almont flung himself at the suit again, which cuffed him away with a swing of a heavy armoured fist, like a batter striking a ball. Almont hit the ground hard and this time didn't move. The suit seemed to remember the gun clutched in one of its mid-limbs. It raised the weapon, preparing to shoot its fallen enemy.

Drake knew he couldn't wait any longer. He didn't throw himself at the Xter as Nate had but stayed on his feet. The guardian seemed to be improving its control over the suits the whole time, but that control still wasn't yet perfect; the suits didn't move with the natural fluidity they would if their wearers were still alive, and Drake drew hope from that.

He ducked under a bludgeoning upper limb that swung at him, and twisted away from a mid-limb that attempted to grasp. He was close enough now, and rammed his cane against the suit's armoured hide, triggering the repellor field. The Xter staggered backwards. Had there been a live wearer inside it might have recovered, might have brought its mid-limbs down to the ground for increased stability, but the guardian was outmatched and the suit crashed backwards, limbs flailing.

The news, however, wasn't all good. The suit had gone over on its back, giving Drake no opportunity to attack its supposed weak spot. Also, as the limbs steadied, so did the Xter's gun, which now pointed squarely at Drake. He didn't have time to avoid, didn't have time to think, he simply reacted, bringing up his cane and ramming it into the muzzle of the gun.

Once again he had reason to thank the cane's non-conductive nature, which didn't stop the resultant explosion from swatting him with the force of a runaway bull. He was flung through the air, crashing into something hard and collapsing to the ground.

Pain and oblivion threatened to overwhelm him but he refused to succumb, struggling to sit up. Agony shot along his left arm and shoulder as he pressed down with a hand to lever himself onto his knees. Blood ran from his nose and into his mouth. He struggled to clear his vision, to see or even to think. Once he had, part of him wished he hadn't.

The suit was there, looming over him. One mid-limb had been torn away and the armoured carapace was scorched around that area, but it could still move and could still reach for him; and there was nothing he could do to stop it.

A frozen second of resignation passed; this was it. This was death. Then he registered that the suit was no longer moving, that its clutching limbs had come no closer but had frozen in mid- grasp. For a surreal moment he couldn't quite accept this was real, but then a familiar voice said, *There, I told you not to worry.*

Mudball?
You were expecting someone else?
No, but… The guardian entity?
Toast. Kaput. Vanquished. Fear not, it will trouble you no more.
Thank the gods… You took your bloody time, didn't you?
Now there's gratitude for you.

Drake climbed shakily to his feet. Looking around, he saw bewildered expressions on the faces of his companions, most of whom looked surprised to still be alive. Leesa in particular, who prodded the suit confronting her as if expecting it to come back to life at any second.

"What the hell just happened?" Pelquin said.

"I think the guardian's burnt itself out directing all these suits at once," Drake said as he limped towards the captain. It sounded lame even to his ears, but let someone else try to come up with a better explanation.

TWENTY-ONE

The clear up was a sobering affair. Anna's death hit everyone hard. They placed her body in a cryochamber – not with any hope of revival this time, she was irrevocably dead. No, they put her in a cryochamber because they didn't want to leave her here and there was nowhere else to put her.

The buggy proved functional despite some minor damage. Leesa took over the driving duties. They completed the task of emptying the cache chamber because they felt obliged to now that they were here, but the joy had gone out of proceedings and the whole process had become an empty one rather than the pleasure it should have been.

The doc made a decent job of patching up the injured – Drake and Leesa being the worst off, though Nate came a close third – and all of them were able to contribute to the work, but the going was a lot slower than previously.

They laboured under the shadow of the guardian entity, afraid that it might return at any moment, all except for Drake, who knew better. "Matching limps," he said to Leesa at one point.

"Yeah, lucky us," she replied, but it was said without any hint of malice. Previous petty differences seemed irrelevant after all that had happened.

Darkness was falling by the time they'd finished. Pelquin took the *Comet* up and parked her in orbit. None of them wanted to spend a night close to the cache chamber or the Xter ship.

The next morning the *Comet* returned to the planet's surface. Spirits aboard had revived a little, but the atmosphere remained muted.

Drake, Bren, Nate and Leesa took the buggy across to the Xter ship. Drake was quietly pleased to note the subtle change in Leesa's status. Any reservations Pelquin or anyone else might have had about her had clearly evaporated, and she was now working as a fully integrated part of the team.

"Pel... You should see this," Bren said over the com as they stepped aboard the alien vessel.

"Yeah, and one day I will," came the reply. "But not today." He and the doc were busy compiling an inventory of what they'd brought out from the cache.

Drake knew that images were being relayed back to the *Comet* via their suits, but Bren was evidently determined to add a personal commentary. "This is… weird; absolutely amazing."

"Almost alien, you mean?" Pelquin said.

"Very funny. There's no 'almost' about it, trust me."

Drake knew what she meant. You might suppose that an empty hold was just a big open space; pretty much the same no matter who had built it, but that failed to take into account what surrounded the space. Considered separately, each individual element might be familiar and logical, but the proportions were all wrong: designed for beings with different frames and a different number of limbs. In combination, the effect was reality-stretching and surreal. Drake had actually been on an Xter ship before, though he had no intention of admitting the fact, but never in its hold. He had to admit that there was something deeply unsettling about it.

"Come on, we've got a job to do," Nate muttered – evidently unfazed.

They found the control room easily enough – a space far more deserving of the term 'bridge' than anywhere aboard the *Comet* – and while Nate and Bren went to deploy the Ptarmigan, Leesa set about trying to fathom the controls. Drake stayed with her to 'observe', interjecting when needed. Between Leesa and Mudball – ostensibly Leesa and Drake – they managed to work out the basics.

I could fly this thing all the way home if you like, Mudball told him. *The systems are far more logical than anything you humans have come up with.*

And that would be far more difficult to explain than programming the ship for a simple planetary orbit, Drake pointed out.

They rendezvoused with the others back at the buggy. Both Nate and Bren were carrying a spacesuit each and an armful of other assorted Xter items. Bren grinned, "Waste not, want not."

Nobody wanted to hang around planetside any longer than necessary, and the *Comet* lifted as soon as possible once they were back on board.

"The moment of truth," Pelquin said, triggering the sequence that should see the Xter ship follow them into the air. Things went without a hitch, and the *Comet* then shadowed the other craft as they headed for the edge of atmosphere.

"You're sure it's stable?" Pelquin asked, as Bren checked the Xter's orbit for the umpteenth time. She was standing in for Nate, who had cried off bridge duties, still recovering from the injuries he had sustained in the cache chamber.

"I'm sure."

"Okay, here goes." Pelquin triggered the Ptarmigan, and the Xter ship immediately vanished from their sensors. He waited a few seconds and then turned it off. The ship reappeared.

"Exactly where she should be," Bren said. "Don't worry, we can find her again."

For future retrieval and salvage.

The enormity of what they'd achieved had begun to sink in at last, and a cautious sense of celebration overtook the crew, though news that Nate Almont was unwell soon put a dampener on things again. The cause of his tiredness proved to be more than just his injuries.

"He's picked up an infection," Doc explained. "I told him he should have worn a slap mask, but would he listen? No, of course he wouldn't."

"How come Pel and I haven't got it?" Bren asked. "We both lost our masks in the chamber."

"Blind luck," the doc told her. "As with any bug, exposure doesn't guarantee infection it merely provides an opportunity and increases the likelihood."

"Can you cure him?" Pelquin wanted to know.

The doc shook his head. "Not with the facilities we've got here. This is an alien virus. I might be able to slow it down, but cure it...? No."

"Will it kill him?"

The doc shrugged. "Who knows? I can't even say for certain whether it's infectious or not. The ship isn't exactly equipped for isolation and we've all been breathing the same air since we came back on board in any case. There's every chance that more of us are going to catch whatever this is."

"Fantastic. Your advice?"

"A hospital, as soon as possible; preferably one capable of dealing with exotic diseases. I've taken the liberty of checking the data base and there's one on a world not far from here, just into human space."

Drake was impressed, not to mention a little surprised by the doc's initiative. Clearly the threat was serious enough to stir him into action.

"We don't really have much choice, do we?" Pelquin said. "Okay, Doc, give me the coordinates."

They delayed only briefly. In a ceremony that harked back to the days of seafaring and burials at sea, they committed Anna's body to space, on a trajectory that would take her into this system's sun.

The journey to the doc's hospital world passed without incident. On approach, they were directed to an isolated landing area and instructed to wait there with the ship sealed until they were contacted again.

Drake sat in the galley. Bren, Doc and Nate were with him. The latter looked far from healthy – his skin pasty and sweaty. Not the most pleasant of sights, but Bren's suggestion that Nate might like to wait in his own bed hadn't gone down too well.

"Yeah, and then again I might not," the big man had said. "Look, if you're going to catch it you've probably already got it by now. No point in making me a pariah at this stage."

The doc had dosed them all with a cocktail of drugs which he hoped might offer some protection from the virus. For all Drake knew, this might have been no more than a placebo, but at least it offered reassurance that something was being done.

In the meantime, they waited.

Drake yawned, feeling unaccountably tired; his limbs were suddenly heavy and he was struggling to keep his eyes open. A delayed reaction to all the excitement? It wasn't like him to crash so completely, no matter how fraught recent events might have been. Then he noticed Bren slump forward, her head cradled in her arms, already asleep; Leesa was nodding off too.

Mudball?

I'm checking… Yeah, you've been drugged; poisoned. Sorry.

Mudball had no access to his body, only his mind. There was nothing the little alien could do to affect his metabolism. Nate Almont finally making his move, it had to be; and a pretty successful one too by the look of things. Fake an illness and bring them all exactly where he wanted them… Then he saw Almont try to stand, only for his legs to buckle, causing him to collapse onto the floor; clearly as much a victim as anyone else. If not Almont, *who?*

By now Drake was struggling to keep his head upright and his eyes open. A contest he was losing. His head felt so heavy it was a wonder his slender neck ever managed to support it. With that thought his chin dropped onto his chest.

As consciousness fled, Drake caught movement in the corner of his eye and strained to stay awake for just a fraction longer, managing to do so long enough to see Dr Ahmed Bariha step forward to examine Bren, as if to check that she really was unconscious. Only then, in the last seconds before awareness deserted him, did Drake finally understand. *The doctor, of course...*

De Souza, Archer, Gant, and two additional heavies – big, solid, thick-set goons hired by Gant to provide extra muscle – rushed towards the waiting ship in a covered truck. Bariha had signalled that he'd taken control of the *Comet* and, true to his word, the loading bay door was unfolding even as they approached. By the time they arrived it was fully opened and they were able to drive straight up its ramp and into the ship. De Souza still had a lingering concern that this might all be some ruse and he was about to be greeted by Pelquin and the rest of the *Comet*'s crew bearing big grins and even bigger guns, but it didn't happen. As Gant brought the truck screeching to a halt, the Jossyren executive opened the door and stepped out unopposed. Behind him, Archer and the hired muscle unfolded themselves from the more cramped seating at the back.

A wall of Elder artefacts faced him. More wealth than most men, most *hundred* men combined, would ever encounter in their lifetimes; and it was all *his*. Well, mostly his.

De Souza took a moment to stand and savour the heady flush of victory.

Footsteps heralded the arrival of someone on the metal stairway leading to the ship's upper decks: Bariha. The doctor looked nervous, as if anxious to get all this unpleasantness over with.

"The crew are up here," he said.

De Souza nodded and went to follow him, pausing as Archer said, "I'll stay here and start loading the artefacts. I know how much would be expected from a minor cache find and I'll put some pieces aside to cover that; enough to persuade First Solar that my own supposed cache hunt was a genuine one."

"Fine, fine. Gant can help you."

Archer looked at him sharply for an instant, as if the idea that de Souza might not fully trust him had never occurred to the idiot before; but he didn't object. De Souza felt a lot more comfortable knowing that the banker and all that wealth were under Gant's watchful gaze.

He followed the doctor up the stairs, the two goons close behind. It never ceased to amaze him how basic these small trading ships were. This stairway, the gantry it led to – the entire living quarters section of the ship – felt impermanent and flimsy, as if the whole lot had been hastily erected to serve the crew for this one trip alone and would be dismantled and packed away immediately afterwards. It was all so claustrophobic. Not even the lowliest miners who worked for Jossyren were expected to spend any length of time in such cramped conditions. And yet people lived like this by choice. It bordered on the barbaric.

Even the galley, which was intended to service the entire crew and act as a social centre for the duration of the trip, was smaller than a single room in the suite he enjoyed aboard his own ship. The low ceiling didn't help; nor did the fact that the room was currently littered with recumbent forms. The scene was almost peaceful. There was no sign of violence or anything nefarious, they all looked comfortably asleep. All it needed was a little contented snoring and the picture would have been complete.

"Are they dead yet?" he asked the doctor.

"No, probably not," Bariha replied. "Soon, though. I made it painless. After all, these were my friends."

De Souza couldn't have cared less, and certainly didn't intend saying anything to help salve the man's conscience. These were people Bariha had crewed with, *lived* with, yet he'd turned on them and murdered them rather than come clean and seek their help and understanding. He'd chosen to be exploited rather than exposed. Whining about it after the event was pointless.

A small form moved, startling de Souza. At first he was afraid it might be a rat, but then he discerned a ball of green-brown fur from which two saucer-like eyes stared at him. The thing rested by the shoulder of a man in a grey suit, whom de Souza recognised from the reception on Brannan's as the banking representative, Drake. What was it with bankers and suits?

"What the hell is *that?*" he said out loud.

"Just the banker's genpet," Bariha replied. "It's harmless."

Reassured, de Souza shifted his focus, taking particular pleasure in seeing Nate Almont among the doctor's victims. Here was a man who had spurned the chance to work with him and instead had run back to his old friend Pelquin and offered *him* the golden opportunity. *Not such a bright move after all, eh?* Almont deserved all that he got and more.

De Souza abruptly realised that something wasn't right. He did a quick head count. "There's one missing. Where's the captain, Pelquin?"

"In the ship's cockpit collapsed over the controls," Bariha assured him. "Don't worry; he's unconscious the same as his crew."

De Souza allowed himself to relax. "Good. How long before…"

It was at this point that one of them moved. Not a genpet this time, or even a rat; a woman, and not someone he could identify. Hard-bodied, still young though not a kid; a moment before, she had been slumped forward over the table, apparently as unconscious as the rest. Not anymore.

There was nothing woolly-headed about the way she moved, no indication that she was just waking up or fighting off the effects of a deadly toxin, far from it. Her actions were swift, assured, and effective, taking everyone by surprise.

Leesa recognised the presence of the poison as soon as it began to affect her body, paralysing nerves and attempting to shut down sections of her brain. The augmented part of her mind analysed the active agent and began to manufacture countermeasures immediately, ruthlessly drawing on her own body for what was required – plundering the components of blood, nerves, tissues – and even utilising elements of the toxin itself. The effects of the poison were neutralised almost before they'd begun to take hold. While everyone else was slumping into unconsciousness around her, Leesa felt bright as a button and pumped with adrenaline; but she determined to play dead, to mimic the other victims and see what developed.

The revelation that the doc was responsible shocked her but she continued to feign unconsciousness, wanting to see the extent of his treachery. This was a delicate game she had chosen to play. The poison wasn't an aggressive one; it had induced unconsciousness by gentle degree and would continue to work at that sort of pace, shutting down the body's functions slowly. As yet, she was confident that all the crew could be revived, but the longer she left it the greater the risk. Still she waited, praying that she didn't miss that crucial tipping point.

When Bahira left the galley to welcome his guests she followed on silent feet, only to scamper back as he returned, regaining her seat in plenty of time to resume her previous position.

As she did so, she noted Drake's genpet watching her intently. Odd, but she almost had the impression that it was about to do something, which was ridiculous.

The doc strolled around, clucking on about making the poison painless and the crew being his friends. It was all she could do not to reach out and strangle him straight away, and eventually, when she'd heard all she needed and couldn't risk waiting any longer, that was precisely what she did.

He was behind her, close to her left shoulder, and she knew that the other man – the one who had spoken in such haughty, hateful tones – was standing just inside the door. She thought she'd heard at least one more set of footfalls approach, but there was no way of telling for certain until she opened her eyes, and by the time she did that she was already committed.

In one swift motion Leesa surged upwards, twisted around and reached out, her right hand clamping around the startled doctor's throat so firmly that she lifted him from his feet, her fingers digging into the soft skin and firmer tendons beneath. It felt good to abandon pretence and to be actually doing something; better than good, it felt great. There were two others, she saw, both near the door and close to Haughty Voice and both reaching for guns.

The doc was struggling, kicking his feet and clawing at her wrist and fingers, making a choking, gagging noise all the while. Leesa turned him towards the door as the first goon freed his weapon and fired. She felt the impact but had her elbow locked and held her human shield steady, feeling the heat where the energy bolt hit home, and feeling warmth spatter against her wrist and face as blood sprayed from Bariha's back. The doc abruptly stopped struggling.

Leesa didn't hesitate but flung his body towards the two goons, charging after it so that she hit them only a fraction after the doctor's corpse. There was blood – the doc's – and a gun which she knocked aside, a knife which she avoided before breaking the arm that wielded it. A knee smashed into her midriff. She rode the blow, jumping upwards so that both feet were off the ground and folding at the waist to lessen the impact even as her left hand reached for the goon's face and clawed for his eyes. Her opponent screamed as she felt something soft give beneath her fingertips.

She was vaguely aware of the slighter, almost dandified man she'd dubbed Haughty Voice slipping out of the room but couldn't spare him any attention just yet, as the second thug – the one with both eyes still intact – came at her with the knife. She had to admire that. His right arm was held cradled close to his chest but he still attacked, holding the knife expertly in his left hand and showing little sign of any pain. Drugged presumably; something to block the alarm messages that would normally alert the brain of damage. He was no slouch, either, keeping her at bay for precious seconds in which she really wanted to be going after Haughty Voice. At last he over-extended, his thrust made awkward by the need to protect the injured arm and compromise his balance. She twisted out of the way, grabbed his wrist before the arm could retract, and broke that one as well.

A blow to the neck with the stiff edge of her hand and he hit the floor. She was free, and raced in pursuit of Haughty Voice.

Too late. She arrived at the cargo hold just in time to see a truck lumber forward and disappear down the loading ramp, gathering speed all the way. Part of her wanted to give chase, wanted to leap in the buggy and hunt down Haughty Voice and whoever else was with him, but to do so would mean consigning everyone else on board to die.

After a deep breath and a quick glare at the retreating truck, she turned and headed back up the steps, knowing that she would have to act quickly even now.

"I don't believe it." De Souza's patience had finally run out. A little belatedly perhaps given the circumstances, but he was somewhat pushed for resources out here and beggars couldn't be choosers. "You couldn't even get *that* right."

Archer's face reddened. "You can't go blaming me for what happened back there. I did my part. I got you an established member of the crew, which is something that for all your money and influence you hadn't been able to achieve. Bariha's dependency on drugs made him vulnerable and it was *me* that uncovered the fact that he's on the run after a wealthy patient died in a botched operation. And that's what sealed the deal, don't forget. Threat and reward; carrot and the stick; we had him where we wanted him, and he performed as promised.

"The girl was a wildcard. We never planned for her and had no way of anticipating what she can do. She's clearly something extraordinary."

"Extraordinary, my foot. Your friend Dr Bariha botched his end of things, there's nothing extraordinary about this fiasco. Somehow he must have failed to administer the poison to that girl. Unbelievable! Mind you, given the incompetence displayed in everything else you've touched, I don't know why I should be surprised."

Archer looked fit to explode. "I've had just about all I'm willing to take of your condescending attitude, de Souza..."

He'd had enough of *him*? The gall of the man. De Souza glanced quickly at Gant, who stood a few paces behind the banker. The bodyguard gave a crisp nod and prepared to step forward. Archer wouldn't be an irritation for much longer. "I don't think you have, Archer, not quite yet."

Then Archer did perhaps the first truly impressive thing he'd managed in the whole of their acquaintance. Somehow sensing Gant's approach, he spun around... and shot him. No hesitation, no unnecessary drama, just a swift and clinical execution.

De Souza hadn't even seen the gun until that instant, and had no idea where the banker had produced it from. A burst of energy and a puff of smoke and blood from the vicinity of Gant's chest; the big man hesitated, glanced down as if unable to believe what had happened, and then collapsed to the ground.

De Souza must have frozen for an instant. By the time his mind had caught up with events Archer had swivelled back around and de Souza found the barrel of the weapon that had just killed his bodyguard pointing squarely at his face. Sleek, black, palm-sized and evidently deadly, the gun monopolised his attention.

"You really are a pompous ass, aren't you?" Archer said. The sneer was unmistakable now; an expression that was so unexpected in the bumbling banker – always so eager to please, always so inept – that de Souza could hardly credit it was the same person. "How you ever clawed your way up to a position of authority *anywhere* is beyond me," Archer continued. "You're incapable of doing anything for yourself; you rely entirely on others and then delight in criticising their perceived shortcomings… Actually, perhaps I just answered my own question. Maybe *that's* the talent that has propelled you to the top: your ability to bully and organise others to do your work for you. A skill, I suppose, though a pretty worthless one in a situation like this, don't you think?

"What use is being a bully when it's just you and the angry man with the gun? Nobody else to call upon now; no one to come to your rescue. Your only resource is whatever you can bring to the party yourself, which, when all is said and done, isn't a hell of a lot, is it, Falyn my old friend."

"Oh, you'd be surprised," de Souza replied, regaining a little composure and determined to keep his body language relaxed and all hint of fear from his voice. "I still have a very great deal to offer."

"Really?Such as?"

"Money. More wealth than you could ever imagine."

Archer stared at him for a second and then burst out laughing. "Oh dear," he said at length, "you really are too predictable. *Money*; is that the best you can come up with?"

De Souza's desperation ratcheted up a notch. This wasn't quite the response he'd anticipated. He struggled to mask his alarm. "Don't be too hasty. I'm not just talking about your standard fortune, I mean *real* wealth, of the sort that only the mega-rich usually catch a glimpse of."

"And this incredible wealth is where exactly?"

De Souza relaxed a little. This was a language he knew well. When it came down to it, everything was always about money.

"Not that it really matters," Archer continued. "The money is only of secondary interest to me."

"Oh come, come. You don't really expect me to believe that, surely?" Bargaining, open gambits and bluffs – familiar territory. De Souza's confidence recovered a little more with every syllable.

"I expect you to believe whatever you will."

"We'll start with my own personal fortune – which is not inconsiderable; it's yours, every penny. Then we'll move on to the *real* wealth. His smile was confident, conspiratorial: they were partners now.

Archer shook his head. "You really don't get it, do you? Even if you did have access to funds at that sort of level – which you don't, or you wouldn't be out here in the back of beyond chasing Elder artefacts – it's not really the money I'm interested in; it never has been."

"Of course it isn't." De Souza refused to contemplate that this wasn't an act, that Archer actually meant what he was saying.

"Is it really so hard to grasp? Is the concept that someone could be motivated by anything other than greed beyond you?"

"*What then?*" de Souza shrieked, losing control despite himself; anger and contempt for the banker overcoming his fear.

"The guardian." Archer's words were chilling in the quiet of their delivery. "The creature that was watching over that cache."

"*What?* You're mad, you've totally lost it." De Souza found courage in his rage, channelling it into reckless defiance. For that instant, he didn't care. Let Archer kill him, just so long as the windbag *got on with it.*

"There's more going on here than you'll ever know. You still can't lift your gaze from the money trough to see beyond your all-consuming greed and realise that the guardian of that cache is centuries upon *centuries* old, that here is an alien intelligence stretching back to the time of the Elders themselves. What's mere *money* compared to that?"

There was no reasoning with this man; he was a fanatic, de Souza suddenly realised, shocked that he hadn't seen it before now. Archer was investing the guardian programmes with some sort of mystical significance, which was absurd. "They're just programmed entities," he said softly, "sophisticated software, that's all. Nothing living could survive this long."

Archer's head was shaking again. "No, you blind fool, you're judging them by our standards – in *human* terms – when they're so far beyond us that we'll never understand them; but I realise I'm not going to convince you, even if I felt inclined to try. And, you know what? I really don't." The grip on the gun tightened, the arm straightened and the barrel, which had wavered a little during the discussion, pointed straight towards the bridge of de Souza's nose once more.

"No, wait," he said desperately, all pretence of calmness gone. "I know where there are more caches. I can lead you to them…"

"I should thank you, all things considered," Archer continued, oblivious to de Souza's pleas. "I always knew that someone else *must* have realised the significance of the guardians, and now I know I was right, and even who that someone is. I should have guessed it before now: Drake, my own dear colleague. A rival in every sense it would seem. *Of course* Drake is my adversary. How could it possibly be anyone else? Thank you, Falyn, dear friend, for making all this clear to me. Now, I really must be off."

The breath caught in de Souza's throat. He couldn't tear his gaze away from Archer's trigger finger, which was in motion just below the gun's muzzle. Time seemed to slow as the finger squeezed, its joints contracting by the tiniest of increments. Fleetingly, irrationally, de Souza wondered whether he would see the beam for a split second before it killed him.

TWENTY-TWO

"The doc, can you believe it?" Nate shook his head. "Damn! I've known the man for years, we all have."

"Yeah," Bren agreed. "It's pretty hard to take."

"Just goes to show that you can never really *know* anyone," Pelquin said. "We were all aware of his little dependencies, but I never thought for a minute..."

"None of us did," Bren said quickly.

They were back on New Sparta, embroiled in all the legal consequences of their departure the last time they were here; but, with a hold bulging full of Elder artefacts, Pelquin was happy enough to let the lawyers earn their keep. He was also glad to see the back of the banker, Drake, who had scuttled back to his precious employer. In fairness, the man had been decent enough for a banker, but it was good to get the ship back to themselves again.

They'd decided to return directly to New Sparta and realise their assets before picking Monkey up at Babylon – which would doubtless please the little mechanic no end, but it had been a unanimous decision. Everyone wanted to get the cache contents safely delivered before anything elsecould go wrong.

The doc's betrayal and their brush with near death had shaken them all, especially coming so soon after Anna's death. It transpired, of course, that Nate had never fallen foul of an alien infection. That was all of the doctor's devising and, had it not been for Leesa...

Pelquin felt a pang of guilt when he glanced at Nate. How could he ever have doubted his oldest friend, even for a moment? They all knew how sound travelled on the *Comet* and how easy it was to overhear others' conversation even when you *didn't* want to. The doc must have heard enough to glean what he needed.

His gaze moved back to Leesa. Now there was an enigma. He still had no idea *how* her body had manufactured an antidote – when asked she'd simply shrugged and said 'it's just something I can do' – but without that handy little talent they would all have been dead. Perhaps he should press the girl about it but that would go against the grain; as he'd once explained to Drake, everyone on board the *Comet* was entitled to their secrets.

He glanced across at Bren – acutely aware that there was unfinished business between the two of them that needed to be resolved. She caught his eye and smiled, but it wasn't their personal situation she chose to comment on. "Everything that's happened does leave us sorely light on crewmembers, even after we pick up Monkey," she said, looking significantly at Leesa.

Pelquin nodded. "That's true."

"And Leesa did just save all our necks back there…"

A fact that nobody was about to dispute, and one that had already been recognised in the decision to increase her entitlement from a half share of the spoils to a full one – with Anna and Doc out of the equation they could afford to be generous. "Also true." He shifted his gaze to their stand-in mechanic. "Well, what do you say? We could dump you back where we found you on Babylon or, if you'd prefer, you could sign up and join the crew formally on a long term basis. Your choice."

Leesa didn't hesitate. "No contest; count me in," and she smiled, which was something of a rarity and an expression she ought to try on for size more often, Pelquin reckoned.

"It'll be good to have two mechanics aboard," Nate said.

"Yeah," Bren agreed. "Especially when the other one is Monkey."

Even Pelquin grinned at that. There was a fair bit of smiling and laughing going on despite all that they'd been through; and with good reason. They were alive for starters. Added to which they'd brought back a momentous haul of Elder artefacts, even after the lorry load pilfered by the doc's associates – presumably agents of Jossyren, although he wasn't about to start making accusations he couldn't prove. There was enough here to make each and every one of them wealthy. At least, there would have been. By the time First Solar had taken their cut and he'd settled all the legal matters arising from their unauthorised take off the last time they were at New Sparta, he wasn't so sure. They would still turn a decent profit no doubt, but 'wealthy' might be a bit much to hope for; which was why he was willing to discuss the composition of the crew. It looked as if the *Comet* was going to remain a place of work for all of them for a while. And their home. Important that. Above all else, the *Comet* was their home.

The bustle of New Sparta's streets always seemed alien to Drake when he first returned from a trip, as if his brain rejected the relentless urgency of those around him. Even La Gossa with all its crowds and traffic jams had been less pressured, less stressful in comparison. After all, traffic jams never go anywhere in a hurry, whereas on the streets of New Sparta *everyone* was in a hurry and everything happened at break-neck speed. Except for Drake, who refused to be harassed out of his own preferred pace; and today that pace was a stroll.

He had filed his report and had no further interest in the *Comet's* haul beyond the commission he would eventually be due, passing all such responsibility onto the bank's lawyers and accountants, but he'd still made an appointment to see Terry Reese in person.

She must have wondered why, so he decided to put her out of her misery immediately upon being ushered in. "I was wondering if now might be a good time for me to take a holiday," he said.

Reese stared at him as if he'd asked for something scandalous. "A *holiday*, really?"

"Yes. Unless I'm mistaken, I think I am owed some time…"

"Certainly you are; a considerable amount, come to that. It's just that I can't recall you *ever* asking for time off before. Normally I have to force you to take some."

He smiled. "Perhaps I've learned the error of my ways."

"I was under the impression you did that the day you first joined First Solar." He refused to rise to that particular bait and stayed quiet. "Of course you can have a holiday. You know we always recommend a few days off following an away trip in any case. How long did you have in mind?"

"Oh, I don't know…" He made a quick calculation, factoring in travel time. "Three weeks ought to cover it."

"Then let's say four weeks just to play safe. I think the bank can survive without you for that long, and you can always come back to work before then if you find yourself at a loose end. I'll book you out starting tomorrow; will that do?"

"Perfectly, thank you."

He turned to leave, but was stopped by Reese saying. "Drake, tell me one thing. Should I be worried?"

He looked back, taking a second before answering, not wanting to lie to this woman who had taken a chance on him and so facilitated this new life. Only when he was certain that he wasn't did he say, "No. No need for you to worry at all."

She nodded, accepting his word. "That's all right, then."

Drake left Terry Reese's office still troubled, not so much by anything that had been said as by what had remained *un*said. In his final assurance to her he had omitted one word, a small but invariably significant one. The word was: *yet*.

Mudball's attention was focused inward, still working at what was proving to be a tricky assimilation. This cache guardian had been powerful and was defiantly stubborn; but at the end of the day Mudball was the stronger and the newcomer was being steadily absorbed. It had hampered him, prevented him from acting in the face of the doc's treachery as quickly as he might have, but fortunately the auganic had stepped in to save the day. This was the biggest addition yet, and he was finding it increasingly difficult to maintain the physically diminished size – something which was essential if he wanted to continue working with Drake. Tiny puffed-up and vaguely cute genpet was one thing; a man-sized sphere of furry xenobiology complete with tentacles was decidedly less likely to be invited onto client spaceships to go cache hunting.

Still, it was getting to the point where he wouldn't need Drake for much longer. Another addition as strong as this, two at the most, and he would be complete. A shame really; he'd grown fond of this human. He would almost regret it when the time came to kill him.

Leesa was surprised to get a message from Drake, especially such a cryptic one: *"This might help you."* The note was accompanied by an attachment.Whatever this was, it was heavily encrypted.

Leesa smiled. If there was one thing she enjoyed, it was a challenge.

She had very little to go on, only what she'd seen of a deliberately reserved individual during the brief time she'd spent with him since joining the crew. Yet why set her a puzzle unless she was equipped to solve it? All it would take was a word – she just needed to identify the right one. She started with the obvious: Mudball; Drake; Firstsolar; Solar; Bank, Banker, Representative, Suit; Grey; Cane: Walkingstick;

Handsome… Now where had that last come from? She shook her head and kept going.

Over the course of the next hour she attempted every word, contraction and combination of potentially relevant words she could think of, all to no avail. Eventually, frustrated and annoyed at not being able to second guess the banker by now, she took a break. She wandered into the galley, to find Bren there.

"My," the other woman said, "you do look serious."

"Sorry, just preoccupied. I'm trying to break an encryption."

"Oh?"

"Something Drake sent me. I've tried everything I can think of."

"Name, job, stuff personal to him – that sort of thing?"

"Yes, yes and yes. Tried it all, but the message remains stubbornly coy."

"Hmm…"

"What?"

"Well, probably nothing, but I was just thinking. If you asked me to describe Drake, one word that would instantly spring to mind is 'observant'. What if you're not looking for something personal to *him* at all but rather something that's personal to you?"

Leesa froze, staring at Bren. "Thank you." With that she turned and hurried from the galley.

She got it at the second attempt: *techorg* didn't work but *auganic* did.

After all that, the file's content was something of a disappointment. It consisted of just four letters and a space: Hel N.

"Not even a proper word," she muttered. Perhaps it was a name, or a clue to a name that required her to figure out what that final 'N' stood for, but either way it meant nothing to her; more frustration.

Was that entirely true though? Hel N resonated with something somewhere, at the very back of her mind, as if this was a piece of the puzzle that ought to fit but wouldn't. Instead it lingered at the margins of her awareness, shadowing her thoughts and refusing to be ignored. Hopefully, this was more than just wishful thinking; perhaps if she gave it time the cryptic message might yet be of value.

Leesa went to bed still absorbed by the issue, hoping that 'Hel N' might at least unlock a dream or two.

It unlocked something, no question about that; a memory that had Leesa sitting bolt upright in the dead of the night, eyes open and mind racing. Starting with a blank slate as she had when waking on Babylon, she'd thought herself prepared for anything and that nothing in the universe could surprise her, but this…

"Now I know you, banker man," she whispered, as if this breath of sound could be carried across the vastness between stars to reach his ears by the power of her will alone. "*Now* I know you."

With that, she tucked down again, a smile upon her lips, and she slept so soundly that no dream troubled her for the rest of that night; nor did she need one to.

Russell Tavistock was fairly typical of a common class of traveller – dubbed by the media 'the Grey Swarm' – men and women of a certain maturity whose last marriage or relationship had dissolved, whose children, grandchildren, and even great grandchildren were too busy getting on with their own lives to concern themselves with their oldest relatives; people who had done their bit and were now taking things easy, who had enjoyed their last rejuve or perhaps never bothered with such things; who had built up a nice little nest egg which they were utilising to travel and to see the stars, visiting the worlds they'd always dreamt of seeing but had never found the time for until now.

Despite the industry of organised cruises that had sprung up to cater for the mature sightseer, many still preferred to set their own tempo and so took a more individual approach. Tavistock knew all this and was not in the least surprised to find himself processed by the port's arrivals system smoothly and efficiently, being gently spat out onto the street within minutes of his arrival.

It was a mild but sunny afternoon. He took a moment to stand and blink as if a little confused or perhaps simply to get his bearings. In fact he was merely savouring the unfamiliar sense of freedom, of being somewhere at his own volition. After a quick scratch of his beard, which had begun to itch a little, and a flex of his back, he shuffled over to the rank of waiting taxis and asked the first in line to take him to his hotel, the Balam Tree. He didn't even mind the somewhat circuitous route the driver took; everyone had to make a living.

Check in was automated though there was a real live Person With Pulse available if you preferred – the Balam Tree was one of the *better* hotels in Victoria – and within minutes Tavistock was able to close the door on the rest of the universe, safely ensconced in his own comfortably appointed suite.

After removing his jacket, he took out a small, slender and surprisingly contemporary perminal from an inside pocket and used it to conduct a thorough sweep of the room, searching for electronic bugs. He didn't honestly expect to find any but was determined to be as careful as possible while here. Only once the sweep had drawn the expected blank did Drake feel able to relax.

He kicked off the shoes with their built-up heals, spat out two cheek inserts that had distorted the normal contours of his face and then, taking a small aerosol, he carefully sprayed along the base of his beard. After a couple of seconds delay the whiskers pulled off easily, without taking any of his skin with them. Exposure to a small UV palm torch removed the grey from his hair and returned it to its natural brown – he hated wearing wigs, particularly for a protracted period. Contact lenses popped readily from his eyes and the application of a simple cream – massaged gently into the skin – returned a young and healthy complexion to his cheeks and forehead, effectively knocking years off him.

When are you going to make the call? Mudball asked, which reminded Drake that the little alien was still sealed in his pouch.

He replied, *patience, patience,* while reaching behind his shoulder and loosening the seam, feeling his companion manoeuvre into a more comfortable position.

It was a risk his coming back to Brannan's World; he knew that. He had history here and more than one person might remember him. Had he taken the trouble to sit back and assess things in his accustomed fashion, he would doubtless have rejected the whole idea of returning as preposterous and foolhardy, but he hadn't. Instead he'd acted on impulse – an approach that was novel to Drake, certainly in recent years. Perhaps the very thing that made Brannan's dangerous was what had called him back: *he had history here.*

There was no point in putting this off any longer. He thought of Laurena, the ravishing beauty who had invited him to call her, and then he thought of Alexis in both guises: the young woman who had approached him at the reception and the child she'd been when he lived here. That inevitably woke memories of her mother...

Two numbers, two choices; calling one would mean reconnecting with a past that had once meant everything to him, while the other was all about the present, the here and now. Throughout the journey to Brannan's he'd deliberately shied away from analysing which of the two was the stronger lure, which of them had *really* called him back here. Only now, as he picked up the perminal and felt its slender moulding in his hand, was he sure.

Having checked himself in the mirror to ensure that no sign of Russell Tavistock remained and that he really did look like Corbin Thadeus Drake once more, he took a deep breath and made the call.

His contact request was accepted almost at once. "Drake, what a wonderful surprise!"

He smiled, matching the expression of the vision of beauty that grinned back at him from the display. Yes, he could see surprise there, but also delight; definitely delight.

"Hello, Laurena." She could easily have refused his call. He'd deliberately made it an open one, which meant that she would have seen his face clearly before accepting. Had she done so, there was always that other number... But here they were, and he wouldn't have had it any other way.

"Where are you?" she asked.

"In Victoria, at the Balam Tree. I'll be in town for the next few days," or maybe a few weeks, depending on how things panned out. "I was just wondering whether you were free for dinner tonight."

Her smile broadened significantly. "I am now."

Yay, at last! said Mudball.

We're meeting for dinner, that's all, Drake insisted. "Excellent!" he said out loud.

Yeah, right, course you are. Can I watch, can I?

Without missing a beat, Drake finished making arrangements for the evening. At the same time he casually reached his left hand to the back of his neck, as if to scratch an itch. What that hand actually did was push Mudball gently down and press shut the pouch seal.

I'm guessing that's a no, then.

ABOUT THE AUTHOR

Ian Whates lives in a quiet Cambridgeshire village with his partner, Helen, and Honey, a manic cocker spaniel. He currently has two published novel series: the *Noise* books (space opera with a twist) via Solaris, and the *City of 100 Rows* trilogy (urban fantasy with steampunk overtones and SF underpinning) via Angry Robot. Some sixty of his short stories have appeared in various venues, two of which were shortlisted for BSFA Awards, while his work has received honourable mentions in Year's Best anthologies. His second collection, *Growing Pains* (PS Publishing), appeared in 2013. Ian has edited a couple of *The Mammoth Book of...* titles for Constable and Robinson and the on-going *Solaris Rising* series for Solaris, one of which found its way onto the 2014 Philip K. Dick Award shortlist. In his spare time, Ian runs multiple award-winning independent publisher NewCon Press, which he founded by accident in 2006.

Ian has served a term as Overseas Director of SFWA (Science Fiction Writers of America) and spent five years as chairman of the BSFA (British Science Fiction Association), stepping down in 2013. He remains a director of the latter.

The Gift of Joy ~ Ian Whates
Introduction by Ian Watson

Eighteen stories of distant futures and disturbing tomorrows, of strange new worlds and others that are uncomfortably familiar. Intelligent science fiction and quirky fantasy, packed with excitement, surprises, humour, and warmth

"Darkly funny tales of the unexpected, with a deft science-fictional turn of the knife."

Ken MacLeod

"Planetary escapades and vivid battle action rub shoulders with charming yet eerie rural tales and with perilous urban nightmares."

Ian Watson

"Ian Whates has a way with words, a storyteller's sensibility...Definitely one to watch."

Jon Courtenay Grimwood.

"It is his characters who live through the story and make the reader need to know just how it's all going to pan out, human characters who may seem familiar but then there's that one thing, that shifted alteration that changes the world and changes the reader too."

Interzone

"The variety is only one of the pleasures on offer; others are the fully rounded, if not always likable, characters, and Whates's knack for taking stories in unexpected directions... This may not be cutting-edge SF, but it is satisfying, well observed and entertaining."

The Guardian

Signed limited edition hardback   £18.99
A5-size paperback edition: £9.99

Paradox

Stories inspired by
the Fermi Paradox

Paradox
Edited By Ian Whates

With introduction by astronomer Marek Kukula and Rob Edwards of Royal Observatory Greenwich, and original stories from:

Pat Cadigan, Adam Roberts, Paul Cornell, Mike Resnick, Robert Reed, Tricia Sullivan, Paul di Filippo, Adrian Tchaikovsky, Eric Brown, Keith Brooke, Stephanie Saulter, Mercurio Rivera, Rachel Armstrong, and more…

The Fermi Paradox is the apparent contradiction between the high probability of extraterrestrial civilizations' existence and the lack of contact with such civilizations.

In Paradox, a selection of the world's leading science fiction authors are joined by physicists and other scientists in writing exciting and original stories inspired by Fermi's famous paradox, daring to ask…

Where Is Everybody?

"*Paradox* lives up to the usual high standards we have come to expect from Newcon Press…. most of the stories here are very good. Four or five are outstanding." – *Amazing Stories*

"Whates has assembled a splendidly diverse collection of stories, ranging from coolly cerebral thought experiments to unashamedly pulpy twist-in-the-tail romps. His real coup, though, is commissioning tales from scientists – space technologist Gerry Webb and biology innovator Rachel Armstrong among them – alongside SF stalwarts."
— *The Financial Times*

IMMANION PRESS
Speculative Fiction

The Moonshawl by Storm Constantine

Ysbryd drwg… the bad ghost.Hired by Wyva, the phylarch of the Wyvachi tribe, Ysobi goes to Gwyllion to create a spiritual system based upon local folklore, but he soon discovers some of that folklore is out of bounds, taboo... Secrets lurk in the soil of Gwyllion, and the old house Meadow Mynd, home of the Wyvachi leaders. The house and the land are haunted. The fields are soaked in blood and echo with the cries of those who were slaughtered there, almost a century ago. Old hatreds and a thirst for vengeance have been awoken by the approaching coming of age of Wvya's son, Myvyen. If the harling is to survive, Ysobi must lay the ghosts to rest and scour the tainted soil of malice. But the ysbryd drwg is strong, built of a century of resentment and evil thoughts. Is it too powerful, even for a scholarly hienama with Ysobi's experience and skill? 'The Moonshawl' is a standalone supernatural story, set in the world of Storm Constantine's ground-breaking, science fantasy Wraeththu mythos. ISBN: 978-1-907737-62-6 £11.99, $20.99

Ghosteria 2: The Novel: Zircons May be Mistaken by Tanith Lee

Sometimes when people die, it comes as a great shock. Even to them…

A group of the dead linger here, in the yellow dwelling on the hill – once a castle, then a stately home, now falling into ruin.These ghosts drift and mingle, and brood on their lost lives. Death can be caused by so many things – war, pandemics, ordinary murder – even suicide or accident. Even time. But after death, surely, one could hope for peace? Not any more.For with 2020 the New Apocalypse began.

Civilisation crashed, and outside this ancient building things terrible, predatory, mindless and unkillable roam and bellow.

Now all the lights have gone out for good –Where do you turn?
ISBN: 978-1-907737-63-3 £9.99 $18.99

Immanion Press
http://www.immanion-press.com
info@immanion-press.com

Ingram Content Group UK Ltd.
Milton Keynes UK
UKHW011813260523
422417UK00004B/205

9 781907 069789